"I never claimed to be wonderful!"

"No, but Josiah claimed it for you!" Rogan replied. "I ask him to find me a sensible woman, someone who wouldn't mind moving out here to the banks, but no, he had this *wonderful* young female he claimed was just what I needed! The only fly in the ointment was that I had to marry her."

"Fly in the— You did *not* have to marry me! I never, *ever* wanted that!"

"Damned if he didn't sucker me good, telling me the last thing I needed was another old woman to worry about. She's young, he said, she'll pull her weight. Plain, prissy, proud as a hog on ice, but the important thing was that you were healthy, a good hard worker with a cool head on your shoulders."

Stricken, Kathleen felt the starch go right out of her defenses. "P-prissy? Proud?"

"And plain," Rogan reminded her ruthlessly. "But since I wasn't looking for a new mistress, that part didn't bother me. It was the rest of it I was interested in."

ΛΛΛΛΛΛΛΛΛΛ

✑FAMILY✑

Bronwyn WILLIAMS

The Mariner's Bride

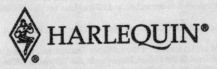

TORONTO • NEW YORK • LONDON
AMSTERDAM • PARIS • SYDNEY • HAMBURG
STOCKHOLM • ATHENS • TOKYO • MILAN • MADRID
PRAGUE • WARSAW • BUDAPEST • AUCKLAND

HARLEQUIN BOOKS
225 Duncan Mill Road, Don Mills,
Ontario, Canada M3B 3K9

ISBN 0-373-82173-5

THE MARINER'S BRIDE

Dear Reader,

For those of us who are blessed with parents, grandparents, aunts, uncles, cousins, siblings, family is a unique bond. Warts and all, we belong to each other. For others it can start with sensing in someone else a kindred spirit, someone to build with, to grow with.

To each of us, whether alone or surrounded with genetic ties, the family represents continuity, something rooted in the past that extends to the future. We're links in a chain, some firmly attached to the links on either side that are our parents and our children. Others must forge their own chains, one link at a time.

Whether it be two lonely people coming together with hope for the future, or a wonderful, noisy reunion complete with dinner-on-the-ground, family is a bond. There may or may not be a genetic component, but *family* is the building block of every civilization that has ever existed. It's something to live up to, to treasure, our promise to the future.

All the best,
Bronwyn Williams
a.k.a. sisters

Dixie Browning & *Mary S. Williams*

To our cousins, the many descendants of
John Burrus, born January 6, 1738,
and his wife, Margaret

Chapter One

1882, Beaufort, North Carolina

The Reverend Josiah Dunwoody sat in his study and thoughtfully nursed the single glass of port he allowed himself each night. A minister's life was truly not his own. Always there were problems to solve. At the moment, there was the letter from young Rogan. Captain Rogan Rawson, Josiah reminded himself with a nostalgic smile. Hadn't he watched the lad grow from a rawboned, hot-tempered stripling into the fine young man he was today?

Rogan was not an official member of Josiah's flock, for the boy had spent his entire life, when he wasn't at sea, on the Northern Carolina Banks. But Rogan's father, Captain Edmund Rawson, had been Josiah's dearest friend back in the days when a green young preacher had paid his dues by agreeing to sail from island to island along the Outer Banks carrying the word of the Lord to the scattered families that had settled there.

Edmund Rawson had been a coaster, one of a number of men making the coastal run, hauling passengers and freight from Charleston and points south all the way up to Boston, with regular stops along the way.

The two men, one city bred, seminary educated and barely into his twenties, the other a rugged, self-taught seaman of some thirty-odd years, had struck up an unlikely friendship that had endured through the years, even after Josiah had been given a land-based church, leaving the circuit sailing to younger men. He had known about Edmund's first wife, Sarah, although she had died shortly before Josiah had come east. He had known that with a five-year-old son to raise and a career that took him constantly away from home, Edmund had had no choice but to remarry or lose his son.

It had been on his regular run to Beaufort, between offloading a cargo of ice and machinery and taking aboard another cargo of rice, corn and indigo for the northward run, that Edmund had contracted to marry Henrietta Beshears, a woman of few means, indeterminate age, but undeniably fine character. Three days after marrying her, he had left her at his home on Hatteras Island, leaving in her care his horse, his house, his five-year-old son, Rogan, and ten dollars to see them all through the rest of the summer.

Now it was Rogan who bore the burden of caring for the woman who had looked after him all those years. According to his letter, that burden had become increasingly difficult in recent months. Neighbors would have helped, but knowing the lad, Josiah suspected he hadn't asked. Too much pride. Even as a boy he had taken his duties seriously, neither asking for help nor offering excuses.

Now he had written asking if Josiah knew of someone capable of dealing with an elderly woman who could outwit the devil himself, yet lacked the judgment of a child.

Lighting his pipe, Josiah allowed the smoke to curl its fragrance around his ruddy face. A few ashes drifted across his paunch, and he ignored them, staring at the half-composed letter before him. He had already put off writing far too long.

My Dear Rogan:

I have in hand yrs. of Mid-June, and was glad to hear that you are faring well. It grieves me some to learn that Miss Hetty is no longer hale and hardy. I well remember the day when your father came to me in search of a woman to take on the care of his five-year-old son. I was glad to be able to recommend Hetty Beshears, for she'd been left in sad situation by the War, her home having been taken from her and all her menfolk killed. It spoke well of Edmund that he was willing to marry her, for she was but a young woman at the time. I could not in all good conscience send her off with any man without the protection of marriage.

Meanwhile, I am pleased to be able to report that the woman I have in mind to look after Miss Hetty is some years older, being I suspect in her middle forties. She is a widow of good character, stout constitution, and quite a tolerable cook, I'm given to understand. I have made arrangements to see her tomorrow to discuss

A timid sound at the door caused him to glance up. His spinster sister was standing at the entrance to the room. "Josiah, I'm sorry to interrupt, but Kathleen Stevens is here and says she has to see you. The poor child is some wrought up. I offered her tea, but I don't think she could swallow a drop, the shape she's in right now."

Sighing, Josiah laid the letter aside. A moment later, as his sister ushered a young woman into his presence, he stood, scattering ashes onto the carpet, and fumbled to button his vest.

Josiah Dunwoody knew little about women, and still less about fashion, but even he knew that the rusty black bombazine gown the poor child was wearing didn't do a blessed thing for her looks, nor did the flapping black bonnet trimmed with the lopsided dove. On her older sister, Alice, whose plump blond beauty had once drawn men the way a sugar bowl draws flies, the same outfit might have looked quite fetching. It made Kathleen, who was pale, thin and freckled, her great gray eyes large and her hands red and rough from housework, look more drawn than ever.

But it was not the gown that held Josiah's attention, nor even that pathetic dove. It was the anguish in those gray eyes. "What's gone wrong, child? Is it Alice? One of the children?"

Kathleen made a valiant effort to pull herself together. She was beyond embarrassment, even though her trunk was lying beside the road in front of the parsonage where Morton's delivery cart had dumped it out. She cleared her throat and drew in a deep breath, visibly bracing herself for what had to be done.

Louisa Dunwoody poked her gray head through the door and said, "There's a trunk out by the road. Is that yours, child?"

Numb with shame, Kathleen could only nod. Alice had come in when she was halfway done with her packing and relented enough to tell her she could stay on until morning, but by that time, Kathleen had wanted only to escape. Too disheartened to try once more to explain that things weren't the way they seemed, she had silently finished her packing, all the while fending off questions from Caleb and the twins, until Morton's delivery wagon had come for her trunk.

Louisa hovered in the doorway, wringing her hands. "Are you sure you wouldn't like a nice cup of hot tea? You look all done in, I declare you do."

In the face of such kindness, Kathleen felt her chin wobble a bit. She hadn't cried when it had happened. She hadn't cried in years. Tears never solved a blessed thing, they only left her with a red nose and a soggy handkerchief. "No. Thank you very much, Miss Dunwoody. Perhaps later?"

Louisa went away mumbling to herself about injustices and looks being only skin-deep and ladies being more than fine feathers, which might have been a bit muddled, but then so was Louisa, as a rule.

Josiah waited, knowing she would get to it in her own time. Meanwhile, his thoughts rambled. The girl was too thin by half, but then, she'd always been more spunk and spirit than flesh and bone. Took after her father's folks, more's the pity. She'd still been playing with dolls when her parents had been drowned in that awful accident back in '69. Her mother's people, the Chadwicks, had taken in the older sister, Alice, leaving Kathleen to go to old Maggie Stevens.

Josiah harrumphed his disapproval. The Chadwicks could easily have afforded to take both girls, but Alice had been the pretty one, showing promise of the beauty she would soon become, while poor little Kathleen, a scrawny stick of a child, all ears, straight brown hair and big wistful eyes, had been her father's child through and through.

Old Maggie Stevens, the girls' paternal grandmother, had lived at Pelletier's Mills. Josiah had lost track of Kathleen for the next few years. Not until later did he learn that the old woman had taken sick soon after Kathleen had gone to live with her and, though still a child, Kathleen had looked after her grandmother until the end.

After that, she'd come back to Beaufort to live with her sister. Alice was married by that time to Morton Kingsley. It had been considered the match of the season, the beautiful Chadwick ward and the handsome son of old judge Urias Humphlette Kingsley, who had died drunk as a lord in the arms of his mistress, but whose mother had been a Davis, after all.

Everyone had said how kind it was of Alice, and her expecting a baby most any time, to take in her poor little sister. The Kingsleys weren't precisely rich. Comfortable, of course. Even well-off, what with Morton's hardware store having just branched out into the chandlery business with a new line of bronze, brass and galvanized fittings.

They could easily afford to pay for help. Morton had hired one girl after another, all buxom and fresh from the country, to help with the large house and the baby, but for reasons Josiah was only now beginning to understand, none of the girls ever lasted more than a few weeks. Thus it was that when Alice found herself in the family way again, only three months after baby Caleb was born, the burden of looking after the Kingsleys had landed square on Kathleen's fragile young shoulders. For the next few years she had served as unpaid nurse, housekeeper and maid, while Alice produced a set of twins and a baby girl to go with young Caleb. Meanwhile, it was common gossip that Morton was carrying on with his wife's best friend, the Widow Rhodes.

"I reckon you're wondering why I've come," Kathleen said finally, and Josiah reined in his rambling thoughts. "The truth is, I've nowhere else to go."

Josiah waited patiently. The child was obviously struggling to compose herself. Her chin had a tendency to quiver, but her shadowed eyes met his with a directness he'd come to expect from her.

"Nowhere to go?" he prompted when she seemed to have forgotten what she'd been about to say. Strange, he mused. She must be nearly eighteen by now, yet he always saw her as a child. The same child he'd caught in his mulberry trees when she was no bigger than a grasshopper. He had lectured her on the sin of stealing, then given her the freedom of his trees. He had tried—just how successfully, he had never quite known—to explain death to her after her parents had drowned, and had come to her defense when she'd stolen a neighbor's skiff and set out to sea all alone to find heaven, where her parents had gone to live.

"I'd never do that. Morton said I did, but I didn't."

Drat his rambling mind! What had she said? "I'm sure you didn't, child," he assured her, wondering what she'd been accused of but not wanting to ask her to repeat herself.

"But Alice believed him, and Patrice did, too. Did I tell you she was there when it happened?"

Morton. If that man had laid a hand on this child— "You say that Morton…?" he began, hoping to lead her into a fuller disclosure.

Her eyes slid away from his, and he had his answer. Choking back his wrath, Josiah made himself ask the question that had to be asked. "Did that wretch dare to lay a hand on you, child?"

"He…he—" She broke off, her face splotched with color. "That is, I'm mindful of the fact that he took me in when I'd nowhere else to go, and—"

"And you've repaid him a hundred times over." Josiah clenched the stem of his pipe between his teeth.

"You see, I wasn't expecting him. Caleb was up the street playing with the Guthrie boy, and the twins were asleep, and Alice had taken the baby over to visit with Patrice. They were planning Alice's birthday party."

"Did Morton know she'd be gone?"

"I suppose so. Yes, she told him at breakfast."

"And he came home and found you there alone?"

"I was out in the backyard, picking figs. Sometimes I— I sing to myself when I'm working. That's probably why I didn't hear him when he came up behind me."

"What did he do? Did he—ah, greet you?"

"Not in words." Her voice sounded extremely small in

the stuffy little room. "He—he came up behind me and put his arms around me, and I think I must have cried out. I was so startled, I dropped the basket, and when I tried to see who it was, he—he laughed. Then I knew, of course, and I—well, I'm afraid I kicked him."

"Good, good, an entirely appropriate reaction, I'd say. Go on, child, get it out of your system, and then I'll have Louisa fix us a pot of strong tea and bring in some of her pecan pie."

Kathleen drew in another deep, shuddering breath. She seemed to have got a grip on her emotions now, for her voice was steadier as she told how she had demanded to be released, and Morton had laughed and turned her around in his arms and tried to kiss her.

"Had he ever done anything like this before?"

"Not—exactly. Sometimes he bumped into me, or— touched me. On the shoulder or the arm. Once on the…" She looked away, and a moment later, she continued. "He used to come to my bedroom late at night."

Josiah tugged at his high collar. Heavenly Father, he didn't want to hear this!

"I always pretended to be asleep, and after awhile, he would go away. I was petrified, hearing him breathing, knowing he was there. If he'd tried to—to touch me, I don't know if I could even have screamed. It was like a nightmare. I couldn't cry out, and I couldn't wake up, and he just stood there, and I could smell the cologne he always wore." She shuddered.

"Shh, it's over now, child, it's ended."

"Once—once he came to the bathing room when I was in the bathtub, claiming he heard splashing and thought it was Caleb."

"The unregenerate bounder! What did you do?"

"Pulled a whole shelf full of dry towels down on top of me, and then had them all to rinse and hang out again."

She managed a wintry smile, and Josiah felt his crusty old heart expand.

"It's over now. You're here, and you don't have to go back if you don't want to. You're eighteen years old, after all."

"Not quite. My birthday's the last of August, but Alice won't have me back, at any rate. You see, while Morton was trying to—um, he was holding me, and—and I'm afraid my shirtwaist had come loose when I'd tried to reach up and push him away, and my hair had come down, too. Morton kept trying to kiss me, and I had my face pressed against his chest so he couldn't, and Alice thought that I—that we...and Patrice did, too. I tried to explain, but they wouldn't listen!"

The Rhodes woman! She would have to be a witness! According to Louisa, she had the busiest tongue in town. If only someone from her late husband's business concern would call her away to Baltimore before she had time to ruin this poor child's reputation!

He would think of something. With the Lord's help, he would contrive some solution. "Well, we've done all we can do for the time being, so why don't you go out to the kitchen and tell Louisa to put on the kettle while I go fetch in your trunk?"

"I mean to find work tomorrow, you know," she told him very earnestly. "I'm good with children, and I've had considerable experience in looking after the sick and the elderly."

Josiah had no doubt of that. Between her grandmother and Alice, who even in the best of health could be extremely demanding, he had no doubt that the poor child had had more than her share of experience. "Well, I don't know about tomorrow. I wouldn't expect a miracle right off," he warned. "Women's work's not easy to come by in the best of times, and since the war, there's been so many widows...." Rising, he placed his pipe in a bowl of wax fruit on the table.

Kathleen followed him into the front hall. "I can sew. I make all the children's things, and my own. I'm counted a right fair cook, and I don't mind turning my hand to the heavy work, either. I'm a lot stronger than I look, Reverend Dunwoody. I'm never ill. My teeth are sound and I'm not given to headaches, and—"

"Child, child, you don't have to tell me all this." He stood in the doorway, hoping to catch the slightest breeze. "We'll find something, never you fear. Meanwhile, Louisa and I will be happy to have you stay on here as long as it suits you."

Josiah wanted to gather her into his arms and tell her everything would come out right in the end. Only he'd lived long enough to know that that didn't always happen, no matter how hard he prayed.

It was tall, thin Louisa, stern of face but soft of heart, who showed Kathleen where she was to sleep. "I can't thank you enough," Kathleen began, only to be shushed.

"There now, if I can't do my Christian duty by one of my brother's flock, why then, I reckon I've outlived my usefulness. Open the window if you've a mind to, it's some stuffy up here. Lordy, if it don't rain soon, there'll not be a thing worth pulling in the garden. Grass is already commencing to turn."

Josiah asked blessings on the fried mullet, grits and tomatoes the next morning. Louisa poured coffee from the graniteware pot, and Kathleen removed the biscuits from the oven and slid them into a basket.

Gracious Heavenly Father, Josiah thought in prayerful irritation, how could a supposedly civilized, enlightened society cast so many of its members out to fend for themselves? And why were they always the weakest ones, the women and children?

They talked of inconsequential matters over breakfast, then Josiah announced that he had a letter to finish writing before he commenced on Sunday's sermon. After that, he was expecting the woman he had mentioned to Rogan to come for an interview. When he'd first spoken to her about the position, she hadn't been all that eager to relocate, but he was counting on changing her mind before Rogan arrived. Which could be most any day now, he reminded himself as he settled into his favorite chair in the study.

As it happened, it was Kathleen who answered the door at half past ten to find a ragamuffin with a note clutched in his filthy hand.

"Preacher home?" the boy asked.

"Yes, he is. May I ask who's calling?"

The boy blinked twice and grinned, revealing a ragged row of brown teeth. "Ain't nobody calling so's I kin hear 'em. Lady says was I to give him this letter, he'd gimme a nickel."

About the same age as Caleb, the boy reminded Kathleen so much of her nephew it was all she could do not to drag him in the house, scrub him and hug him and ply him with milk and molasses cake. Instead, she said coolly, "I believe a penny would be sufficient."

Unrepentant at being caught out, he shrugged. "Maybe she said a penny. Gimme it, an' I'll gi' ye this letter."

"Wait right here." A moment later, she appeared with a penny and a large slice of cake wrapped in a scrap of kitchen cloth. "Now, do we have a trade?"

"Yes'm!"

Oh, my mercy, he reminded her so much of Caleb, it hurt! How was she ever going to get by without seeing her babies? Surely Alice couldn't mean to keep her from her own niece and nephews!

"Kathleen, is that someone for me?" Josiah called from the study.

"Sir, it was a boy with a note. He said some lady asked him to deliver it." She took it to him, and when she started to leave, he waved her to a chair while he scanned the few lines. "Is there something wrong?" she asked on seeing the furrows appear between his bushy eyebrows.

"Hmm? No, I suppose not. Leastwise nothing I can do anything about now. Kathleen, I've been thinking, and I believe I know what it is you need."

She sat on the edge of her chair, her spine ridiculously straight. "You do?"

"What you need, child, is a husband."

Kathleen's wide gray eyes widened even more. "No, thank you. Thank you kindly, sir, but a husband is precisely what I *don't* need."

"But a woman alone—" Josiah began. Never having been married, he was not in a particularly strong position to defend the breed as a whole. Nevertheless, he felt compelled to try. "Not all men are cut from the same bolt of cloth as your sister's husband, my dear."

"I'm sure you're right, but if it's all the same to you, I intend to be independent. In these modern times, women can do all kinds of interesting things to support themselves. It's just a matter of finding the right position."

Josiah sighed. "In Atlanta, or Charleston, or New York or Chicago, perhaps that's true, but I'm afraid that here in Beaufort, a woman's opportunities are fairly limited." Then, taking in the set of her small, stubborn chin, he said, "Well, promise me you'll give it some thought, that's all I ask."

Kathleen nodded, and having promised, she set herself to thinking about it. She thought of the only beau she had ever had. Marshal Partridge had come calling twice on a Sunday afternoon, and he had offered to be her partner at the fourth of July cakewalk, but when the time had come, two of the children had been sick, and she'd kept them all home, knowing it was only a matter of time before the other two succumbed.

Marry Marshal? He didn't frighten her the way Morton did, but she couldn't abide the scent of his hair pomade, and the way it melted and dribbled down the back of his neck on hot days.

"I thought about it," she told Josiah that evening at supper.

"Marriage? You'll consider it then?"

Sitting painfully erect, she replied, "No, sir. I don't believe marriage would suit me, Reverend Dunwoody."

"But, child—"

"Hush, Josiah, let the child be," Louisa remonstrated. "I never married, and I'm still here to tell the tale."

Josiah sighed. Kathleen stirred her she-crab soup and wondered where she could go when she left the haven of the parsonage. Louisa made up her mind to get her brother alone and tell him to quit his meddling. It was plain as the nose on your face that the poor child was scared to death of men. The very last thing she'd be wanting to do was to jump into bed with some strange man just so's she could be assured of a roof over her head and food in her belly.

After supper, Josiah repaired to his study, as was his habit, to enjoy his glass of port. He still had the letter to Rogan to finish, only now it seemed he would have to begin his search all over again. The good widow had already found a position that would not require relocating farther than Morehead, across the bridge.

He read the letter he'd received nearly a month before, in which Rogan had deemed he would take it kindly if Josiah could have someone ready, willing and able to sail with him on his northward journey. Hetty desperately needed a companion.

"Companion!" he snorted. The poor woman sounded as if she needed a keeper. A woman whose mind was slipping its mooring would require someone strong and quick-witted, preferably someone young enough to stay one step ahead of her.

Stroking his jaw, he drew noisily on his pipe as a smile began to kindle in his eyes. What that young man needed, whether or not he was ready to admit it, was a stout young woman who would bear him half a dozen sons and daughters, not some middle-aged woman to act as nursemaid to a sickly old woman. Hetty wouldn't be around forever. Once she was gone, Rogan would be completely alone. And that, as Josiah well knew, was a sad fate for any man.

Oh, he had Louisa now to look after him, and a finer sister no man could ask. But he'd often wondered what it would have been like to have married. There were things a man could share with a wife that he could never share with a sister, especially not with a sister who had never married herself. Besides that, a lusty young man had certain needs, and if he were any judge, Rogan was a lusty young man in every respect.

Kathleen, on the other hand, was a complete innocent, despite her recent unpleasantness. After what had happened, a man would have to go easy there, but in time, the rewards might be well worth the wait.

Josiah nodded slowly, his eyes closing in a satisfied smile. He was a minister, not a matchmaker, he reminded himself. On the other hand, when two members of his flock were in desperate need and came to him for help, and when a solution to both their problems presented itself in one neat and tidy package, who was he to quibble?

"My dear," Josiah announced the next morning at breakfast, "I've been giving your situation considerable thought, and I believe I've come up with just the solution. Pass the salt pork, Sister.''

"You've found me a position? Where? Are there children?"

"Now, now finish your breakfast and we'll go into my study and I'll tell you about it."

Louisa gave him a stern look. "When did you have this blinding revelation, if I may ask? You've had enough of that pork, Josiah, I've already moved the buttons on your vest as far as they'll go."

The morning meal ended quickly, and Kathleen asked if she might be excused for a moment before washing the dishes.

"You run on, girl. You already scrubbed the pots and pans. I'll be done in two shakes with the rest. Run on, now, hear what that brother of mine has to say."

Josiah was filling his pipe when Kathleen joined him, and he waved her to a chair. "Now—" He jammed the stem between his teeth and lit the thing, and Kathleen waited, her short nails biting into the palms of her hands. "I know you said you weren't looking for a husband, child, but there's times when a situation comes along that—"

"Please, you're not asking me to—to marry some man, are you?"

"Not right off, and not in the way you're thinking. Let me tell you about a problem I've been asked to solve for the son of an old friend." He gauged her wariness and knew he'd better make it convincing. Carefully, he described the man he had sailed with all those years ago, and the woman that man had married to be a mother to his motherless son. "So now that same young lad has grown up, and the woman who looked after him has grown old and needs a companion. My friend is looking for someone willing to move to the Outer Banks and live in his house while he's at sea, someone with the patience and experience to look after an ailing old woman. Someone he can trust not to run off and leave her alone just because she gets cranky or troublesome. Someone honest, capable, dependable and kind.''

"And you think I might be that woman?"

"I'm sure you would suit admirably, my dear. You've had experience with the elderly before, and after these last few years of keeping up with your sister's children, I believe you could take on one old woman easily enough."

"Yes, but—you said something about marriage?"

"Hmm, yes, I did, didn't I? Well, let's forget that for the time being. For all I know, Rogan might have already found someone, and we'll have to start all over again on you."

"Oh, my mercy, I hope not," Kathleen murmured, and Josiah settled himself deeper in his chair, his smile hidden behind the hand that cupped his pipe.

"Have another glass of that port, boy," the reverend urged. "Louisa won't allow me more'n one in the evening, but that don't mean you have to go thirsty. Where were we? Oh, yes, I believe I was telling you that the widows hereabouts are all taken. There was one I thought surely would do, but bless me if she didn't up and take another position over across the bridge. Had two more in mind, but one's sickly, and one's not but a year or two younger than Hetty. No, son, what you need is someone younger, someone you can leave behind without worrying that she'll sicken on you, or up and go back to her own people. Women have this thing about family, you know."

"Fine. Young, old, I don't care as long as she's able, decent and not a mean sort. Before I'd see Hetty mistreated, I'd install her aboard the *White Witch*." Rogan frowned. "Although come to think of it, I seem to recollect Pa telling me how sick she was on the trip up the banks."

Josiah drew on his pipe. Rogan sipped his port wine. The two men were a marked contrast in looks, the one being squat and grizzled, the other tall, with a powerful build and the farseeing look of a man who'd spent most of his years at sea.

Rogan Rawson could not be called a handsome man, yet few women could resist turning for a second glance when he strode by. There was something about the intensity of his dark eyes, the strength of his jutting jaw and the firm cut of his lips that more than offset the fierce slash of his dark brows and the thrust of his twice-broken nose.

He was not a handsome man, yet women had been known to take one long look at him and forget the vows of a lifetime. To his credit, he had never misused this gift. Half the time, he was not even aware of it, although when it came to women, the chase had long since ceased to be a challenge. He treated the decent ones with the deference they deserved, gave the not-so-decent ones what they wanted when it suited him and avoided those who had fallen so far as to be a threat to a man's health, although he was never unkind about it.

"Now it just so happens that I do know of a woman who might serve," Josiah said. "She's had experience with the elderly. Nursed her grandmother until the old lady passed away, and then she went to, uh, another position. Children, sickly mother, large house to manage. Her sister's family, actually. Did a fine job of it, too."

"Then why is she leaving?"

Carefully brushing a trail of ashes from his vest onto the carpet, Josiah chose his words carefully. "Hmm, now that's what you might call a delicate situation, m'boy."

"She steals? Lord knows I can't have that, Josiah. One in the family's enough."

"No, no, that's not it at all. See, the thing is, she's young. Not what you might call pretty—plain, I guess you'd say.

Proper as a pope—nothing havey-cavey there. A mite prim, but that's to be expected in any decent young woman. The thing is, when a man begets so many children on his wife that she's always big as a house, and sickly on top of that, sometimes what's right under his nose gets to looking pretty good to him."

"Oh, hell, he didn't!" Rogan made no effort to hide his disgust.

"No, I don't believe he did, but he came close enough on a number of times to scare that poor girl out of her wits."

"Why the devil didn't she scream bloody murder?"

Josiah shrugged. "Why knows? Maybe she did and no one heard her. Maybe she thought no one would believe her. Maybe she was afraid of losing the only home she had."

"So what happened?"

"The bounder caught her alone and tried to take advantage of her, and his wife happened to catch him. Unfortunately, she was with a neighbor at the time, the town's worst gossip, so there was no way they could hush it up, even if they'd wanted to. The sister kicked poor Kathleen out on her ear, and she came to me because she didn't have anywhere to go."

"Why didn't she defend herself? No backbone?"

"Oh, she's got backbone enough to run a railroad, but when a woman's hurt or frightened, maybe she don't think too clear. Maybe, too, the wife knew which side her bread was buttered on and came down on the side of that no-account husband of hers, in which case her sister didn't stand much of a chance."

"Josiah, I don't know about this. She sounds—"

"Now, don't make up your mind too quickly, boy. You're in need of a worker, and Kathleen's in need of a home. Seems to me this situation is— Yes, what is it, Louisa?''

''I'm sorry to interrupt you, brother, but Mrs. Rhodes is here, asking to speak to you. I told her you were busy, but she said it was important.''

Josiah would rather have taken a dose of castor oil. He had a fair notion what the widow was up to, nosing around for more gossip. He'd like to have sent her packing, but he was a minister, and while she wasn't a member of his flock, she was still one of God's creatures.

''Would you mind waiting a few minutes, Rogan? The backyard's right pleasant this time of day. Leastwise, there's some shade under the mulberry trees. You can go out through the side door there.''

Rogan stepped outside with no purpose in mind other than to wait until he could continue his conversation with Josiah. When he saw that he was not alone, his first feeling was one of irritation. On the heels of that came curiosity.

The woman striding along the side of the road toward the back gate with a market basket over her arm was kicking up dust with every step. She was garbed all in black, but it was an unbecoming shade of black in an unbecoming style that put him in mind of a rusty poker. She was thin, too thin. She was pale, her small face completely colorless except for a smattering of freckles that were shaded by the most god-awful hat he'd ever beheld. The thing was enormous, and apparently anchored to a wad of hair on top of her head so that it flapped with every step she took. Smack dab in the middle of the crown was a heap of gray feathers that resembled a pigeon that had been run over by a speeding carriage. The poor thing seemed to be struggling to launch itself.

In the process of withdrawing a cheroot from the pocket of his shirt, Rogan froze. She was coming into the yard. She was coming *here!*

Plain, prim, proper, and with enough backbone to run a railroad. That would describe her perfectly. That spine of hers wouldn't have stretched any stiffer if she'd been hanging from a white oak tree.

"Miss, ah…" He stepped forward, out of the shadow of the mulberry tree, just as it occurred to him that he'd never heard her last name.

Kathleen glanced up warily. She'd gone to Mr. Davis's store for a peck of potatoes and a quarter's worth of side meat. Louisa had said they'd be having company for supper. "You're the company," she said, her eyes wary as she sized up the stranger and found him too big, too dark, too *everything*.

"Rogan Rawson, miss. Josiah called you Kathleen, but I'm afraid he didn't tell me your last name."

"It's Stevens," Kathleen whispered. She clutched the basket with both hands, wondering whether to shove past him or to ask him to step aside. He was standing directly between her and the house, on the narrowest part of the path, with the dewberry patch on one side and the privet hedge on the other.

"Miss Stevens," Rogan Rawson repeated, and she was struck by the timbre of his voice. He spoke quietly, but with an authority she had never before heard from any man.

"Are you a minister, too?" she blurted. The words just popped out. His eyebrows reacted first, and she stepped back. They were black as soot, straight as an arrow, tilted over eyes so dark they defied description. They puckered, and she tried to remember what it was she'd just asked him, but for the life of her, she couldn't.

My mercy, the man was intimidating! Just as she'd been getting her nerve up to go forth on her own and find herself a position, she had to run into someone like him—someone who could scatter her wits with no more than a frown!

"What makes you say that?"

"Say what?"

"What you said," Rogan repeated, his earlier impatience back in force.

What did I say? Kathleen thought frantically. Oh, yes, I asked him if he was a minister. "Well, what's so wrong about that?" she demanded, clutching the basket handle until the knuckles of her red, rough hands showed white.

Then he grinned, and the starch drained right out of her, leaving her feeling limp. "Why, nothing, I reckon, only I'm about as far removed from a preacher as you could ever hope to find."

"You're a devout sinner, then?" Dear Lord, what had rattled her brain? Here she was trading impudent remarks with a stranger as if she'd been doing it all her life. The plain truth was, she was so far out of her element, her tongue was running away with her.

It had to be the heat. If she didn't get out of this dratted gown soon, she would melt right down to her shoe tops.

And if he didn't get out of her way, she was going to—to hit him with a potato!

"I'm a sailor, Miss Stevens, and not all that devout, I'm afraid."

"I'm sorry about that. About calling you a sinner, I mean, not a minister. I expect it was your voice," she explained to the dusty pale ground between them. "I mean, you sounded as if you could—well, that is, you sounded..." She gave up. She'd never lacked for wit, it was just that her brain seemed to be lagging about two beats behind her tongue.

Rogan waited, intrigued by the beady eyes on what must be the head of her pigeon. They were uneven. The beak was even worse, one part being so far out of alignment that if the poor bird hadn't come to grief under the wheels of a carriage, it would surely have starved to death.

"I'd better get these potatoes in to Louisa," she muttered, and shot him a stern look from under the brim of her hat. Move, she willed silently. Move out of my way before I tromp right over you!

Her eyes were gray, too, Rogan noticed. Not gray like the pigeon, but a soft shade that hinted of smoke and cool rain. They were set in a bed of lashes so dark and thick they almost obliterated the lavender shadows around them. Almost, but not quite.

Without comment, he stepped aside and let her pass, turning to watch her as she made her way to the back stoop. Josiah had been dead on course. She was prim, all right. On the hottest day of July, she was dressed in an ugly black frock with long sleeves and a neck high enough to strangle a giraffe. He knew enough about fashion, having dressed more than a few mistresses over the years, to know that a frock like that, while it might have once been expensive, was too far behind the styles ever to catch up.

Besides which, the poor little twit couldn't have carried herself any stiffer if she'd had a poker rammed up her back.

But plain? He wasn't so sure of that. Yeah, all right, so she was plain. If she'd had a touch of pink cheeks in that pale little face of hers, or a pair of sweetly curved rosebud lips—maybe if she'd had golden curls instead of straight brown hair that slipped its mooring a bit more with every step she took, and if her eyes had been blue instead of gray...

Yeah, she was plain, all right. She was all the things Josiah had said she was, but somehow Rogan had a feeling that that wasn't the sum total of Kathleen Stevens. And it was the rest of who she was that intrigued him.

Chapter Two

Patrice Rhodes left, having learned little more than she already knew, which was irritating, but then, she already knew enough. What she didn't know she could surmise. Perhaps now that she'd caught them together, Alice would remember other suspicious instances. Patrice would invite Alice over for lemonade and cakes this very afternoon, and between them they would sort it all out. Although Alice, poor twit, had the brains of a cabbage.

As for Morton, Patrice still hadn't decided to forgive him for straying. And with that pathetic stick of a girl, at that! True, he'd been growing rather boring lately. She'd been thinking of replacing him, but there was no denying the convenience of having one's lover so discreetly situated. Out one back door and into the other, and no one the wiser.

Turning the corner, she caught a whiff of smoke from an expensive cigar, usually a sure sign of an interesting masculine presence. There was nothing like the smoke of a good cigar mingled with the scent of a masculine cologne to set a lady's heart to fluttering.

Under cover of her ruffled pink parasol, she glanced around, but there was no one in sight, male or female. Noticing a faint drift of smoke from the Dunwoodys' backyard, she began to dawdle. Old Dunwoody smoked a smelly old pipe. Perhaps, after all, she had not been mistaken in thinking she'd seen a man slipping out the side door as Louisa showed her into the study.

Her delicate nose twitching, Patrice stepped through the parsonage hedge and began to call softly, "Here, Spotty, here now. Come to Mama, you bad doggy."

A man stepped out of the shadow of a nearby mulberry tree, and she nearly keeled over. Glorious day, but the man was magnificent! A stallion on two stalwart legs, if she was any judge of men. And of course she was.

"Oh, dear, you startled me," she gasped with an appropriate flutter of her hand.

"Beg your pardon, ma'am. Have you lost your dog?"

"Oh, have you seen him?"

"No, ma'am, I can't say as I have."

Those shoulders! And she simply must—*must*—touch that wonderful chest! Dear Lord, just looking at the fit of those tight seaman's trousers was making her ache in the most delicious way! She would have cheerfully given a year's dividends to have him in her bed, naked and eager, just for one night.

"Oh, that little wretch." Looping the ribbon of her parasol over her wrist, she planted both hands on her hips in a manner designed to show off her nineteen-inch waist and the swell of her full bosom. "Do you suppose he could have gone on home without me? I do so count on Spotty for company. Since my dear husband passed away, I'm all alone, you know." Casting him a glance to evaluate the effect her disclosure was having on him, she sighed heavily and watched his eyes settle on her bosom.

Oh, ho, she had him now. All she had to do was reel him in. "I don't suppose you could...oh, no, I shouldn't ask."

"Ask what, ma'am?"

"Oh, please don't keep calling me ma'am. It makes me feel so old." Which was his clue, of course, to deny any such thing.

She waited, but he said nothing. Her Cupid's bow lips tightened imperceptibly. She was thirty-three, and in all but the cruelest sunlight, she could easily pass for twenty. Well...perhaps twenty-two. Of course, the pink parasol helped.

With another heave of her whalebone-elevated bosom, she opened the thing and twirled it over her head, even though they were standing under the shade of an enormous mulberry tree. "My name is Patrice," she confided. "Actually, it's Mrs. Rhodes, but if you'll whistle just once for Spotty for me, you may call me Trice. I never could learn to whistle, even though I've heard some women can do it quite well. Something about the pucker—" She demonstrated. "I could never get it quite right."

Once more she licked her lips and pursed them in what was surely an irresistible manner, but the dratted man was peering under the hedge and whistling for a dog that didn't even exist. Oh, the fool! Did she have to hit him over the head?

He whistled several times and called, as well, but there was no sign of a dog. Patrice would have swooned away if there were. She couldn't abide the smelly things, but then she'd had to have some excuse to accost a strange man. A lady couldn't simply stroll up and ask to feel a man's muscles.

"You must be related to dear Reverend Dunwoody, Mr. ah..."

Rogan turned to the overblown blonde. "No, ma'am. Rogan Rawson, and pleased to make your acquaintance, Mrs. Rhodes. The reverend was a friend of my father's."

He'd been on the point of going inside, hoping for another glimpse of that prickly little thing Josiah was trying to foist off on him, when this woman had barged through the hedge. Why didn't she keep her dog on a leash if she couldn't train the thing to obey?

"And are you a minister, too, Mr. Rawson?"

"No, ma'am, I'm a coaster. That is, I sail the coastal route between Beaufort and Baltimore."

"Oh, how exciting! I can just see you, climbing masts and doing all sorts of dangerous things while the sea rages around you!"

Rogan, distracted by the sound of women's voices in the kitchen, spoke without thinking. "Nothing exciting about it, ma'am, it's damned hard work, and as for climbing the rigging, I leave that to my crew. Uh—if you'll excuse me?"

Stunned, Patrice watched him disappear through the back door. Her face mottled with angry color, she turned and stomped off toward Ann Street, the palms of her hands sweating under her lace mitts as she clutched the bamboo handle of her pink parasol. Damn the man! Not once had he called her by her given name! Not only had he not asked where she lived, he had turned his back on her!

Ah, but she could be understanding. Young men were inclined to be volatile, to be—unexpected. It was one of the things she found so exciting about them. She could just picture that magnificent young creature standing on a rolling deck, those powerful legs of his spread wide apart as he used his whip on some hapless member of his crew. Jutting her lower lips, she blew at the film of moisture that suddenly blossomed on her face. Wasn't it a lucky happenstance that she had been planning a trip to Baltimore in the autumn to see the manager of her late husband's business?

Briskly, she turned the corner onto her street. Suddenly, Morton's perfidy didn't seem half so distressing. She made a mental note to ask a few discreet questions of her shipowning friends about a young captain named Rawson.

* * *

Kathleen remained in her room as long as she dared before going downstairs to supper. She had spend the past hour dicing and frying salt pork to go on top of Louisa's boiled fish and potatoes, and she feared the smell of it still clung to her hair.

Stripping, she quickly bathed in the tepid water on her washstand and changed into her thinnest underwear, leaving off all but a single petticoat. Then she sprinkled a few drops from her precious bottle of attar of roses onto her hairbrush and commenced to drag it through her long brown hair.

Fifty strokes for now, and another fifty before she went to bed. She had long since given up hoping that one day her hair would show signs of waving, the way Alice's did. According to her grandmother, tidiness and good moral character were the most important attributes a woman could wish for. All the same, she'd gone on hoping for a miracle until well past her fourteenth year. By then she'd been so busy that even tidiness was sometimes an impossible goal.

After the requisite number of strokes, she laid the brush aside and began braiding. Then, coiling the heavy rope on top of her head, she pinned it all around and offered up a small prayer that it would hold until bedtime. She had the slippery sort of hair that refused to hold. Her grandmother, in despair of keeping it out of her eyes, had cut a fringe when she was ten, and she'd worn it that way ever since. It wasn't particularly becoming, but it was neater than having it slither over her face.

The evening meal was an ordeal that seemed to go on far into the night, although it was still light outside when the menfolk finally wandered out to the front porch for a smoke.

"Cat got your tongue?" Louisa teased as they made short work of the dishes.

"What? Oh. I'm afraid I'm not a great talker."

"Wouldn't have nothing to do with the fact that Josiah's angling to fix the two of you up, would it?"

Kathleen covered the sugar bowl and sat it in a dish of water against ants. "He mentioned something about taking on the care of Captain Rawson's mother, but..."

"Stepmother. Took care of him when he was a boy. All the family he has left, poor thing. I'll say this about Rogan Rawson—he might've cut up wild in his younger days, but once he settled down, he's been a credit to his raising. Works hard, don't drink above the ordinary, and never a journey does he make but what he don't stop off and see to Hetty's comfort. Buys her gifts right out o' the blue. Pretty shawls, store-bought candy and suchlike. Why, he couldn't think more of her was she his own blood kin, and that's the gospel truth."

Absently, Kathleen shoved a pin into her topknot and reached for the dish towel. "I don't know, Louisa...I hadn't thought of going so far away."

"Hatteras? Why, it's no more'n a good hard day's sail up the banks. You could come back and see your sister's children whenever you took a notion. That's what's eatin' at you, isn't it?"

That was only a part of it. Rogan Rawson was the other part. By far the greater part, for he had the strangest effect on her. She'd been around men all her life. Josiah, little Caleb, old Dr. Koonce back at Pelletier's Mills. Morton.

"He's a fine-looking man," Louisa said quietly, and Kathleen nodded.

"I suppose. Not that that matters, of course."

"No, I don't reckon it does. He'll be gone all save a day here and a day there on his way up to Baltimore and back. Likely, you won't see him more'n a few times a year."

Moving slowly, Kathleen placed the cut-glass pickle dish on the shelf, her mind distracted by just what it was about Rogan Rawson that made her react so strongly.

Well, there was his size, first of all. As tall as she was, he towered over her. He looked strong enough to bend a cold iron bar with his bare hands...yet he didn't frighten her. It wasn't precisely the way he looked. At least, she didn't think it was. Nor the way he acted, for he'd done nothing at all to alarm her. Nor even the things he'd said, come to that.

Horse biscuits! She was imagining things. After lying awake half the night, reliving that awful scene with Morton and Alice and Patrice, after going over and over in her mind every word spoken, wondering what she could have said to make them understand that she had done nothing wrong, she'd woken up feeling lost and miserable, her nose stopped up and her eyes all wet, and now she was getting fanciful.

"Didn't half sleep last night, did you?"

Startled, Kathleen dropped the towel and bent to pick it up. It wasn't the first time the elderly woman had seemed to read her mind.

With a small laugh, she admitted it. "To tell the truth, I can't recall the last time I slept through the night. If it wasn't Caleb's sleepwalking, it was the baby's colic. With the twins, it was even worse. They still haven't sorted themselves out. One of them will be sleeping while the other one plays, and turn about, until I didn't dare shut my eyes more than a few minutes at a time."

"Couldn't Alice look after them?"

"She needs her rest. She's increasing again, you know."

"Harrumph!"

Josiah took turns talking to Rogan and Kathleen. At first he spoke to them singly. Once he convinced Rogan that he needed someone young, quick-minded and responsible to keep up with a woman in Hetty's condition, he set out to talk Kathleen into taking on the job. That done, he tackled the next hurdle.

"Now don't go flying off the handle, boy. I'm not talking about your usual kind of marriage here. Fact is, considering what that poor girl's been through, I doubt she'd have any man under those conditions. I'm talking about a good, solid, sensible arrangement where you agree to give her the protection of your name and she agrees to take over your shoreside responsibilities, leaving you free to go your way. Seems to me like you both get what you're wanting."

"I guess I could hire her," suggested Rogan, shifting uncomfortably in the hard oak chair.

"But then you could turn her out. Or she could walk out on you when she'd had enough of Hetty's foolishness."

"I'd be willing to sign a contract," he offered a little desperately.

"That's just what I'm suggesting, boy. But you see, there's only one kind of contract suitable for a young lady to sign that won't blight her reputation, and that's a marriage contract."

Rogan tugged at the collar of his white cotton shirt. In deference to the heat and humidity, he had left off his coat. He wished to God he could have left off all but his drawers, but certain things were expected of a gentleman in the presence of ladies. "Yes, well, you see, that's where I run aground. I don't have anything against marriage, Josiah—leastwise, not for other men. But the truth is, I never planned to marry. It just don't suit my nature."

Much to Rogan's growing unease, the elderly man beamed. "There, there, I knew it would work out just right. Don't you see, boy, it's the perfect solution. You need a woman in your house, but you don't want a wife. Kathleen needs a roof over her head, but the last thing she wants is a husband. You both sign the contract, I'll read the service, and you'll both get your wish."

Rogan was on his feet like a shot. "Now, hold there! Just a blasted minute there, Josiah, I figured you for better than a fast-talking hustler! What do you mean, we both get our wish? How can we get our wish by marrying one another when she doesn't want a husband and I don't want a wife?"

Thus it was that two days later, Kathleen found herself standing beside a stern-faced Captain Rawson in the Dunwoody parlor. Josiah had wanted to marry them in church, but they'd both spoken out against that simultaneously. When Josiah had backed down, they'd looked at one another with no small degree of satisfaction.

As hot as it was on the twenty-first day of July, with not a cloud in the sky, Rogan had worn his best black suit, a black tie and a new white linen shirt. Billy, his cabin boy, had polished his tall black boots and the gold braid on his black leather-brimmed hat, but he'd left that on the hat rack in the hall.

He'd bought her a plain gold band, but he hadn't thought to bring flowers. It wasn't that kind of a wedding. However, Louisa had picked everything that was blooming in the yard and gone across the street to beg the last of Bertha Willis's sweet William, which was enough, with her own petunias and a few odds and ends, to make a right pretty bouquet.

Kathleen had taken great pains with her grooming, even though it was no more than a business arrangement. She had hung her best gown on the back stoop to air, after sponging it with vinegar water. She'd polished her shoes, rubbing Vaseline into the cracked leather until it gleamed almost like new, then she'd tackled her hat.

"Here, I thought you might like to wear this," Louisa said, slipping into the cramped guest room with a forget-me-not-trimmed Italian straw. It was lovely! Small, feminine, it was not quite the latest fashion, but certainly far closer than Kathleen's best bonnet, which had been Alice's fourth best three years ago.

"Oh, you're wearing black?" the older woman exclaimed.

"I only have black, if you don't count my gray skirt and brown shirtwaist."

"Looks more like mourning than marrying."

"It is." Kathleen managed a small smile, surprised that her face didn't crack. She'd felt as if it were frozen ever since she'd heard herself agreeing to this farcical wedding. A hundred times she'd wanted to run back into Josiah's study and tell him she couldn't possibly go through with it. Two things had stopped her. She was a woman of her word, having had responsibility drilled into her all her life. And she had nowhere else to go. She couldn't impose on the Dunwoodys any longer. They had been kindness itself, but she knew for a fact that a parson's stipend would only stretch so far. "Alice had closets full of lovely things she wore after Grandmama died. When I was fifteen, I suddenly shot out of everything I owned, and she gave me the whole lot to make over. The taffeta is particularly nice, I think, don't you?"

Louisa did not look convinced. "Perhaps a spot of color...a scarf, or a pretty bunch of flowers up at the neckline. Why don't I take these forget-me-nots off—"

"Oh, no, please don't ruin your beautiful hat!"

"Pshaw, child, they're only pinned on. One week I pin on fresh jonquils, the next week a bunch of wax cherries and a ribbon or two. Come September, I have a nice dark red velvet rose."

So there she stood, her black taffeta still smelling ever so slightly of vinegar, her shoes glistening with Vaseline and Louisa's forget-me-nots pinned under her chin. In case Captain Rawson thought she was too frivolous, she had insisted on wearing her own black hat with the gray dove, but then Louisa had spoiled the sober, businesslike effect she'd hoped to create by handing her at the last minute a bouquet of petunias, sweet William, boneset and horsemint.

The flowers trembled so that a few petals fell to the floor. Near the door, Bertha Willis and Fanny Gillikin, who had come by to see about the altar flowers for Sunday's service and stayed on as witnesses, began to sob. Louisa played "Lohengrin" on a wheezing old pump organ, and Josiah began to speak.

Chapter Three

Watching her trunk being carried aboard the schooner *White Witch*, Kathleen fought against a wild surge of panic. Going to sea was bad enough, but leaving Beaufort? Never in all her seventeen years and eleven months had she been farther away than Pelletier's Mills, and that by way of farm wagon.

As for the rest of it—well, her mind simply refused to deal with it. Married? She couldn't be! Last week at this time, she'd never even heard of Rogan Rawson. Could she have dreamed the whole thing?

Hardly. She could still see her reflection in the gold-framed mirror over the mantel as she stood there like a gray-faced ghost beside the tall, sun-browned stranger. They'd both been dressed almost entirely in black. He'd worn a white shirt that had made his skin look the color of a copper penny, and she'd worn Louisa's forget-me-nots under her chin. Something borrowed, something blue, she'd said. The flowers had served as both.

Married. But it was only a business arrangement, she assured herself. They had argued long and hard before they'd come to an agreement. Kathleen had been against it from the very first, but no less than Rogan had. Neither of them wanted marriage. It had been Josiah who had worked on first Rogan, then Kathleen, arguing that marriage was the only sensible course of action.

Homesick, heartsick and frightened, Kathleen had let herself be convinced. In the end, she'd had little choice. Positions for women were hard to come by. There was never a guarantee of lasting employment, no matter how rosy things looked in the beginning, and she had nothing of her own, no money, nowhere to go.

"Do you want me to talk to Alice and see if she'll have you back?" Josiah had asked.

"I'd rather work on a chain gang than live under Morton's roof."

"I doubt if that's an option, my dear."

It was Louisa, a spinster herself, but one who, as a parson's housekeeper, had seen much of life, who had finally made the young woman see that, while marriage had its unpleasant side, at least it was permanent. A wife could hardly be let go as easily as Morton and Alice let go one maid after another.

"A smart woman earns a man's respect right away. You set about making yourself indispensable to that boy and you'll have a secure place for life. A man knows when he's well-off. Why, Josiah couldn't get along without me."

A wife and a sister were two different things, Kathleen thought wryly. Still, there was something to what Louisa had said. A permanent home where one was respected and needed... Kathleen had never expected to be loved, but she desperately longed to be needed. Perhaps marriage would not be too great a price to pay, after all.

Oddly enough, it had been Rogan's reluctance that had tipped the scales. It was quite obvious from the way he looked at her whenever she was in the same room that he was no more anxious to be saddled with her than she was with him.

Rogan had had his own last-minute doubts. In an earlier day, he might've been called a rake. He thought of himself as a man who worked hard and played hard. A man who liked women and enjoyed the freedom to pursue them.

The problem was, as he'd explained privately to Josiah, that he could no longer trust Hetty alone, and there was only so much a man could ask of his neighbors.

"Like I told you, boy, the only sensible thing to do is find a healthy, biddable young woman, someone plain enough and poor enough to be grateful for a good home, and marry her."

Sensing defeat, Rogan had argued that the last thing he wanted was a wife hanging around his neck, to which Josiah had replied reasonably that a woman could hardly hang around his neck if his neck was not there to hang onto.

"That's not the whole of it, though."

"You can't afford another mouth to feed?"

"Dammit, it's not that, Josiah!" Downing his port, Rogan had commenced to pace restlessly around the cramped study. "The *Witch* is more than earning her way. Just last year I bought a third interest in a four master running dyewood from the Indies to New York. The *Arduous* is already earning us twenty-nine dollars the ton just for hauling, and I put my first profits into a small packet that runs freight out to the banks."

"Then what's the matter, son?"

Rogan tugged at the collar of his shirt. He flexed his shoulders, looking like a man who felt himself hemmed in and didn't care for the feeling. There were some things a man didn't discuss with a minister. "The thing is, when it comes to women…uh, well, you see, Josiah, there's this widow woman in Pasquotank County…"

Josiah nodded thoughtfully. Not for a single moment had he doubted that there'd be women aplenty willing to warm the lad's bed. As a man of God, he didn't condone adultery, all the same, when a man stood in need of a good woman and there was a good woman in need of a protector...

Well, sometimes the Lord worked in mysterious ways.

Thus it was that, with no family of their own present to wish either of them well, Kathleen and Rogan had heard themselves pronounced man and wife, for better or worse, until death did them part.

Now, standing beside her scowling husband on the waterfront, Kathleen braced herself against a brand-new fear. The last time she'd set foot in a boat of any kind was five days after her parents had been lost at sea. That had been a skiff. "It's big, isn't it?"

"She's some over sixty foot long, eighteen foot athwart and about thirty ton burden. There's three passenger cabins, and not but two of them let, so you'll have a room to yourself."

That was a relief, although she'd been willing to share with another woman passenger if need be. Wistfully, she glanced over her shoulder, hoping against hope that Alice had brought the children to see her off. She'd written last night, and Louisa had sent the note around by Bertha Willis's youngest boy. She knew for a fact that he'd delivered it, but evidently her family had decided against further contact. It was just as well, she supposed. She didn't know whether to be shamed before her family to be marrying a perfect stranger, or shamed before her new husband that none of her family had cared enough to come see her off.

"Are you sure you're all right, ma'am? You look a mite green about the gills to me." Rogan's broad shoulders blocked the sun from her face, and Kathleen managed a creditable smile. "I'm quite well, thank you, Captain Rawson."

Looking vastly relieved, he took her arm and steered her along the wharf. "Glad to hear it. Blessed if I know how I'd have got you home if you couldn't tolerate the sea."

Home. The word rang in her head, making her blink hard against the sudden humility. But before she could lapse into self-pity, Rogan steered her up the gangplank, holding her arm as if he feared it might break.

Once aboard, she had to stop and stare. It was chaos, but orderly chaos. Men were everywhere, rushing about. One was dancing along a massive boom, another swinging from a line overhead. Some were cursing, some were laughing, but all seemed to be in wonderful spirits. Even amidst all that, she could see that the ship was clean and tidy, which she took as a favorable sign, for she could never abide slovenliness.

Suddenly, the deck gave a slight lurch as an enormous crate was trundled on board. Her belly responded with a lurch of its own, and she gripped Rogan's hand.

With a look of surprise, he glanced down at her, and she instantly released him. "I'm sorry. It—I was startled, that's all." She adjusted her hat, which was anchored to her top-knot, which unfortunately was beginning to slide. "Perhaps if I could go to my cabin?"

With a look of relief, Rogan signaled a gray-haired seaman who reminded her somewhat of a weather-beaten Josiah Dunwoody. "Mrs. Rawson, I'd like to present my first mate, Dick Styron. Dick, show my wife to number three and then rout out Billy and send him below to see to her needs. I'll have your trunk sent down soon's it comes aboard, ma'am." And with that pronouncement, he left her.

Kathleen looked at the grizzled first mate. She looked up at the three sharply raked masts, back to the crew jockeying the crate into position to lash down, and then back at Dick Styron. Before they'd even left the harbor, she was already feeling as lost as if she'd been stranded on a raft in the middle of the ocean.

"If you'll permit me, Miz Rawson," said the first mate.

He offered her a bow that would have done credit to a beruffled courtier and shot out an elbow.

Resolutely, Kathleen nodded, causing her hat to shift another degree to the starboard. "That would be lovely, Mr. Styron." Accepting the proffered arm, she confided, "I'm afraid I'm unfamiliar with boats."

"Begging yer pardon, ma'am, but she's a ship, and as fine a schooner as you'll find anywheres on the coast. Cap'n Rogan, he'll keelhaul a shirker quicker'n you can say scat, but he's a fair man and as fine a seaman as ever commanded a coaster. Taught him from a boy, I did. Betwixt me an' ol' Captain Edmund, the boy's father, young Rogan knows ever' shoal and slough from Beaufort to Baltimore. I seen that boy come through many a hurricane on a jib and a spanker when stouter vessels was getting mommicked something fierce."

By the time Rogan's first mate had finished his little eulogy, they had reached the passengers' section of the stern castle. Scant light filtered through the small portholes, but there was enough to see that the *White Witch* was as tidy below decks as she was above.

"Yes, ma'am, a ship is sure enough female, and that's the Lord's truth," Dick Styron went on as he ushered her along a narrow, darkly paneled corridor. "Like a good woman, she takes a strong hand at the helm to keep her from going to hell with all sails a-flying. Er, begging yer pardon, ma'am, no offence intended."

"None taken, Mr. Styron," Kathleen assured him. Remarkably enough, she was feeling considerably better about embarking on this mad venture. At least she was until, peering from under the brim of her bonnet, she caught sight of her husband striding along the narrow passageway, looking even more grim than usual.

Without so much as acknowledging her presence, he cornered Dick Styron and commenced talking rapidly about a bill of lading and some clearance or other that the customs officers were fussing over.

While the two men conversed, Kathleen took the opportunity to study the man she had so recklessly tied herself to for better or worse. In the angular light that fell through the porthole, illuminating his rugged features, she was struck afresh by his uncommon looks. How had the Reverent Dunwoody described him? A well set-up young gentleman of comfortable means who would be a good provider without making any undue demands on her position.

A gentleman? Now that it was too late to reconsider, she could see that his mouth was too sharply chiseled ever to be considered truly gentle. His means may be comfortable enough, but his eyes were far too intense for comfort; the granitelike structure that shaped his face from cheekbones to jaw fairly shouted stubbornness. And unless she was badly mistaken, that nose of his had been broken more than once. In a fight, more than likely.

Had she completely taken leave of her senses?

"What bee is buzzing around under your bonnet now, Mrs. Rawson?" Rogan suddenly demanded, turning to confront her.

Before she could answer, they were forced to step aside to make way for a man carting two steamer trunks and one of the new humpbacked Saratogas. The battered one on the bottom was hers.

Kathleen felt Rogan's hand at her back, and she arched as if he'd touched her with a hot poker. It wasn't that she was unused to being touched. Having had the full care of four children since birth, she was accustomed to being jumped upon, climbed upon, tugged at, clung to and embraced. Usually with sticky fingers. Yet the lightest pressure of the stranger's hand had burnt right through three layers of cotton and one of silk as if they weren't even there!

"M-my trunk. He's taking it away," she said, her voice as thick as a pauper's porridge.

"Dick, see to it, will you? I've got to go back and straighten out this business with customs. Report to me as soon as you get Mrs. Rawson settled. By your leave, ma'am."

He tipped his hat. Not waiting for her leave or anyone else's, he was gone. For a long moment, she stared after him, still reeling from the force of his vitality. It was more than the way he looked. It radiated from the very core of the man. He had removed his tie before they'd left the parsonage. Now he'd shed his coat and vest as well, leaving only the thin white shirt and a pair of close-fitting trousers that hugged his limbs like a glove. To come face-to-face with a man like Rogan Rawson was intimidating enough. To have married such a man was simply beyond belief.

They reached a narrow door with the polished brass number three mounted on it. Dick Styron reached for the knob, but before he could grasp it, the door swung open. A tall man with black beetling brows and a bushy mustache glared at the first mate, then shifted his attention to Kathleen. The mustache twitched as his gaze began working its way down her body. Before he had completed the course and begun the return journey, he was smiling broadly to reveal two gold teeth and one black one.

Kathleen was stunned into momentary silence, but not so her companion. "Egleston, this here cabin's been assigned to the lady," Styron informed him, with emphasis on the last word. "Yours is two doors down."

"I booked and paid for first-class accommodations—"

"All our passenger cabins is alike, so if you'll—"

"Except for number one. The bed's wet."

Kathleen was tempted to tell him to turn the mattress and sleep on the dry side, but she was still stinging from the look he'd given her. It was a look she was unfortunately all too familiar with.

Men! It wasn't as if she were pretty, or even fashionably dressed. Nor had she done anything to warrant such attention.

While Styron and the passenger went to examine the bedding in the cabin he'd been assigned to, Kathleen looked down the short passageway, locating two more cabins and another door that was unmarked.

"Sorry, ma'am," said the first mate as he rejoined her. "I think Egleston must have spilt something on it, meself, but he's a regular, and it don't pay to rile a regular. They'll spread tales like you wouldn't believe. Bad food, dirty quarters... Seen it happen before. Me, I'd rather haul freight any day than people. Freight don't make no demands on a man."

They passed by the other passenger cabin and stopped at the unmarked door. At this point, Kathleen would have settled for a pallet in a broom closet. She was suddenly exhausted. She couldn't recall the last time she'd had a full night's sleep.

Styron opened the door with a flourish to reveal a surprisingly spacious, well-appointed room. "Here you go, Mrs. Rawson, I'll see to having your things delivered right away."

"Please don't hurry on my account, I'm sure you're busy." That glorious bed! Oh, to sleep for hours without having to go fetch a glass of water, or pat up a bubble, or change a wet bed. Tomorrow would be soon enough to think about the future. For now, all she wanted to do was close her eyes and switch off her brain.

"I'll round up Samson with the trunks and see that yours gets to you right away, Mrs. Rawson, but first I'll send Billy down with tea and biscuits and a pail of warm water. It'll be a while till first sitting, but if you're hungry, I could—"

"Thank you, Mr. Styron, but I believe I'd like to rest now. You've been most kind."

The door closed behind him, muting the varied noises of the busy ship until they were no longer intrusive. Through an open porthole, Kathleen could hear the soothing sound of lapping water and the occasional cry of a gull. With a heavy sigh, she sank down on the plump feather tick, her whole body sagging. She was quite simply too tired to think, too tired to worry about anything beyond this moment.

It took the last bit of energy she possessed to get undressed. She removed her hat. The pins had been gouging her all morning. Next came her shoes, and she wriggled her toes in the neatly mended cotton stockings. Her toes relished their newfound freedom. Both her petticoats were old and soft. Her cotton lawn petticoat and her muslin pantalets were comfortable enough to sleep in. Thank heavens she didn't have to wear stays!

Folding back the sheets, she crawled into bed and snuggled down on her stomach, poking the pillow until she'd shaped it to suit her. Her last conscious thought was that the bed was much longer than the one she was used to, and it smelled of some elusive scent that was strangely exciting.

More than an hour passed before Dick Styron had time to explain to his captain that Mr. Egleston, the leather-goods salesman assigned to number one, was now in number three on account of a wet bed, which could have been because the porthole over the bunk was left undogged and salt spray had soaked the mattress, but was probably because the man had spilled his drink on the thing.

"Damnation! There's times I'm tempted to convert the passenger space to another cargo deck and be done with it! Leastwise bales of cotton don't complain about wet beds, cold food or rolling when the wind blows and the lack of speed when it don't.''

"Yes, sir. Ain't that what I been saying all along?''

"I quit listening to you when you wanted to turn this thing into a floating crap game. Where'd you put my wife?''

"In your quarters, and word is that Amos's boy's doing all right with his floating crap game.''

"Happens I'm a coaster, not a gambler. You want to ship out with Callum, I'll pay your passage down to New Orleans. How about number two?''

"The Crottses is in there.''

"Oh, hell, I forgot. Maybe you'd better plan to shift your gear to the crew's quarters until we get to Hatteras, Dick. I, uh—that is, Mrs. Rawson and I—oh, the devil, hadn't you better make ready to get underway? That business with customs is all cleared up. Damned clerk can't read.'' He swore again and turned away, leaving a smirking first officer to see to the last-minute preparations.

Watching the sails fill some forty minutes later, Rogan unconsciously caressed a spoke of the wheel, sensing the drag of current, the wind and a dozen other variants, just as he'd seen his father do countless times in the past.

While all his senses were alert to the business of getting his ship safely through the inlet and around the cape, another part of his mind was plagued by an altogether different matter.

That woman. That damned ugly bonnet! Was there something wrong with the shape of her head that she had to wear a hat all the time? He had nothing against women's hats in general, but that black thing was an abomination.

Josiah had warned him that she was plain. Under the circumstances, her looks didn't make all that much difference. It wasn't as if he had to live with her or anything. Still, he'd have thought a woman's wedding day would have called for something a little special in the way of a hat or a gown. He had had Billy black his boots till they shone like glass. He'd put on a vest with his black suit, surely a concession on the hottest day of the year!

What the devil was she hiding underneath all that ugly black taffeta? God knows, she had no call to hide herself from him. He'd had no designs on her even before Josiah had explained why she'd had to leave her sister's house. Married or not, the poor girl was safe as a door lock as far as he was concerned. He liked his women plump, blond, pretty and experienced. The Stevens girl didn't fit on a single count.

Maybe for a wedding gift he'd buy her a mirror so she could see for herself that she was no great temptation to any man, husband or not. Hell, she was skinny as a bird dog, and those great, gray eyes of hers were far too big for her bony little face.

All right, so he might've been the least bit moved by the shadows in those eyes. That had been before he'd figured out that they were probably just caused by her lashes, which were long and thick as a privet hedge.

And then there was her mouth. While he could hardly deny that her lips were full and soft and moist-looking, with none of the dryness that came from using stains, she wouldn't know what to do with them. A woman's mouth could be a wondrous thing, properly taught...

What was he thinking? Prim and skinny? All right, so maybe her waist *was* so small a man's two hands could easily span it...and slide down over gently rounded hips. Or upward, over soft, incredibly white breasts...

Swearing under his breath, Rogan glared at a packet that was overtaking, showing every sign of meaning to pass in the narrowest part of the channel. As if he didn't have enough on his mind, he had to keep an eye out for green seamen.

He'd better concentrate on maneuvering his way through this mess that glib-talking preacher had landed him in!

Dammit, he had gone ashore intending to hire a woman and ended up taking on a wife! How the bloody hell had Josiah managed to talk him into such a thing? He couldn't even blame it on rum! He'd been stone-cold sober the whole time he'd been ashore.

The trouble was, it had been too long since he'd taken the time to visit Della, his mistress of some two and a half years. A few hours in port now and again was hardly long enough to see to his cargo, much less hire a buggy to take him out into the county, where she lived, and to tell the truth, he didn't particularly care to drop in on her unannounced and discover that she was entertaining another man.

Josiah had hinted that Rogan might want to think of getting himself an heir now that he owned not only a home and an elderly schooner, but a packet and an interest in a four master. An heir he could live without. A *wife* he could live without, and fully intended to. But that didn't mean he intended to go around with a bone in his britches. A man needed a soft, willing woman underneath him from time to time—not some skinny prig in faded black taffeta who looked as if she'd break before she'd bend, for all her big eyes and soft mouth and fragile white throat.

Discovering that he'd been fondling the spoke on the wheel as if his hands were around a woman, Rogan swore under his breath. At this rate, he'd pile them up on a shoal before they left sight of land!

Guiltily, Rogan glanced around to see if anyone had noticed, but all hands were occupied with their duties. "Styron," he growled when the first mate swung up onto the quarterdeck.

"Aye, sir!"

"Take the helm."

"Hand 'er over." The old seaman grinned. He'd seen Rogan Rawson through many a storm, but this was one storm the boy was going to have to navigate by himself, snags, shoals, rips and all.

Rogan stood over the bed and stared at his bride for several minutes, feeling a growing curiosity. Asleep, she looked damnably young, with none of the primness that had irritated him so much. Not nearly as plain, either, he added with grudging honesty.

Had he really bettered his position by marrying her to look after Hetty, or had he simply added to an already intolerable burden?

Time would tell. Meanwhile, he would make a point of stopping off to visit Della on the no'thard run. A widow of some twenty-six years, she was even-tempered, discreet and a skilled lover, if not overly intelligent. He paid her well, and if she took other lovers between his visits, he could hardly blame her. As long as she was available to him when he needed her, he had no complaints.

His gaze strayed back to the woman asleep in his bed. Her lips were parted slightly, yet she didn't snore. Della snored like a sow—her only fault.

He caught the faintest drift of roses, which was surprising, considering they were several hours out to sea. Come to think of it, he'd been smelling a lot of roses lately.

Would a prim little thing like Kathleen wear scent? Somehow, he'd thought a woman who didn't seem to care how she looked would lack the vanity. But damned if he didn't smell roses, and there were none within twenty miles, as far as he knew.

Primrose, he thought, gazing down at the slender sleeping woman. He leaned closer and inhaled deeply of the warm, spicy fragrance, noticing as he did so that her skin was as smooth as the finest silk, her freckles no more than the lightest scattering of gold across a short, straight nose. He'd promised Josiah he wouldn't touch her unless she gave some sign of welcoming his attentions, and he was a man of his word. Still, he couldn't help but be curious. She was sleeping in his bed, after all. She bore his name. Soon she'd be living in his house.

What did *she* think of all this? Had she truly wanted to marry him, or had she seen a way to feather her nest? Some women never found pleasure with a man, he'd heard it said. Some considered lying under their husbands a duty and bore it with varying degrees of stoicism.

Would Kathleen be one of those? According to Josiah, she had neither invited nor welcomed Kingsley's attentions, but then, Josiah had heard only one side of the story. Perhaps there was another side. Perhaps all her nose-in-the-air primness, her high collars and drab garments were only a pose. Perhaps his little bride was really a wanton who had stirred up a hornet's nest under her own roof and then, when her family had turned her out, had gone in search of a safe haven.

It might explain why she didn't think twice about marrying a man she'd scarcely met. A man with a comfortable income, at that. Could she have been seeking to…?

Oh, hell, he'd be the last man to claim any real understanding of the female mind.

Straightening slowly, Rogan came to a decision. For better or worse, the deed was done. He was a fair man; he would give her the benefit of the doubt. As long as she kept her side of the bargain, he would keep his. He had never promised her more than that, after all.

But as he shut the door of his cabin silently behind him, the memory of those long silken lashes fanning out on her pale cheeks fresh in his mind, he couldn't help but wonder if he had made the biggest mistake of his life.

Chapter Four

Despite the increasing winds, which resulted in an uncomfortable rolling motion, the three other passengers as well as the captain were at dinner. Kathleen was seated at Rogan's right hand, with a Baltimore merchant named Crotts on her right. Mrs. Crotts sat across from her, between Rogan and Mr. Egleston, whom Kathleen had consistently ignored except for the most commonplace exchanges. She could hardly refuse to pass the man the salt, but she didn't have to like him.

She had woken from her long nap thinking of the children. Only now she was coming to realize quite how drastically her life had changed. What if she never saw them again? For all she knew, Captain Rawson might maroon her on his island home and leave her there until she was too old even to remember that she'd once had a family of her own.

"Don't you agree, Mrs. Rawson?"

"Don't I..." She stared at the flushed face of the round little woman across from her. "I do beg your pardon, I'm afraid I was wool-gathering."

With a decided gleam in his eyes, Rogan said, "Mrs.

Crotts was asking if you don't agree that sucking on ginger-root is an excellent specific for a rollicking belly.''

Kathleen was spared the need to answer as Mr. Crotts, a patent-medicine drummer, held forth on various nostrums throughout the corn chowder, the baked bluefish and half-way through the raisin pie.

Just as coffee was served, a crew member came and whispered in Rogan's ear. The captain excused himself and left. After that the spark somehow seemed to go out of the evening.

Styron joined them before they could adjourn. "Cap'n says if you'd like to come up on deck for a spell, there'll be a full moon rising directly. Might be yer last chance. Wind'll probably pick up some before the next watch.''

Mrs. Crotts allowed as how that sounded most entertaining. Mr. Crotts murmured something about posting his ledgers, and Mr. Egleston flashed his gold teeth around the table and offered to escort the ladies on deck.

"Thank you, but Mrs. Crotts and I are ready now. Mr. Styron, if you'll lead the way?" Surely in the company of another woman, she should be safe enough, especially as Dick Styron was with them. She might have had an unpleasant experience, but she was sensible enough to know that not all men were like Morton.

The air was decidedly cooler now that they were well offshore. Already there was a stiff breeze blowing. The first mate showed them to a sheltered place near the bow and left them there, claiming the call of duty. Egleston stood some distance away enjoying a cigar, and Mrs. Crotts, a cheerful tub of a woman who resembled her husband to a remarkable degree, chattered about her grandchildren and her garden and her neighbor's dogs. Kathleen began to relax. The long rest had helped. Knowing she was safe from Morton helped even more.

She made what she hoped were appropriate comments

from time to time, but in truth, her thoughts were elsewhere. Her gaze wandered from the faint glow of light on the eastern horizon to the ghostly gleam of canvas overhead and back along the shadowy length of the ship. Not that she was looking for anyone in particular.

Besides, he would be busy.

Turning her face to the wind, she watched the lightening horizon. To think she'd been uneasy at first. Why, sailing was really quite pleasant. All her troubles had been left behind, and she was drifting out of reach in a mysterious world filled only with the sound of rushing water, the creaks and groans of the rigging and the occasional snap of canvas overhead.

This was splendid! The damp air felt deliciously bracing, and not even the ceaseless prattle of Mrs. Crotts could disturb her overmuch. She was beginning to understand why so many men took to the sea. It had a way of lulling one's mind, as if the rest of the world had suddenly ceased to exist.

"My, did you feel that? I do believe it's getting rougher. Either that or it's commencing to rain," Amanda Crotts said as she drew her shawl closer around her plump shoulders.

"Rain? It couldn't be, the sky's still clear...although I do believe we've begun to roll a bit more." A shower of spray flew over the bow, wetting her face. Laughing, Kathleen stepped back just as the deck dropped sharply under her feet. Staggering a bit, she caught the railing. "Oh, my mercy, isn't this exciting!"

"Oh, la, my poor belly don't call it exciting," the older woman moaned.

"I've never done much traveling," Kathleen confided.

"To my sorrow, child, I have. If you'll excuse me, I'd best go get my gingerroot while I can still keep it down. Are you coming?"

"In a little while. You go on ahead, I'll just stay out here until the moon shows on the horizon." For the first time in years she felt completely free. Why, this was an adventure!

As Amanda Crotts scurried for cover, Kathleen clasped the wet railing and leaned forward eagerly. Another burst of salt spray dampened her gown, her face and her hair, which was now blowing wildly around her head, but not even that could dampen her spirits.

Suddenly, the future didn't seem quite so grim. Somewhere there was a lonely old woman waiting for her. A woman who needed her. Kathleen knew her limitations. She'd been reminded of them often enough. But she knew her worth, too. Captain Rawson would never regret having hired her. Having married her, she amended quickly.

"Ah, so this is where you got to, little lady. Don't you know it's dangerous for a beautiful woman to be out here alone at night?"

Kathleen stiffened. Clutching her skirts, she held them aside as if to avoid touching something unpleasant. "Good evening, Mr. Egleston, I thought you'd gone below."

"Can't think how you can stand the flap of that old fool's tongue. She does go on, don't she?"

"If you'll excuse me, I was just on my way to my cabin."

"Now, don't go rushing off, Kathy—it is Kathy, isn't it?"

"No, Mr. Egleston, it's Mrs. Rawson." Telling herself there was no reason to be frightened, she stepped back, but he reached out and caught her arm. She jerked it away and stepped back again, only to collide with a hard and surprisingly warm wall.

"Sorry I was so long, darling. Trouble in one of the holds, but it's all taken care of now. You were just leaving, Egleston? Don't let us keep you."

Rogan's arm had gone around Kathleen's waist to steady her. It remained there, like an iron corset. His voice, speaking over her shoulder, was deceptively soft, but there was no mistaking the edge to his polite dismissal.

Egleston mumbled a hasty good-night and fled, and Kathleen tried to move away. To her surprise, Rogan continued to hold her tightly against him, her back against his chest. His feet were spread against the roll of the deck, and she found herself in the awkward position of being nestled between his muscular thighs.

Face blazing in the darkness, she said, "I'm grateful you came along when you did, Captain Rawson. That man makes me uncomfortable."

"Then in light of the fact that I just rescued you from discomfort, do you think you might allow yourself to call me Rogan?" The hard edge of his voice had been replaced by an undercurrent of amusement.

Kathleen made another attempt to step away, but succeeded only in arching her back at an unnatural angle. "Would you mind releasing me?"

He chuckled. "Are you sure you'll be all right? I'd hate to go to all the trouble of securing myself a bride, only to lose her overboard before I even get her home."

"I assure you, Captain Rawson, that I—"

Just as he obliged her, the ship rolled to the port, lifted, then plunged forward into a trough. Both her arms and one of her legs flew upward, and she would have tumbled backward had not Rogan caught her again.

"Blast!" she muttered, grabbing for the hat she was no longer wearing.

Still laughing, Rogan held her with both arms as she regained her balance. "Spread your legs, madam," he suggested.

"I beg your pardon!"

"Part your limbs. If you plant your feet far enough apart

to give you a better purchase on the deck and take care not
to lock your knees, you'll soon master the proper stance.''

"Oh." She tried it, and indeed, it did help. By easing
first one knee and then the other, she was able to compen-
sate for the roll, but when the deck suddenly dropped out
from under both feet again, there was little she could do
except grab on to the closest thing at hand. Which happened to be her husband.

"I suppose you find this amusing," she accused after a
few such near disasters. She was getting better, but just
when she thought she had learned the waltz of the *White
Witch,* the flighty thing did something altogether unexpected.

"You've mastered the roll readily enough. Now we'll
work on the pitch and yaw. I'll have to admit, though, I'm
glad Mrs. Crotts went below. Don't know that I could have
managed the pair of you slipping and sliding all over me.''

"You should have warned us it was going to storm.''

"Storm? If it is, I'll be greatly surprised, ma'am.'' He
was allowing her more freedom now, catching her only
when the deck gave an unexpected lurch, but Kathleen's
every instinct told her he was enjoying her discomfort altogether too much.

"I'd like to know what you call it," she snapped, raking
a tendril of damp hair off her face.

"Ideal sailing weather. If the wind drops too much, we'll
be wallowing like a sick whale. If she picks up, there's
always the chance of water in the holds, and with a cargo
of rice, that's never something I care to risk. The only cargo
more dangerous in a storm is dried beans.''

"You're mocking me, sir.''

"No, ma'am. I've seen many a fine coaster split asunder
after water got to a cargo of dried beans. Swole up to five
times their size, they did. When the hatches flew off the
holds aboard the *Bessie, Mae and Annie* out of Wilmington,

they had so much force behind 'em that they tore through a main, brought down half the shrouds and carried two men overboard.''

Kathleen scowled at him over her shoulder. While she couldn't swear he was grinning, there was a suspicious gleam of white where his mouth should be. ''I don't believe a word of—'' she began, when another wave of spray struck her in the face. She gasped and stepped back from the rail, and once more he caught her.

His face was buried in her wet hair, his hands biting into her waist like hot iron pincers, and she gasped for breath. ''Roses,'' she thought she heard him murmur. And then something about…primroses?

''I b-beg your pardon?''

He stepped back, dropping his hands. ''You'd best go below, ma'am, before you get any wetter. If you catch a chill, Hetty'll not be much help to you, and I'll be on my way north as soon as I get you settled ashore.''

''But I haven't seen the moon yet.'' The moon! Dear Lord, had she lost what few wits she possessed?

''Cloud bank's settled over the horizon now. Likely there won't be much of a moon showing tonight.''

His curt voice was even more chilling than the wind against her wet skin, especially after those brief, unexpected moments of teasing. If he'd wanted to remind her of the businesslike nature of their arrangement, he needn't have bothered. She was well aware of it. She wouldn't have had it any other way.

''Kathleen? You do understand that I'll not be abiding ashore, don't you? We haven't had much time to talk, but Josiah assured me that you understood.''

Wrapping her arms around her shivering body, she nodded. ''I understand perfectly well, sir. You need someone to look after your mother—''

''Stepmother.''

"Stepmother, and I need—I need..." Unexpectedly, she sneezed, was blessed, then Rogan took her arm in a firm grip and steered her toward the companionway.

"Come below now, ma'am, you're wet as a barrel of eels. You change into your nightshirt and get under the blankets, and I'll send Billy down with a mug of hot sugared rum to warm you up."

"I'm perfectly all right." Kathleen, holding her skirt above her ankles, hurried along in his wake. It was either that or have her arm disjointed, for the man had a grip of iron, and though she was a fast walker, the length of his stride was more than a match for hers.

He shot a dubious look. "Then I'll just collect my gear now so I won't have to bother you later," he said. Releasing her arm, he opened the door and followed her inside the cabin. *His* cabin, which Dick Styron had assigned to her.

While Kathleen watched, Rogan went about gathering up a book, a wooden instrument case and a few items of clothing. He added several toilet articles to the small heap, then turned to where she stood beside her open trunk. Her hat was at the foot of the bed where she'd left it when she'd dressed for dinner, and they both stared at it now.

"Are you particularly fond of that bonnet, Kathleen?"

Startled, she told him the truth. "I detest the thing. It happens to be my summer hat, though, so I'll wear it until the weather turns. It serves well enough. Why?"

"Because I'd greatly appreciate it if you'd launch the thing over the stern come morning. Why d'you wear it if you hate it so?"

"I should've thought that would be obvious. I wear it to cover my head." She tapped her foot in irritation, the effect largely lost as her shoe, sole and all, was damp. "It just happens that I have the sort of hair that needs anchoring, and a bonnet helps." Not to mention the fact that she freckled if the sun so much as touched her skin. "In case you were unaware of the fact, Captain Rawson, a lady doesn't go about bareheaded."

His lips twitched, drawing her eyes. "Rogan," he stressed. "As I hope we'll be dealing together for many a year, I would appreciate it if you could bring yourself to call me by my given name."

Kathleen took in a deep breath, too late aware of the danger. The room was small, and it bore his essence. Tobacco, leather, pine soap and something subtly personal, subtly masculine. She was the alien here, and they both knew it. "Rogan," she said grudgingly.

"There, that didn't hurt a bit, did it?" He smiled. To her dismay, Kathleen found that she couldn't look away from him. The man was far from handsome, yet there was something compelling about him...

And she didn't like it, not one little bit! Handsome men were not to be trusted. Morton was generally considered to be handsome, although Kathleen had never been drawn to men with small, even features and small, even teeth. Of the pair, it suddenly occurred to her that Morton at his best had never affected her half as much as Rogan at his worst.

"Yes, well...good night, then," she muttered. What *was* there about the man? His nose was crooked, his cheekbones were too sharp and his jaw entirely too angular. And then there was the matter of his eyes. They were dark, deep set, and they had a way of looking right through her so that, no matter how much she wanted to, she was hard-pressed to ignore him.

"Do you always wear black?"

"Do I— Why, no. Sometimes I wear gray."

"Don't you like colors?"

"This is hardly the time to be discussing my likes and dislikes, Captain—Rogan. If you must know, I like colors well enough. I'm right partial to yellow, but my clothes all happen to be black or gray, so that's what I wear. Now if that's all…''

"Why?"

"Why what?"

"Why don't you wear yellow?"

Arms crossed over her breasts, Kathleen clasped her elbows and traded level stare for level stare. It never occurred to her to dissemble, her only thought being to answer his questions and be rid of the man. "I wear black and gray because my sister had a great many perfectly good mourning gowns after first our grandmother and then Morton's parents died. She was generous enough to allow me to remake them for myself when I outgrew my old things. Now, is that all, or would you care to examine my teeth? I assure you, they're all my own, and sound as a double eagle."

"Kathleen…" Rogan turned away, as if thinking better of whatever he had been about to say. At the door, he paused. "I'd like to assure you that you have nothing at all to fear from me. Josiah explained your—uh, your circumstances. You do understand, don't you, that I married you only because I needed someone to look after Hetty?" She made a strangled sound in her throat, and he went on as if determined to get it all said before he left her. "Just so you know that I don't intend to—that is, I'm not expecting—uh, that is, unless you wish it otherwise, I'll not be bothering you, ma'am."

Kathleen could feel the heat rising from her chest to the top of her head. Afraid to look for fear of seeing steam billowing up from her damp gown, she closed her eyes. Unless she wished it *otherwise?* Saints in heavens, why did he think she'd married him, if not to escape from the unwelcome attentions of a man?

"I'll not wish it otherwise, Captain Rawson, you can rest assured on that count," she managed to say.

He waited, and when she didn't elaborate, he nodded curtly. "Well. Then, uh…then I'll say good-night again."

No sooner did the door close than Kathleen's conscience began to squirm. This was his cabin she had taken over. If all the others were occupied, where was he to sleep? Cramped up in a corner somewhere on a heap of stiff canvas and coiled rope?

Before she could think better of it, she threw open the door and called after him, "Rogan? Where will you sleep? At least take your pillow and blanket—I can easily do without."

Looking over his shoulder, he favored her with a smile of such great tenderness that she felt it all the way down to her cold feet. "Thank you, Kathleen, but you've no call to do that. There's always a hammock and enough bedding to spare." Grinning for no real reason, Rogan strode off down the dimly lit passage. He would be bunking in Dick Styron's comfortable cubby, with Dick moving in with bos'n, along with the spare ropes and canvas. However, he saw no point in telling her that.

Just past midafternoon on the second day, the *White Witch* lay off the inlet that had been cut between Ocracoke and Hatteras Islands some thirty years earlier. The seas were just beginning to crash against the bar that nearly blocked the entrance as the tide began to flood. Pausing in his duties, Styron stood beside Kathleen at the forward rail and pointed out a break in the white water, explaining that within the half hour, they would be able to ease through the inlet with enough centerboard for steerage and water to spare under the keel.

"Captain Rawson don't trust many men to pilot her through. There's many a widow been made in this inlet, and it not but a few years old."

"I wondered where he was," she said before she thought.

"Schoolin' young Billy at the moment, ma'am. Taught 'im his letters and numbers, and now he's teaching the boy to read."

"Rogan?"

"Why, yes'm. See, Billy's ma wouldn't allow him to go to school 'cause she needs the money he earns, and Rogan, he couldn't make her take his money and leave the boy in school, so he give the boy a job of work to do, and on the side he teaches him what he'd a'been learning had he stayed ashore. Worked out right good, it did."

Kathleen covered her surprise and pretended an interest in a flock of gulls working a shoal of fish just off the starboard beam. It did speak well of the man she'd married, though. Perhaps she hadn't made such a bad bargain, after all.

With the weather holding fine and fair, all passengers were on deck, scanning the low, nondescript land on either side of the inlet for something of interest. There was little to see, but Kathleen continued to strain for a first glimpse of her new home.

To her great relief, since that first evening, Mr. Egleston had kept his distance, with no more than a polite nod in passing. She had no way of knowing that Rogan had as good as told the man that if he so much as looked at Kathleen Rawson, he would end up walking the rest of the way to Baltimore, beginning from where they happened to be at the time, which was three miles offshore!

Clapping a hand on top of her head to keep her hat from blowing off, Kathleen stood at the rail and drank in the first look at her new home.

"Them lumps of peat over yonder is all that's left of Fort Hatteras. Fort Clark's over on the other side, with Camp Wool tucked into a neck inside the inlet. Place was plumb overrun with Union forces. Couldn't move without stepping on one of the poor devils. Troubles, troubles,'' the grizzled first mate muttered, as if the land itself were responsible for all the woes of mankind.

Staring at the sliver of sand, Kathleen waited for her own troubles to come back. She'd lost her home, after all, and what little family she had left. Likely her good reputation, as well, knowing the malicious way Patrice Rhodes could weave a scandal out of thin air.

Yet all that seemed irrelevant now, as if time and distance had cast a magical spell. Truly, she had much to be grateful for. She could almost hear her grandmother's rasping voice telling her to quit sniveling. ''Forget what can't be changed, child. There's work aplenty for the least of God's creatures, so get on with it!''

Somewhere up ahead was an elderly woman in desperate need of what she had to offer. When they had stood before Josiah Dunwoody exchanging vows that had no real meaning in their particular circumstances, she had made God a promise. She might not love the man she had married, but she knew that he loved the woman who had raised him, and she could respect him for that. As long as she was able, she would do her very best to look after Hetty Rawson as if she were her own mother. Rogan Rawson would never have cause to regret his choice if she had anything to do with it.

''We're coming about!'' someone shouted, and she realized that the first mate had long since left her side.

''Let fly the first jib!''

''Mind yer noggins, she's a-layin' over!''

Suddenly, the crew was bustling about like ants in a ruined hill. The *White Witch* heeled over and took the wind, flying through the narrow channel. She veered sharply eastward, running some distance off, but still within sight of the long, low body of land that was Hatteras Island.

Kathleen strained for the sight of a town. She had seen quite clearly the dark, misshapen ruins of the first captured fort Styron had pointed out to her, and caught a glimpse of what might be another. The smudge of darkness that represented woods and perhaps a town was looming larger every moment.

What sort of town was Hatteras? Would the people like her? Would she like them? Suppose Hetty Rawson took an instant dislike to her? And what about Rogan's friends? Was there some particular woman who might be heartsick when Rogan brought home a wife?

Probably more than one. Kathleen was no authority, but it did seem to her that Rogan was the sort of man any woman would admire.

"I reckon we won't be seeing you once Captain Rawson sets you ashore," Amanda Crotts said. Now that they were in the more protected waters of the Pamlico Sound, the older woman seemed to have recovered her good health, although she did smell rather strongly of gingerroot. "How long did you say you two have been married?"

"Oh, it's been a while now." All of two days, Kathleen thought, bemused. Then she asked, "But won't you be coming ashore, too?"

"Not likely, dear. There's naught there but a handful of fishermen. No inn, not even a tavern where a body could refresh herself. We always sleep aboard when Captain Rawson stops off overnight. It's generally calm, and he anchors out of range of the pesky insects. Ashore, they're like to gnaw you to the bone. Hiram, see if you have some citronella samples you can give Mrs. Rawson. Here, fetch me that case of yours and let me see what this child needs." Turning back to Kathleen, she said in an undertone, "A change of water can overset a body's system if she's not careful, and you'll not find much in the way of a decent physic in this poor, godforsaken place, begging your pardon, my dear.''

A bleaker, more barren place Kathleen had yet to see. With sinking spirits, she walked beside Rogan through the loose scattering of small, weathered houses that seemed to huddle under the shelter of huge dark cedars and sprawling live oaks. There were none of the tall, grand buildings she was used to seeing in Beaufort. As to the streets, they were little more than cart tracks through the sand.

Rogan had sent her trunk ahead in a pony cart, but suggested they walk so as to point out to her various places of interest along the way. The nearest store. The nearest windmill. A road that led to a church.

People stared. Shaggy, unkempt horses browsed unfettered. Two men tying net in front of a house nodded to Rogan, and he touched his cap, but no one seemed overly inclined to visit.

Unconsciously, Kathleen closed cold fingers around Rogan's hard forearm. Crooking his arm, he covered her fingers with his own, patting them reassuringly. "Folks around here don't see many strange women," he explained. "During the war, the banks were overrun with soldiers, mostly Union forces, but other than that, we've been left pretty much to ourselves. They'll come around."

Suddenly, Kathleen wasn't sure she wanted them to. They seemed a rough sort, men and women alike, from what she could see. Dressed plainly in serviceable clothing, they had a way of looking directly at a body as if to say, who are you and what are you doing on my island?

"D-does Mrs. Rawson know about me?" she ventured as he turned them into a narrow lane that edged past a marsh.

"The other Mrs. Rawson, you mean? Call her Miz Hetty—we all do. There's a dozen Rawsons in the south village alone, a dozen Burruses, another dozen Ballances and a like number of Austins, Willises, O'Neals, Stowes and suchlike. We go by given names, not family names, or we'd never get one another straight.'' A smile broke the barriers of his stern face. ''In the case of two men holding the same name, one's called old, or young, or big or little. With a woman, it's easier. She's called by both her own and her husband's given name.'' His eyes twinkled down at her as she tried to sort it all out. ''In your case, you'd be called Kathleen Rogan.''

Kathleen Rogan? Somehow, that seemed far more personal than Kathleen Rawson, and she hadn't even got used to that yet.

By that time they had come upon a whitewashed house perched on pilings, much like others she had seen. Roughly a story and a half, the roof swept down unbroken by gables to cover a deep, sheltered porch. At one end stood a chimney, and jutting from the back was a covered boardwalk ending in a small, square room with another chimney, obviously the kitchen. There were no elegant columns, no handsome brick foundation, but the place was neat and well kept, like all the other houses she'd seen. And, like the rest, it showed signs of having weathered a few storms.

''My father built it for his first wife. There's a sitting room and a bathing room on the back, a spare room that used to be a parlor and a bedroom downstairs. The kitchen's out in the back. I sleep in the loft, and Hetty uses the bedroom, so I'll hang a curtain across the loft for tonight. Later on, you might want to turn out the old parlor and make a place for yourself. There's a few things out in the shed, or I can bring you a bed and a dresser down from Baltimore when I come south again.''

Kathleen was still trying to assimilate all that when Rogan led her up onto the porch. Without bothering to knock, he flung open the front door and called out,

"Hetty?" When there was no immediate response, he tried again. "Probably out in the kitchen," he said, but Kathleen didn't miss his look of uneasiness. Perhaps he wasn't quite as confident of her welcome as he'd led her to believe. She might not know her husband well, but she had been reading the expressions on little boys' faces for too many years not to know when one of them was hiding something.

"I expect she's off visiting Amos. That's Amos McNair, over across the marsh. He'll be your closest neighbor, so count on him for whatever you need." Taking her by the hand, he led her through the house and out the back door. "Hetty! Are you out here?"

Out of the corner of her eye, Kathleen caught a flicker of movement. "Rogan, is that—" Unconsciously, she rubbed the hand he'd dropped, staring past a large, fenced-in chicken run. Oh, my mercy, this couldn't be... "Rogan?" she whispered uncertainly.

She heard him sigh, then heard him swear, then he left her and strode toward the woman who was daintily picking her way along a plank over a swampy creek, a homemade bonnet in one hand, a dead chicken in the other. Sunlight glinted off the baldest dome Kathleen had ever beheld on man, woman or child.

"Hetty, what the galloping blue blazes happened to your head?"

Chapter Five

By any standards, Henrietta Beshears Rawson was a small woman. Compared to Kathleen, who was taller than average, she was child-size. She could have been any age between fifty and seventy, with leeway on either side. Her complete lack of hair made it remarkably difficult to judge. The faded gingham gown she wore had been patched in a variety of colors and patterns, and rose well above what was considered a decent, much less a fashionable, length. Her sturdy men's brogans were worn over cotton stockings that had been patched, not darned, using squares of gingham and calico and a veritable spiderweb of stitchery.

Kathleen's opinion of her new husband dwindled rapidly as she compared his impeccable black broadcloth suit, his fine linen shirt and his gleaming black boots with the pathetic costume this poor woman was wearing.

She moved away from his side, her back rigid with disapproval.

Ignoring her, Rogan said, "Hetty, what the devil have you done with—"

"Who's that, one of your fancy women?"

Under his perennial tan, Rogan's face grew red. "This is my wife. Her name is Kathleen, and she's come to stay."

To Kathleen's critical ears, there seemed to be some kind of warning implicit in the innocent-seeming words, but by the time he had completed the introduction, she was no longer sure of who was being warned about what. She was murmuring something she hoped was appropriate when Rogan broke in.

"Hetty, what in God's name happened *this* time? Your clothes and—what the hell, did you finally manage to set fire to your own head?"

"Well, I tried kerosene and I tried manure! What's a body to do, take a shotgun to the little devils?"

That was only the beginning. Within minutes, Kathleen learned that the poor elderly woman she was supposed to care for had not only shaved her head to rid herself of lice, she had come close to burning down the kitchen to get rid of an infestation of caterpillars, the latter having hatched out of the myrtle branches she'd spread over the floor to keep the fleas down, the fleas having been brought in by a family of raccoons that had taken up residence in the wood bin just inside the door.

"God almighty, woman, have you taken complete leave of your senses? I warned you to get rid of those damned raccoons!"

By the time they sat down to supper, Kathleen was ready to rescind her marriage vows and face the hornet's nest of gossip in Beaufort. It could hardly be worse than this bedlam. Hetty Rawson didn't need a nurse companion, she needed a keeper!

"Could I trouble you for the salt, Mrs. Rawson?" Hetty asked just as politely as if they were taking tea with the parson. She had dressed for the occasion in a gown of tarnished black sateen of a style that had been dated even before the war. On her head was a length of calico, wrapped turban fashion and sporting a feather that looked suspiciously like it might have come from the tail of the chicken she'd been carrying earlier.

Kathleen passed the exquisite crystal salt dish and watched while Hetty scraped at the lumpy salt with a pewter spoon. "You don't like boiled chicken, Mrs. Rawson?" the older woman asked, arching white eyebrows over a pair of wickedly glinting eyes.

"No, I—that is, of course I do. My—I, uh, don't seem to be very hungry tonight, that's all." She was conscious of Rogan's glare, and wondered if she could plead sudden illness and leave the table. Or leave the house. Or leave the island!

She, too, had dressed for dinner, wanting for reasons that escaped her now to make a favorable impression on the man she would probably not be seeing again for many a month. Rogan was still wearing his black suit and white shirt, although earlier he had shut himself into the bathing room with a towel and a bar of soap, then disappeared up the stairs.

She had waited until he'd come down, a scowl on his clean-shaven face, to go up and change her travel-worn gown, but for all the attention he paid her, she might as well have stayed as she was instead of changing into her second-best outfit, which consisted of a gray serge skirt cut down from one of Alice's old gowns and refashioned in the latest style. With it she wore a brown lawn shirtwaist with a becoming neckline and a cameo that had belonged to her mother. With no time to wash and dry the salt from her hair, she had simply brushed the surface, rebraided it and coiled it on top of her head. It was not a particularly becoming style, but it was neat. At least in the beginning. She fancied it made her look suitably capable and mature.

At the last minute she had unpacked her hand-painted bottle of attar of roses and dabbed a bit behind each ear. It was only to bolster her spirits, she told herself. Only because the stuff would soon turn if she didn't use it up, and she could never abide waste.

She might as well not have bothered. Hetty sniffed once, sneezed, admired her boots and asked whether she wore stays. She then proceeded to ignore her except for the occasional necessary remark.

Rogan didn't even show that much interest. Indeed, she wondered why he'd stayed on for supper at all, when he was obviously itching to get back to his precious ship.

"Hetty, about my books," he began, and both women looked at him.

"Packed 'em away."

"Hetty," he said warningly.

"Now, Rogan, you know you never read any of them books."

"And that rig you were wearing earlier? What happened to all your good clothes?"

"Washed 'em. That's what I did, I went and washed the lot of 'em. They're still wet."

Kathleen watched a small muscle in her husband's jaw clench and unclench. She heard him say in a suspiciously quiet voice, "Soon's you're done here, Hetty, I'd like a word with you, please. *Alone.*"

"Oh, me, now you're mad with me, aren't you, boy?"

Kathleen looked from one to the other of them, her sympathy, not to mention her loyalty, on the side of the woman she'd been hired to look after. Married to look after, actually, but she was past quibbling. Nor did it occur to her that her loyalty might be misplaced. Rogan Rawson was certainly capable of looking out for his own interests. Hetty Rawson obviously was not.

Kathleen, her jaw set and her eyes sparkling, was ready to do battle for her charge when Rogan utterly disarmed her by saying, "No, love, I'm not mad with you. Worried, if you'd know the truth."

Kathleen sank back into her chair as the other two stood up. As courtly as any polished knight, Rogan took the arm of the frail old woman, then turned and asked if Kathleen would excuse them for a moment.

Nodding wordlessly, she told herself that she didn't really know either one of them. How could she judge? So Hetty had packed away a few books and washed her own clothes. Was that any reason for Rogan to fly off the handle?

On the other hand, he was obviously fond of the old woman. As angry as he had sounded, his eyes had softened when he'd looked at her, and his voice had quickly lost its stern edge. And after all, he had gone against his own wishes and married so the poor dear would have someone to look after her. How many men would trade away their freedom just to have someone to look after an old woman who was no blood kin?

In the process of clearing off the table, Kathleen reminded herself sharply that just because a man took himself a wife, it didn't necessarily mean he had given up his freedom. Quite the contrary, if her own observations were to be believed.

Thoughtfully, she cleared away the remains of the meal Hetty had hurriedly prepared for them. Rogan had devoured without comment the indifferently boiled chicken, lumpy mashed potatoes and stringy beans, as if he was afraid of hurting Hetty's feelings. Kathleen had managed a few bites, but that was all.

Aboard the *White Witch,* silence prevailed, broken only by the creaking of the rigging and the lapping of water along the hull. Billy, all of eleven years old and the sole support of his widowed mother, lay awake in his hammock in the fo'c'stle. "Hey, Josh, you 'sleep yet?"

"Tryin' hard."

"Why d'you think Cap'n Rogan stayed ashore tonight? He don't normally do that once he sees to Miz Hetty's comfort."

"He don't normally take himself a wife, neither. Go to sleep, Billy, some things you ain't old enough to understand."

"Is she coming back with him tomorrow?"

"Nope."

"Why not? She's his woman now, ain't she?"

"Maybe she is. Maybe she ain't. Go to sleep, Billy."

Silence. Then, "Josh, why couldn't we've took 'er with us? She don't take up all that much room."

"You want to make sure an' ask the cap'n about that when he comes aboard tomorrow, Billy. I 'speck he'll be real glad to have your nose a-pokin' around in his business."

Rogan lay awake and glared through the darkness at the quilt he'd hung between the two ends of the attic loft. Damned lumpy thing cut off the draft so he was fair sweltering! No wonder he couldn't get to sleep. Maybe now that *she* was asleep, he could shove it aside.

Was she asleep? Or was she lying on that pallet, afraid to move, half-afraid to breathe, wondering what the devil she'd got herself into?

He couldn't much blame her if she was. If he'd been smart, he'd have sent Styron ashore to let Hetty know he was bringing someone home with him. Maybe then she'd have been on her best behavior. It might not be fair, but...

No. It was better this way. Kathleen needed to know what she was up against, and it wasn't the kind of thing a man could easily describe. Fair weather one day, stormy the next, with never a hint as to which was coming. What could he say? That she stole? That she lied? That she hid things and sometimes set fires? That she was as good a woman as ever lived, but she was batty as a barn?

All that was true. She'd been a good mother to him. He owed her more than he could ever repay, and what was more, he cared for her. But if he'd confessed that the poor old thing had long since lost her rudder, Kathleen would've turned him down flat.

Gazing at the quilt that hung from a line across the middle of the long loft, Rogan swore softly in frustration. Damned stiff-necked little twit, she'd refused the loan of his bed, claiming a captain of a ship owed it to his crew and passengers to get a good night's sleep. So there she lay on a pallet, crowded as close to the wall as she could get. And here he lay, as wide-awake as ever he'd been in all his twenty-eight years.

Hellfire, why hadn't he insisted that Josiah find someone more suitable? An older woman. Someone who wouldn't stare at him out of a pair of cloud-gray eyes until he couldn't latch onto a single sensible thought. Someone who didn't stiffen up like a ramrod and hoist that stubborn little chin of hers in the air because she was scared stiff and determined not to show it.

Why did she have to smell like roses and soap and warm, sweet woman, for all she was so starchy she fairly crackled? What the devil had he been thinking of, to touch her the way he had that first night out, to hold her against him and inhale the sweet fragrance of her hair? Just because it had been his wedding night, and he'd been restless. That scum Egleston had been pressing her, and he'd used it as an excuse to leap to her defense, when a word would have been sufficient to send them both to their cabins.

But he'd been in a strange mood. After all, it was not every day that a man got married, no matter what the reasons. And so he'd used any excuse to touch her, and now he was lying awake, remembering how warm and fragile she had felt underneath all that starchiness, and he couldn't quit wondering what it would be like to really hold her. To hold her the way a husband was supposed to hold his wife.

"Ah, devil take it!" he muttered, and rolled onto his back. At least after tonight he'd not be missing any more sleep on her account. He would make it a point to see Della before he came home again. There was no reason his life should change just because he'd signed a legal document. Promises made under duress weren't binding. Or at least they shouldn't be.

Kathleen slept heavily, the past week having taken its toll. She didn't hear Rogan arise, never knew he parted the barrier quilt and stared down at her for several long moments. The first she knew he was fixing to leave was when she heard his voice near the bottom of the stairwell. He was bidding Hetty farewell and cautioning her to be on the very best behavior.

"I'll be needing my heavier clothes before too long, and for God's sake, see if you can remember where you put my books, will you?"

There was a low murmur, then Hetty's laughter rang out. While Kathleen was still scrambling into the clothes she'd taken off the night before, she heard Rogan say, "Look after the girl, old dear. She's young yet, she'll need you. Take her over to Amos's, make her known around the village, and both of you try to stay out of trouble until I get back home."

"She got a bun in the oven, boy? Are you fixin' to fill this house up with grandbabies so old Hetty won't find time hanging heavy on her hands? Don't you worry about the two of us, we'll fare well enough. You just go on off to your fancy city women and leave that girl to me. I'll take care of her and any young'uns she drops same way I took care of you. What's more, I don't need any here-and-gone sailor to tell me how to go about it! Never did. Don't now. Won't tomorrow.''

"Hetty, you wicked creature, you don't know near as much as you think you know." Hetty's thin cackle rang out clearly against the pleasant background of Rogan's deep chuckle. Smoothing her hair with both hands, Kathleen put on her haughtiest face to make up for the fact that she had pulled on her gown over her nightrail. Her shoes were still unbuttoned, but she couldn't think where she'd put her buttonhook.

"Mind my wife, Hetty, for I believe she's got a good head on her shoulders in spite of her looks."

In spite of her looks? Halfway down the stairs, Kathleen froze.

"You go to Amos if you need anything, you hear? I'll try to stop in on my way south, weather and passengers permitting."

In spite of her looks? Furious, Kathleen hoisted her skirts and fairly flew the rest of the way down. It was one thing to be plain. It was quite another to hear herself discussed as if she had no more pride than a pig in a mud hole.

At the foot of the stairs, she came to a halt. If he wished to leave without doing her the courtesy of telling her good-bye, then who was she to deny him the privilege? He meant nothing to her.

All the same, there was a wistful look on her face when she stepped onto the porch to see him striding away down the path, a newly risen sun glinting off the gold braid and patent-leather brim of his black wool hat. Stiffening her back in an instinctive attitude of pride, she was still standing there when he turned and stared directly at her. Across a barren stretch of weed-dotted sand, dark eyes met gray ones and clung for what seemed an eternity.

Unconsciously, Kathleen lifted one hand to her breast. A light wind from the southeast picked up the sweet, dusty scent of drying fig leaves and goldenrod, carrying it to her nostrils. It stirred a tendril of dark hair across her cheek, and she brushed it away and tossed her braid over her shoulder, where it hung past her waist.

A rooster crowed. From some distance away, a dog barked. From the kitchen behind her came the sound of metal clanking against metal, and Kathleen suddenly came down to earth once more.

Good heavens, no wonder he was staring. She hadn't even taken time to wash her face. It was probably still flushed with sleep, the marks of her fingers pressed into her left cheek, as they usually were when she first awoke.

She bit her lip and tried to look away, but some power in Rogan's eyes held her ensnared the way a blacksnake ensnares a sparrow. He was only a man, she reminded herself. No more, no less. He'd made it plain that she had nothing at all to fear. He'd gone to Beaufort to find himself a nursemaid for his elderly relative, and that was precisely what he'd got. It was as simple as that.

A bubble of irreverent laughter, caused, perhaps, by too many restless nights, trembled at the corners of her generous mouth. Suddenly, as unexpectedly as it had begun, the spell was broken. Shrugging her shoulders, she lifted a hand in a careless gesture and turned to go into the house. If Rogan lingered to stare after her—which he did—she never knew it. Would not have known what to make of it, if she had.

"Reckon you'll have to do without your young rooster for a spell, won't you, girl?"

Startled, Kathleen turned to the woman who had come silently into the room. Wearing a man's ancient bathrobe, with head and feet bare, Hetty was a sight to behold.

"My rooster? Oh. You mean Rogan."

"Marry a mariner, do without. I did. Never loved me, Edmund didn't. Needed a keeper for the boy. Now the boy needs a keeper for me. Reckon we're two of a kind, ain't we, girl?'' She cackled again, and Kathleen found herself wondering what kind of woman Hetty Rawson had been in her youth. She couldn't always have been bald, wrinkled and slightly potty.

''He warned me not to be a trial to you,'' Hetty said with a remarkably childlike smile.

Kathleen's answering smile was immediate and sincere. ''Then I'll try not to be a trial to you, either.'' It occurred to her for the first time that Josiah Dunwoody had shown a remarkable degree of insight when he'd sent her here. She needed to be needed. Her grandmother had needed her, then Alice, then the children.

Well, now Hetty needed her, whether or not the poor old dear cared to admit it. Her duty clear in her mind, Kathleen determined to carry it out to the very best of her ability.

''I don't want to intrude, Mrs. Rawson, but I do need to know—''

''Call me Hetty.'' Eyes twinkling wickedly, the old woman said, ''Reckon we'll get on well enough. I got my ways, that's all.''

''I'm sure you have, and I have no intention of interfering with the way you do things. You just tell me what chores you dislike most, and I'll take them on.''

''Rogan left you a list of things that need tending. Left it on the kitchen table under the pepper vinegar. First thing you got to do is quit mooning over that boy. He'll turn up when it suits him, just like his pappy did, and it won't do no good worrying what he's up to when he's away. A rooster's a rooster. He'll strut and crow and tread his hens, but it's them that does all the work.''

''I assure you—''

''Don't need to assure me. Assure yourself, girl. Rogan's as fine a man as ever forked a pair o' trousers, but he's still only a man, for all that. Wild as they come, him and

Amos's boy, and don't think the women don't chase after 'em. Just 'cause Rogan married you, that don't change the nature of things. No, sirree, Bob! Bees and honey, flowers and bees, you mark my words.''

"Hetty, I assure you I'm not—"

"Just so you understand, girl. That boy's used to buzzing around every flower from here to Baltimore and back. It's a man's nature, that's all. Nary a thing you can do about it. You buttered your bread, now you're just going to have to lie in it.''

With those muddled words of wisdom, the old woman strode off, leaving Kathleen with a vision of a giant slice of bread swimming with butter and honey and swarming with buzzing bees.

The days flew past as Kathleen learned to deal with Hetty Rawson's eccentricities. The old woman walked to the beach each morning, a distance of nearly a mile, to gather gravel for her chickens. The entire island was made of sand, but when Kathleen questioned her, Hetty gave her a look of disdain and said, "Sand's sand, gravel's gravel. Sand don't make good eggshells. Gravel does.''

Near the end of the first week, Kathleen went calling on their nearest neighbor, Amos McNair, with a basket of eggs and a loaf of Hetty's baking-powder bread. She had met him the day after Rogan had left, but at that time, Hetty had completely dominated the conversation, telling Amos that Rogan's new bride was fixing to clean out the house, scrub down the kitchen and weed the late onions and collards Rogan had hired Billy to set out earlier. After that, she was planning to clear out the front room.

It was the first Kathleen had heard of her agenda. Rogan's list had mentioned seeing that Hetty ate well, slept in her own bed each night—that one had given her pause, for she couldn't imagine whose bed he expected to find her in. And last of all, he had exhorted Kathleen not to allow Hetty to bring home too many gifts from the neighborhood, which was the silliest thing she'd ever heard.

Dismissing Rogan's list, Kathleen had accepted her alternate agenda in good grace. Indeed, the house needed a good turnout, and the grounds were almost beyond hope. Aside from that, she intended to take Rogan up on his offer and clear out the spare room downstairs for her own bedchamber.

Meanwhile, she'd keep an eye on Hetty to be certain she didn't wear herself out.

Amos, a wiry man with a crooked back, a pair of incredibly blue eyes and a thicket of white hair that hung past his shoulders, took great pains to inform Kathleen that he would be looking after both the Rawson women in Rogan's absence.

"O' course, it ain't like Rogan had to ask me special or nothing. I been doing for Hetty ever since Edmund passed on to his reward. Just a-cause the boy's got two womenfolk to do for now, that don't mean I can't take care of 'em both."

"Mr. McNair, I'm sure Rogan didn't mean to trouble you," Kathleen said hesitantly, not wanting to wound the old man's pride, yet not wanting him to feel responsible for their well-being. He was at least as old as Hetty, and bent besides. Perhaps Rogan had intended her to keep an eye on him as well as on Hetty.

"Storm season comin' on. I'd best see to oiling the hinges on them shutters of yours."

That sounded safe enough. "Yes, that would be nice, thank you," she replied. The old dear probably needed to feel useful. Goodness knows, Kathleen knew all about that. "Well, I'd better not stay too long. I left Hetty raking out the chicken house."

"She does fancy them chickens o' hers. Reckon if her'n

Edmund had had a chick o' their own, she'd not worry so over a flock of dumb fowl.''

Kathleen murmured something appropriate. One day, she might find herself surrounded by dogs and cats or even chickens for exactly the same reason. She would dearly have loved a family of her own, but of course, that was out of the question now.

As if privy to her thoughts, Amos said, ''Come o'er here and allow me make you known to my family, Miz Kathleen.''

She needed to go, but the old man seemed to enjoy company so much. Another few minutes couldn't matter. Standing before the mantel, Kathleen tried to show proper appreciation for the several faded tintypes arranged there, along with various artifacts, ranging from a tarnished astrolabe to an exquisite porcelain vase.

''This here's my Maudie. She were the finest woman ever to walk these banks, God rest her soul. Lost her'n a daughter, Rose, and two sons, Abner and Robert. These is their pictures. They were fourteen and fifteen at the time, fine, strapping boys. Storm took 'em. They were out a-mulletin' when it blew up something fierce. Found their bodies a week later, caught in the ma'sh up near King's P'int.''

There was nothing of self-pity in the words, but Kathleen didn't miss the fine tremor in the hands that carefully set the pictures back on the mantel.

Her eyes moved to the last frame and she beheld a face that was almost shockingly handsome. ''My youngest boy, Callum,'' old Amos said with a quiet pride that made Kathleen's heart constrict painfully. He still had this one, then. At least he hadn't lost all those he loved.

''They was a pair, all right, him and Rogan. Thick as fleas on a hound dog, growing up. What them two didn't think to get up to weren't worth bothering with. Remind me sometime to tell you about the old skeleton them two found washed out of a bank over on the sound side. Injun, more'n likely. Leastwise, it weren't nobody I recognized.'' Kathleen couldn't quite manage to swallow a burst of horrified laughter, and encouraged, the old man continued. ''Them two limbs of Satan snuck out after dark and sunk the thing into Edmund's oyster bed and then like to died laughing when poor old Edmund hauled that skull up in his rake!''

Kathleen shuddered, more at the thought of the gruesome act than at its shameful irreverence. ''That's awful! I hope they were suitably chastised.''

''Chastised!'' Amos crowed, slapping his thigh as he rocked back in his chair. ''Me'n Edmund, we chastised the pair of 'em till their britches fair smoked! Then we made 'em go fetch a spade and dig a grave, and then fish out ever' last one of them old bones. Gave the poor old sot, whomsoever he be, a right fair send-off, we did, with Edmund reading scripture and Hetty and my Maudie singing over 'im until half the dogs on the island joined in.''

Remembering some of Caleb's worst pranks, involving toads and small snakes and the occasional mouse, Kathleen told herself that life on the Outer Banks might be a bit rawer than she had bargained for.

''Growed up to be a right fine-looking boy, if I do say so,'' Amos went on. ''Folks say he's the spittin' image of me when I was a young man, but I don't know... My eyes is not as blue as Cal's.'' Taking the small framed tintype down from the mantel again, he placed it in Kathleen's hands and stood back as if to invite comparison. Helpless to ignore him, she compared the two men.

''I believe there is a resemblance. Of course, your hair's paler now....'' It was white. White, long and unkempt. Callum McNair's was obviously blond and well trimmed. He had a beautiful smile. In fact, he was a remarkably attractive man.

"What you waiting for? You took up with Amos a'ready, girl?" Hetty came through the open door, hands on her hips, and surveyed them both. She was wearing her slat bonnet, which helped disguise her bald dome. On entering, she removed it and stood there as unselfconscious as a child. "Been showing off yer boy, I see." She nodded to the row of pictures on the mantel. "He tell you what a rascal that Callum is? Between him and my Rogan, there ain't a girl on the banks from Currituck to Caswell that ain't had her heart bruised and her petticoats lifted. You recall that time that mainlander come out here, a-smokin' out both ears? I thought we was going to have us a wedding for sure, didn't you, Amos? Onliest thing was, he couldn't figger which o' them rascals to go after, for they'd both been sniffin' round his eldest girl."

The pair of them roared with laughter, and Kathleen smiled uncertainly from one to the other. Was it true then? Was Rogan a complete womanizer? Could he change now that he was married?

Would he even want to?

For the first time, as she lay in Rogan's bed in the loft that night, Kathleen tried to envision their marriage from his point of view. It was no marriage at all, she concluded, and wondered what, if anything, she would change about their relationship if she had the power.

Eight days later, Rogan surprised everyone by coming home again. With the house spanking clean, the garden weeded and the lawn in better shape than it had been in years, Kathleen had started in on the unused parlor, intending to have a bedchamber of her own before he came home again. There were scores of boxes of all sizes, shapes and descriptions, all coated with dust and draped with cobwebs.

She had gone through the first few dozen, finding some empty, some filled with crumbling, yellowed newspapers, others filled with tangled bits of embroidery thread and moth-eaten yarn. She'd intended to work her way to the windows today so that at least she could throw them open to have some air while she dealt with the rest, for it had been stifling hot all week.

Only Rogan had come home too soon. The moment she heard his firm tread on the porch, she knew who it was. Blood rushed to her face, and she froze where she was for an instant. It turned out to be an instant too long. Just as a shadow blocked the light from the open doorway, she scrambled to her feet and began yanking at her skirts, which she had bundled up and tied in a knot like a bustle, the better to crawl about. Her sleeves were rolled up past her elbows, and her hair had collected half the dust and cobwebs in the room.

Standing in the doorway, Rogan was torn between laughter and a sudden, completely unexpected desire to lift his wife into his arms and kiss her furious, flushed face until she begged for mercy. From years of practice, he hid every emotion except for cool politeness. "Good afternoon, Mrs. Rawson. Have I caught you at an inconvenient time?"

She swallowed visibly, and her head bobbed in a nervous gesture. "Mr. Rawson. Captain, that is."

"Have you, ah…lost something there on the floor?"

My mind! Quite definitely, my mind! "I was—that is, I thought, if you don't have any objection, that is, well, you told me I could—that is, Hetty did—and so I thought I would!"

The look he gave her defied interpretation. "Then maybe I'd best go find Hetty. Any idea where I might look?"

"Try the henhouse," Kathleen retorted sharply, mortified at being caught in such a wretched condition. "Evidently she prefers their company to mine."

After another long, thoughtful look, he turned on his heel and left. Kathleen mopped her brow with a filthy forearm and wondered where she'd misplaced her temper. It wasn't like her to be so cross. It had to be the heat. Besides which, for someone who'd always made a point of good grooming, having been told over and over by her grandmother that when a body was born plain, neatness was doubly important, she wasn't making a very good showing.

By the time Hetty came in from feeding the chickens, leaving Rogan to make a walking inspection of the outside of the house, Kathleen had disappeared up to the loft. The first thing she did was rehang the heavy, lumpy quilt over the rafter, separating the long room into two separate sleeping places. She had taken it down the day Rogan had left to create a draft between the small windows in either end of the attic, for in spite of a few cool days, the weather would likely be stifling well up into October.

A pallet. She would have to make up another pallet. And then put fresh linens on Rogan's bed.

But first of all she needed a bath!

The house wasn't meant for three adults, especially when one of them was a stranger. There was no privacy at all, and while she appreciated the fact that Rogan thought enough of his stepmother to build her a bathing room instead of making do with a basin, a ewer and a thunder mug, like most people, she did wish it didn't open directly into the sitting room.

At least it was handy to the kitchen for toting hot water.

The kitchen. Oh, drat. Supper! Having gradually taken over the cooking rather than suffer constant indigestion from Hetty's poor efforts, she had planned on serving the leftover mustard greens and corn bread, but there was hardly enough for three. Nor was there time to soak out a side of corned mullet. It would just have to be bacon, greens, biscuits and—

"Hetty, is there water in the kettle?" she called down when she heard the older woman pass near the stairwell.

"Not now, there's not. Rogan took it into the bathing room to sluice off with."

Well, that was just fine. That was just peachy! He came home all spruce in his black suit and polished boots, with his hair slicked back and his fingernails all trimmed and clean, and here she was in her stocking feet, with her skirts knotted up under her buttocks and her dress limp with sweat! Her hair was flying every which way, and to top it off, she probably smelled like a blasted whaler. And *he* took all the hot water!

Leaving her pride behind her, Kathleen tromped down the steep staircase and marched through the house. While he was safely in the bathing room she would stoke up the fire and heat herself a kettle of water. Two, in fact, one for her hair and one for her—

"Need some help?"

Kathleen spun around. A chunk of split pine slipped from her grasp, and Rogan leapt forward to catch it before it hit the floor. Her heart hammering, she glared at him as if he'd committed the veriest sin. He was naked from the waist up. Wet, his powerful bronzed chest and shoulders gleamed in the late sunlight that slanted through the windows. There was an edge of soap on his left temple.

He stepped closer, and she stepped back. Shrugging, he opened the stove and poked in the firewood, along with several more pieces. "Need another kettle of water. Never did like a cold bath, even in the summertime, did you? By the way, you wouldn't happen to have come across my spare shirts and smallclothes, would you? Looked for them when I was here before, but never could lay hands on them."

Staring at the solid wall of masculine flesh before her, at the swirling pattern of dark hair, Kathleen found herself mesmerized by the sight of a flat male nipple. She opened her mouth to reply, then closed it again, quite certain that anything she uttered at that moment would be sheerest nonsense.

''What's the matter, haven't you ever seen the naked male body before, Mrs. Rawson?''

If she'd cared to look up, Kathleen might have read both mischief and tenderness in the black eyes that watched her so closely.

But she didn't dare. Not with her face on fire and her brain as muddled as a bowl of suet pudding. The best she could do was blurt out the truth, which was that of course she had, more times than she could recall. Caleb and the twins were male, after all, and she'd bathed them all at least once a day.

But there was male, and then there was *male*. And nothing she had seen before, certainly not her three young nephews, or Morton, or even handsome Daniel Bell, who worked bare-chested all summer at the gristmill at Morehead, had ever affected her the way Rogan did. She felt quite simply as if she were in the presence of some rare and untamed creature who threatened her in ways she couldn't even begin to imagine.

"Kathleen?" Rogan said softly. "Darling, the kettle?" Laughing, he held it out to her, and she took it and turned blindly to the sink.

Something in the water, Amanda Crotts had warned her...but there'd been nothing in Hiram's sample case for the malady that had afflicted her in the three weeks since she'd set foot on Hatteras Island.

Chapter Six

Tension hammered out between them until Kathleen could hardly breathe, but if Rogan was affected, he did an admirable job of concealing it. Kathleen looked everywhere but directly at him, while he couldn't seem to take his gaze off her pale face, with the scattering of freckles and the small patches of color high on her cheeks. Her eyes glittered with anger, and her hair was like a dark silken jungle laced with torn cobwebs.

It was Hetty who broke the spell. "Thought I'd cured you of coming in to supper half naked, boy. Reckon I can do it again if you've forgot." Turning the scrap bucket down over a stump on the back porch, the old woman examined the soles of her shoes and stepped into the room.

Rogan grinned, and Kathleen, released from bondage, began filling the kettle. "Believe me, I've never forgotten it, Hetty, darling," she heard him say. "I'll put on a shirt as soon as I can lay hands on a clean one. I seem to have misplaced my clothes. Kathleen, where'd you put them when you unpacked your trunk?"

"Where did I put what? Your clothespress was empty, so I hung a few of my gowns there. As to the rest, I would certainly never go into your drawers."

"Oh, of course not," he said dryly, leaving her to wonder whether he mistrusted her in particular or women in general, or whether he had never outgrown the sort of crude masculine remarks that passed for humor among adolescent males.

Setting the kettle on the range, she turned to go, her head held high as if a regal attitude could make up for the sad state of her grooming. "I'll be down in a little while to start on supper."

Unable to help herself, she made the mistake of glancing over her shoulder. He was leaning, bold as brass, against the door frame, a thumb hooked under the waist of his black broadcloth trousers, with one booted foot crossed over the other, grinning as if he could see right into her addled brain. Her face burning, she hurried along the passageway and into the house.

Two hours later, Kathleen was mentally rearranging furniture to make room for the dining table in the sitting room, where at least a body could breathe. By the time she had sliced off a hand's width of side meat and fried it crisp, baked a pan of buttermilk biscuits and heated the greens, she might as well not have bothered to bathe and put on a clean gown. She had brushed cobwebs and dust from her hair and pinned it up into a neat roll, but it was already beginning to slide free.

Hetty wiped her lips with her yellowed damask napkin, then used it to fan with, scattering crumbs across the floor. Kathleen blew a strand of hair off her cheeks and enjoyed the momentary feeling of coolness on her damp skin.

Seeing Rogan's attention taken up by buttering and dribbling molasses on his seventh biscuit, she surreptitiously twisted a hairpin and shoved it in again. The high-banded collar of her black lawn gown grew damper by the moment, and she felt a trickle of perspiration inch down between her breasts.

Unbidden, her eyes lifted to Rogan's broad chest, clad in the same limp shirt he had taken off before he bathed. The garment was loose-fitting, thin and laid open to capture whatever feeble breeze found its way into the overheated room. The sleeves were rolled up to reveal powerful, bronzed forearms, but it was on his throat that her wistful gaze lingered longest. It was bare all the way down to where the dark hair commenced to curl flat on his chest.

There were times when modesty demanded an unrealistic price from a woman, Kathleen thought irritably as she passed the breadbasket to Hetty and the last slice of bacon to Rogan. While he helped himself, she tugged at her collar and stretched her neck a bit. Come bedtime, there would likely be a band of heat rash girdling her throat. In an effort to distract herself from the oppressive heat, she said brightly, "Hetty, what did you mean earlier this evening when you said you'd cured someone of something?"

"Cured?" Hetty paused in the act of fishing the drowned biscuit out of her coffee cup and looked up.

"I think my wife is speaking of the way you cured Papa and me of coming to the table without our shirts," Rogan nudged gently.

"Did I do that?" The old woman blinked in surprise.

"Yes, you did, ma'am. And very effectively, as I recall."

Taking pity on the woman, who had evidently had another of her frequent small lapses of memory, Kathleen sent Rogan a speaking look. She'd only been making idle conversation. It had not been her intent to cause embarrassment to either of them, but Rogan refused to let the matter drop.

"If I recollect rightly, it was August—one of those days when the air's so wet a man needs gills to breathe," he began, tilting back his chair. "Papa and I had been down to the landing all morning, scraping the bottom of the yawl boat. It's hot, dirty work, ma'am, in case you don't know it. We'd washed off outside at the pump and left our boots on the porch, but it just didn't occur to us to button ourselves into clean shirts in the middle of the day. Hetty had baked a flounder for dinner, all layered over with salt pork, and I'm afraid we hove to and commenced to eating without waiting to be prayed over or even invited to partake.''

He grinned slowly in remembrance, and Kathleen watched, fascinated in spite of herself by the remarkable change a broad smile could make in his hard, irregular features.

"Then Hetty here, she came in and took one look at the pair of us and turned tail. I'm ashamed to say we didn't take much notice. Or if we did, I reckon we thought she'd just forgot to fetch something to the table." He chuckled and shook his head. "We noticed a few minutes later, all right. She marched back into the kitchen and sat down to dinner, naked as a—that is to say, bare from the waist up.''

Kathleen almost strangled. A vision of the scene rose before her, and she darted a quick look at the bald-headed woman who was daintily picking crumbs off her plate with her thumb and licking them off. Her gaze slid to Rogan's, and at the look of barely concealed mirth in his eyes, it was all she could do not to explode.

Rogan watched his wife's expressive gray eyes dance with laughter, saw her lips twitch and saw her suck in her cheeks in an effort to contain herself. As cool as you please, she turned to Hetty and said, "It's been my experience, ma'am, that children and hound dogs remember a simple demonstration a lot longer than they remember any amount of preaching. Don't you find that to be true?''

A few hours later, the kitchen long since tidied and the bread set to rise for morning, Kathleen stepped out onto the porch for a last breath of air before heading upstairs to her pallet. It would be stifling up there with the heat of the day trapped under the roof and the quilt preventing the free flow of air.

"Hear that?" Rogan spoke quietly from the shadowy area near the railing. "Poor Will's widow." It came again, the soft, distinctive cry of the evening bird, and Kathleen stepped closer to the rail.

"I thought you'd gone to visit Amos," she said quietly.

She sensed rather than saw his nod. "Did. Came back when he dozed off. I'll be gone again come morning, but I wanted a word with you before you went up to bed."

Kathleen refused to credit the feeling of disappointment that swept over her at his announcement that he'd be gone so quickly. It was illogical, to say the least, for there was more work to do and less freedom in which to do it when he was home. Besides that, he made her uncomfortable. "Hetty's faring quite well, if that's what you're concerned about. She's up with the sun every morning, after her gravel. She eats well, and enjoys fussing with her chickens. Sews a lot, too. I don't believe she even noticed when I took over the housework and cooking, she's so busy working on those quilts of hers. She finished two more this past week. I, um, bought a dollar's worth of calico from Mr. Stowe's store for her. I hope you don't mind."

Rogan removed a cigar from his pocket, rolled it between his fingers and replaced it. "No, I don't mind. Whatever makes her happy, that's all I care about. We've an account with A. J. Stowe, so buy what you need."

"Does she make them to sell?" Kathleen persisted.

"The quilts? Not to my knowledge."

Standing beside the tall, sinewy figure, close enough to feel the heat of his body but not close enough to risk brushing against him, Kathleen nibbled on her lower lip. "I only wondered. Seems to me that we've more than enough quilts for a family of twelve." And then she felt her face begin to burn in case he mistook her words for a hint that she would welcome a larger family. "I suppose she's making them for your crew and passengers." She thought about the wet bedding Mr. Egleston had complained of.

But then she also recalled that the blanket on Rogan's bunk aboard the *White Witch* had been tightly woven of creamy wool, with a pale blue band worked into the borders. Indeed, she could hardly conceive of anyone with a choice in the matter choosing to use one of Hetty's lumpy creations. They were patched together of scraps in no discernible pattern, tufted rather than quilted, and so heavy that a body would be crushed under their weight.

Rogan shrugged. "God only knows why she insists on making the things, but as long as it keeps her out of trouble, I'll not complain."

"I should hope not," Kathleen said defensively. "I'm not sure what you mean by trouble, but I do know that handiwork has gotten more than one woman through a bad patch in her life. Busy hands have a way of lulling troubled minds." That much she knew from personal experience.

Beside her, Rogan shifted so that his arm momentarily brushed against her shoulder. Remembering the way Morton used to invent excuses to touch her, to brush against her seemingly by accident, she stiffened and moved farther along the rail.

"Don't let her good behavior fool you into dropping your guard, Kathleen."

Her guard?

"Hetty can be a holy terror, but she's still my mother. Leastwise, she's the one I remember best. My own mother died when I was no bigger than a minute. Papa gave the running of his ship over to another man so he could stay home and take care of me, but when the *Witch* took to losing too much money, running into bad weather and suffering damage, losing entire crews to crimps and such, Pa left me in the care of neighbors and took her over again.

Truth is, I ran wild until the day he came home with Miss Hetty.

"From that day on, though, my life changed. Hetty fed me, clothed me and managed to keep me from breaking my fool neck or landing in more trouble than I could handle. She did her best to civilize me before turning me loose on the world, and for that alone, I'll forever be grateful to her. Try to have patience with her, will you, Kathleen? She'll drive you up a tree if you let her, but for all her wily ways, she's a good woman. She gave up any family she might have had when she married Pa and moved out here. She took care of me when I needed it most, so for my sake, look after her for me, will you?"

Impulsively, Kathleen laid a hand on his arm, more touched than she cared to admit by the unexpected revelation. While he might look hard as bedrock, Rogan was not invulnerable. "We get on very well," she told him. "I'm sure Hetty is a dear woman, for all her ways, and I want you to know I'm not a bit put off by her—by the way she—"

"The way she looks?" His smile was a flash of brightness in the dark. "I can't say I wasn't shocked when I saw her looking like a peeled onion. And here I'd especially been wanting you two to make a good impression on one another."

Remembering her own shock at the sight of the bald-headed woman who had greeted them that first day, Kathleen laughed softly, and as if startled by the sound, Rogan stared at her through the darkness. "Kathleen?"

A hollow place opened up in her chest for a single heartbeat. But then the spell was broken. Rogan stepped back, and Kathleen moved away and smoothed her skirt over her hips with unsteady hands. "My, it's warm tonight," she murmured nervously. "I'd best be sure Hetty's window's open. Sometimes she forgets."

Rogan watched her disappear into the house, her slender figure with its impossibly tiny waist and delicate shoulders swaying slightly despite the almost militant stiffness of her bearing. Yes, sometimes poor Hetty forgot. Forgot to open her window to the sunshine, forgot to close it to the rain. She desperately needed someone to watch over her when Rogan was away.

As for Rogan himself, he'd better make damned sure he didn't get to feeling too needy himself and forget why he had married the girl and brought her here. He might find himself wondering now and then what it would be like to take her to bed, but he needed her too much to risk it. He respected her. Hell, he even *liked* her. All of which meant that he'd best leave well enough alone.

The storm struck with stunning fury. Kathleen bolted up from her pallet in one movement as a blast of thunder exploded over her head. A ball of blue fire danced in through the open window, circled the room, bounced off the chimney, then disappeared.

With her thin muslin night rail clinging like a second skin to her damp body, Kathleen stood trembling, her feet tangled in her rumpled bedding, a fist crammed against her mouth to keep from screaming in terror.

"You all right?" Rogan pushed aside the curtain between them and stared at her, his face that of a stranger in the flickering illumination. Lightning flashed continuously, the thunder, aside from a single ear-shattering burst, seeming to come from some distance away.

Abruptly, she remembered to breath. "Yes... At least, I think so. Do you think it did any—any—d-d—"

"Damage? I expect we'd know if it'd struck a chimney. Might have got a tree, but at least it didn't come through the roof."

Kathleen swallowed hard, then fought to suppress a giggle. In the brief glimpse she'd had of her tall, stern husband, with his naked chest and nether regions half-hidden behind one of Hetty's more dreadful quilts, this one of sulfur yellow, snuff brown and faded pink, Rogan had looked rather like a Roman emperor clad in the world's ugliest toga that dropped alarmingly low on his left hip.

She was still trying to recall the exact image when a deluge of rain struck the side of the house with a deafening roar.

"Oh, the window!" she gasped and turned to slam down the sash over her pallet.

"It's not raining in on this end," Rogan shouted over the noise. "I'll leave it open for air."

"Hetty!" Kathleen cried, remembering that the bedroom downstairs was on the wet side of the house.

"What else is open?" Rogan's voice was muffled. In the constantly flickering lightning, she could see that the quilt had been dragged aside, and Rogan was fastening his trousers. "You check on Hetty. Be sure her bed didn't get wet. I'll check the rest, all right? Watch the stairs! And take that lamp with you, that's what it's there for."

Already three steps down and feeling her way, she came back for the lamp that stayed on the shelf at the top or the bottom of the stairs. Sudden squalls made her edgy, though she wasn't afraid of them.

Hurrying through the dark house, they crossed and bumped into each other several times as they slammed windows shut all around. The wind switched back and forth. Rogan dashed upstairs and shut the other attic window, and by the time he came back downstairs, Kathleen had lit another lamp and was lowering the chimney.

Between the kitchen and the house proper, Rogan had got himself drenched, his shoulders glistening warmly in the yellow light. Kathleen did her best not to stare. Curling her bare toes on the cool floor, she was conscious of the gritty feel of the sand that had blown in through the open window just before the squall had struck. The damp muslin felt clammy against her bare skin. Her heightened senses quivered with awareness of Rogan's flickering shadow as it climbed the opposite wall; of the dusty smell of thirsty ground and coal-oil from the lamp.

Last of all she became conscious of the way Rogan was staring at her. He had gone very still, his feet braced slightly apart, his arms hanging at his sides. "What are you... No, Rogan. Please, no," she whispered, her eyes widening as she noticed his gaze moving over her body. Damp muslin could be far too revealing.

Crossing her arms over her breasts, she began to edge toward the stairwell, but to reach it, she would have to pass within inches of where he was standing. "Please," she whispered again, her eyes wide and more appealing than she could possibly know. Unconsciously, she was shaking her head from side to side in denial of the inevitable.

How could she have been so stupid! By the time she was thirteen years old, she'd known better than to show herself in Morton's presence unless she was covered from head to toe and aproned on top of that! Men took advantage. They always did. Alice had told her that. Alice had warned her, not about Morton, but about other men. About all men.

It had been one of the maids who had warned her about Morton, but by that time, she already knew. Each time she caught him watching her that way, his wet lips gone slack, his pale eyes glittering, she had felt like scrubbing herself all over with lye soap. More than once she'd asked him not to look at her that way, only to have him threaten to send her off to the orphanage.

"Kathleen, I—"

"No. Don't come any closer. You can't send me away, Rogan, I'm too old. And besides, I know my rights as a wife."

"And I know mine as a husband," he countered.

Arms still crossed over her bosom, she narrowed her eyes at him, not trusting the teasing note in his voice. "We have an agreement, sir," she reminded him.

"I'm well aware of that, madam. You were to shut Hetty's window and see to her bedding, and I was to do the rest. I trust you've fulfilled your end of the bargain?"

The air left her lungs in an audible whoosh, and she continued to stare at him suspiciously. Was he serious or was he teasing her? For the life of her, she couldn't tell which. Alice had no sense of humor at all, and as for Morton, his brand of teasing had always made her feel somehow soiled. With Rogan, it was different. Almost as if he were inviting her to laugh with him.

Warily, she ventured a smile, then quickly bit her lip when he didn't smile back.

"Kathleen, if you're frightened of storms—" His voice seemed to surround her in the dimly lit room, raising goose bumps on her flesh.

"Frightened? Of a little rain? I haven't seen rain in so long, I assure you, it's most welcome." Her voice sounded almost calm, not easy under the circumstances. "As for being frightened, we've storms aplenty in Beaufort, every bit as fierce as this. If that's all, then I'll bid you goodnight."

"The floor's wet. Mind you don't slip on the stairs." There was a velvety quality in his voice that made her even more uneasy than the weather.

"If you're hinting for me to mop your floor, I do believe I'll wait until morning. For all I know, your roof leaks like a sieve."

He chuckled, and Kathleen fought to suppress a nervous laugh. For some reason, she felt unusually vulnerable. His smile was enough to knock her defenses tail over topknot.

Shared laughter in the middle of the night was more than she could handle.

For the rest of the night, Kathleen lay awake, stubbornly refusing to admit that her pallet was too damp for comfort. Stiff as a board, she was alert for the slightest sound from beyond the quilt. The rain had ended, all but an occasional flurry. The air was close, but not nearly so hot as it had been. For that, at least, she was grateful.

Long before Hetty's favorite rooster walked to the end of his pine bough and stretched his neck to crow, Kathleen was up and quietly gathering her clothes and shoes. She sorely missed the privacy of having the loft to herself. She would have to get dressed in the bathing room, which was scarce big enough to swing a cat. Taking time only to brush out her hair and rebraid it, she felt for her hairpins, added them to the stack, and tiptoed downstairs, heading for the kitchen to collect the kettle of warm water.

Rogan was already seated at the table, chair tipped back as he cradled a tankard of coffee between his large, capable hands. The range was crackling hot, the kettle steaming, and a fresh pot of coffee was sending off a tantalizing aroma.

He looked around when she entered the room. "I tried to be quiet, but I reckon I didn't do a very good job of it. You should have rolled over and gone back to sleep to make up for last night."

"I slept perfectly well last night, thank you." Embarrassed at being caught a second time in a state of near undress, she spoke more curtly than she might have. It was a lie, as well. She'd lain awake for hours.

He sent her a mocking grin. "Funny...I could've sworn that was you rushing around slamming windows in the middle of the night, but maybe I dreamed the whole thing."

"I meant afterward," she mumbled. She reached for the kettle, intent only on escaping.

"Hetty slept through everything. I looked in on her a few minutes ago and opened her window again. Bully'll sound the alarm before long."

"Bully?"

"Don't tell me you haven't met old Bully. He's her pet rooster."

"The one who's always causing trouble?"

"That's Bully. I think Hetty raises up young cocks just for the pleasure of seeing that old rascal beat the living daylights out of them. That was one of the losers we ate your first evening here."

Kathleen's stomach threatened to turn on her. She remembered the chicken well. It had been tough and stringy and ill seasoned. "I could never name an animal I raised for the table."

Rogan merely shrugged. "Any last questions about how to go on?" he asked as she headed out of the kitchen with the steaming kettle.

"None at all. If you've any complaints, then I'd as soon hear them now as worry about hearing them later."

He smiled, and she was uncomfortably aware of everything about him—the way his cheeks lifted, causing his eyes to narrow. The way his sharply chiseled lips pulled slightly to one side when he smiled, revealing one chipped tooth among all the perfect ones. The way his eyes seemed to dance like light reflecting on dark rippled water.

The way *she* seemed to glow inside whenever he looked at her the way he was looking at her now.

Slowly, he shook his head. "No complaints. No commands. One caution—no, make that two cautions."

She braced herself, gripping the wooden handle of the heavy copper kettle. Rogan unfolded his length from the table and removed it from her nerveless fingers, replacing it on the stove.

"I wanted that, Rogan! I haven't even washed my face yet."

"Slack off, girl, you make me nervous. Put me in mind of a cat I once rescued from the tide when she came floating past the back door on a chunk of firewood. No matter what I said, no matter how I tried to fish the poor wretch out of the water, she kept digging her claws into that firewood, facing me down like she expected me to knock her off her raft and drown her."

"A cat? I remind you of a *half-drowned cat?*"

He grinned. "Scared stiff, she was. Oh, I managed to rescue her, all right, but she near about tore me up before I could bundle her into a blanket. Never could abide cats after that."

"Captain Rawson, I—"

"Rogan."

"Captain—"

He drained his coffee cup, then slammed it down on the table. "Look, woman, we've already settled the matter. You're to call me by my given name. Now that that's understood, heed my words again. First off, let me caution you against taking on too much and making yourself ill. With Dr. Brachum gone, there's not a physician nearer than the mainland, and nobody here who can spare the time to take you across the sound. Secondly, don't let Hetty fool you. I'll not say she's batty, but—"

"Batty!" Kathleen was furious that he would even suggest such a thing. She was disappointed in him, too, for in spite of the way he teased the poor woman, and even lost his temper with her, she had never before had cause to doubt that he loved her.

"I said I *wouldn't say* she was batty," he began, then he swore. "Dammit, woman, don't twist my words!"

"I didn't twist anything! You said she was batty, and she's not! She's simply—not young any more."

They were both standing now. Kathleen's arms were once more crossed over her bosom, her chin thrust forward and her eyes as hard as flint. Bracing himself on his hands, Rogan leaned across the table to confront her, his eyes narrowed to glittering slits. "It'd serve you right, young lady, if I let you find out for yourself! If you're so almighty wonderful—"

"I never claimed to be wonderful!"

"No, but Josiah claimed it for you! I ask him to find me a sensible woman, someone who wouldn't mind moving out here to the banks, but no, he had this *wonderful* young female he claimed was just what I needed! The only fly in the ointment was that I had to marry her."

"Fly in the— You did *not* have to marry me! I never, *ever* wanted that!" The fringe on her forehead was standing on end where she'd slept on it, and her braid had already unraveled halfway down her back.

Ignoring her, Rogan grumbled, "Damned if he didn't sucker me good, telling me what a blasted wonder you were. The old goat had me believing that the last thing I needed was one more old woman to worry over. She's young, he said—she'll pull her weight. Plain, prissy, proud as a hog on ice, but the important thing was that you were healthy, a good hard worker with a cool head on your shoulders."

Stricken, Kathleen felt the starch go right out of her defenses. "P-prissy? Proud?" She'd never been proud in her life. Leastwise, not *proud* proud. Not the kind of proud that goeth before a fall.

"And plain," Rogan reminded her ruthlessly. "But since I wasn't looking for a new mistress, that part didn't bother me. It was the rest of it I was interested in. The part about having good health, a strong back and a cool head on your shoulders."

Kathleen snatched up the kettle, sloshing water over her

wrist. She gasped and tried to ignore the stinging pain, but Rogan was too quick for her.

"What the devil have you done now?" he grumbled, reaching for her arm.

"Nothing!"

"Don't be childish, give me your wrist."

She snatched her arm away, endangering herself again, and he removed the kettle, sat it back on the stove, grabbed the back of her night rail before she could get away. "Dammit, woman—"

"I told you to leave me alone! Don't you have a ship to sail or something?"

"If you've burned yourself, you'd damned well better take care of it before it goes septic! I told you we didn't have a doctor out here." Taking her by the hand, he yanked her arm under his and clamped it against his body, holding her wrist toward the light.

Kathleen fought, but she might as well have done battle with a tidal wave for all the good it did her. "Don't make me hurt you, Rogan, I'm warning you." The hard hand that cradled her arm burned her skin even more than the scald, but she could hardly tell him that.

"You're warning *me?*" Reaching for the flour bin with his free hand, he tilted her a quizzical look. "Darling, if I'd known you didn't have the sense God gave a barnacle, I'd have married Louisa and left you right where I found you. Now hold still while I damned well make a poultice out of this stuff."

"I don't think I want you poulticing me. What do you know about medicine?"

"A damned sight more than you do, I vow. Who d'you think mends broken heads when my crew goes ashore up in Baltimore?"

"I'd sooner trust Billy than you," she muttered, not because it was the truth but because she would die before admitting that the flour paste he'd just spread over her scalded wrist had leached the pain right out of it. The trouble was, if he'd cracked her arm like a piece of kindling, she probably wouldn't even have noticed. All she was conscious of was how strong he was, how gentle his touch and the strange effect his nearness was having on her.

Racking her brain to remember what she'd been so upset over, she blurted, "She—she's not batty, you know. Just because she quilts a lot and wears strange clothes."

"Or none at all. How about shaving her head?"

"She had reason for that, and her hair will grow back. It's already started to grow."

"Just be warned, that's all I'm asking."

Releasing her hand, he stepped back, studying her face as if searching for any sign of weakness. Kathleen tilted her chin, only too aware of her plain cotton night rail, her tangled hair and her bare feet. Never again, she vowed, would he catch her this way, if she had to sleep in her clothes!

"I reckon I'll be leaving then. If you're sure you'll be all right?"

"Of course I'll be all right."

He continued to study her silently for another moment, then, as if making up his mind about something, he nodded. "That's it, then. If you need anything before I get back, call on Amos."

Perversely, now that he was actually going, Kathleen found she didn't want him to leave—not quite yet. She told herself that it was only because she wanted a chance to prove him wrong about her, then she told herself she was the batty one, not poor Hetty. "You may set your mind at rest, Rogan. I'll take very good care of Hetty for you."

He reached for the hat that was hanging on a peg by the back door. "I reckon you will, at that."

And before she could think of an excuse to keep him there, if only for another few moments, he was gone.

This time she refused to watch him go. There was something about that man that set her mind atilt, and she hadn't the least notion of what it was. He certainly wasn't the handsomest man in the world. Nowhere near as handsome as that son of Amos's. There was nothing fancy about his clothes—in fact, judging by the way they hugged his body, he'd outgrown them all years ago.

She sighed. At the sound of the rooster's crowing, she collected the kettle and headed for the bathing room to ready herself for another day.

Rogan paced the deck on his way across the sound. It was not his own deck, and he blamed most of his restlessness on that fact. With the business of off-loading a consignment of manufactured household furnishings at Elizabeth City and taking on a deck load of machinery bound for Morehead, he had taken a sudden notion to leave the *Witch* under Dick Styron's command and hitch a ride on a packet bound out to the banks to deliver a piece of equipment for the new Hatteras lifesaving station.

By the time they left the Pamlico Sound and headed up the Albemarle, Rogan had been unable to rid his mind of the image of Kathleen as he had last seen her, dressed in a shapeless cotton tent that covered her from chin to toe, with her hair in a rope down her back, her face still flushed from sleep and her eyes—those great gray eyes that were nestled in the thickest, longest, silkiest lashes any mortal had ever been blessed with—snapping fire at him for daring to tend her wound.

Don't make me hurt you, Rogan. Was that truly what the little baggage had said? A slow smile spread across his face. Squinting against the sunlight, he recalled the way she'd stiffened up and jutted that little chin of hers, like a doe sensing danger. Oh, he knew her secret, all right. That starchiness, that confounded pride of hers, was her only defense against the world, her defense against being hurt.

God knows he was no threat to her. He might tease her now and then just to get a rise out of her, but surely she knew he meant her no harm.

Had Kingsley teased her, too? Had that been his way of throwing her off guard?

His fists curled at his sides. From what Josiah had said, she'd had a narrow escape. She might not be an eye-catching beauty, but no man with eyes in his head could call her plain. A woman with skin as fine as silk, with lips so soft a man wanted to reach out and touch them...a woman with eyes like the shadow of rain, so large, so clear, so full of dreams and fears—

Well, dammit, she might not be pretty in the ordinary sense, but no man could call her plain!

Forcibly shifting his thoughts to a safer channel, Rogan made up his mind to pay Della a visit before he took the *Witch* up the canal to Virginia. There'd be time to spend at least one night with her, and another on the return trip. That ought to help him hold a steadier course the next time he went home.

Chapter Seven

Rogan, his coat unbuttoned and shoved back by the hands rammed into his trouser pockets, stared down from the second-story window and wondered what the devil he was doing there. He'd arrived that evening with the clear intention of burying himself between Della's plump white thighs as many times as it took to drain the neediness out of his system, then getting a decent night's sleep before heading downriver at first light.

Instead, he had insisted on having a meal sent up from the boarding house kitchen, eaten twice as much as he wanted of food that was not half so well prepared as it should have been for the price, and now, as he listened to Della's rustlings and splashings in the next room, he was wondering why the notion of bedding his mistress of long standing didn't appeal to him more. God knows, it had been far too long since he'd had a woman. Celibacy was an unhealthy condition. It spoiled a man's powers of concentration and undermined his general constitution. Everyone knew that.

Rogan had an even more compelling reason for needing a woman. All the way across the Pamlico and Albemarle sounds and up the Pasquotank River, he'd been thinking about Kathleen. When he should've been thinking about securing enough new cargo for the run down the coast to replace what had been off-loaded in Elizabeth City, or whether the frayed tops'l halyard was due to faulty rigging or simple wear, or any of a dozen other important matters, he'd find himself gazing into space and wondering what Kathleen was doing at that particular moment.

Kathleen. He thought of her as Primrose. She might smell like a rose, but she had all the prickly pride of one of those fancy breeds of cat that were all the rage in Baltimore now. Yet underneath, he suspected she was as vulnerable as a kitten. Perhaps all she needed was a bit of feeding, reassuring, stroking…

But dammit, theirs was a business arrangement, no more, no less! They had spelled out the rules and reasons beforehand, and both had been well satisfied with the bargain. He had agreed to a legal arrangement that would provide good care for Hetty in her failing years in exchange for his protection and security for the one giving that care. As for himself, all he wanted was peace of mind. He'd never had the least intention of tying himself down with a lot of unwanted restrictions.

A wry smile twisted Rogan's face as he remembered a day nearly twelve years before when he, then only fifteen, and Callum McNair, a year older, had entered into a solemn pact. Having only recently discovered women, neither of them could conceive of any man's willingly giving up his freedom for the sake of any one woman. They'd watched many a young rakehell change overnight after taking on a wife; watched many a fetching young girl turn into a drab, given to boring monologues on such tedious topics as canning turnips, turning collars and the proper way to train a babe to use the chamber pot.

It had been the next summer that Amos had tried to make a deal with the father of a spinster of some twenty-odd

summers. Had he succeeded, he would have been the richer
by a half interest in a sixty-nine-foot Chesapeake bugeye,
and Callum would have found himself saddled with a saber-
tongued wife who considered anyone unfortunate enough
to be born on North Carolina's Outer Banks a heathen at
best and a savage at worst.

Between them, Callum and Rogan had managed to convince the poor girl that not only were all bankers heathens,
most were not above a discreet bit of cannibalism should
the fishing season be poor. After that narrow escape, they
had reaffirmed their oath never to shackle themselves to
any woman.

Three years later, Amos had lost his small coaster and
half his crew when she foundered in a storm off Cape Hen-
lopen. As the last man to leave the ship, he had survived
by clinging to a spar, but by the time he had recovered,
he'd lost his taste for the sea. Taking the insurance money,
he'd built himself a snug house on his father's property and
retired.

By then, Callum had been busy cultivating one of his
more outstanding talents. A gambler's career had taken him
from one end of the Mississippi River to the other, earning
him outright ownership of a gaudy stern-wheeler and part
interest in a gentleman's club in Mobile. More than once
he'd written, urging Rogan, who was sailing with his father
aboard the *White Witch,* to join him there.

Rogan might have considered it, for he was young, and
hauling freight up and down the coast under Edmund Rawson's stern command lacked excitement, to say the least.
But before he could bring himself to tell his father that he
wanted to strike out on his own, the old man had suffered
a sudden seizure of the heart and died.

Shocked, for at that age, Rogan had considered his father
immortal, he had taken the *Witch* home, where it had laid
over until after he had buried his father. Under Dick's guid-

ance, Rogan had taken command. He could have sold her a dozen times since then, but the crew would not have been guaranteed a place under a new owner.

And there was Hetty to look after, as well. He couldn't just go off and leave her on her own. With the first mate's help, and a crew that was both mature and experienced enough to make up for his lack of both qualities, they had made a go of it. After a few years, Rogan had expanded his interests into the West Indies trade by buying into the *Arduous,* and later a steam packet.

Over the years there had been little time for play. He saw Callum infrequently, and then only briefly, when they happened to be in the same city. Neither of them ever mentioned the pact. Rogan had all but forgotten it, and judging from the type of women Callum usually surrounded himself with, he was no more ready to settle down now than he had been at eighteen.

"Sweetums? You're still wearing your coat," Della Hester purred against his back. She'd come up behind him silently while he'd been staring out the window, lost in thought. Now she slipped her arms around him, pressing her full breasts and soft belly into his backside, and ran the backs of her fingers over the fly of his britches.

Moving restlessly, Rogan grimaced at the scent of her stale perfume, repressing the unwanted memory of Kathleen's clean, soap-and-roses scent. "Sorry, Della. I was just wondering if I've put too much off on Dick. The man's long past retirement age, and I've left him to find me a deck cargo, deal with the broker and see to the loading."

"Hmm, age don't have anything to do with whether a man's still a man, sweety." She laughed softly, her fingers now busy on the buttons of his shirt. She was wearing a lacy wrapper of peach-colored silk that he'd given her for her last birthday, and suddenly, visualizing Kathleen in her plain cotton nightshirt, he felt guilty.

Dammit, a man had a right to a mistress! He treated her better than most men treated their wives, so why should he feel guilty? Just because she wasn't the kind of woman he would ever consider marrying—just because he'd married a woman he had no intention of bedding...

"Is there any coffee left in the pot?" he growled.

"Coffee!"

Rogan couldn't see her face, but he knew she would be pouting prettily. Della made an art of pouting prettily, just as she did everything else prettily. That, after all, was to her advantage, he reminded himself, considering her profession.

"Did I tell you I brought you a bolt of silk from Baltimore?" he blurted, regretting the words the moment they left his tongue. He'd bought the silk for Kathleen, intending to take it to her the next time he had reason to stop off to see Hetty.

"Ooh, lovely! What color is it? Blue? I adore blue!"

Della's eyes were blue. Against her pink and white skin and her guinea-gold hair, they suddenly struck him as infinitely less interesting than gray eyes. Gray eyes, and a short, straight nose dusted with freckles, and a gleaming crop of mahogany-colored hair that was straight as a waterfall and never quite tidy.

"Blue? Yeah, I reckon you might call it blue," he muttered. He had called it gray, and pictured it made up into a gown such as the fashionable ladies of Baltimore were wearing, with that little puckered thingamabob on the stern, and close-hauled in the front so that a twitch of the skirt showed a flash of ruffled petticoat.

"Why don't we take the carriage into town so you can fetch it for me, and then we can come back here and decide how to have it made up, hmm? We can lie down and get real comfortable while we talk about what you like best in a woman...that is, in her gowns."

Rogan closed his eyes, knowing he had set the trap and baited it too well. He had only himself to blame for the fix he was in. Nor did it make sense to feel guilty for being unfaithful to the wife he had no intention of ever bedding, with the mistress he'd kept for more than two years. Still, there was no denying that guilt was his problem.

One of his problems, at least, the other being that unless he got his mind off his wife and back where it belonged, he was going to have one very unhappy mistress on his hands, not to mention explanations that no man enjoyed having to make.

Kathleen lifted the bright red flannel drawers from the washtub and peered closely to make sure she'd gotten the stains out. She couldn't believe it! What on earth had Hetty been thinking of, stealing Amos's brand new underwear right off his clothesline, then hiding it in the henhouse? If she hadn't needed another egg and gone out to see if she could find one, she would never have known.

Reacting to the deed and not the doer, she had demanded an explanation, as if Hetty were no older than Caleb.

"Well, now, I'm not certain sure just what that pair of drawers was doing there, and that's the truth," Hetty said as guilelessly as if she'd never laid eyes on them before. "Did you ask Amos to see if he'd left 'em in there?"

Exasperated, Kathleen hung onto her temper by a shred. "Hetty, Amos has never set foot in your chicken house, and you know it! Why would he do such a thing? Why would anyone in their right mind hide a pair of drawers under a nesting box?"

She regretted the words the minute they were out. Hetty might not be bright as a button every moment of the day, but that was no call to hurt the poor woman's feelings. "Never mind, I suppose there's no real harm done."

It was the sort of pisky-mindedness she'd come to expect

from Hetty. It would have helped if Rogan had warned her, but then perhaps he'd tried, only she'd misunderstood. "I'm sure Amos appreciates your taking in his wash for him. I'll just wring these out and hang them back on his line, and with any luck, they'll be dry by night." With any luck, he'd never know they'd been stolen!

With her skirts blowing around her sturdy limbs and the mid-August sun shining down on the wispy white fuzz that covered her head, Hetty looked like a wrinkled child as she scowled and grumbled. Kathleen, thinking to spare her, had taken over the wash along with the rest of the chores, but Hetty never hesitated to criticize the way she did things. "I always use the other tub there to rinse in. Does a better job of it."

"I'm sorry, I'll remember that. Thank you for telling me." The tub in question was rusted through on the bottom, but Kathleen saw no need to mention that fact.

"And don't steal no more o' my eggs, girl. You want eggs, you come ask me. They'll cost you a penny apiece."

Kathleen's jaw dropped. Collecting herself, she gave the long drawers one last hard twist and nodded meekly. "I'll remember that, too, Hetty. I'll pay you as soon as I run over to Amos's and hang these out. One more egg and I'll have enough to make a pan of spoon bread for supper."

Callum had forgotten how small his old home was. He had forgotten how old and frail his father was. Suddenly, he felt guilty for having stayed away too long. He'd felt cramped, as if the close-knit little community was choking the life out of him. The last straw had been when Amos had bargained to trade him for a half interest in a dammed schooner!

He'd been back for visits since then, but it had been some time since the last one. "How long has it been,

Paw?'' he asked now, tenderness creeping into his voice in spite of his resolve to deny it.

"How long has what been, since I whupped you last, or since you been home?" Amos took another sip of the smooth bourbon whiskey his son had brought him and admired the rich amber color. "This here tastes considerable better than what John Robert makes in his fish house. Charged me a whole half-dollar for the last gallon I bought, and him me own blood kin, too."

Callum grinned. Half the island was blood kin. A man had to make a living the best way he could, and when fishing was slow, why, then he had to use a bit of ingenuity. "I was in Memphis last Christmas, Paw. Remember, I sent you that chesterfield coat?"

"Damned silly thing. You think I'd wear a coat with a velvet collar out where God'n ever'body could see me?''

"Before that, I was in St. Louis. Or maybe it was Mobile. I kept thinking to take a train to Charleston and book passage up the coast, but somehow, it never seemed to work out."

Amos snorted and took another sip of his whiskey, but his eyes were filled with pride, even watering a bit, as he stole quick sidelong glimpses at his only living son. "Don't take time out from all your fancy clubs and wild women on my account, boy. I got all I need right here."

"Level with me, how've you been getting on, Paw?"

"Good. Better some day'n others, but I ain't complaining."

"You and Hetty still look after one another the way you used to?"

"Some," Amos allowed. "Some. Rogan's woman helps out."

"Rogan's woman?" Leaning forward on the mule-eared chair, Callum repeated, "*Rogan's* woman? What the blue blazes are you talking about, Paw? Things can't have changed *that* much in the past two or three years!''

"Don't know what you call change, but Rogan brought him home a woman, all right. Name of Kathleen. Beaufort girl, she was. Cooks real good bread."

"You mean he hired a housekeeper."

"Nope. Up'n married her. Told me afore he left to keep an eye on the pair of 'em, on account o' he didn't want to scare her off by telling her too much about Hetty's ways."

Callum whistled softly under his breath as he thought of his friend's vow all those years ago. They'd both declared their intent to remain single. At the time, Callum had just had the devil scared out of him by a close call. Fortunately, the lady involved had been as disinclined to have him as he had been to have her, so there'd been no real loss on either side.

Other than his father's, he thought now. Poor Paw had had his heart set on buying into that fine bugeye, but even then his rheumatism had been coming on. He'd not have been able to sail many more years, no matter how many ships he'd owned.

"So Rogan's got himself a bride," he mused. "What's she like? Pretty?"

"Like I said, she makes good bread. Hard worker, too."

"I can't see the Rogue marrying a woman on the strength of her bread alone. He could have half the women on the eastern seaboard dangling from his watch chain if he wanted 'em. Always did have the devil's own luck with women, damn his salt-cured hide."

"Not much to choose betwixt the pair o' ye, come to that."

Although Amos would never have admitted it to the boy, he'd always been secretly proud of Callum's success with the ladies. To tell the truth, Amos himself had never been

above fair to middling when it came to good looks, but
Callum took after his mother, rest her soul.

"Still, she must be pretty special, or Rogue'd never've
looked twice at her."

"As to that, I reckon she's a decent enough woman. Not
what you'd call downright pretty. Not like your ma was.
She's a worker, all right, but the truth is, she's kind of puny.
No meat on her bones, not much color to her cheeks and
eyes. Still, she comes over regular to bring me a pot of
soup or a plate of biscuits. Does right well by the old
woman. There she is now, out in the backyard a-hanging
my new flannel drawers on the line. Hetty took 'em for one
of them confounded quilts of hers, an' I didn't have the
heart to make her give 'em back. You gotta watch her
around red. Likes red above ever'thing."

Callum threw back his head and laughed. "You mean
that loony old goose is still robbing folks' clothes off their
lines and making 'em up into quilts? Godamighty, Paw, it's
a wonder you're not all running around stark naked." Idly,
he stood and wandered over to the tall, narrow window that
faced the backyard. Just as idly, he drew back the limp,
dry-rotted drapery that had hung there for as long as he
could remember.

He whistled softly under his breath. "Taller than average, would you say? Tidy little stern and long, dark hair?"

"I reckon you could say that," Amos agreed.

"Wears black stockings, black boots and white drawers
with pink bindings around the knees?"

"Well, now, I can't say as to that, boy. She don't go
lifting her skirts, leastwise not on my account. Wears a lot
of black, and when she's not wearing black, she'd got on
something gray. I've always favored color onto a woman.
Your ma was right partial to blue, and I don't reckon a
woman lived but what looked as pretty as she did in a blue
frock. I recollect this one she had…bought it for her up in

Boston, I did. Ready-made, right there in the store. It had a..."

But Callum was no longer listening. Thoroughly capti-vated by the sight of a trimly rounded bottom in thin knee bloomers, surrounded by a billow of skirts and petticoats, he watched, entranced, as a tall, slender woman with wind-blown hair and patches of color in her cheeks wrestled to hold down her flying skirts while she pegged Amos's draw-ers onto the clothesline.

"I always did enjoy a fresh northwest gale," he mur-mured, rocking back and forth on his handsome French leather boots.

Kathleen unwrapped a clinging wet leg from around her forearm while she fumbled for the peg she held clamped between her teeth. Her tubs were set up on the southerly side of the house, between the kitchen and the shed. She hadn't realized how chilly it had gotten, or how much the wind had picked up since morning, but then, that was the exciting thing about this time of year. Just when you'd had enough of one kind of weather, it went and turned on you.

She was thinking about whether to tackle a few more boxes after she set the bread to bake when she sensed a presence behind her. Grabbing her skirt, which was whip-ping wildly about her legs, she wiped her hair out of her eyes and glanced over her shoulder.

And gasped. "Oh, my," she cried softly. "That is, I know you." And then she blushed. "No, I don't, but I know your face. You're Amos's boy. His Callum."

"Amos's boy," Callum repeated, sounding thoroughly bemused. "It's been a while since anyone called me a boy, Amos's or anyone else's. You, I take it, are Rogan's woman."

"I'm Kathleen Stevens. Rawson, that is. I mean, I'm Mrs. Rawson—uh, Rogan's wife. Yes," she added for good measure, leaving him, she was quite certain, in no doubt that his friend had married an idiot.

A gust of wind plastered her gown to her body, and she held down her skirt with one hand and brushed back her hair with the other. She'd given up on trying to keep it pinned up while she worked around the house, and settled for one long braid. "You are Callum, aren't you?"

Blue eyes dancing with good-natured amusement, he deliberately looked her over, from the toe of her oldest boots to the crown of her tangled hair. "Callum McNair, gambler, rakehell and general layabout, at your service, ma'am. Where the deuce has Rogan been hiding you all this time?"

While he might not be actually flirting with her, the man was surely teasing her. Kathleen was not so green that she didn't recognize that right off. But he was such an utterly charming scamp, she couldn't bring herself to call him down for it. He was Rogan's friend, after all. And Amos's son. "Your father must be over the windmill to have you home. How long have you been here?"

"Just long enough to be lectured for staying away too long. How long have you been here?"

Kathleen bent over to pick up the basin she'd used to carry the wet underwear to Amos's backyard, and Callum took it from her. For an instant, their hands rested side by side on the graniteware pan, and the difference between them was startling. Her own, while small, were embarrassingly red and rough, while his were soft, pale and well manicured.

"What? Oh. I've been here—well, I suppose it's been nearly two months now. Goodness, I've lost track."

"Still on your honeymoon, then, are you?"

Once more she could feel her cheeks burning, and it had nothing to do with the brisk wind. "Would you—are you— that is, I thought I'd bring Amos some spoon bread and stew for supper. I'll bring over enough for two."

"Why don't we all get together for supper, you and Rogan, Hetty, Paw and me?"

"Rogan's not here."

"You mean he left you here on your own?"

He sounded shocked. He also sounded as if he knew very well that Rogan was not at home. "Callum—that is, Mr. McNair, if you'll give me my basin, I'd best get home and start on the bread. It takes a while to bake."

There were elongated dimples in his lean cheeks when he smiled, and he was smiling now. It occurred to Kathleen that any man this handsome, this charming and this forward could have been dangerous, yet oddly enough, she wasn't afraid of him. Perhaps she'd grown up in the few months since she'd been married.

Or perhaps she sensed that he didn't take his looks too seriously, nor did he expect her to. As for his charm, it was so comically overdone that it had no effect at all on her, other than making her want to laugh. That, in itself, was a wonder, for she seldom found much to laugh about.

Rogan, on the other hand, could send her into shock with a single look from those compelling eyes of his.

"Mrs. Rawson? No, I believe I'll call you Kathy," he dared, his smile robbing his words of any impertinence.

"Mr. McNair, you might as well know right off that I've heard all your darkest secrets. I know about the sisters you and Rogan wrote love letters to, and signed each other's names. I know all about that awful skeleton, and the flowers you stole from the delivery boy and sent to his girl with your name on the card, and the time you—"

"Alas, I was easily led astray in my youth. Kathy, darling, I was an innocent pawn for Rogan's wicked schemes, didn't they tell you that? They don't call him the Rogue for nothing, you know."

By that time they were strolling toward the Rawson house. When they came to the plank across the shallow creek that twisted through the marsh between the two houses, Callum went first and extended his hand, leading her across and then tucking her hand against his side as if they'd known each other for years.

"You don't have to see me home, you know," Kathleen said, her voice husky with brimming laughter.

"Hetty would never forgive me if I didn't pay my respects, and I'd never forgive myself if something happened to you between Paw's house and Rogan's."

She laughed outright at that. "My mercy, what could happen?"

Sending her a teasing sidelong glance, he said, "Don't rush me, I'm trying to think of something."

"You know, you do remind me of someone," Kathleen murmured as they approached the house from the back way. She tucked the basin under the bench outside the kitchen door, alongside the clothes pegs.

"Your first love, perhaps?" Callum suggested outrageously. "They say a woman never forgets the first man to touch her heart."

They had come to a halt outside the kitchen door, and it occurred to Kathleen that, banker or not, Callum McNair looked about as much at home in the weathered little village as a South American parrot would in a nest of sparrows. Holding her hair with one hand and her blowing skirt with the other, she smiled at him, cheeks glowing from the wind and eyes sparkling like sunlight on stormy waters.

"Not my first nor my last, I'm afraid. To tell the truth, you remind me of my nephew, Caleb."

"Your nephew? I'm crushed, absolutely crushed!"

Kathleen laughed aloud at his crestfallen look. "He's going on six, and he's a wicked little imp." But her laughter faded quickly as she turned to go inside. "And sometimes I miss him so much I hurt," she said softly. "Thank you for seeing me safely home, Callum. I'll send Hetty over after awhile with your supper."

Chapter Eight

Kathleen laughed more during the week that followed than she had in years. Hetty and Amos were a pair when they got to yarning, and Callum liked nothing better than to lead them into one tale after another about Rogan's early misdeeds, which as often as not had included his own participation.

My new family. My new friends, Kathleen thought, one of the circle, yet apart. Hetty was the age her grandmother would have been, but the two women were not at all alike. Her grandmother had seldom smiled. Life was too serious for smiling. It occurred to Kathleen that she'd never heard her laugh—not the head-thrown-back, full-bodied cackling laugh she heard from Hetty at least a dozen times a day.

As for Amos, he was simply Amos. An irreverent old man who was lonely without his Maudie, his babies and his only remaining son.

Kathleen's gaze fell on Callum, and she caught herself studying him with no more personal involvement than if he were a lovely sunset or a particularly fine painting. How handsome he was, with his dark gold hair and his deep blue eyes. If now and then those eyes took on a look of...was it regret? Sadness? Whatever it was, the moment always passed quickly enough for Kathleen to wonder if she'd only imagined it.

Callum had been home for a week and a day when word came that the *Witch* had been third in line to unload and take on new cargo at Beaufort three days before, and would probably have cleared Cape Lookout and taken a northeast heading by now. Whether or not Rogan would stop off at Hatteras was anyone's guess.

"I reckon I'll be heading out with the *Eagle* tomorrow morning," Callum remarked as he finished his morning coffee. He and Amos had been discussing some of the newer ships being built on the islands at Hatteras and Kinnakeet, farther up the banks. The *American Eagle,* a small Hatteras built schooner of some six tons net burden, was presently running material for the new lifesaving station being built up the beach, and taking the occasional passenger, as well.

"You'll not stay over to see Rogan?" Amos pressed. "I'd lay odds he'll be stopping off to see his bride."

Callum rose and crossed to the stove, pouring himself another cup of coffee. In spite of the fact that he'd have liked to stay and see Rogan, he had pressing business of his own to attend to. He had decided to make a long overdue visit home in the first place because it had seemed important to make himself scarce until a certain redhead's husband cooled down and called off the dogs.

It had been a stupid miscalculation on his part. Who would have dreamed the man had a brother with the Pinkertons? If the redhead hadn't been so damned beautiful, and so obviously interested, Callum would never have considered dallying with her in the first place.

But she was, and so he had. Taking great care first to see that her husband was involved in a high stakes card game. How the devil was he to know the gentleman would throw in a losing hand and go rushing up to his stateroom to check up on his wife's headache?

Callum had been doing well at alleviating the redhead's discomforts, real and imagined, when he'd heard the key in the stateroom door. He had spent an extremely unpleasant ten minutes squeezed into a clothes locker with two black suits, three full-skirted gowns and a number of ruffled petticoats.

All the way upriver he had borne the gentleman's suspicious looks with admirable aplomb, but it had taken something out of him. He'd left the *Sunset Queen* in Memphis and taken a train east, vowing never again to dally with a married woman.

Not that he considered the time spent with Rogan's bride in the same light as a dalliance. It was no such thing. Somewhat to his surprise, he'd found that he enjoyed her companionship. Friendship with a woman was a new experience for him, but much as he was enjoying it, he didn't relish having to satisfy Rogan that it was all quite innocent.

It had been eighteen months since the two men had last met. The edge had already gone off the old friendly rivalry that had existed between them ever since they'd first taken turns blowing dried peas through a hollow reed at Miss Marthenia's tomcat. As they'd grown older, they'd competed at hunting, at horse racing, at gaming and finally at the gentlemanly sport of seducing women. It added zest to the game, and since neither of them had ever had anything resembling an honorable intention toward any of the women they flirted with, who were invariably older and far more experienced than they themselves had been at the time, where was the harm?

Of course, if the girls in question had been innocent...but then, at that age, innocence had been the last thing to attract them.

The last time they'd vied for a woman's favors had been

nearly four years ago. Coralann had been outrageously beautiful. The two men had outdone themselves competing for her favors. The young widow of an elderly shipping magnate, she had entered the game with every sign of enjoyment, spurring them on to outdo one another in compliments and gift-giving.

Rogan had been in Newport News having the *Witch* refitted at the time, while Callum had been running a gaming table in one of Norfolk's better establishments. Each had strived to present the merry widow with the lushest hothouse flowers, the sweetest candy and the most impressive jewelry, all of which she had accepted as her due. In return, there'd been a few ardent stolen kisses, and that was all.

For a pair of experienced men-about-town, they'd been magnificently duped. Afterward, they'd agreed that it was the combination of jade eyes and red-gold curls that had done them in, but in the end, neither of them had won more than a glimpse of lacy undergarments, a squeeze, a tease and a kiss or two.

Not to mention a few personal injuries. They'd wound up fighting, and when the match was over, Callum had been sporting not one, but two black eyes, Rogan a broken nose and a fist that resembled a fresh hamhock. Meanwhile, before they could recover enough to come calling once more, the young widow's stepson waltzed off with the prize, thus keeping his father's fortune intact.

Disgruntled, they'd gone their separate ways. For the next year or so, Rogan had been busy enlarging his Atlantic shipping interests and Callum had headed west to examine his latest acquisition, a fancy floating gambling palace that plied back and forth on the Mississippi River.

From time to time their paths had crossed and they'd shared a few drinks and the latest news from home, but the old closeness seemed to be missing. Occasionally Callum wondered if any of the women they had vied for had meant more to Rogan than he'd let on.

"Took a shine to Rogan's woman, didn't ye, son? Just like the old days."

His father's jarring observation brought Callum up short. Was it? He didn't want to think so. Despite the rather hedonistic path he'd followed, he preferred to believe that his integrity remained intact.

Turning away from the window, he shrugged. "Kathleen? She's a nice enough woman." She was a wonderful woman. Not his usual style, but then, he wouldn't have thought she was Rogan's style, either.

"Bakes right good bread."

"That she does. Hetty seems to be faring well."

"Still up to her old tricks. Steals things. Hides 'em, and then forgets where she put 'em. Scares the pants off'n all the young'uns tellin' 'em the devil can't wait to get his hands on 'em."

"Same old Hetty," Callum observed.

"Same old Hetty, Lord love 'er scrawny carcass."

During Callum's visit, Kathleen had found it all too easy to let her work slide. There were so many more interesting things to do, and for the first time in her life, she was completely free to enjoy them. With Hetty's blessings, Callum drove her in Amos's horse cart to show her where the Indians used to live. He showed her where the wild horses holed up in a storm, and where they dug along the shore for fresh water. Together, they climbed Trent Hills in search of wild grapes, which were still shudderingly tart to taste.

One rainy night, while Hetty and Amos sat dozing, he introduced her to the game of poker, then taught her to cheat. Unfortunately, no matter how skilled she became at dealing off the bottom of the deck, she couldn't do it without giggling. Callum said she was hopelessly moral, a lost cause, and she giggled all the more. It quickly became obvious that what he didn't know about games of chance wasn't worth knowing, for he could deal from the bottom, the top or the center of the deck without batting an eye.

For perhaps the first time in her life, Kathleen felt she had found herself a best friend, albeit a rather unlikely one. She'd never had much time to cultivate friendships before, what with first her grandmother, then Alice's brood. The fact that her new best friend was a man instead of a woman seemed completely irrelevant. They talked avidly about anything and everything.

Of course, there were some things she would never reveal, even to a best friend. Such as how she hated always having to wear things that had been cut down for her, or her fears of suddenly finding herself homeless again for the fourth time in her eighteen years. Or the way she was coming to feel about the man she had married—and how much those feelings confused her.

But they laughed together. She found herself telling him all about Alice's children. They compared some of Caleb's pranks with Callum's boyhood memories. Being able to laugh together and share a few memories went a long way in relieving the homesickness that still plagued her in the quiet hours of the night.

The evening before Callum left, the two families shared a meal in the Rawsons' kitchen. Amos had entertained them with tales of Blackbeard's activities around Ocracoke, which led to more recent stories of blockade-running through the inlets bounding Hatteras and somehow wound up with a tale of the time the sound had frozen over. Callum and Rogan, it seemed, had built a brush hut on the ice, then tried to warm it up by building a fire. They'd ended up nearly drowning themselves, as well as a poor dog who'd been fool enough to tag along.

While the two elders finished their meal and headed for the sitting room, Kathleen told Callum, who had remained to help her carry out the lemonade, her own ice story, about the time Caleb had tried to sell the twins to the man who delivered ice so that he could buy licorice whips with the money. Near the end of the telling, she had to blink several times and swallow hard.

"You miss them, don't you?"

Nodding, she didn't pretend to misunderstand.

"Why did you leave? Hetty says Rogan brought you here and left the next day, and he's not been back but once since then. That strikes me as a lonely sort of marriage."

"Lonely? I can't think why," she said with spurious brightness. "My mercy, I have Hetty, and if she's not enough to keep me hopping, there's Amos. Your father and I have got to be great friends. Can you carry all the glasses? I thought we had a tray, but I can't seem to find it."

Callum's smooth hands closed easily around four of Hetty's best glasses, and Kathleen picked up the white porcelain pitcher. "What about children of your own, Kathy?" he persisted. "Seems to me you'd make a wonderful mother."

Ignoring the question as if she hadn't heard it, she led the way to the sitting room, her best black taffeta skirt rustling with every step. Perhaps it had been a mistake to get on such cozy terms quite so quickly.

Lonely? Her chin went up as she placed the pitcher on the little spool-legged table. Certainly she was lonely. But then, even when she'd been surrounded by Alice's babies, she'd been lonely deep inside, where no one could see. Perhaps she'd been born with that kind of loneliness. Perhaps everyone was, only no one dared admit it.

"Kathy?" Callum said quietly. He had come up behind her to place the glasses on the table, and she began to pour. "It's none of my business. I'm sorry if I upset you."

"Upset me? I can't imagine why you should think that. Here, give this one to Hetty. Amos likes a drop of whiskey in his, but he'll have to do without. I think Hetty must've given away Rogan's supply."

The talk was impersonal, and the McNairs said good-night soon after that. Callum said his goodbyes, as well, for he was leaving early the next day. He hugged Hetty and whispered something in her ear that set her off. While she was still cackling, he grabbed Kathleen's hand, tugged her into his arms and planted a noisy smack on her cheek. They both laughed, although the laughter didn't spread as far as Callum's eyes. But Kathleen didn't notice. Before he'd reached the foot of the path, he'd already faded from her mind.

Rogan was on his way home again! Why, he might be dropping anchor this very minute. The trip to shore in the launch didn't take long, and he might borrow a horse...

The glow in her eyes faded. Unless, she cautioned herself, he decided not to stop off on his way north. He didn't always. Just because someone had seen the *Witch* in Beaufort and suggested that she might be on her way north by now, it didn't really mean anything. Rogan could be half-way to Baltimore by now, without a single thought in his head for her or Hetty.

Well...perhaps for Hetty.

That night, before she went to bed, Kathleen dragged out a dozen or more boxes, dumping their contents to be sorted out later. She stacked them, smallest into the next size up and so on, until they took up only a fraction of the space, and carted them out to the shed, thankful that it was definitely turning cooler now. Autumn was in the air, even here where there were few trees to turn color.

Early the next morning, she climbed out of bed, having lain awake half the night thinking of all that had to be done before Rogan came home. *If* he came home. Still, sooner or later, he would have to, and when that time came, she was determined to have her own bedchamber.

Even after she cleared out the last of the years' accumulation of clutter, there was a world of scrubbing to do before she could even think of moving her belongings downstairs. She had already rummaged through the shed and set out the few pieces of furniture she'd be needing. Nothing matched. It was as if they'd been collected from half a dozen different sources, but that was neither here nor there. A bed, a three-legged dresser and a row of pegs on the wall would serve quite well. Perhaps a small table and a chair if she could find something that wasn't too far gone to rescue. The odds and ends she'd unearthed looked as if they'd been through the wars.

Perhaps they had.

By nightfall, the room was reasonably clean, the musty smell overlaid by the scent of Hetty's strong lye soap and oil furniture polish. Kathleen's hands were chapped redder than ever, but she soothed them with a coat of carbolated arnica salve and covered them with her oldest cotton gloves. On impulse, she sprinkled a few drops of attar of roses on her pillow, so that the last thing she thought of before she dropped off to sleep was the tea roses that grew along Alice's back fence.

But it wasn't the thought of roses that followed her into her dreams.

Rogan. Since when had she begun to dream about him? It wasn't the first time, she realized the next morning. There was a certain familiarity about the warm, glowing feeling that had suffused her when she'd woken. Like all dreams, it faded in the cold light of day.

"Oh, my mercy, as if I didn't have enough to do without mooning around all day!" she grumbled, ruthlessly yanking a brush through her tangled hair.

It didn't take a great amount of rationalizing to conclude that her best black was the only possible thing to wear. The old black bombazine was wearing on the grain. Her gray skirt was dusty around the hem. Both that and her second-best black needed a good brushing and airing, but she'd been too busy to take care of it.

After breakfast, she hurried to her new room, which was all ready to move into. She'd left the windows cracked open the night before to air out any lingering mustiness, and now it smelled fresh as sunshine. And it was hers! No cradle at the foot of her bed, no cot for an ailing to child to bed down on. It was her very own, and she intended to waste no time in moving her things into place.

She was on her fourth trip from the loft, her arms laden with bedding, when she heard the front gate squeak. Suddenly, her feet went cold and her face caught fire. Her heart commenced to leap about like a frog in a pail, and she pressed a feather pillow hard against it, for all the good it did.

With a soft oath, she tossed the bedding onto her trunk, which served as a blanket chest, and turned just in time to see Rogan enter the house.

The front door, the door to the loft and the door to Kathleen's new room were all within a few feet of one another. When Rogan entered the house, he usually dropped his seabag near the stairs and headed for the rooms at the back of the house.

Instead he stood frozen, his seabag sliding slowly to the floor as he stared at the woman in the doorway. Barriers clicked into place. He stared at her softly gleaming eyes, her pink cheeks, at the expression that seemed compounded of hope, fear and a good measure of uncertainty, and all his old survival instincts stirred to life.

Neither of them spoke. Then both spoke at once.

"You're looking well, Kathleen." She looked wary. She

also looked...not precisely beautiful, but something far more intriguing.

"I—I'd better go get Hetty," she said, not moving a step.

"I brought you something," he said, and watched the wariness increase twofold.

"You did? Why?"

Why? Rogan had asked himself that question a hundred times since he'd left Della, having given her the bolt of silk he'd purchased for his wife. They'd quarreled after that, and Rogan knew it was mostly his fault. He'd been in an irritable mood. As things stood now, he doubted if he'd be seeing her again, which meant that sooner or later, he would have the task of finding himself a new mistress.

Damn! He wasn't usually such a bumbler!

"Hetty, too," he said, and cleared his throat self-consciously. "That is, I brought her something, too."

"Oh. Of course." Kathleen stared at the tips of her boots. Her face was still burning, she could feel it. And the angrier she grew at herself for being so foolish, the more it burned. Hell and drat!

By suppertime, Kathleen complimented herself on having largely recovered her composure. She had changed into her old gray and brown, never mind the dusty hem, and covered it with an apron. The rest of her clothing, including her few winter things, hung from pegs in her new bed-chamber, looking like a flock of bedraggled crows. She was so blessed tired of mourning! What was more, she was tired of hand-me-downs, and one way or another, she was going to buy herself a new coat before cold weather came. If she had to wear that cut-down cast-off melton of Morton's one more time, she'd burn the blasted thing!

As if on signal, the smell of burning stew assailed her nostrils. Her stirring hand had kept time with her thoughts, splashing stew onto the stove. She uttered a mild oath, reached for a cloth to clean up the mess and decided to let it burn dry, then brush it off. So what if it filled the kitchen with the smell of burned food? Hetty would hardly be likely to complain, and Rogan had left almost immediately after telling her he had brought her a gift. Since then she'd not seen hide nor hair of him or his gift!

He probably had a dozen girlfriends on the island and had brought them all gifts. After hearing all the tales Hetty and Amos had told, not to mention Callum's, it wouldn't be hard to believe. Nor would marriage change *that* particular situation. Their marriage wasn't a real one, and besides, Rogan wasn't the kind of man any woman would be likely to forget.

Then let his other women feed him, she thought, having worked herself into a fine state of temper. When she heard a door close in the main house, she filled her lungs, and without bothering to look around, yelled, "Hetty! Supper's done!"

"Sorry, but she's decided to take her evening meal with Amos. Anna Quidley brought him a mess of stewed crabs."

"Oh." It was Rogan. Sensing his presence immediately behind her, she steeled herself against being affected. She could smell the subtle wool, tobacco, male scent of his body, feel the warmth radiating from him. It was a dangerous combination. She took a deep breath, then wished she hadn't, for it went straight to her head. Moving too quickly, she dropped the cooking spoon and tried to catch it again. Instead, she brushed her hand against the stove.

"Hell and drat!" she gasped, sucking her fingers.

Immediately, Rogan practically surrounded her, taking her hand from her mouth and examining the injured area. The skin on the pads of her first two fingers was red and shiny, and when he drew them into his own mouth, Kathleen felt her consciousness waver.

"Maybe I should forbid you the use of a stove. Seems you can't be trusted around fire."

"If you'd just stay out of my way, I'd be fine!"

Ignoring her, he led her to the sink and held her fingers under a stream of water. After the initial shock, the pain eased, and she expelled her breath in one long gust, blowing the fringe off her suddenly damp forehead.

"Hell and drat?" Rogan repeated, sounding mildly amused. "And here I thought I'd married myself a genuine 'my mercy' lady."

"I'm sorry. Please, I can take care of it myself."

He held her hand up to examine the damage, then turned her hand over to examine her wrist. Other than the shadowy tracery of veins, the skin on her fragile wrist was flawless. Rogan smiled, making her feel doubly vulnerable. "There, what'd I tell you? The old one's as good as new. At the rate you're going, you'll soon stop letting me come home. You seem to get burnt every time I get near."

Did she ever! "It was my own fault," she said stiffly. "I'll take care of it." But Rogan was already dipping flour into a saucer and wetting it down for a poultice.

Shaken and feeling somehow threatened, she stared at him. As usual, he was clad in black, the close-fitting trousers and jersey no different from what any ordinary seaman might wear. Only there was nothing at all ordinary about him. It occurred to her that a man like Rogan didn't require starched linen and brass braid to set him apart from his crew. His authority was in his very bearing, an innate part of the man himself.

"Give me your hand," he commanded, reaching for the fist she was clutching to her chest. "Come on, Primrose, it's messy, but it'll take the sting out. When I'm not here, you may do as you please, but as long as I'm home, you'll do as I see fit."

"Aye, aye, sir," she muttered.

His dark eyes snapped with amusement as he glanced up from the task of carefully smearing her fingertips with paste. "I'll remind you, Mrs. Rawson, that insubordination is a punishable crime."

"I thought floggings had been outlawed, Captain." It was all she could do to keep from gasping as his thumb clamped onto the palm of her hand to hold it in position.

"A man writes his own laws in his home and on board his ship. Shall I bind you up?"

Her eyes widened in alarm before she realized that he was offering to bandage her hand. "I could hardly get supper on the table wrapped up like a mummy."

"I could serve. Come to that, I could feed you," he said with a wicked glint of a smile. "Smells burnt, anyhow. Maybe we'd better go over and see if there's any stewed crabs left at Amos's house."

"It's not burnt at all. What you smell is what I splashed on the stove, but perhaps you'd rather eat over at Amos's."

"I'll take my chances here with you." He was teasing her, and she was still unused to being teased. Certainly by him. But the smile faded and he said, "Kathleen, if you're not content with our arrangements, say so. I prefer plain speaking to holding things inside."

"I'm not holding anything. Inside, that is. What I mean is, I'm perfectly content, but if you have any complaints, I'm sure I'd like to hear them. Perhaps you're the one who's not cont—"

He placed a finger on her lips, and the effect was roughly like being struck by lightning. "Shh, I'm sorry, Primrose. Didn't mean to get to the wind'ard of you. Josiah told me you were known for your even disposition, so I reckon if you're riled up, it's my fault. I'm truly sorry, but there's not a whole lot I can do about it. Sometimes it happens between two people that way. They strike sparks off one another. Get under one another's skin without meaning to."

"But I don't—that is, do I strike sparks off you? Have I done anything to get under your skin?"

For the longest time, he didn't reply. And then, with a thoughtful look, he said, "No. Leastwise, I don't suppose it's intentional."

Kathleen was crushed. An even disposition was one of the things she had cultivated all those years she had waited on an irritable, ill old woman. By the time she'd gone to Alice's house to live, she'd been able to take most anything in her stride. Anything except Morton, at least, but that was another matter.

"I'm sorry. I don't know what gets into me sometimes." She wouldn't let him drive her away. There was nowhere else to go. More to the point, she wasn't sure she could bear to leave him.

"No need to apologize, Kathleen. I reckon I'm not the easiest man to get along with...although deuced if I know how we manage to set each other off so fast."

She sent him a wary look, then moved to the gleaming cast-iron four-holer. "Would you—that is, if you'd care for a bowl of turtle stew, I'd be glad to serve you. There's cold biscuits left over from dinner. I'll put a dab of butter on them and run them in the oven again—or if you'd rather, I can fry up some journey cakes."

One thickly arched brow rode high on Rogan's tanned forehead, giving him a decidedly diabolical air. "Kathleen, just because I took you to task about—"

"Which was no more than I deserved," she put in hastily, although it galled her. Humility. That was the ticket. Her grandmother had drilled it into her that a woman must always be humble and know her place around a man, for that was the Lord's will, else He would have made Eve first, then given her Adam as a handyman.

The trouble was, humility was so blasted uncomfortable.

It was like trying to jam her foot into one of Caleb's boots—it just didn't fit.

"Biscuits sound fine. Don't go to any bother on my account."

She sent him a suspicious look. "You're sure? It wouldn't be much of a bother. I can rake the coals under the oven and have it hot enough in five minutes."

"What, and collect another burn?" Crossing to the cabinet, Rogan took down two large bowls, then got out napkins and the spoon jar. "Where are the soup spoons?"

"In the jar."

"Kathleen, if they were in the jar, I'd not have asked where they were."

She expelled an impatient sigh. "Unless they've sprouted wings, they're right there in the jar where I put them when I washed them this morning. All three of them. Hetty had oatmeal, I had oatmeal, and the other one was used for—"

"Six."

"Six what?"

"Papa had six spoons. We always had six spoons. If you haven't got around to washing them all yet, then why not just say so?"

That tore it. Kathleen whipped her apron off, flung it in the floor and rounded on him, fists planted on her hips. "First you accuse me of a lack of humility, and then—"

"Humility! Who the devil said anything about humility? All I said was—"

"It's the same thing! All right, on rare occasions, I do tend to raise my voice above the purely polite! I admit it, but when you accuse me of *stealing*—"

"I did *not* accuse you of stealing!"

"I'd like to know what you call it!"

"I call it—I call it…" Rogan tilted his head back, closed his eyes and let the fire drain out of him. He had never in his life met anyone, man or woman, who could light his fuse as fast as this woman. "Damned stiff-necked female," he muttered. "I'd have done better to shut up the house and load Hetty on board the *Witch* and make her ship's cook. Might've starved to death, but leastwise, I'd have kept my sanity!"

Chapter Nine

Chapter Nine

It occurred to Rogan, not for the first time, that one of the reasons he'd been so edgy of late was that he hadn't had a woman in entirely too long. Common sense told him he couldn't afford to look at Kathleen in that light. He needed her too much to use her and risk losing her.

The trouble was, his body hadn't a grain of common sense. At the first touch of her soft skin, the first hint of her spicy, womanly scent, it reacted with embarrassing enthusiasm.

Dammit, he had but to think of her to set his juices to flowing! All he'd done was smear a flour paste over her burnt fingertips, and he was suddenly hard as an oar handle!

He should've gone on up to Baltimore. He had no real business here, now that Hetty was being cared for. He'd leave this minute if only he hadn't blurted out the fact that he'd brought her a gift. Now he had to produce it. Just thinking about the slither of soft silk on her even softer, silkier body was enough to get him so done up he couldn't see straight.

A gown. What the bloody hell had made him buy her a gown?

Well, he knew the answer, all right. He'd felt guilty toward Della because he'd known he'd be breaking it off with her, and so he'd given her the bolt of silk he'd bought for Kathleen. That had made him feel even guiltier. With half a dozen drinks under his belt, he'd set a course for town and picked out a yellow frock with little bands of black velvet ribbon on the collar and around the bottom. That done, he'd gone to the milliner's shop next door and bought her a yellow hat all covered with silk flowers and some scraps of net. It was prim and feminine, and the yellow roses had reminded him of her, and before he'd had time to think the thing through, the deed was done.

In the midst of congratulating himself for his taste and his generosity, he'd remembered her plain little boots with the cracks across the instep. He'd wanted to go back and buy her a new pair of those, too. Something lighter, with little heels and pointed toes. She needed something dainty. Only by the time he thought of it, he'd been well up the coast with a perishable cargo bound for Baltimore and a load of gristmill machinery waiting to be collected before the end of the month.

He hadn't gone back for the boots, and now he was wishing he'd settled for a book or a box of candies instead of something so personal. He'd been giving gifts to women for longer than he cared to recall, and not all of them innocent. Very few of them innocent, in fact.

The trouble was, he hadn't the least notion of how to handle an innocent young lady. Especially when that lady was his own wife.

He heard the back door open and close and breathed a sigh of relief. Maybe she'd gone over to Amos's place to fetch Hetty home. Maybe he would pretend he had forgotten and left them aboard the ship. Maybe he could——

Exasperated, Rogan dug his fingers into the back of his neck. Women! To be sure he'd enjoyed his share of them, but once a man let a woman get past his guard, there was bound to be the devil to pay. His father used to say that. It was about the only piece of advice the old man had ever given him on the subject of women, though he'd handed out plenty on just about every other topic under the sun. On the subject of money, ships, men and drink, he'd been dead on course. Was there a chance he'd been right about women, too?

In all the years Edmund Rawson had been married to Hetty, Rogan never recalled seeing a sign of tenderness between the two of them. He'd provided for her needs, entrusted her with his young son, and that had been the extent of their relationship. On the rare times when he came home for a spell, the two of them had never even sat down to table together, Hetty serving the old man first, then eating alone. They had shared a bed, but for all Rogan knew, there'd been a bolster down the middle, dividing off the space.

Not until after Edmund had died and Rogan had done a good bit of maturing, some of it damned painful, had it hit him that he, Rogan, was all the family Hetty had left. All she would ever have. Whether she'd ever cared above middling for the old man he didn't know. Personally, he didn't believe in love, and he couldn't imagine his father ever loving a woman the way the poets and songwriters went on about it. He'd married her, given her the care of his son and left, and that was about it. Then Rogan had gone to sea, the old man had died and now, God help him, he had sentenced another woman to the same barren life, without even so much as another woman's child to call her own. Never once looking beyond his own selfish interests, he had offered Kathleen a lifetime of servitude to a man who could never love her, in exchange for her keep and a roof over her head. He tried to tell himself she'd been a damned fool to take it, but what choice had she had?

On the other hand, if he was using her, she was sure as

hell using him. He told himself it was a fair trade. If he hadn't come along, she'd have trapped herself another victim.

Only he didn't believe it. Some women, maybe, but not his Kathleen. In the first place, she didn't have the proper equipment to attract a victim. In the second place, she lacked the cunning to take advantage of one even if she did manage to trap him. She was as different from the women he had amused himself with over the years, the Coralanns and the Dellas, as night was from day.

The back door slammed again, jarring him from his uncomfortable thoughts. "Kathleen? Everything all right out there?"

"I was just shutting the henhouse. Hetty forgot." Entering the kitchen from the little vestibule that sheltered the back door from the northeast wind, she looked first at his face, then at the pile of bundles on the table, then at his face again.

"I told you I brought you a gift. I'm, uh…sorry."

She continued to fix him with a steady gaze, making him aware all over again of the depth and clarity of those remarkable eyes of hers. He had the uncomfortable feeling she could see right through him.

"Sorry?" she echoed.

"Well, I imagine you'd rather have picked out something for yourself, something more…sensible."

Sensible. Of course. She smiled just as brightly as if she didn't long to throw his glib words right back in his face. Sensible. What had she expected, frivolous? Feminine? Beautiful?

Horse biscuits. "I'm sure whatever you've brought me will be lovely, Rogan. You needn't have bothered."

"It's no bother." Oh, hell, would you listen to him! He'd done a better job of impressing the little Gaskins girl some fifteen years ago when he'd brought her a bouquet of collards and green onions. Stolen ones, at that!

Cautiously, Kathleen moved past him to examine the parcels, and when she accidently brushed against him, he backed into the pie safe.

Suddenly, unexpectedly, her chin began to wobble. She took a deep breath and blurted, "Thank you, Rogan, it was most thoughtful of you to bring me a gift. No one ever—" She bit off the words, but it was too late.

"No one ever what? Don't tell me no one ever gave you a gift before?"

"Of course I've had gifts. Lots of gifts. And now I have one from you, and I—"

Stop babbling, you idiot! Next thing, you'll be telling him about the time Grandmother forgot Christmas, and then raised sweet Jericho with you for wasting your pennies on a tin of sweet pea scented talcum for her!

Pulling out a chair, she sat down and began fingering the knotted string of the largest package. There was a box of some sort under the brown paper, that much she could tell. She poked at the other parcel. It was soft, like a shawl or a length of woven goods. One was tiny. It could be a piece of jewelry, and she avoided that like the plague. "Isn't one of these for Hetty?" she asked, hoping it was, embarrassed at finding herself the recipient of so much attention. She truly wished he hadn't bothered. She hated being beholden. All her life she'd owed everything she possessed to someone else.

"Speaking of Hetty, I reckon I'd better go pry her loose from Amos's if I want to see her before I go." He was standing beside her chair, and Kathleen tried to think of an intelligent response. It was crazy, the way the man affected her! He had only to walk through the door to set her blood to running hot and cold. Just let her try to hold a reasonable conversation about the most ordinary matter and she ended up either completely tongue-tied or clattering like a flock of guineas.

Still he didn't leave. She wished he would. At the same time, she wished he wouldn't. Irritated with herself, she broke the thread and tore the wrappings off a spanking-new hatbox. It looked expensive. Too expensive.

"Oh," she wailed softly. "I wish you hadn't."

"Is it that bad? I can take it back next time I'm up that way if you don't like it."

He sounded so anxious that she made the mistake of looking up at him. Damn his careless kindness, she wouldn't let him do this to her! Time after time she had loved someone, only to lose them. First her parents, then her grandmother, bitter old woman that she was, and finally Alice's children. The last time she'd vowed it would never happen again, and heaven help her, it wouldn't.

Schooling her voice to hide any sign of emotion, she toyed with the shiny black-and-eggshell papered hatbox. "No, it's lovely. That is, I'm sure it will be. I just—I wish you hadn't, that's all. I have two perfectly good hats, you know, one for summer, one for winter."

"So now you have three. Well? What are you waiting for, a block and tackle? Lift the blooming lid off, woman!"

He was back to his old arrogant self, face flushed, jaw clenched, eyes glittering like obsidian. If she'd thought he'd softened toward her, she'd been sadly mistaken.

Sensible. He'd probably bought her a slat-brimmed calico bonnet like Hetty's to wear while she worked in the garden.

Sitting ramrod straight in her mule-eared chair, Kathleen untied the grosgrain ribbon that held the two parts of the oval box together. If she was clumsier than usual, it was only because of her burned fingers, not because of the man who was hovering over her like a great black cloud. "Rogan, why don't you sit over... Oh, my. Oh, my mercy," she whispered reverently.

Rogan cleared his throat. "It was a foolish notion. You probably don't even like flowery bonnets. Look here, why don't I go fetch Hetty home?"

Ignoring him, she lifted the flowered confection carefully from its nest and held it up before her. A wealth of yellow silk roses began to tremble as if a light spring breeze had just brushed over them. Quickly she sat it down in the nest of tissue and stared at it. "It's lovely. It's the loveliest thing I've ever seen, Rogan." She lifted her head to stare at him, and he was stunned to see moisture beading her thick lashes. "How can I ever thank you?"

"You might start by sailing that damned black thing into the nearest swamp. I've never liked the look of black on a woman, especially one with your coloring."

Too late, Rogan sensed that it had been the wrong thing to say. Very carefully, she lowered her gaze to the silly confection of silk and flocked veiling, making him wish to God he'd brought her a plain calico sunbonnet instead. In the milliner's shop on a sunny Thursday morning, the thing had looked young and feminine and pretty, and he'd wanted to give it to her because he'd been feeling guilty. And maybe because he'd sensed that underneath all her prickliness she was still awfully young, and...well, if not precisely pretty, at least feminine.

But here in the smoky old kitchen, between the black iron stove and the galvanized sink, it looked as out of place as a butterfly in a boiler room. Besides which, he was beginning to feel like a perfect idiot, a feeling he'd never been partial to. Unfairly or not, that feeling quickly translated to anger.

He had already turned to leave when Kathleen, carefully replacing the hat in its box and smoothing the tissue over the top, said, "Thank you, Rogan. It's the nicest thing any-one has ever—"

"Forget it! I told you how I feel about all that black you wear around here. If you don't want the damned thing, give it to Hetty. She'll likely put it out in the henhouse for a nesting box!"

But for once, his harsh words rolled right off Kathleen's back. He didn't fool her for a minute. He wasn't quite as tough as he'd like her to believe. Perhaps if he hadn't re-minded her quite so much of a little boy who'd done some-thing truly awful and was trying desperately to bluster his way through it, she would never have dared do what she did next. He was too old, too big and far too sure of himself in the ordinary way of things, while she was far too timid.

But he'd reminded her so of Caleb. Already made vul-nerable by his kindness, she was touched by his attempts to deny it, and before she could think better of it, she rose and hurried across to where he loomed in the doorway, intending only to give him a proper bread-and-butter kiss on the cheek. After all, he had just presented her with the loveliest, most generous gift anyone had ever given her in her entire life. She had no more than laid a hand on his arm and lifted her face to his when he jumped back as if she'd been about to slap him.

She could have withered and died on the spot. Lifting her chin, she stiffened her spine and looked him right in the eye. With a graciousness befitting a grand duchess, she said, "You're most generous. Tell Hetty I hooked the hen house door, and if you need a blanket, you'll find one in the chest at the other end of the loft. Good night, sir."

If Kathleen had thought she'd sleep better for having a room to herself, she was sadly mistaken. Her eyes burned dryly as she went over in her mind every nuance of every word and each laden look that had passed between them.

What on earth had gotten into her to make her behave in such a way? He'd brought her a gift. Surely not an extraordinary thing between a husband and a wife. She had thanked him, then somehow everything had seemed to come apart.

It was her fault, not his. Why the devil couldn't she have simply said thank you and let it go at that instead of rushing up and throwing her arms around him? Why couldn't she do *anything* right? It wasn't as if she was given to emotional displays. Just the opposite, in fact. So why was it that the smallest remark from Rogan Rawson invariably led to her sailing off on a tangent and making a fool of herself? His rejection had hurt her more than she dared to admit, even to herself.

The last thing she thought of before she finally fell asleep sometime between midnight and dawn was that there'd been several more packages lying on the kitchen table. Thank heavens she hadn't opened another one. After that little performance, he'd probably crammed the rest back into his seabag and lit out for God knows where!

Up in the loft, Rogan lay awake and wondered for the hundredth time if she would really have kissed him. He pictured her mouth, wider than was considered fashionable. He pictured her lips, soft, full, with just the shadow of a valley centering the lower one. They were deep pink, and he knew for a fact that there was no artifice involved, for he'd seen her with her face still flushed from sleep. He'd seen her before and after she'd washed her face of a morning, and there was never any difference.

Sometimes she smelled like roses. Sometimes she smelled like soap and cinnamon, after she'd been baking. But it was the way she smelled when she was hot and dusty and damp with perspiration that made him so blasted restless he couldn't sleep. It was that same restlessness that had made him go seeking out Della, only to beg off bedding her with an excuse so feeble she'd looked at him with more pity than scorn.

Damn that stiff-necked female, anyway! He should have stuck to his guns and hired a middle-aged widow to look after Hetty. Then he could have fired her, and that would have been the end of it. As it was, he was stuck with his bargain for good, and that was bad.

Because, much to his disgust, he'd just discovered that he was not a man who could vow before God to cleave himself only unto one woman, and then turn around and cleave unto any damned petticoat that caught his fancy!

It was called adultery. An old-fashioned word for an old-fashioned urge, one that was as old as mankind. How the hell was he to have known that he would turn out to be that singular oddity, a man for whom it was impossible? And where the hell did that leave him now?

In spite of his plans to set out first thing in the morning, Rogan stayed on for another day. He had no business laying over. He was already behind schedule, but the crew didn't give a good damn. They'd be paid either way, and laying over like this, at least half of them would get an unexpected shore leave. A home-cooked meal and whatever other benefits a home could provide.

Which his couldn't. Or didn't.

"For the last time, where the devil did you put my books, Hetty?" he demanded as soon as he'd dressed and come downstairs for breakfast.

"Mice ate 'em."

"Same as they ate my winter clothes?"

"Where's my present? Kathleen showed me the bonnet you gave her. Is this mine?" Before he could stop her, she was tearing into the largest of the packages he'd left on the table the night before, ignoring the one that held a black wool shawl and the smaller one that held a small silver thimble in a silk-embroidered case. When she held up the yellow gown, with its crisp black velvet accents, he opened his mouth to explain, then shut it again.

Josiah, you owe me for this. I don't know what the penalty is for wringing a preacher's neck, but whatever it is, it will damned well be worth it!

Chapter Ten

Hetty gawked at the yellow silk gown. Kathleen looked from the gown to Rogan. Rogan, his face flushed dark red under its perennial tan, gazed up at the smoke-stained ceiling.

"Lord love us, boy, the mites have got to your brain! Why'd you bring me a frock that don't even fit?" She held it up to her short, plump body and spread the skirt with one gnarled hand. "Did you ever see anything so pretty in all your born days? Too long, though. I was never that tall, even before I commenced to sink in on myself." Gazing down at herself, she whispered, "Oh, me, if this ain't the prettiest thing I ever set my eyes on."

"But I never meant... That is, I meant it for Kathleen—" Rogan began, but Kathleen cut him off.

"What Rogan means is that he meant it for me to make over to fit you, since that was the only size they had it made up in. He thought I could let it out a bit and take up the hem, didn't you, Rogan?" Her steady gray gaze dared him to argue.

Rogan looked from Hetty to Kathleen, his look of exasperation giving over to one of resignation. "I reckon that's just what I did mean, darling," he told the proud old lady as she kicked out first one foot and then another to hear the soft swish of the flared skirt. "I was given to believe that Kathleen was a right fair hand with a needle, but just in case she'd left her thimble behind, I brought her a new one." He sent the younger woman a look of apology. "And a black woolen shawl."

"A shawl!" Hetty scoffed. "If that's not just like a man, taking the easy way out. I got shawls enough to stretch from here to the lighthouse and back. Pieced 'em into quilts, most of 'em. A woman don't need but three shawls, a warm one for everyday, a pretty one for Sundays and a black one for burying in. When my time comes, you can lay me away in my new yellow silk frock, and don't you dare cover up one speck of it with any old shawl, either, you hear?"

Before he left, Rogan managed to steal a few minutes alone with his wife. Hetty had already set out on a round of visits to spread the news of the yellow silk gown her stepson had brought her. Rogan only hoped she hadn't stopped to fill her apron pocket with the rest of his mother's silverware on her way out the door. It was downright embarrassing to have to go around to the neighbors and ask for the return of it. Mostly he didn't bother, although he tried to keep count of what was missing and where it had most likely gone. He knew as well as did the neighbors that anything they returned would be given away again. When one of her "giving spells" took her, Hetty was apt to give away the feather tick right off her bed.

"I'm sorry about the gown, Kathleen." There was no point in pretending. They both knew it had been meant for her. Kathleen did her best not to mind, but she couldn't help but wonder how she would've looked wearing something so fine, something so bright and pretty. Something that hadn't first belonged to someone else.

"She adores it. It pleasured me enough just to see her face when she held it up to her, Rogan. A woman never gets too old to care about pretty things."

"And you, Kathleen, do you care about pretty things?"

She began nervously twisting a button on her sleeve. "Oh, I—why, surely I do. My new bonnet is so beautiful I can scarce take my eyes off it." She had tried it on a dozen times already.

"The gown was meant to go with it. I wanted to see you all in yellow, not in those drab colors you always wear, so that when I pictured you, I could—" He broke off, looking almost embarrassed, and Kathleen told herself she must be mistaken. Why should he be embarrassed just because he didn't like the way she dressed? It wasn't as if he hadn't voiced the same opinion before at every conceivable opportunity.

Nevertheless, thinking to ease over the awkward moment, she assured him that she did indeed need a new thimble. "My old one showed signs of rust. And the shawl is—"

"It's black, dammit! I don't want you wearing any more black. Next time I'm able to stop over, I'll bring you another dress, something with some color to it."

He was obviously embarrassed, and Kathleen wanted to ease his mind. Truly, she didn't mind about the dress. Not now that she'd had the night to get over it. Not so terribly, awfully much. "Hetty will look—"

"Ridiculous."

"Not at all. She'll look just fine once I get it altered to her size. What I take off the length I can piece into the sides so that it will fit her well enough."

"Just see that she keeps her bonnet on," said Rogan, and a smile twitched at the corners of his mouth. "You're a kindhearted woman, Mrs. Rawson."

Kathleen shook her head quickly and stared at the button

she'd just twisted off the sleeve of her second-best blouse. She'd dressed this morning in her gray skirt and the brown shirtwaist that had once been the top of one of Alice's day dresses. It wasn't a particularly fashionable pairing, but at least it wasn't black.

"Kathy?" She looked up at the sound of her shortened name, and Rogan lifted a fist under her chin, tilting it higher. "Did you really like the hat?"

"Oh, yes," she whispered. "It's beautiful." Her eyes tangled with his and clung there. When his smoldering gaze began to move over her face, it was like being stroked with a raven's feather.

"So are you," he said in a gritty whisper. She felt his warm breath on her face just before his mouth touched down on hers. Touched, lifted and returned in a tentative caress that shattered her beyond recovery.

In the first instant, her lips quivered, uncertain whether to pucker or clamp shut, then it was too late to do either. His hands braced her cheeks, fingertips moving across her temples and into the edge of her hair. Tilting his head first one way, then another, he explored the soft terrain of her lips until she was trembling all over. When she felt the first touch of his tongue, the briefest licking caress, she moaned and might have collapsed had he not caught her to him.

Slowly, Rogan released her and stepped back. She was breathing as if she'd just run a mile uphill. As for Rogan, he looked as if he'd seen a ghost and was trying to convince himself they didn't exist.

For the longest time, they stared at one another, then his face sealed over and he was once again the stern man she had stood beside in a stuffy parlor in Beaufort, North Carolina, and pledged her lifelong allegiance to.

Ever practical, Kathleen was first to recover. Drawing herself up to her tallest height, she lifted her chin and said with only the slightest trace of unevenness, "Will you—that is, I suppose you have to get back to your ship?"

He nodded. "I hadn't planned on staying this long. Dick'll likely be coming after me if I don't head out directly."

"You'd think he was the captain instead of you," Kathleen murmured.

"Aye, you would, wouldn't you?" he said absently. Rooted in place, he stared down at her. He swallowed hard, and she saw a muscle in his jaw tighten. She'd been dimly aware that his seabag was resting beside the front door. Abruptly, he turned and swung it up and over his shoulder in one fluid motion. At the door, he paused to say, "Take care, little Primrose."

Primrose. He'd called her that before, although she had no idea what it meant. Sighing, she watched him amble off across the front yard. In his lean black pants, his black knit jersey and leather knee boots softened with age and wear, he was a striking man. Not storybook handsome like Callum, perhaps, but there was something about him, all the same. Something far more arresting than a simple arrangement of flawless features.

Rogan had been gone three weeks when rumors of the first storm of the season reached the banks. It was Callum who brought the first real news, although Amos and all the men of the village had been muttering for days about unseasonably warm weather and the greasy look of the surf.

"Count 'em," one man said. "Ever' seventh one is a boomer. If it don't change by tomorrow, I'm taking up my nets."

"Me, I'm putting out my flounder net first thing in the morning. I'd welcome a hard shift, we've not had no wind to speak of all season."

"She'll veer off to the no'thard afore she hits the Carolinas," opined a fairly young fisherman.

But Callum didn't think so. After spending an hour or so with his father, he came to warn the Rawson women. "The word is that some of the islands down the Caribbean have already taken a beating, Kathleen. She might blow herself out or cross over into the gulf, but it won't hurt to be ready just in case."

"But the weather's so lovely! Almost like summer again," Kathleen protested. She set out coffee and a plate of sagamite cakes she'd baked the day before, using brown sugar and parched cornmeal.

They talked of what had gone on since Callum had last been home. Kathleen omitted to mention that Hetty had been more forgetful than ever. Just that morning she'd taken a small spool-legged table from the sitting room and carried it all the way over to Dosher and Achsah Burrus's house, claiming she'd never liked the thing anyway, and Achsah had offered her seventy-five cents for it.

Calling out to Kathleen when she walked by on her way to the store, Achsah had advised her to let it pass. "After a week or so, I'll tote it back. Poor Hetty, she'll have forgot all about it by then. Course, if she sees it in my parlor, she's just as apt to accuse me of stealing it, but then, she'll forget that, too."

Poor Hetty. On her bad days she was like a crow, picking up whatever caught her fancy and hiding it away. On her good days, she reminded Kathleen of a cat her grandmother had once had. The pesky thing was forever presenting them with small gifts. Usually small dead rodents, but occasionally a half-dead snake.

In between forays to give or to take, she seemed perfectly content to sit in her room in the bentwood rocker she claimed Edmund had given her, but which was a suspicious match for Amos's, and sew on her quilts. Kathleen had given up on cleaning the older woman's bedchamber. It was crowded with trunks, chests and boxes, a layer of lint and dust over all, but Hetty pitched a fit if she dared enter with mop or dust cloth.

Callum got up and poured them more coffee. "You're looking fit," she told him. "I thought you'd be back on the river by now."

"Thank you. I wish I could say the same, but you're looking tired."

Kathleen didn't take offense. She was tired.

"As for why I'm back, I was on my way south from New York when I heard about the storm, and I thought maybe Paw could use a hand. It surprised me to see how old he's gotten when I was here last. I guess I expected everything to stay the same while I was away."

They talked of this and that. Kathleen was wearing her oldest dress, and that none too clean, but she gave her appearance no more thought than she would have if she'd been sitting across the table from Caleb.

While Callum regaled her with tales of fast horses and fancy women, of fortunes won and lost on a roll of the dice and hearts broken and mended in a single night under the Mississippi moon, he devoured more than half the cakes and drank two more cups of coffee.

By nature fastidious to a fault, he had long since dropped all pretense of formality with Kathleen. Such was the easy friendship between them. Now, vest unbuttoned and shirt collar loosened, he watched as she set about putting the kitchen to rights, lazily entertaining her with a few more of his outrageous tales.

Not that she would ever tell him, but most she dismissed out of hand as bold exaggerations, if not outright fabrications. "How on earth did you come to be a gambler? I'm sure it's nothing you learned from Amos," she said as she smoothed the dish towel over the rack.

"You know how it is with black sheep. We follow the scent of gold and adventure. Can we help it if others occasionally follow along behind us, hoping our incredible luck will rub off on them?"

"In other words you've dedicated your life to leading other poor souls astray," she teased with mock sternness.

"No, dear heart, I only meant that being a dedicated black sheep is a lonely business. It helps to have company along the way." He grinned, and she shook her head. The man was obviously something of a scamp, but she had an idea he wasn't nearly so depraved as he pretended. Now and then she caught a glimpse of something under the surface—a sadness, a wistfulness, perhaps—that made her wonder if he was truly happy with his chosen life.

"If there's a storm coming, and if it's as bad as you say, then I'll have to be up early in the morning to get ready. Go home, will you, Callum?"

"I thought we might have a game of cards now that you've got the table cleaned off."

"What, and have you starve us all? You've already won half a peck of black-eyed peas off me, and that's half a peck more than I can afford to lose."

"Coward," he teased with a wickedly handsome grin. "I'll be over first thing after breakfast to help you batten down."

"Take care of Amos first, then if there's still time, I could use a hand. This place is different from what I'm used to. It's a lot lower for one thing."

After he left, Kathleen went about closing up for the night, her mind darting around like a devil's darning needle. Where was Rogan? Was the storm really headed their way? Had Hetty hooked the chicken house door? Where was Rogan? Had Hetty gone to sleep with the lamp burning?

She should have sent Amos some sagamite cakes. She'd have to remember to send some over tomorrow. And she'd better kill a chicken and boil it down, and get in plenty of firewood before the rains commenced.

Rain barrels. She'd have to see to that, because if the tide came up over the cistern, they wouldn't be able to drink the water until it was cleaned out again. Kathleen was no stranger to typhoid fever, nor to hurricanes, having lived at Beaufort most of her life. But Beaufort, even though it was exposed, had the advantage of being on the mainland. If the terrible tides threatened, one could always pile everyone into a buggy and head inland.

Here on the banks there was no such option. Half a mile in one direction lay the ocean. A stone's throw in the other was the Pamlico Sound. There were creeks and marshes winding all through the village, and in the short time since she'd been living there, she'd seen the tide come up over the road in less than an hour when the wind backed the sound water up into the creeks.

Where was Rogan? Would he worry about them, or would he trust her to look after everything? A dozen times as she got ready for bed, she wondered such things. Once she even stood still for a moment, a bath cloth in her hand, shut her eyes tightly and willed him to come home to her.

Which was ridiculous. Unless, perhaps, she added an amen at the end, in which case it might pass for a prayer.

Moving with the quiet efficiency indicative of her nature, she closed windows, blew out Hetty's lamp and set the damper on the stove so as to keep the coals alive for morning. Rogan was in no real danger, she assured herself. He'd been sailing all his life; surely he knew how to take care of himself and his crew by now.

But what if he hadn't heard about the storm? Offshore, out of sight of land, who would tell him? A passing ship? What if no ship passed within hailing distance? Daily newspapers were of no help at all to a man who was constantly at sea, and there were no seagoing telegraphers that she'd ever heard of.

Carrier pigeon? Carrier *sea gull?*

That night, Kathleen lay awake worrying until finally, long after midnight, her innate good sense took over, reminding her of all she had to do the next day. If there was a storm coming, she'd be far too busy looking after Rogan's home and his family to waste time worrying over something she couldn't help. He was a grown man. No doubt he'd been through storms aplenty before this. She couldn't afford to dwell on the thought of a flimsy little cockleshell bobbing on top of a furious sea, subject to crushing waves and mast-snapping winds.

She couldn't and she wouldn't. Rogan had married her to look after his shorebound interests. She would do the very best she could, and when she'd done everything she could think of, she'd just have to pray. The Lord might have trouble placing her voice, for it wasn't one He heard on any regular basis, but by the time she got done with Him this time, He'd probably be willing to grant her almost anything just to shut her up. If there was one thing Kathleen knew about herself—and actually, there were several—it was that she was no quitter.

As the storm raged up the coast and reports of the devastation left behind passed from tongue to ear, Kathleen worked feverishly to prepare. Thank God for Callum! He made her laugh when she was too tired even to smile and smile when she was so tense with worry she could scarce function.

He and Amos helped anchor her rain barrels to the porch railing after lifting them up out of reach of the tide. The very first thing Hetty had done was to see that her new silk gown was safe on the highest shelf in the house, well wrapped in oiled cloth. After that, she made trip after trip to the loft with bundles of quilting material.

Kathleen had carried her own belongings upstairs. She paused to gaze regretfully at her lovely clean room, all freshly scrubbed and refurbished. Perhaps the storm would veer out to sea at the last minute, and she wouldn't have it all to do over again.

Then again, perhaps it wouldn't. With Callum's help, she stacked furniture. "What about the rugs?" she asked.

"Later. Where's that little spool-legged table that used to sit over by the window?"

"Achsah Burrus is, uh, borrowing it for a spell."

He sent her a look of understanding as he stacked a small wooden chest onto a table. "Oh, well, that won't be the only thing misplaced if this storm comes right up the coast. Folks'll be spending a good part of the next week tracking down their belongings and toting them back home again."

"Mercy, I hope not!" She lifted out the bottom drawer of the heavy linen chest and looked around for a place to put it. "Maybe it'll go on out to sea." And then she bit her lip. Given the choice, she'd rather have it slam into the island full force than to know that Rogan was somewhere out there fighting to stay alive.

Callum took the drawer from her hand and stacked it with the others on top of the chest. It was the best he could do. The stairs were already so full they were scarcely passable. "Poor old Rogue," he said, shaking his head. "Bad enough to have to go chasing all over creation after boats, water barrels and sections of fence that have floated off without having someone on the inside handing out your belongings right and left."

Kathleen brushed the hair off her face and took a moment to flex her shoulders. "They all seem to understand. I'd better start on the pantry."

"I'll lift the barrels. Would you care to place a small wager on how high the tide will come in the house?"

"With the man who once bet on the number of pickles in a barrel? And *won?* I'm tired, Cal, not daft."

Callum, looking every inch the dandified riverboat gambler despite the casual open neck of his ivory silk shirt, grinned unabashedly. Kathleen flopped down on one of the few chairs left on the floor and mopped her forehead, leaving her soft fringe standing on end.

By the next morning, the house was as secure as she could make it. Kathleen had cooked up enough to feed an army, sending more than half of it over to Amos's house. She was taking a breather while Callum and Hetty set up the quilting frame in the loft. That had been Kathleen's first suggestion when Callum had come over that day. Kathleen had come to realize that usually when the old woman acted up, it was because she was upset with Kathleen over some real or imagined offense. Therefore Kathleen took pains to make sure the chickens and her quilting apparatus were safe, and that Hetty had everything upstairs she wanted upstairs, regardless of how many trips it took to get it all up there.

"Are you sure Amos isn't needing you?" she asked as Callum came downstairs, smoothing his flawlessly groomed hair.

"Paw? He's been through this drill so many times he could do it in his sleep. The rugs next, I reckon. Off your duff, lady."

"Do we roll or fold?"

"Roll. Hope you haven't swept too much dirt under here."

"I think I've just been insulted. Forgive me if I don't get on my high horse. Too much of an effort."

She was tired. She was filthy. The hair she'd put up so neatly that morning was now tied in a lopsided twist with a scrap of yarn. Her shirttail had come loose, and the apron she'd put on clean a few hours ago was torn in two places and not fit for the scrap bag.

Thank goodness there was no one here to see her except Callum, she thought, not even wondering at her own lack of vanity around what must surely be the handsomest man in the world.

The rain had begun more than an hour before, a fine, warm mist that blew almost horizontally. "You'd better think about getting home before the tide comes up in the marsh and catches you here," she said as she finished rolling up a small Turkey rug and dusting off her hands. "How do we get the plugs out of the holes, knock them through or pull them out?"

"Knock 'em through," said Callum. "After the tide goes down, you can shove a corncob in them until Rogan can fit another set. And Kathy—if the water comes up too fast and you feel the house start to shift, for God's sake, open the doors, will you? I'd hate to wake up tomorrow and find your house sitting on Paw's front porch."

"I'm not worried about the house floating, I'm worried about the varmints that might come in before I can plug up the scuppers again." Kathleen waited until Callum finished rolling up the large rug, then looked around for a place to put it. Every surface above the high-water mark on the walls was already full.

"Quit worrying, the snakes are no more thrilled with the idea of sharing a house with two squealing women than you are. Now I, on the other hand—"

"Are an inveterate scamp. I never squeal. I do believe I'd rather have a nest of snakes for company than a riverboat gambler who can talk a body's ears off even while he's eating her out of house and home."

"Ah, you wound me vastly!" He tried to look vastly wounded, but kneeling on the floor in a pair of filthy buff britches, his blue eyes sparkling with mischief, he didn't look vastly anything, except devilish.

By the time the rugs were put out of reach of the tide and Kathleen had made a fresh pot of coffee, the water was halfway up to the porch and rising rapidly. "Not that I want to seem inhospitable," she said, "but hadn't you better get on home while you still can? You're not exactly dressed for swimming." The wind was beginning to whine now, whipping the long boughs of the live oaks around in an unnatural direction.

"I hate to leave you all alone here."

"I'm not alone, I have Hetty, and we'll be just fine, thanks to your help. I do thank you, Callum. I don't know what I'd have done without you."

"You'd have done just fine. Rogan would be proud of you."

For some reason, the thought saddened her. "I suppose. He knows I'm sensible. It's why he married me, after all."

Callum's nicely arched brows climbed in surprise, but all he said was, "The roof'll probably leak, you know."

"Won't matter all that much, since the floor leaks, too." Tired as she was, she managed a cheeky grin.

"We could always stay up all night and drown our sorrows while we play cards," Callum suggested. "I'd let you win. Storm rules are different from ordinary rules. They favor the fair sex."

"At the moment, I hardly feel fair, much less—" She broke off, her cheeks reddening under a generous layer of grime. Callum chuckled, and she could cheerfully have crowned him with her best skillet.

Instead, she bundled up the last few sagamite cookies and shoved them across the table. "Here, these are for Amos. Mind you don't devour the lot before you even get home."

"My dear, you do me an injustice. Do I look like the

kind of man who would steal the food out of his own father's mouth?''

"I'd say that was a pretty sound description."

With the indolent grace so typical of him—and so very different from Rogan's coiled-spring tension—Callum wandered to the back door and opened it to look out. "Hmm, I'm afraid I've already waited too long. The water's up another six inches in the past hour. It's all the way over the wood bin and halfway up the—"

"Oh, my mercy, I plumb forgot about laying in more wood!"

"Then we've best get at it, else you may have to burn the furniture, and poor Hetty wouldn't have anything left to give away."

"But you said—"

"Perhaps I exaggerated just a bit. There's still a few splits on the top, under the eaves of the shed, that aren't too wet."

"Oh, horse biscuits," Kathleen muttered, striding into the pantry to snatch her jacket from behind the door. It was an old spencer of Alice's that was snagged, pulled and mended. Tugging it on, she thought about the gloves she wore for rough work, but hadn't the slightest notion where she had put them. There was no time to waste looking.

"Where's your coat? Oh." He was wearing it. After struggling with furniture and rugs and all Hetty's odds and ends, he was still so well put together, she felt like a scarecrow beside him.

"I was wondering where my work gloves were, but even if I'd found them, I'd be bound to offer them to you." She lifted one of his well-kept hands in her own workroughened one and shook her head ruefully. "There ought to be a law against men like you," she snapped, a smile threatening in spite of her irritation.

"Probably is." Callum removed his boots and stockings.

Reluctantly, for she'd never much cared for wading in murky waters, Kathleen followed suit. Thinking of all the creatures that could be crawling or swimming unseen, she left on her stockings. Any protection was better than none.

"I can fetch in the wood by myself, you know. I won't melt."

"Quit trying to be so damned independent and get a move on, will you?"

"What about Amos? Won't he be needing you?"

"Paw? All he wants is a checkers opponent. That's all he does during a storm. Drink, sleep and play checkers. Believe me, the way he plays it, it's no game of chance."

The rain had ceased for the moment, and holding up her skirts, Kathleen bravely stepped off the bottom step and into the swirling dark water. It wasn't particularly cold, but the thought of what might be lurking in its depths made her hurry to the shed and load her arms with as many sticks as she could carry.

They made two trips, shoving the damp wood inside the kitchen door to be dealt with later. "Thank goodness the rain's stopped," she observed.

"For the moment. Wind's picked up some, though."

"The tide's already up to the—oh, my mercy!"

"That high?" Callum teased as he bent to roll his trousers up another two turns.

"I clean forgot to feed the chickens! Hetty always gives them something before they go to roost, and I promised her faithfully I'd give them an extra measure of corn, and now—"

"Let me do it for you. Tell me where you keep everything, and I'll be glad to—"

"I can do it quicker than I can tell you how, but thank you. Hetty'll ask after every one of her hens by name, and if I can't tell her, she's apt to come out here and see for herself, and that's the last thing I need."

"Then I'll come along. If you're bound and determined to be a martyr to a flock of silly birds, I may as well go watch."

Rather than stand there arguing with him, she allowed him the privilege. Knowing too well how snakes swam about in search of higher ground as the tide began to rise, she wasn't particularly anxious to wade to the henhouse alone.

In no more time than it took to fill the water containers, put out fresh corn and run her hand into the seven nest boxes on the off chance of finding a late-laid egg, the tide had risen still higher. Kathleen, her skirts by now unabashedly pulled between her legs and tucked under her waistband, hooked the door behind her and stared at the turgid water that covered her garden, the small fig trees she'd set out and both steps to the kitchen. Oblivious to the fact that her muslin drawers were shamefully exposed, she hitched her skirt more securely and started down the ramp, where Callum was waiting.

"All done?"

"Thank goodness, yes. I'd have let them go hungry for once if I didn't think Hetty would get up in the middle of the night to go feed the poor stupid things."

"Chickens don't eat in the dark. Even I know that much."

"Try telling Hetty that," she said with a grin. Making her way carefully down the barred ramp, which was more slippery than ever, she was glad she'd left on her stockings.

"Ever ride piggyback?"

"I've been the piggy, but never the rider."

"Then we'd better do it the old-fashioned way." Without giving her a chance to open her mouth, he swung her into his arms and stepped into the moving tide.

"Cal, put me down! I'm already wet through," she protested, giggling as she threw her arms around his neck and hung on.

"Quit wriggling or I'll drop you."

"You don't have to do this, honestly! I've been wading all my life!"

"In hurricane tide? All full of noxious vermin you don't even want to think about? Ever had your toe grabbed by an oyster toad?" And when she shuddered, he laughed and said, "No, I thought not."

The wind tugged at her hair, blowing it across both their faces. Her stockings had come undone from where she'd anchored them at her knee and were slowly slithering down her calf, showing more skin than most decent women ever showed another living soul.

"We'll go around to the front door, since we've all but blocked the back one with firewood."

"Just mind you don't step in a hole and drop me!" It occurred to her that if the fine citizens of Beaufort could see her now, her reputation would be sunk beyond repair.

The thought provoked another giggle, which in turn provoked a response from Callum as he struggled against the wet wind toward the house. To make the going more treacherous, the soft, driving rain had started up again. "What the devil are you laughing about, woman? And watch that elbow!" But he was chuckling, too, as he waded around the corner of the house holding her high against his chest.

Her face buried in his neck against the rain, she said, "I was just thinking—" He came to an abrupt halt, and she peeped out to see why. "Thinking..." she repeated mindlessly. Her eyes widened. "Rogan?"

"Kathleen! What the hell is going on here! Callum, dammit, that's my wife you're—"

"Kathleen *Stevens?* Is that really you? Goodness, you poor dear, so this is where you've been hiding. Why, the

whole town was talking—that is, we were wondering what
had happened to you after... Well, I mean, Alice said you'd
run away and married some sailor, but I never *dreamed*...''

Patrice Rhodes's avid gaze moved from Callum's face
to Kathleen's and back again. Both her arms were clinging
to Rogan's neck, and she turned to look at him. "But you
said—surely, Rogan, *you're* not the sailor she married? Not
our poor little Kathleen!"

Kathleen had heard that same tone of overdone innocence too many times to be taken in by it now. Patrice had
known, all right, but knowing, why had she come? More
to the point, what did she want?

The tide swirled around the muscular thighs of both men
as they confronted each other, each holding a woman in his
arms. Rogan glared impartially at both Callum and Kathleen. Patrice, looking beautiful and helpless and everything
Kathleen despaired of ever being, gazed speculatively from
one to the other.

Kathleen had eyes only for Rogan. He was safe. After
all her worry, he was safe and secure!

So why did her heart feel like a lead weight?

It was Callum who finally broke the impasse. "Shall we
go inside, or would you rather stand here a while longer?
Kathy's no real weight, but I'm afraid she's wet halfway
up her, ah, limbs. I'd not like to see her catch a chill."

A chill! Judging from the way she felt, Kathleen thought
it far more likely she might burst into flames!

Chapter Eleven

Our little Kathleen. If that woman called her that one more time, Kathleen was going to crown her with the butter crock! She was no one's little anything, surely not Patrice's. Ever since Morton had built the new house directly behind the Rhodes mansion, Kathleen had had to tolerate the woman. Alice had been flattered by Patrice's offer of friendship. She'd been completely taken in, but then, Alice had been taken in by Morton, too.

"I just can't get over what a lovely coincidence it was, finding you this way after all these months, dear." Patrice fluttered a pale hand over her prominent bosom, calling attention to the ruffle-edged cutout that showed an inordinate amount of cleavage. To Kathleen's way of thinking, the pink and maroon velvet gown was more suited to a ballroom than riding out a hurricane in a three-masted schooner!

Except that she wasn't going to ride out the storm aboard the *White Witch,* she was going to sit it out right here in Rogan's sleeping loft.

By the time Kathleen could think of a suitably polite response to Patrice's remarks, the widow had already turned her attention to Rogan, joining him at the window to stare out into the wild darkness.

Stiff with irritation, Kathleen turned to Rogan's bed, where Hetty had long since settled herself. "Hetty, do you need another blanket? I can feel the draft all the way over here."

"My feet's already warm as hot biscuits. Tell Rogan to crack the leeward window a mite more, will you?"

In spite of herself, Kathleen had to smile. If she had imbibed as much French brandy tonight as Hetty had—purely to ward off the rheumatics, of course—she'd likely be complaining of the heat, too. "Unless you want to get wet clean through, you'd best make do with what's already open." It was only open an inch, and that only to keep the walls from giving way when the storm pressure changed suddenly. If it weren't for that, Kathleen would have shut it long before now to keep out the dreadful sound of the wind.

Lord, but it was wild out there! Seated on an improvised pallet between the quilting frame and a stack of Hetty's boxes, Kathleen found her attention straying to the couple standing by the far window. They made a handsome pair, she had to admit, with Patrice so blond and fragile and Rogan so dark and rugged. Each time the wind screamed louder than usual, or a branch broke off and struck the side of the house, Patrice grabbed Rogan's arm and buried her face against his shoulder. She'd been practically hanging around his neck ever since they'd got home.

Not that Kathleen cared. It was nothing to her if he wanted to wear the silly twit around his neck, but she'd have thought a grown woman would have more pride. Noise alone had never hurt a body, and what's more, Patrice Rhodes was old enough to stand on her own two feet!

The more Kathleen thought about it, the more peculiar it seemed that Patrice had picked Rogan's ship to travel on.

There were any number of ships that could have taken her to Baltimore. For that matter, she could have gone inland and caught a train.

Kathleen told herself she was not simply being churlish. She wouldn't have begrudged giving shelter to a cur on a night like this. All the same, why did it have to be the one woman in all the world who had witnessed that scene with Morton? She wouldn't have minded if Rogan had wanted to bring home someone like Amanda Crotts. Or even that awful Mr. Egleston.

Instead, he'd brought Patrice, and there wasn't a blessed thing she could do about it. Putting the best face on the matter, she had asked about Alice and the children, and been given only the briefest accounting. Alice was fine. The children were fine. The baby was due in a few months, and Alice was big as a house.

With a knowing smirk, Patrice had volunteered the fact that Morton was doing well, too. "I do believe he misses you, though."

Counting to ten, Kathleen had offered to make coffee and was asked for tea. She had offered molasses cakes and was asked if that was all she had to offer.

"There's cold chicken and pickles, but I'm afraid that's all until the tide goes down and I can get to the pantry. Maybe you should've stayed aboard the *Witch*." Which was hardly hospitable, but at that point, Kathleen was past caring.

"Oh, dear, I'd have been simply terrified," Patrice said with a delicate shudder.

"I'm sure Rogan would've been happy to stay aboard and take care of you." She could've bitten off her tongue the minute the words slipped out. Patrice pouted, looked helpless, wounded and unbelievably beautiful, in spite of the water spots on her pink velvet. Her hair was the kind that curled even more when it was damp.

Kathleen tried to force an apology past her lips and found she wasn't generous enough to do it. With a vicious twist, she rammed an escaping hairpin home.

Rogan scowled. "You'd both best get some sleep while you can." He was watching Kathleen, deliberately trying to make her feel ashamed of her shrewishness, she told herself. Jutting her chin, she sat up straight on her pallet and crossed her wet stockinged feet at the ankles and her arms over her bosom.

Something flickered in Rogan's eyes, but she made no effort to interpret his feelings. She'd be better off not knowing.

"Wind's falling off some now, but we'll catch the back of it before long," he said calmly.

"The eye, you mean."

"Right. Is there anything you need done during the lull? I'm going down to check on things below."

Rogan shrugged, but the Rhodes woman still hung on like a barnacle. The same way she'd been hanging onto him since the storm had first caught them just south of Ocracoke. His first mate had as good as threatened to drown her if Rogan didn't take her ashore with him.

He continued to stare at the strange little creature he'd married. If she had a worry in the world, she kept it well hidden, sitting there cool as you please in her filthy wet stockings with her bedraggled skirt spread primly over those long, shapely limbs of hers. Her hair had long since slipped its mooring, she'd collected a smudge of soot on her cheek, and she still managed to look as if butter wouldn't melt in her mouth.

Damned if he wouldn't like to know what it would take to get her ruffled! A hurricane obviously couldn't do it. What would it take to have her clinging to him the way the Rhodes woman did? The way she'd been hanging on to

Callum when they'd waded around the corner, laughing up into his face as if they'd known each other all their lives.

Or maybe known each other considerably better than she knew her own husband.

At the sound of a snore from the corner, three pairs of eyes swiveled toward the bed. "Well, would you look at that! The old sot's gone out like a light," Patrice said with a breathless giggle.

"Hetty's joints ache when the weather turns," Kathleen said evenly. "She only uses her medicine when it hurts too much to sleep." The medicine in question being Rogan's French brandy, but she saw no need to elaborate.

Patrice shrugged. Rogan glowered. Kathleen locked her spine into place and stared straight ahead.

Suddenly, there was no sound at all. It was eerie, as though they were shut in a gigantic tin with the lid sealed on. And then Hetty snored again, and Kathleen became aware of the sound of splashing water somewhere below.

Rogan strode across the room to the stairwell. "Stay back, I'll check it out," he said, shaking off the woman who hurried after him and was still clinging to his arm.

"Ahoy! You still kicking up there?" The voice came quite clearly through the door that had been wedged open to allow the tide to flow freely without lifting the house off its foundation.

"Callum? What the bloody hell are you doing out and about?"

They heard a scraping sound, then the splash of footsteps, and then there was Callum, grinning up at them from the bottom of the stairwell. Swinging his lantern around, he glanced behind him. "Looks like you're about six, seven inches under. We're no more'n five. Guess we got lucky on this one."

"Yeah."

Ignoring Rogan's growled response, Callum started up

the stairs, pausing to squeeze the water from his trousers. "I'd have been back sooner to help out, but I thought I'd best wait for the wind to drop. I don't fancy having a shingle come sailing off a roof and slice my head off my neck."

Patrice had edged in beside Rogan at the head of the stairs. With one hand resting on his shoulder, she stared avidly at the man who paused to hang his lantern on a nail, then stepped up into the loft. He was wet to his waist, his once-pale trousers hugging his trim form like a second skin. Kathleen, amused, saw Patrice's hand slide off Rogan's shoulder, watched her eyes widen as they played over Callum's neatly constructed form.

"I don't believe we've officially met," she murmured. "You rushed off so fast earlier. I'm Patrice Rhodes. I was traveling north with Captain Rawson when the storm caught us."

"Callum McNair, ma'am. Real pleasure." He turned and grinned at Kathleen. "How're you faring, my dear heart? Oyster toads been nibbling at your toes?"

If the careless endearment had been designed to inflame, it succeeded. Rogan's face hardened as he looked from one to the other, but before he could react, Callum clapped him on the back and said cheerfully, "Good to see you again, Rogue. Well...looks like she's already passed the high-water mark."

In Beaufort, Patrice was well known for stirring up trouble for the sheer pleasure of it. Pitting one man against another for her own amusement was just the sort of thing she excelled in. "Could you see anything on the way over?" Kathleen asked, hoping to deflect the rising tension.

"Not much. Just the usual. Skiff lodged in a tree. Chickens perched on tombstones. Got a towel up here, love? I seem to have gotten a bit damp around the edges."

Rogan threw him the towel he had used earlier when he'd come upstairs after reconnoitering below. It was wet and slightly muddy. "This isn't a damned hotel, you know."

Kathleen spoke up quickly. "Is Amos all right?"

"Sound asleep, just like I told you. Took forty-seven dollars off me in a checker match, finished off the bottle of bourbon I brought him and turned in. I got to thinking about poor old Rogan over here with all these womenfolk to look after, and it occurred to me that he might be in need of reinforcements."

Rogan snorted. "Go wake up Amos and get your money back, I don't need any help."

Cheerfully ignoring him, Callum said, "I shut your door when I came in. Scuppers'll take care of the flow from now on. I ran into half a dozen muskrats on the way over, looking for a dry place to set up housekeeping again."

"Oh, heavens, do tell me you're not serious," Patrice said with a gasp and a delicate shudder.

Both men ignored her. Kathleen ignored her. She'd had about all she could take for one day.

Patrice moved over to a stack of Hetty's quilts and cut her eyes at Callum. "Perhaps you'd better cover up with one of these. It would be a pity to catch cold." She was still taking an active interest in the masculine attributes revealed by the clinging trousers, Kathleen noticed, amused. If there was one thing the widow was noted for even more than her penchant for stirring up trouble, it was her insatiable appetite for masculine attention. She'd managed to lure Morton away from Alice, and Alice had once been considered the most beautiful girl in Beaufort.

But then, Kathleen wasn't supposed to know about Morton's late-night visits through the back fence. For Alice's sake, she'd always pretended not to.

From the far corner of the loft, Hetty snorted and let out a long, loud groan. Kathleen quickly rose to go to her, but by the time she'd crossed the room, the old woman was snoring peacefully again.

Callum settled down on a hastily made pallet beside Kathleen's. As his coat was damp, he removed it and tossed it aside. "Excuse my shirtsleeves, if you will, ladies. Kathy, my love, you look ravishing with your hair all down over your shoulders." Kathleen made a face at him, and he grinned. "Don't she look ravishing, Rogan? I purely enjoy getting her riled just to watch her eyes throw sparks and that lovely little chin shoot right up out of her collar. Enticing little female, this wife of yours. How the devil did you talk her into marrying you, anyway? I'll lay odds you forgot to tell her about your glass eye and your fits, and the time you were near about hanged for a horse thief down in Georgia."

"Behave yourself, you wicked gambler," Kathleen muttered in a voice too low to be heard by the others. She was used to Callum's horseplay, but this was neither the time nor the proper circumstance.

Stealing a swift glance at Rogan to see how he was taking it, she encountered a look of anger so fierce she caught her breath. So they were all tired. Was that any reason for Rogan to get his hackles up? He more than anyone else present should know that Callum was only teasing.

"Rogan, I'm sure Callum didn't mean any harm. He was only—"

"Madam, would you please stop chattering long enough to go open the west window?" Eyes blazing, Rogan turned and stalked the length of the loft, slammed down the sash on the east end, then continued to stand there, scowling out into the pitch black night.

No one moved. Patrice's small mouth had fallen open, and her busy eyes were glittering like pale blue tourmalines. Whistling silently under his breath, Callum gazed speculatively from Rogan to Kathleen to Patrice and back again, making Kathleen feel like spanking him. He was as bad as Caleb. But unlike Patrice, there was no malice in his brand of mischief.

In one graceful flow, Kathleen rose and moved to the other end of the loft, opened the window a hand's width and took several deep, steadying breaths. The only sound to be heard was a steady dripping of water off the roof. The rain had stopped. The wind wasn't blowing. One might almost have thought the storm had passed on.

She knew better. The tension was a palpable force, nor was it all due to being suspended in the eye of a hurricane.

Flexing her shoulders, she allowed some of the stiffening to flow out of her spine. If a body don't bend, he'll break. Someone had told her that once. Josiah Dunwoody? Probably. When she wouldn't cry after her grandmother had died. Her grandmother had disapproved of tears, and Kathleen had long since learned that they never solved anything. So why did she feel so much like throwing herself down on that pile of quilts and bawling her eyes out?

Storm nerves. No. More likely it was Patrice's unexpected appearance. The last time she'd seen Mrs. Rhodes, her whole world had been falling apart around her, with Alice and Morton accusing her of terrible things and Patrice gloating and spurring them on.

Not a pleasant memory at the best of times. Too bad she had to be reminded of it when she already had more on her plate than she could say grace over.

Speaking of plates, it had been some time since any of them had eaten. Grateful for a duty that would occupy her hands, if not her overactive imagination, she pinned on a smile and turned to face the long, narrow room. Hetty was still sleeping. Callum and Patrice were talking in undertones, and Rogan was running the palms of his hands over the sloping ceiling, feeling for leaks.

"Would anyone like something to eat? This seems like

a good time to go down and put together a picnic basket. No hot coffee, of course, but there's buttermilk.''

Callum looked up and smiled. "Now that sounds like a lovely idea. Rogan, why don't you go downstairs with your wife and help her while Mrs. Rhodes and I talk about mutual friends?''

Rogan nodded with, as it seemed to Kathleen, less than good grace. Was he so taken with that velvet-covered viper that he couldn't bear to let her out of his sight?

Kathleen unrolled her damp stockings and peeled them off, flinging them into the corner. "I really don't need any help, thank you. You can both stay up—''

Rogan took her elbow in a firm grip and said, "Mind your step, madam, the stairs are cluttered. I'll go first and hold the lamp. Put your hand on my shoulder.''

She didn't, of course. If the wind had come right through the walls and threatened to carry her off, she wouldn't have grabbed onto his shoulder to save herself.

But she couldn't help remembering another stormy night when the two of them had raced downstairs together to shut the windows. Unexpectedly, her eyes dimmed and she blinked several times and stiffened her back. *Boiled chicken, Kathleen! You have guests and they're hungry, and this is certainly no time to—to come down with something!*

She could have wept real tears at the sight of the parlor, awash in muddy water. Something bobbed just under the surface, and she leaned over to pick it up when Rogan caught her arm. "Don't. Time enough to sort out the rubble tomorrow, when the water's gone down and you can see what's what.''

"But it might be—''

"A rat,'' he finished for her. She'd been going to say a book, one of his precious books that had disappeared before she'd ever met him.

She prided herself on not flinching. "You're right, of course." Holding her skirts above the water, she sloshed through the sitting room and into the passage. She didn't have the heart to look into her new bedchamber. Things were bad enough in the rest of the house, with furniture stacked up like children's blocks and boxes, trunks and drawers full of linens and clothes on top of that. The curtains were doubled up and looped over their rods, but they were wet from the rain that had beat in around the window frames.

Rogan held open the door to the kitchen, forcing her to brush against him to pass through. She caught her breath as his touch set her nerves to jangling. Glancing up, she saw the dark glitter of his eyes. His smile was less than reassuring. "You had a lot of work, getting ready. I should have been here to help you."

"Callum was a real blessing," she said without thinking, then could have kicked herself.

His hand closed over her arm, halting her progress, and when he swung her around to face him, her heart gave a terrified leap and began to race. "We'd better hurry," she managed to whisper.

"You're in that big a rush to get back? What's the matter, don't you trust them together?"

"I don't know what you mean." Water raced past her ankles as the wind-driven tide began to ebb. There was a pungent aroma of mud and marsh and broken pine boughs, and Kathleen drew in a deep, shaky breath.

Something bumped against her ankle, and she gasped. "Kathleen? What is it?"

"I—nothing. I felt something, that's all. Let's hurry, all right?"

Rogan could have said something more about the pair they'd left upstairs, but he didn't. The lamplight was casting intriguing shadows on her face, dusting the tips of her long lashes with gold. He drew in a deep breath and smelled woman, tidewater and the faint, unlikely fragrance of roses.

With a deep groan, he tightened his grip on her arm and drew her unresisting form against him. "Kathleen, I—"

Once more his body reacted to her nearness in a way that was both untimely and inappropriate. How could anything that looked so prickly feel so incredibly soft and yielding? His mind raced out of control, painting vivid pictures of all that was concealed under her drab gown.

He wanted her. He wanted her so damned much he could taste it, and the longer he stayed away from her, the worse it seemed to get. Seeing her in the arms of another man had just about ruined him. Only by reminding himself forcibly of the circumstances surrounding their relationship, and the likelihood that nothing was going on between her and Callum, had he been able to keep from beating the hell out of his best friend and dragging her inside to stake his claim.

Josiah had warned against doing anything to frighten her, and he'd given his word. What's more, he'd keep it for as long as he had to, but dammit, someone had to warn her about Callum. She might be an innocent, but McNair wasn't!

He opened his mouth to speak, shut it again and shook his head. How could he warn her without putting ideas in her head? If they weren't already there, he'd be a fool to plant the seeds.

Besides, his own motives were not all that blameless. Where women were concerned, there wasn't a lot to choose between the two of them.

But women like Kathleen were not fair game. Neither he nor McNair had ever ruined an innocent girl, nor had they ever broken up a marriage. Which was not to say that when a woman let it be known that she was available—

But that was another story. And this was Kathleen. And dammit, she was definitely not available!

"Kathleen, this friendship of yours with McNair—just how far has it gone?" He had to ask. He didn't want to alarm her, but he had to know.

"How far?" Kathleen was puzzled.

"Look, I'm not accusing you of anything, but I think you should know that—"

"Accusing me! Accusing me of what?"

"Dammit, I said I *wasn't* accusing you of anything, I merely—"

"You are so! Ever since you came home today you've been glaring at me—and snapping at me, and…" Her voice wavered, and she wished she knew enough profanity to tell him what she really thought of him.

Rogan was not so handicapped. Gripping both her shoulders, he shook her and then brought her hard against him, eyes burning through the gloom at her pale face. "When I want to accuse you of something, woman, you'll damned well know it! All I wanted to know was—"

"And that's another thing, I wish you'd stop swearing at me! I've done nothing but follow your orders, and if that doesn't suit you, then you can—you can just go *fly!*"

"Kathleen," he warned, but she wasn't finished.

"What's more, I'll thank you to get that woman out of my house the minute this storm is over, do you hear?"

"*Your* house! What woman?"

"You know very well what woman!"

Rogan linked his hands together behind her back and stared at her, distracted, but not distracted enough to release her. Not when she felt so good—so right—in his arms. "Now, what the bloody hell does Mrs. Rhodes have to do with anything? I was trying to warn you about Callum, and suddenly, here you are, carrying on like I'd insulted your honor instead of trying to protect you."

The wind began to pick up, causing the lamp to flicker. She was looking at him as if she'd just opened a sack of flour and found a litter of kittens, but at least she wasn't trying to get away.

He must have been blind to have considered her plain. What she was was beautiful, with the kind of timeless beauty that would still be hers when she was an old woman.

And God help him, he would probably still be wanting to take her to bed. He reminded himself that they'd both agreed to a marriage of convenience. Hell, his own pa had done the same thing, hadn't he? That was what marriage was for—convenience.

Only it wasn't quite so convenient when a man wanted to bed his woman and he'd promised not to.

Her eyes were silver in the moonlight. Silver and suspiciously bright. For all she could tilt her chin and snap that spine of hers into an upright position at the first hint of a threat, she was no warrior. She was as prickly as a cactus, but even a cactus was soft inside. What was it about this particular woman that lured him into wanting to taste her sweetness, to lose himself in her soft, delicate petals?

"Rogan?"

Releasing her as if she'd suddenly burned his hands, Rogan stepped back and reached for the lamp he'd left outside the door. She must take him for a fool, standing here ankle deep in water with the tail end of a hurricane fixing to whip around on them any minute now. "Yeah. Right. We'd best be getting whatever we need from the kitchen. The wind's already picking up. Tell me what to do, and I'll do it."

How many times in his life had he made that statement, Kathleen wondered, pulling herself together. "Something to drink," she murmured, then set about putting bread, chicken, pickles and cheese into the basket.

Had she only imagined what had just happened? One

minute they'd been at each other's throats, the next she'd been standing there in his arms as if they were the best of friends. As if they were far more than friends; as if they were lovers. If he ever guessed what she'd been feeling, what she'd been wishing for, he would likely die laughing.

"Scuppernong wine, ale or buttermilk?"

She looked up, hoping he couldn't read her mind, and said, "Wine would be nice, but perhaps you and Callum would prefer the ale." She wished they didn't have to go back upstairs. She wished Callum had stayed home with Amos. And, oh, how she wished Patrice Rhodes's late husband's business interests had been in Baton Rouge instead of Baltimore!

"Both, then," Rogan said, reaching for the basket she'd loaded almost to the handle. "Can you carry the lamp? Watch that broom."

Kathleen bent and retrieved the broom that had floated across the passageway and lodged in the latticework. Tomorrow, and for a lot of tomorrows after that, she would have her work cut out for her, but right now all she could think of was the man beside her. It was uncanny for a body to be so affected by another mortal, as if one were steel and the other magnet. She prayed it wasn't a lasting condition, because she didn't know how she could go on forever pretending that he was no more to her than any stranger.

Long afterward, Kathleen would remember the night of the hurricane. It was the night she'd learned that her instincts about people were remarkably accurate. Without any particular reason, other than that she was a known gossip who enjoyed stirring up a tempest in a teapot as long as it was someone else's teapot, Kathleen had always disliked Patrice Rhodes. Patrice claimed to be a great friend of Alice's, but Kathleen was almost sure that Patrice and Morton were lovers.

Could that be the reason Patrice had been so furious that day she'd seen Kathleen with Morton in the backyard? At the time, Patrice had been the least of Kathleen's worries. She'd been far more concerned for Alice, who had a blind spot where her husband was concerned. If Alice had ever learned of Morton's philandering, her marriage would have been in ruins. That had been one of the reasons Kathleen had been willing, albeit reluctantly, to take the blame on herself and leave Beaufort, even though her leaving was hardly likely to cause Morton to change his ways.

During the long night's vigil she was able to think clearly about the situation she had left behind when she married Rogan. She was convinced it had been the right thing to do for Alice's sake. Although unless she could come to terms with the turbulent feelings Rogan aroused in her, she would be little better off.

Callum had been a godsend. He'd stayed until daybreak, entertaining them with his usual bag of gambling stories, distracting Patrice when she seemed inclined to curl up against Rogan for the night.

Where Kathleen was concerned, he'd been his old teasing self, helping her to forget that after an endless day and a sleepless night, she looked like a scarecrow. Patrice had taken great pleasure in calling attention to the contrast between her looks and Kathleen's. Freshly brushed and powdered, the older woman had looked lovelier than ever to Kathleen's tired eyes. It had been the last straw when Patrice had insisted on having Rogan hold a mirror for her so that she could pin up her hair.

Tiresome woman! Kathleen was glad she'd soon be leaving, even though it meant that Rogan would be leaving, as well. "I'd better let out the chickens," she muttered.

Patrice dabbed a bit of perfume in the cutout triangle

below her collar. Flipping her skirt up to reveal at least three lace-trimmed petticoats and a length of silk stocking below white silk pantalets, she drew the glass stopper slowly behind each of her knees. "Where are the men?"

"They're checking the damage. Callum's probably gone home."

"I can't possibly walk to the wharf, you know, and I'm not about to ride on one of those great shaggy beasts. Someone will have to carry me."

"Don't look at me," Kathleen said, and marched down the stairs in time to hear Rogan saying, "Don't bother. I'll have someone from the village come help her mop out the house and put back the furniture. You'll have enough to do digging Amos out from under the mud."

"No need for that." Callum stood beside the front gate, which hung at an angle. "I'll be more than glad to help her get straight, seeing's you probably need to get on back to see to the *Witch*."

"Don't put yourself out on my account, I can easily make other arrangements. I imagine you're anxious to find out how the *Sunset Queen* fared in the blow. Be glad to give you a lift across the sound."

"No hurry. The *Queen*'s up in Missouri. Doubt if they got much damage up that far."

Sensing an inexplicable tension between the two men, Kathleen waited until Callum had left before making her presence known. "Oh, my mercy, it's even worse than I thought."

Utterly daunted, she stood in the doorway and stared at the ruins of the sitting room. There was mud everywhere. The floors were slimy underfoot. A brown line marked the walls and table legs some seven inches above the floor. Puddles stood in the uneven places, and already the planks were beginning to buckle.

Rogan came to stand behind her. "I'll get help. I don't

want you tackling this by yourself," he said, and she shook her head.

"Don't. I can manage perfectly well by myself. Everyone's going to have their own messes to clean up."

"Kathy—"

"I said I'll do it, Rogan, and I will!"

His lips tightened. His chest seemed to swell. Kathleen knew she sounded shrewish, but she couldn't help it. She was tired, dirty and discouraged, and if anyone crossed her, he might just discover that she wasn't quite as meek and dutiful as she'd been made out to be.

"Kathleen, about Callum," Roger began, but she cut him off with an impatient gesture.

"I don't want to hear about Callum, I don't want to hear about help, I don't want to hear about anything. I have more than enough to do, and the sooner you and your *friend* are on your way, the sooner I can get on with it."

Every plane in Rogan's lean face seemed to flatten. Every angle suddenly grew sharper. Never before had he seemed quite so essentially *male*. "All right, little Miss Ramrod, I'll leave, since you're so damned anxious to get rid of me. I've better things to do than stay here and keep you in line, but before I go, hear me out."

Without seeming to move, he was looming over her, his shoulders crowding her, the heat of his body singeing her soul. "There's no great rush to get anything done, other than making the place livable. I'll open the windows before I go, to dry things out. As for you, you're to go back to bed. You look like hell."

Kathleen moved away, crossed her arms and said, "I'll sleep when I get sleepy."

"You'll damned well sleep now, or you'll fall flat on your face. Another word of caution, lady. About Callum."

"What about him? I heard you telling him he was no longer welcome here." She knew better than that. What drove her to force the issue, when she knew very well it would only set him off?

"Callum knows what I'm getting at, and so do you. He's a man, and not all men are to be trusted. I should think you more than most would know that."

As if she needed the reminder. Patrice Rhodes had been reminder enough, but Kathleen refused to give him the satisfaction of agreeing. "Cal's not like that. We're very good friends. As to that, he was your friend even before he was mine, and I think it's most ungenerous of you to forget it!"

A tendril of hair slipped free of her braid and fell over her right cheek. Rogan reached out and tucked it behind her ear, and she felt her cheeks grow warm. Suddenly, it was as if the whole world eclipsed into a pair of glowing black eyes as they stood face-to-face, staring at each other.

What might have happened next she would never know, for Patrice chose that moment to come downstairs. "Oh, no! How am I ever to walk in this mess? My skirt! My shoes! Rogan, dear, you'll have to carry me again. At least your ship won't be muddy."

Rogan looked ready to explode, and Kathleen took advantage of the distraction to go to the kitchen. There was wood to be dried if she was ever to get a fire going, and right then she wanted nothing quite so much as a cup of steaming hot coffee.

With Patrice complaining about everything under the sun, Rogan didn't linger for coffee. As soon as he'd satisfied himself that there was no structural damage to the house, he swept the complaining widow into his arms and stalked off across the yard with her, splashing mud with every step.

Kathleen watched them out of sight, wanting to cry, wanting to curse, wanting to call them back and keep Rogan with her until she could get to the bottom of whatever was between them. Because something was. Something most definitely was, only he didn't seem to want to explore it, and she didn't know how to begin.

With a resolute set to her shoulders, she turned and went back inside to collect a pail and a mop. Duty came before daydreams.

Chapter Twelve

"You're in love with the Rogue, aren't you?" Callum asked. They were placing the chairs around the kitchen table, having washed down the walls and scrubbed tons of mud off the floors. Now the handsome gambler leaned on his mop, looking uncommonly dapper in spite of his bare feet and filthy clothing.

Never one to prevaricate, Kathleen ignored her burning cheeks and faced the question squarely. "I think I must be," she replied. "Not that I'm any great authority on the subject."

"Goose bumps? Trouble catching your breath? Bothersome dreams that leave you wanting something you can't put a name to, much less a face?"

She grimaced and wiped a smear of mud off the hearth. "What about tripping over your own tongue when you particularly want to make a good impression? Or being hot and cold at the same time, wanting to laugh and cry or pick a fight for no reason at all? Are you saying that's love?"

"Never having been seriously afflicted, I can't swear to it, but I'm pretty sure it's not indigestion. I had six weeks of that the first time I ever went down to New Orleans, and believe me, it's not the same thing at all."

Kathleen laughed, as she was meant to do. "Thank you, Cal. One thing about good friends—they keep a body from falling into the doldrums. Now, if you'll help me get Hetty's quilting frame down the stairs, I'll send you home with half a chicken and a custard pie. The hens laid right through the storm, and the eggs piled up on me, so I baked two this morning before the sun was even up good."

Busy work. She'd had to do something after Rogan had left. Scrubbing wasn't enough, she'd craved a more expressive outlet. As her meager talents were limited to cooking, sewing and singing off-key, she hadn't a whole lot of choice.

That day passed like the one after it, with Callum commandeering whatever help was needed from the village to set things right at both houses. Amos's skiff had turned up missing, and a section of someone's fence had come to rest across his front door, but other than a few missing shingles from each house, both places had weathered the storm well enough.

Hetty found a family of mice in the coffee grinder. Unable to bring herself to kill them, Kathleen had taken grinder and all to the far side of the Green Pond and dumped it out, praying the poor creatures would never find their way back.

The next evening, Callum came calling again. It was close to dark, and Kathleen had just finished clearing away their supper things. "I've come to say goodbye, ladies," he told them as he poured himself a cup of coffee from the pot at the back of the stove. "Hetty, I found these spoons of yours in Pa's spoon jar. Must've been washed over there by the tide."

"Reckon they were," said the old woman without batting an eye. "Don't happen to have a bit of red flannel you're done with, do you? I need a touch of red for my quilt."

"Red was never my best color, love, but I promise I'll send you a bolt of the finest red serge once I get to the mainland." Then, after dutifully admiring the log-cabin pattern she was working on, Callum followed Kathleen out to the chicken yard.

While she felt in the nests for late eggs, he said, "The *Eagle* came in this morning. She's due out tonight, and I'll be on her as far as Elizabeth City. From there, I'll catch a train."

"You could've gone with Rogan."

"I could've. Fact is, Paw still needed me." He reached out to take the single egg she handed him, then waited until she dropped the bar across the door. "So I reckon I won't be seeing you again for a spell."

"I'll miss you. It's been like having a big brother. Even better. We don't fight like brothers and sisters do. Caleb and the twins are forever picking on little Margaret, and she's not even two yet."

"A brother," Callum repeated with a rueful smile. "There's the gambler's luck for you. Can't lose at cards, can't win at love."

"Oh, pshaw! Is your indigestion kicking up again?"

"Gad, woman, you don't know when to quit, do you?" he teased. "I envy Rogan, y'know. Why didn't I meet you first?"

"Because you weren't shopping for a wife."

"Well, there's that, of course," he agreed. "But believe me, if the Rogue hadn't already claimed you, we could have had us a season of wild, uninhibited passion that would have raised eyebrows and temperatures for miles around."

"What a shocking notion, Mr. McNair! If I thought for one minute that you meant it, I assure you, you'd never have tasted the first bite of my custard pie."

Callum chuckled, and Kathleen took the egg from him

and strolled toward the house. How strange. She'd always been rather awkward with members of the opposite sex, and here she was swapping jests with the handsomest creature in three states, and she was no more self-conscious than a day-old biddy. Marriage must have lent her a greater degree of sophistication than she'd realized.

Well, perhaps not true sophistication, she reflected more seriously. All the same, she had changed. She was no longer a timid mouse, too frightened to squeak, who had snatched the first chance to escape an intolerable situation, for all she looked the same.

The amethyst glow of a waning day cast a magic spell on the weathered house, the gnarled trees and the bleak marsh to the east. Blind to the beauty around her, she thought about Rogan. Was it love she felt for him? Or did she tremble inside and forget to breathe out of respect and admiration? She couldn't deny feeling all that and more, but if she admired and respected him so much, why did they always seem to fight?

Callum broke in before she could reach a conclusion. By then they had reached the back steps. "Remember to let Paw know if you need anything, Kathy. There's not a man, woman or child in the village but what wouldn't come to your aid if you were needy. They'd have done it even if Rogan hadn't put out the word."

"Oh, I—well, actually, he always leaves us well-fixed. John Quidley and Bun Stowe keep us in fish, and Zorie Burrus brought us a goose and a haunch of venison just last week."

"Good. They're not real outgoing, especially since the war, but they'd never allow one of their own to go needy. I reckon it was the same everywhere, even before all those years of occupation. Out here on the banks there was scarce enough food to keep a tick alive, much less to feed half the Union Army."

"Yes, well...that was years ago, and we're hardly needy now."

Callum nodded. For a handsome, debonair gambler who probably had more women after him than sugar had flies, he looked surprisingly ill at ease. "Did, uh, Rogan say anything to you about me before he left?" he queried.

Kathleen fingered the large brown egg in her apron pocket. Actually, he had issued some sort of a veiled warning that she'd hardly understood, but then that Rhodes woman had come swishing down the stairs, and the moment had passed. "I'm sure he must have mentioned your name, but I don't recollect anything in particular."

"Yes, well...I was only wondering if he thought— What I mean is... You see, Kathy, there was a time when Rogue and I used to make sport of going after the same woman. If I saw her first, then he'd make a dead set for her, trying to win her off me. I did the same thing with his women. From the time we were fifteen, it was always a match to see who could steal a lady off the other one quicker."

She'd heard about this, of course, from Hetty and Amos and Callum himself. "And who usually won?"

With a shamefaced grin, he admitted, "Rogan. Don't make sense, does it? That face of his looks like it was put together from spare parts. If he ever wore anything fancier than a plain black suit, I've yet to see it, and Lord knows he's never been much of a hand with pretty words. The more he tries to sweet-talk 'em, the worse he gets. Best I could figure, the women must have felt sorry for him."

Kathleen could have told him otherwise. She didn't even pretend to understand Rogan's unique appeal, but it had nothing to do with pity.

Pausing beside the back steps, Callum propped one foot on the top one, calling attention to his trim, muscular build and his flawless grooming. Even his boots were freshly shined. "Well...I reckon I'd best be going, love. I just wanted to make sure there was nothing else you needed before I left.''

''We'll be fine, Cal. I can't tell you how much I appreciate all you've done for us. I'm sure Rogan does, too.''

Tilting his gray beaver hat at a reckless angle, the gambler said, ''I wouldn't lay odds on that, darling Kathleen. The one time when it really matters, that lucky devil gets there first. Oh, well, I'll likely win my passage all the way to New Orleans before I'm halfway across the sound. By the way, Paw says if your collards don't thrive, help yourself from his patch.''

''I'm sure Hetty won't hesitate one minute.'' They both laughed, and Kathleen moved back until she felt the edge of the steps press into the calf of her leg. ''You take real good care of yourself, Cal. And hurry back home. I'll— Hetty and I will miss you.''

Callum stepped closer. Kathleen knew what he was going to do before he ever touched her. Knew it and made no move to avoid it. Something about the look on his face touched her heart, and she laid a hand on his arm. Such a handsome, teasing face was never meant to look sad, nor wistful, nor any of the things she fancied she saw in his eyes now.

Lifting her chin with a long, sensitive forefinger, Callum brushed a kiss on her lips, then stepped back. ''Nothing, huh? No fireworks? No stomachache? No palpitations?''

It had been like kissing Caleb. Warm and sweet, but that was all. ''The trouble with you, Callum McNair, is that you're spoiled. You're used to having every woman in sight tumble right into your hands.'' She smiled, wishing she could feel more for him, although under the circumstances, it would be disastrous. ''Who knows, perhaps I might have tumbled right along with all the rest if Amos and Hetty hadn't told me what a wretched little heathen you were as a child.''

"Oh, sure. And the fact that you're head over heels in love with that thick-skulled husband of yours has nothing to do with it, I suppose."

"I thought we'd decided that was only indigestion, after all." Laughing, she waved him off and let herself inside.

If only it were as simple as that. If only what ailed her could be cured by a simple dose of soda, she thought as she lay awake into the night wondering where Rogan was, and if he'd given her a single thought since he'd walked away three days before. Was he on deck right this very instant watching the moon rise with Patrice Rhodes?

"What can't be cured must be endured," she whispered into her pillow. Another of her grandmother's homilies.

The house was sparkling again, but it still smelled musty. On fair days Kathleen sent Hetty over to sit with Amos, bundled herself up in her ragged old spencer and threw open all the windows so that it could air out.

Hetty was squirrelly again. Muttering under her breath, she came and went with lumpy little parcels half-hidden under her apron. Kathleen tried to think of some way to discover what she was carrying off, but she didn't dare ask. Hetty seemed to take umbrage at the least thing lately. She'd accused Kathleen of trying to poison her chickens, accused her of stealing the soap because it had taken so much to clean up the aftermath of the tide, then accused her of snooping because she'd cleaned out all the boxes to make room for herself downstairs.

For the most part, Kathleen ignored it. Five minutes after Hetty had made one of her accusations, the whole thing was forgotten. Sunny one moment, cloudy the next, just like the weather.

After a few weeks, things seemed to have settled into a comfortable rut, with Hetty spending more time quilting and far less thinking up accusations.

One wet and blustery morning Hetty presented Kathleen with the yellow silk gown and demanded that it be fitted properly. "I'm aiming to wear it Christmas, you know."

"That will be lovely, Hetty," murmured Kathleen. Privately she hardly thought December a time to be wearing yellow silk, but one didn't reason with Hetty Rawson. Kathleen was a skilled seamstress, thanks to years of sewing for the children and cutting down Alice's gowns for herself. Lately, she'd been toying with the notion of buying a dress length of calico from Mr. A. J. Stowe's store and making herself a dress in a bright, pretty color.

If she had enough money left over after that, she might buy a piece of good quality linen and make Rogan a shirt to replace the ones Hetty had hidden and they hadn't been able to find. She'd never before tackled a man's shirt, but it couldn't be all that difficult. Besides, if she botched it, he need never even know. She would give it to Hetty for quilting scraps.

By keeping her bow to the wind and a lively watch for waterspouts, Dick Styron had brought the *Witch* through the storm safely enough. It was not the first storm he had ridden out at sea, nor, God willing, would it be the last.

Afterward, there'd been plenty for all hands to do. Both the jib and spanker he'd used to maintain steerage had suffered damage, and a section of railing had been lost when a water barrel had washed over the side. Thank God Rogan had forgone a deck cargo in light of the predicted storm, or they'd likely have lost that, too.

After surveying the damage and settling his grumbling passenger into her cabin with a warning to remain below until the railing was repaired, Rogan set about jury-rigging the broken railing and mending the sails as they made their way up the coast toward their first scheduled stop, only three days overdue.

The sea was still rough. According to Billy, the Widow Rhodes was not enjoying the journey, but inevitably, as the seas grew calmer, her condition improved, and Rogan found it impossible to forbid her the freedom of the ship. As captain, he had certain obligations, one of which was to insure the comfort and safety of whatever paying passengers might be aboard.

As it happened, Patrice Rhodes was their only passenger, but that didn't alter his responsibility. The first two days he'd taken his meals in his cabin, leaving Dick to entertain the widow at the table. On the morning of the third day, both Dick and Patrice sought him out separately to register a complaint.

"God help me, Rogan, if you leave me alone with that woman again, I'll jump ship the first time we touch port! Weren't one dadblasted thing we ate enough for her! The meat was tough, the turnips was stringy, the stewed apples was too sour and the bread weren't worth snuff! To hear her go on, you'd think she was used to a house full of servants a-sucking up to her."

"Reckon maybe she is. Her husband was Claude Rhodes."

"Would that be Claude X. Rhodes Chandlery up to Baltimore City?" And when Rogan nodded, "Yeah, well, no wonder the poor man turned up his toes. Reckon she plumb whined him to death! I never saw the mess cleared so fast in all the days I been sailing. Otis left without even waiting for second helpings."

Rogan sighed in sympathy. The bos'n's appetite was formidable, as was his intolerance for dinner conversation. "All right, Dick, you've made your point. I don't want a mutiny on my hands."

The strange thing was that Mrs. Rhodes was a good-looking woman, if somewhat past her prime. Not a one of his men but what didn't like women. She must have really been on her high horse.

Breathing a soft oath, Rogan stood and reached for his coat. He'd best go pour a bit of oil on troubled waters if he wanted to be left in peace. Women passengers could be more damned trouble than they were worth. Maybe after this trip, he'd limit his passenger service to males only.

Reluctantly, he prepared to leave his cabin, where he'd been working on his logbook. His hand was on the door when someone knocked on the other side. "Oh. Mrs. Rhodes. I was just on my way—that is, good morning."

Her blue eyes were snapping, and her cheeks held even more color than usual. In the filtered light below, Rogan couldn't tell if it was anger or rouge. While a few women of Mrs. Rhodes' social standing actually painted their faces, Rogan suspected the rest weren't above chafing their cheeks with a scrap of coarse muslin.

"Oh, Rogan, dear, I was afraid you weren't feeling well when you missed so many meals." Her eyes seemed to focus on his entire body at once.

"My, uh, duty, ma'am. I mean my log. That is, I've not posted my books since we last left port, and I'm afraid the *Witch* doesn't run to a clerk."

Not waiting for an invitation, she brushed past him in a cloud of cloying perfume, and Rogan, resigned to hearing her out, indicated a chair. She sat, smoothing her skirts prettily over her lap. "I'm sure you're the kind of man who personally oversees the smallest detail. My dear late husband was that way. The mark of a successful businessman, I always say."

Get to the point, madam. You didn't come in here to talk business with me, and we both know it. "I'm sorry about the delay in your journey, Mrs. Rhodes. I'm sure you're anxious to get on up to Baltimore, but I thought it best to put you ashore for the duration. Bigger ships than mine have been upended by a hurricane, with all hands lost.''

She fluttered her surprisingly dark lashes. ''Are you always so protective, sir?'' She rearranged her skirts in a flurry of pink and white ruffles, sending up, in the process, another wave of heavy perfume. ''I can't tell you how safe it makes me feel.''

''Yes, ma'am. Well, if that's—''

''But can you *imagine* my surprise at finding poor little Kathleen Stevens in a place like Hatteras! I didn't want to say anything while I was there—I mean, the poor child's probably so ashamed as it is, but of course, we all knew she'd run off. Not that she had much choice, with the whole town—''

Rogan's eyes were suddenly glacial, and she covered her small red mouth with one hand. ''Oh, my clumsy tongue! It's my worst failing, you know, speaking without thinking. But as long as I've blundered this far, please let me tell you how wonderfully generous you are to have actually married the poor thing after all the scandal and everything. She'd have had a perfectly wretched time of it if she'd been forced to stay around Beaufort. Naturally, none of the women would have anything to do with her, and the men… Well, you can imagine the way she would have ended up. I couldn't have borne it for poor Alice's sake. Her only sister, and after all Alice and Morton had done for her, too.''

Rogan's fingernails bit into his leather-hard palms. He wondered if smoke was actually pouring out of his ears, or if it only felt that way. If Patrice Rhodes had been a man, she'd have long since been laid out cold on the deck! The bitch was making it sound as if Kathleen were to blame for the whole wretched business!

Taking a deep breath, and then one or two more, he said carefully, ''Mrs. Rhodes, I—''

"Oh, Patrice, please! Surely we know one another well enough for that. After all, I've been a guest in your home. We've actually spent a night together." Under a sweep of lashes, she sent him a piquant look then added, "In a manner of speaking, of course."

"Right," he said grimly. "In a manner of speaking, Mrs. Rhodes, just why did you choose my ship for your journey? Surely you could have gone more quickly by train?"

"Oh, but I could never abide trains! All the noise, and the cinders, and the rushing along at breakneck speed—oh, dear me, no, I'd have stayed home first and conducted my business by mail."

All of which led Rogan to wonder why she hadn't done just that. What business would the woman be conducting, anyhow? Personally, he'd sooner conduct business with a man-eating shark.

"Even so, there are larger ships than mine making the regular run, most with far finer passenger accommodations." He watched, amazed, as she swatted her eyelashes again. Damned if he wasn't beginning to think the things were made of horsehair! Either that or she'd used enough soot and grease on them to black a stove.

"Oh, dear, you've caught me out. If you must know, Captain, I asked about you, and was told you were one of the most respected coasters in the trade." The truth was, ever since she'd seen him in Josiah Dunwoody's backyard, she'd been unable to get the man out of her mind. God, he was magnificent, in his black boots, his lean black trousers and a shirt that seemed bound to split at the seams across his broad shoulders. He had been the subject of so many of her daydreams since she'd first laid eyes on him that she felt as if she knew him. Intimately!

The fact that he had actually married that little Stevens tramp was no great problem. Kathleen appeared to be running true to form, with another man already in hand. What on earth could they possibly see in her? Other than her youth, that was. At least her taste was remarkably improved. Well, little Miss Mealy Mouth could play around with her pretty gambling man all she wanted. Personally, Patrice preferred this exciting young stallion.

She leaned forward, lips pursed in a charming moue, and suddenly Rogan remembered where he'd seen her before. It had bothered him when she'd first come on board, but he'd dismissed it. She was pretty. She was blond. So were countless other women, and this one hadn't all that much to set her apart.

"I remember now," he said. "You're the woman with the dog, aren't you?"

"The woman with the...?"

"In Dunwoody's backyard in July. You'd lost your dog, and you asked me to help find him, only we never did. Did he go home?"

"My— Oh. That naughty darling, he never did come home, you know. I wept for days."

Rogan realized with amazement that she was staring directly at his crotch. Against his will, he felt his body begin to react. She licked her lips slowly, and he dragged out his handkerchief and mopped his brow. Before he could make a jackass of himself with a woman he was fast coming to despise, he rose and opened a porthole, staying to allow the cold air to play over his flushed face.

"Rogan, I feel I must confess something." She had come to stand behind him, so close he could feel the heat of her on his back, and he sidestepped away. Whatever she thought she had to confess, he didn't want to hear it. But without being openly rude, he didn't see how he could shut her up.

"I told you Alice Kingsley was my very best friend, didn't I? The Kingsley house backed up to mine, so we saw a lot of each other over the years. Mr. Rhodes was still alive when poor little Kathleen came to live with them. I felt sorry for her, of course. We all did. And I'd be the first to admit she was good with Alice's children. Actually, she made herself quite invaluable to the whole family. Poor Alice never had the least notion what was going on right under her nose, but the neighbors all knew. Things like that are hard to keep secret.''

Anger blazed from Rogan's dark eyes. "Dammit, woman, if you knew what was going on, why the devil didn't you do something about it?"

One hand fluttered to her silk-clad breast, and Patrice shook her head slowly. "I know. You can't blame me any more than I blame myself, but I didn't want to hurt poor Alice. She would have been devastated, you know. She adored Morton.''

The fluttering hand moved to Rogan's chest, but he stepped sharply back, causing it to fall to her side. "Mrs. Rhodes, if you're trying to tell me my wife encouraged Kingsley, then you're wasting your time. My wife was little more than a child when that bastard started hounding her. He as good as told her if she so much as hinted to her sister what he was up to, she'd be thrown out on her ear! She was a child, dammit! Why didn't you help her?"

"She was no child, Rogan," Patrice said softly. "No matter what you'd like to believe, Kathleen was a woman in all the ways that count. She was thrown out when Alice discovered that she was making up to Morton the same way she'd been making up to anything in britches ever since she was fourteen years old.''

His eyes were burning holes through her. "You're lying."

Shaking her head gently, Patrice said, "Only this time the fools had the poor judgment to carry on right out in the backyard in broad daylight. I saw it. Alice saw it. We both came out and confronted them there, and if your wife told you anything different, I'm afraid she's trying to pull the wool over your eyes, knowing that you'd—"

Rogan's control snapped. He strode to the door and flung it open. "That will be all, Mrs. Rhodes. I'd appreciate it if you'd book your return passage on another ship. The *White Witch* won't have a vacant berth."

Patrice managed to look prettily flustered. "Oh, dear, I'm afraid I've gone and hurt your feelings, haven't I?"

"My feelings are none of your concern, madam! But if you've the least regard for your own, you'll cease your troublemaking from this moment on. If I ever—*ever*—hear so much as a *whisper* about my wife's good name, you'll regret you ever learned how to talk, is that clear?"

Undaunted, Patrice ran her hand up his arm until it curved over his shoulder. "Rogan, please be reasonable. I never meant to—"

"Reasonable!" he roared. "If I weren't a reasonable man, you'd be sailing over the rail by now!" He removed her hand as if it were a bit of filth clinging to his jersey.

"I can't help it if you don't believe what's there before your very eyes. All Beaufort knew what was going on, and whether you believe me or not, Kathleen Stevens was never the innocent she made herself out to be. If her own sister saw through her and threw her out, surely that tells you—"

"Good night, madam. Until we put into Baltimore, I'll have your meals sent to your cabin." He held the door open wider, and with no other choice, she left.

The whole cabin reeked of her after she'd gone, and Rogan paced it like a caged lion. Damn the painted bitch! What did she have against Kathleen? Where the hell did she get off, coming to him with a pack of lies like that? Josiah wouldn't lie. He'd said that Kingsley had chased after the girl practically ever since she'd been living under his roof, and if that didn't make him a miserable, worthless scum of the first order, Rogan didn't know what it would take!

Saw it, indeed! So that snake-tongued witch wanted him to believe she'd caught them in the act! He might not know Kathleen as well as most men knew their wives, but he knew she could never have done the things the Rhodes bitch had accused her of doing.

A vision swam before his unwilling eyes, of Kathleen laughing with Callum as if she'd known him all her life. Of Kathleen in Callum's arms, being carried to a dark house...

Slamming a fist into his palm, Rogan continued to pace. Finally, he stopped and swore. He needed air. The whole cabin reeked of that meddlesome female's perfume! Undogging the other porthole, he left them both open, blew out the lamp and headed topside.

In her cabin, Patrice heard him go by and smiled. What would he do if she opened the door and invited him inside?

Shoot her, probably. She'd spread it on a bit thick, but she'd been bored. Besides, she owed the little twit something for trying to take Morton from her. And then, for her to end up with Rogan.

God, but he was a tempting devil! The other one, Callum Something-or-other, was twice as handsome, but there was something almost primitive about Rogan Rawson. Something fierce, raw and shockingly masculine. After Morton, she was rather bored with handsome men. To tell the truth, she'd begun to tire of him even before he'd lost interest in her, but after all the years she'd given him, both before and after she'd been so fortuitously widowed, *she'd* wanted to be the one to end it. He owed her that much, at least.

Wrestling with the last few buttons on her bodice, Patrice let the gown billow down around her legs and stepped out of it. She'd have that cabin boy, Billy, or whatever his name was, brush it and steam out the creases before she repacked her things.

Placing her hands over her ample breasts, she lifted them and stared critically in the mirror. Were those creases across the top where they rose out of her corselet?

Of course not! It was only the wretched lighting in here. One small porthole and two lamps, both of them bolted to the walls. How was a woman to see well enough to apply a discreet touch of rouge and kohl?

Impatiently, she reached for the largest of the collection of pots in the drawer of her trunk and began massaging scented cream into her bosom. After awhile, a lazy smile spread over her face. They hadn't reached Baltimore yet, and once they did, surely he wouldn't be sailing right away. That gloriously wicked-looking creature with the enormous shoulders and the powerful thighs hadn't bedded his wife, or any other woman, since she'd boarded his ship in Beaufort more than a week ago. For a man in his prime—and that one most certainly was—a week could be a long time. Let a hungry man smell food, and first thing you knew, he was starving!

Even if he managed to hold out against all her best efforts, she'd still have the satisfaction of knowing she'd evened the score for Morton. That skinny little wretch with her flat chest and her haughty ways would have a taste of her own medicine the next time she crawled into her husband's bed, only to have him kick her out again. If the seed she'd planted in Rogan's mind tonight bore fruit, then that was exactly what he would do. No man wanted a wife with loose morals. She prided herself that there'd been just enough truth in what she'd told him to make the story utterly convincing.

For all she knew, it might even be the truth.

Kicking off her shoes, Patrice sprawled across her bunk, propped her feet against the wall and admired her ankles.

Her feet weren't quite as pretty as they used to be, but she still had wonderful ankles.

And God, was she good! The world had lost a wonderful actress when she'd decided to marry that old goat, Claude Rhodes, but she'd never once regretted her decision. Beauty didn't last forever, and a woman had to think of tomorrow.

Chapter Thirteen

The waterfront was bustling. It would be hours before Rogan would be in position to commence unloading. With a view to avoiding his passenger, he went ashore by launch and spent the morning conferring with the harbormaster and various warehousemen and shipping agents, including the agent representing the ship in which he owned an interest. He was pleased to learn that on her last voyage, the *Arduous* had turned a fine profit.

Late that afternoon he watched from the dock as the *White Witch* was warped alongside, confident that by now Patrice Rhodes was miles away, comfortably ensconced in surroundings that were far superior to anything he had offered her. When there was a delay in docking, passengers usually chose to be ferried ashore by launch, leaving their trunks to be delivered at a later time.

Suddenly his eyes narrowed against the glare of late afternoon sun glinting on the Patapsco River. Wasn't that…? Dammit, he'd given her all day to leave, but unless his eyes deceived him, there she was, bold as brass, traipsing down the gangplank with Billy toting a stack of hatboxes taller than he was and poor Dick struggling with three valises.

Rogan turned away, but it was too late. She'd already seen him.

"Oh, Rogan. There you are! Were you waiting for me?"

Like he was waiting for a case of the cramping flux. "Mrs. Rhodes." He nodded. Steeling himself to be polite, he touched the brim of his cap, his face stony. "I thought you'd be long gone by now."

Something in the smile she barely suppressed told him she knew exactly what he'd thought.

"By your leave, ma'am," mumbled the first mate as he dumped the heap of luggage onto the dock. Turning to Rogan, he said, "The men want to know when we'll be sailing, sir. I've put Almy, Calvin and Maurice on watch. Your leave to let the rest go ashore soon's we stand down?"

"With the usual restrictions. Billy stays on board unless one of us is with him, and any man I have to stand bail for will have his pay docked and be restricted to ship for the rest of the journey."

"Fair'n square, sir. See you directly!"

With Billy on his heels, Styron made his escape, leaving Rogan to deal with Patrice and her baggage. Nor did she seem in any great rush to leave. "If you're not being met, I'll see about securing a carriage for you, ma'am."

The widow's dense black lashes leaped into play. In the clear light of day, they weren't nearly as impressive. "Rogan," she teased. "Are you so very anxious to be rid of me? Oh, me, I'm afraid I upset you, didn't I?"

He stiffened. "Not at all, ma'am. Did you say you were being met, or shall I fetch a conveyance for you?"

"No, I am not being met," she snapped. She was dressed all in blue, a velvet princess line coat trimmed with white fur and a small matching hat. "As a widow alone in a strange city, I suppose I'll have to get used to fending for myself." She eyed him consideringly. "I don't suppose—"

Rogan didn't wait for her to finish. "I'll have your trunk sent on soon's we unload if you'll give me your direction."

She sighed and tunneled her hands deeper into her fur muff. "Oh, well, if you're going to hold grudges, I suppose I must." Naming one of Baltimore's oldest and most respected hotels, she added, "I don't suppose you're free for supper tonight?"

"Mrs. Rhodes—"

"No, I was afraid not. Please, Rogan, let's not part this way. Call me Patrice, won't you? I only meant to offer a word of advice, you know. I was afraid you were worried about leaving Kathleen all alone with that ridiculously handsome young man of hers. If I spoke out of turn, it was only out of concern for you, but of course, I should have realized that with Mr. McNair being a friend of yours, he'd be much too loyal to—"

"Just so, ma'am." Rogan's words were too clipped for politeness. Overcoming a powerful urge to throttle the woman, he turned and waved to a hired conveyance. With more speed than grace, he ushered her into the black leather-topped carriage, spoke to the driver and handed him a few coins. By the time the reins slapped the back of the spavined bay mare, Rogan was halfway down the dock, his long legs eating up the distance. Long before he reached his destination, more than one longshoreman, on seeing the look on his face, hastily stepped out of his way.

There was the cargo to be unloaded, checked over and signed for first. Meanwhile, as one hold after another was emptied, he set his men to pumping the bilges dry. That done, Rogan directed Dick Styron to go below with the ship's carpenter to check carefully for any leakage since the storm. They'd taken in surprisingly little water under the circumstances, thanks to good maintenance, careful stowage and a seasoned crew. All the same, Rogan ordered the hatches left off until the new cargo was ready to load. It didn't take much to start damp rot. The *Witch* was as sound today as she'd been the day she'd slid off the ways in Hatteras back in the fall of '72, with stem, sternpost, inner post and knees of Kinnakeet oak and a centerboard taller and thicker than two stout men. But a ship, like a woman, could go downhill in a hurry unless a man kept a close watch on her.

While the crew, save for a skeleton watch, enjoyed a few days of respite in port, Rogan did his best to forget Patrice's sly insinuations.

Callum? Oh, hell, that was crazy! Kathleen had better sense than to be taken in by that sharpster. The Rhodes woman was just trying to make trouble, that was all. Maybe she was one of those females who couldn't abide any man who didn't instantly fall at her feet. Or into her bed. Hell, she'd spent more time staring at his crotch than she had at his eyes.

And, dammit, his traitorous body had been just hungry enough to react, in spite of his dislike of the woman herself, which had probably given her all the encouragement she needed!

Driven by an increasingly familiar restlessness, Rogan set the time of departure a good twenty-four hours short of what had been scheduled.

"Hell, boy, that don't even give us enough time to get the holds loaded, much less secure us a deck cargo." In moments of stress, the first mate was apt to forget their relative positions. "Besides, that milling machinery ain't even come in yet. I checked at the depot no more'n a hour ago."

"It'll be in on the night train from Chicago. If it's not on the dock by six in the morning, we'll damn well sail without it."

"What the Sam Hill's got into you, anyhow?"

"Dammit, Dick, if you can't manage to oversee the loading, I'll find a man who can!"

"Now, come on, boy, this ain't like you," the grizzled first mate protested. But after a second look at his captain's grim face, he flicked a finger to his cap. "Aye, sir! Number one's near about loaded, only I left the hatch off like you said. I'll top 'er off, batten 'er down and get on with number two. Should be ready to take on a deck load by morning. Once we're cleared to sail—"

"I've already handled that."

"Then I reckon there's no need to tarry, once we hoist them machines on board and lash 'em down good. I'll have Luther rig some kind of protection in case we run into a spell of weather."

"They'll be crated. A tarp lashed over the top will be sufficient."

"Aye, sir! With your permission...sir!"

The next few hours were far too busy to spend time worrying over what might or might not be happening back home. Exhausted from too many sleepless nights, Rogan managed to convince himself that he didn't give a damn. If Kathleen was no better than she'd been painted, what difference did it make? She took good care of Hetty, and that, after all, was what he'd married her for. If he wanted a woman, he had plenty to chose from. There was the Rhodes woman.

Oh, hell, no! He'd sooner bed down with a coral snake.

There was still good old Della. Maybe he'd stop by for a visit with her on his way south. If she'd already got around to finding a replacement for him, there were plenty of other women around. Pretty women. Available women! There was no reason to deprive himself of a woman, he thought, dismissing his earlier conviction that he just might be one of that rare breed of men who couldn't bring himself to be unfaithful to the woman he'd married, no matter what the circumstances.

And then, his convictions swinging like a weather vane, he would manage to convince himself that Kathleen deserved his protection no matter what she'd done. She had sought sanctuary at the parsonage, and from there she'd been placed in his care. And no matter what she'd done before or after that, he had given his word to Josiah that he would not press her to share his bed unless she gave him some sign.

Actually, he'd assured Josiah that she wasn't the sort of woman he even thought of in that way, having always preferred blondes and redheads with a comfortable amount of flesh on their bones. How the devil could he have known that a smile from a prickly little brunette, a casual touch, even a sharp exchange of words, could cause him to swell up until he near about burst the buttons off his britches?

Primrose. He couldn't remember when he'd first started calling her that in his mind. The first time he'd laid eyes on her he hadn't been all that impressed. He'd been downright dismayed, in fact. She'd struck him as almost comically starchy. Proud as a clipper ship, proper as a British admiral in her plain black frock, with her nose in the air and her hair screwed up in a lubber's knot and anchored down with the ugliest bonnet he'd ever laid eyes on.

Slowly, a look of bleakness replaced the warmth that had kindled in his eyes. A bitter parody of a smile curled his hard lips as he stared at the bustling wharves of Baltimore harbor. Damn her wicked heart, she hadn't looked quite so prim and proper laughing up into Callum's face, her arms battened around his neck as if she couldn't bear to turn him loose.

She'd made the same promises that he had in Dunwoody's parlor back in July, all that business about obeying and honoring and cleaving only unto. Hers had lasted just about as long as it had taken McNair to come sniffing around.

"Well, we'll just see about that," Rogan muttered. He'd kept his word a damned sight longer than she had, so if he decided to change the rules, she had only herself to blame.

The deck cargo had barely been set in place before they cast off. With a steady twenty-knot wind out of the northeast, they made excellent time, arriving at Norfolk dead on their original schedule, in spite of the layover during the storm. With time in his favor, Rogan had already made up his mind to lay over at Hatteras on the way south, although if anyone pressed him for reasons, he'd have a hard time coming up with one that made sense.

But that was before his schedule began to fall apart. Easing into the harbor under half canvas, he found coal schooners lined up as far as he could see, waiting to fill their holds.

Damn!

A day passed, and then another. Rogan paced the deck. He spat out orders only to rescind them before the echo had died away. His crew took to hiding from him. His first mate watched and listened, shaking his head in silent commiseration.

Woman trouble, Styron thought. It never failed. It had been his experience that any man was a fool to marry, leave alone sailors. Just let a seaman marry himself a pretty young thing and then go off and leave her alone for weeks at a time, and trouble was bound to follow.

Long before their turn came to warp alongside and commence the process of unloading, Rogan had lost whatever small advantage he'd gained by leaving Baltimore a day early. Frustrated to his wits' end, he tried to convince himself that he was relieved. He'd been planning to walk in and take her by surprise. But what if he'd been the one to be surprised? What then? What happened after he'd wrung Callum's neck and kicked his fornicating carcass out of Kathleen's bed?

He'd be right back where he'd been when he'd landed himself in this mess in the first place. Needing help, not knowing where to turn. Losing too much time in stopping off to see to Hetty's well-being. Wondering each time he left if the poor old soul would give away everything he possessed and set fire to the house before he could get back again. He'd done what he'd thought best for her. It just hadn't turned out right.

But it wasn't concern over Hetty's plight that was eating holes in his gut, and Rogan knew it. He'd been dealing with Hetty's problem for years. All the neighbors knew and understood. They did their best to look after her, but dammit, a man could ask only so much of his neighbors.

In the dark watches of the night, while he waited for his ship to be ready to sail again, Rogan examined his situation dispassionately, wondering where he'd gone wrong. Inevitably, it all came back to Kathleen.

The trouble had started when he'd let her get under his guard. Even now he didn't know how she'd managed to do it. In her drab, shapeless dress, with her hair every which way, she certainly hadn't gone out of her way to make herself appealing. Just the opposite, in fact. So why did he spend so damned much time thinking about her, remembering those steady gray eyes, the way she smelled, the way she smiled, the infrequent sound of her laughter?

He remembered the way she'd felt when he'd held her against him that first night out, when she'd gone out on deck to watch the moon rise. His emotions caught in a treacherous riptide, he recalled the look in her eyes when Hetty had snatched that yellow silk gown out of the wrappings and held it up to herself. She'd known. They'd both known, yet she'd done the only decent thing. And dammit, he didn't want to think about that, not now!

Nor did he want to think about how she'd felt in his arms, the way her lips had softened under his when he'd kissed her. She'd been startled at first, almost as if she'd never been kissed before. Remembering the way her lips had quivered uncertainly for an instant, he felt the old familiar fullness in his groin, and he swore.

How had she felt in Callum's arms? he asked himself, deliberately inflicting the pain he could not escape. Stiff and prickly? Or soft and yielding? Had she pushed the raunchy bastard away? Or had her eyes widened and her lips parted eagerly, joining in the game? What other games had they played? Had McNair succeeded where Rogan had failed? God knows the silver-tongued devil had enough experience with women to melt the heart of a wooden figurehead!

Already running late, Rogan decided it was all for the best. Another week and he could lay to rest the demons that rode him relentlessly, day and night.

But the demons still rode him eight days later when the *White Witch* dropped both her anchors in the lea of Hatteras village on the upper Carolina banks.

"Not again," groaned Dick Styron. "Damn all, boy, we were due into Norfolk yesterday! At this rate we'll end up hauling coal like half the coasters in the business, and I'm a-telling you, we've not got the freeboard for it!"

Rogan glared at him. Only the fact that Dick Styron had taught him more about sailing than any other man, living or dead, had saved him from instant dismissal. "Have I missed out on a single scheduled consignment?"

"Not yet, but you've been late more times than I care to dwell on."

"Trains haul quick. Coasters haul cheap."

"Or not at all when they've got a skipper who can't keep his mind off his—"

"Set the watch, dammit, and quit trying to tell me how to run my business!" But the old man was right; he'd spent more time at home in the past few months than he had in the past few years, and it wasn't all on account of Hetty.

"Dammit, some things are more important than a few tons of rice and another load of yellow pine!" he grumbled, and barked out an order to lower the launch.

The peach-colored calico with the tiny bunches of blue flowers was her favorite. Kathleen had studied the bolts of cloth at Mr. A.J.'s store, comparing quality and color. At fourteen cents a yard, she dare not make a hasty decision. It had been between the red and the peach, and in the end, she'd chosen the peach, two spools of white thread and a dozen bone buttons for the bodice. The glass ones would have been far prettier, but they were too dear. In all, she spent more than three dollars on herself, and another four for enough linen to make a shirt for Rogan. She'd chosen mother-of-pearl buttons for that. They cost more than the bone but less than the glass.

That had been four days ago. Since then, she'd stayed up long after Hetty had gone to bed each night making first the shirt and then her gown, which was all done but for turning up the hem.

When Rogan pushed open the door and walked into the house, she was on her knees with a mouthful of pins.

"Kathleen, I'm home."

Her mouth fell open, the pins scattered on the floor, and she gaped at him in utter astonishment. Ever since that day nearly a month before, when she'd watched him stride out with that witch, Patrice, in her ridiculous pink gown, wrapped around him like a poison ivy vine, she'd been trying her best to bring her wayward feelings under control.

"How are you, Rogan?" He was glaring at her, and she asked herself guiltily what she'd done to rile him *now*.

Besides spending his money on herself, that was. In a weak moment, she'd managed to convince herself that he'd be glad to see her in something other than black, brown or gray. And then, because she wasn't quite convinced, she'd spent even more for material to make him a new shirt, hoping it would ease her conscience.

It hadn't. "You're looking well," she said. He was looking magnificent! All muscle and sinew, browned by the sun and honed by years of hard work, he was garbed in his usual black. Callum was twice as handsome, and far better dressed, yet all Rogan had to do was walk in the door and she fell apart.

Ducking her head, she hurriedly picked up the pins she'd dropped.

"Working late, aren't you?" Rogan slung his worn canvas bag into a corner and sauntered into the room to offer her a hand up.

"The, um—the hem needed turning up." What was so wrong about making herself a new dress? Surely she'd earned that much! But if he'd noticed the bright splash of color spread over the gate-legged table, he didn't let on.

"I thought you'd have found something more exciting to pass the time with by now."

Exciting? She was more excited this very moment than she'd been in weeks, but she could hardly tell him that! "I enjoy sewing. I—it's good to see you, Rogan. Hetty's fine now. She suffered a bit of a fall a few weeks ago, but her leg mended good as new." As usual when she was nervous, her tongue ran away with her.

"A fall?" Rogan frowned as he continued to hold her hand.

Kathleen's palm was tingling. Her fingers curled instinctively around his hard, capable hand, and she caught her bottom lip between her teeth. Hetty! What was she going to do about Hetty? She hadn't been expecting Rogan, and now Hetty was sound asleep in Kathleen's bed, snoring like a sawmill, and Kathleen had spread her personal things all over Rogan's loft, never dreaming he'd be coming home so soon.

"Yes, that is—" Suddenly realizing that he was still holding her hand, she snatched it away and smoothed the hair that had long since come loose from trying on her new gown so many times to get the length just right. "Well, you see, there was this dog, and—"

"What dog?"

"Oh, didn't I tell you?" she asked brightly. "We have a cat now."

Rogan's eyebrows shot up. "A cat? I thought you said it was a dog."

"Yes, well, that's how it all started, but—" She broke off, noticing for the first time the look of strain around his eyes, the deep grooves at either side of his set mouth. He looked tired, as if he hadn't slept for weeks. "Rogan, are you sure you're all right? Come out to the kitchen and let me fix you some supper. There's a bit of turtle stew left, and I can fry some corn bread to go with it."

"Coffee'll do," he said tiredly. She led the way, and after only the briefest hesitation, he followed. "Tell me about Hetty's fall. I've warned her about that chicken ramp. The thing gets wet and slippery, and—"

"It wasn't the chicken, it was the cat. At least, first it was the dog, and then—" She dipped a bowl full of stew and placed it before him, unasked, then poked up the fire under the coffeepot. "It'll be hot in no time," she promised. "You see, this cat took up here a few weeks back, and Hetty let him sleep in her bed."

His stony face revealing none of his suspicions, Rogan

finished the stew and accepted a cup of hot black coffee. "Hetty never could abide cats."

"Well, that may be, but she likes this one. I think she sort of enjoys having something to make over. Anyway, Rags—that's his name, Rags—he was out taking the sun one morning when Marthenia Willis's big yellow dog came around, and the next thing I knew, they were both out of the yard and gone, with Rags yowling and that old dog barking his head off."

She ladled the last of the stew into Rogan's bowl, then set the pan to soak. "Well, the upshot of it was that the dog treed poor Rags in that dead cedar down by the Green Pond, and the more we called, the higher the poor thing climbed. Hetty was all for going up after him, but I made her stay on the ground."

"I thought you said that was how she broke her leg." Rogan was looking considerably more relaxed, Kathleen was pleased to note.

"Wrenched it, not broke it. As it was, I was the one who went up the tree. Hetty stayed down below. I finally managed to get my hands on that stupid animal, but he lit into me like a wildcat, clawing and biting until I was mad enough to feed him to the dog and be done with it."

Rogan finished his coffee and eased the chair away from the table, stretching his long legs halfway across the kitchen. Kathleen caught herself staring and looked away, mortified at the way her thoughts were running. Dear Lord, she should have made him another pair of trousers instead of a shirt. Big ones! Gathered at the waist so they'd not reveal the very parts they were meant to conceal!

She dropped the dish towel, bumped against the corner of the table and started talking faster than ever. "So I threw him into the pond."

"The cat?"

"Certainly the cat! I could hardly hold him in my arms,

scratching and clawing the way he was. I called down to
Hetty to grab him in her apron when he came ashore, but
blessed if she didn't try to catch him bare-handed, so he
scratched her, too, and when he ran, she took off after him,
and before I could get down and see to everything, she'd
gone and tripped over a root and fallen over that old dead
tree that came down in the storm.''

She ended out of breath and embarrassed at having rattled on a mile a minute. It was all Rogan's fault. If he
hadn't come home so unexpected—if he hadn't pinned her
down with those devil-dark eyes of his, as if he knew precisely how many hours she'd wasted thinking of him when
she should have been looking after his interests...

"Any more coffee?"

She turned and glared at him. "Yes, but it's gone cold
by now! I reckon I'll have to poke up the fire again!"

"Try breathing on it a few times. That ought to be
enough to melt the stovepipe."

"I *beg* your pardon."

"And don't go all huffy, you'll throw your backbone out
of joint. Just pour me another half cup and I'll drink it
cold!"

"I'll make fresh," she snapped.

"The hell you will!"

"Don't curse in my presence, Rogan Rawson!"

"Then don't go flouncing around like a—"

"I am not flouncing!"

"The hell you're not! Before I even get my boots off,
you're off spinning some farfetched faradiddle about dogs
and cats that don't make a bit of sense, then when I asked
for a cup of coffee, you start slamming things around like
I'd insulted you or something, and I damn well want to
know why! Could it be you have a guilty conscience?"

"A guilty conscience?" she squeaked. "Why should I

have a guilty conscience? It was hardly my fault that Hetty—"

Rising, he moved around the table, and Kathleen edged away. "That's what I'm asking you. Maybe if you stop trying to throw me off course with a bunch of fairy tales, we can get to the bottom of just why you're so nervous."

"I am not—"

"You damned well are! Look me in the eye and tell me what you've been doing all these nights to entertain yourself, and don't tell me you spent all that time sewing, dammit! You could've ruffled the whole damned house by now!"

He allowed his eyes to play over her, making her painfully aware that she was wearing her oldest gown because it was easy to take off and put on again when she was fitting her new one.

"Well? I'm waiting," he sneered. "Have you missed me, wife? Or have you been too busy?"

"Oh, I missed you, all right," she shot back. "Almost as much as I'd have missed the plague! And as for how I've been keeping myself busy, I've managed to do that the same way I've kept busy since I was nine years old. With chores!"

Rogan's jaw tightened, but for the moment, he remained silent. Kathleen tossed her head and stared boldly at him, her stormy eyes nearly as dark as his. She refused to be the first to drop her gaze, but if he didn't back down soon, she might break in two. Her spine was so rigid she was shaking all over. Never in her life did she remember being so furious!

Rogan's fists clenched and unclenched. He ground his teeth. Didn't the little fool know enough to quit while she still could? The greenest seaman aboard the *White Witch* would have long since run for cover. His crew, right down to the last man, knew him far better than did his own wife.

But that was about to change.

"I take it Callum's still around?"

"Then you take it wrong." Kathleen was furious with him, but even more furious with herself for allowing him to get under her skin. Why was it that she always overreacted to every single thing he said or did?

"So...when did he manage to tear himself away?"

"You mean the precise day? Do you want the hour and the minute?"

Truth to tell, she couldn't remember when he'd left. She didn't care. What made her so spitting, fighting mad was the fact that she remembered to the minute when Rogan had walked out that door. Over and over she'd pictured it, wishing he'd trip and tumble that nasty-minded female into a ditch. Wishing he'd drop her in the muddiest puddle around and walk back up the path, onto the porch, and take Kathleen into his arms.

She was a fool. Evidently, she'd been born a fool, and it was beginning to look as if she'd die a fool. To think that she'd once dared to hope...

Chapter Fourteen

Rogan finished his coffee in silence. Kathleen stalked around, wiping off surfaces, putting away dishes. She closed the damper and banked the coals in the stove for morning, then stood, arms folded over her breasts, daring him to say one more word to her.

"Thank you. It was good stew." Easing his lithe, muscular body from the chair, he flexed both shoulders and exhaled heavily.

Poor darling, he was tired.

She didn't *care* if he was tired!

Oh, drat, she couldn't even keep her head on straight where this man was concerned, and it drove her wild, it purely did! "You're welcome."

"Go ahead, I'll take care of the lamp."

Without waiting for a second invitation, she fled. She should have made a fresh pot of coffee, then while he was drinking it, she could have raced upstairs and gathered her things and been down before he knew what she was doing.

"Where is Hetty? Gone to bed already?"

He'd come up behind her before she even got to the other end of the passageway. No man that large had any right to move as silently as he did. Another mark against him. "She goes to bed right after supper lately."

"I'll just look in on her in case she's still awake." He turned toward the room where Hetty had always slept, and Kathleen had no choice but to tell him the truth. "She's in the front room. My bedchamber. Hers is—that is, Rags..."

"Rags?"

"You know, the cat. The one Marthenia's dog chased up a tree. I just told you about it, for heaven's sake!"

"She's a bitch, you know."

Kathleen spun around, her jaw hanging. "I *beg* your pardon."

"A female canine, Kathleen. What did you think I meant?"

"Oh, well...of course I knew that." Rattled, she turned too quickly to escape those wicked eyes of his and bumped her knee on the door.

"Did you?" His skeptical tone rattled her all the more. Damn, damn and double damn! She'd never had one whit of control over her own life, but at least she'd never before felt like a puppet. All he had to do was twitch her strings, and she danced to whatever tune he whistled.

"If you'll give me a minute, I'll get your bed ready."

"Don't go to any special trouble on my account. I don't mind sharing."

"Well, I do!"

"What were you saying about Rags?"

"You mean the cat?" she asked inanely. *Well, of course he means the cat, you ninny!* "She—that is, he—he committed an indiscretion in the middle of Hetty's bed, and I had to scrub the feather tick and air it out. It—it's not dry yet."

Rogan began to chuckle. And then he stood there in the middle of the sitting room, feet spread wide apart, hands braced on his lean hips, laughing as though cat poop in the middle of someone's bed were the funniest thing in the world.

"Oh!" Spinning on her heel, Kathleen strode across the room, skirts swishing around her ankles. Not until she reached the stairwell did she realize that he was one step behind her.

"Your room's not ready yet."

"I'll take my chances," he said, still grinning. Then he sobered, as if some unpleasant thought had occurred to him. "Or maybe you need time to clear away the evidence."

Evidence? Did he mean her comb and brush, her gown and her few toiletries? "Why don't you go wash while I collect my things?"

"I washed aboard ship, thank you." She had backed up onto the bottom step, and now he crowded her up the next one.

"The door! Did you think to latch it?" He was making her exceedingly nervous, practically breathing down her neck that way. And when she was nervous, she was apt to do something foolish. Like babble a mile a minute. Or hurl herself into his arms.

Oh, yes, that would be just wonderful, wouldn't it? First she'd bore him to death with every tedious detail of her uneventful life, and before she was done, she'd have made an utter ass of herself by blurting out how much she—

Not that she did. Love him, that was. Not really. You couldn't love a man and fight with him over practically everything and nothing at all.

She backed up three more steps, with Rogan pacing her step for step. She was breathing as though she'd raced up them backward and forward. The more he looked at her, the more nervous she grew. There was something in the way his eyes glittered over her, lingering on first her mouth, then her breast, that made her exceedingly uneasy.

"Rogan, I'm warning you—"

"Are you, darling?"

Darling? The endearment lodged in her heart and sent it soaring. Surely that meant something. Unlike Callum, Rogan had never been free with careless endearments.

She felt for another step, and when there was none, she floundered and would have fallen had not Rogan reached out and caught her arm. "Don't fall."

Too late. She had already fallen, if he only knew. Shaking off his hand, she stepped back, eyeing him nervously.

Rogan watched her through slitted eyes, enjoying her growing uneasiness. The prickly little thing. He'd see how starchy she was when he finished with her. "Were you sleeping in my bed, or did you make yourself a pallet?"

"I—that is, I—"

"Never mind, Primrose, I don't mind sharing." It occurred to him then that unless he meant to take her by force, something he'd considered more than once on the long voyage home, he'd best begin to soften her up.

She was shivering visibly, her arms wrapped over her bosom. The loft was cool, but not cold, as the heat from the fireplace downstairs seeped up the stairwell.

A pulse was beating frantically just under her right ear, and he reached out and laid a finger over it. Her eyes widened. Her lips parted, and she stared at him as if she'd never been touched by a man before. Maybe Callum wasn't quite as effective a lover as he'd always claimed to be. Maybe the Kingsley fellow—

But he wasn't going to think about them. They weren't here; he was. And before he left her, his wife was going to know which one of them she belonged to!

The lamplight cast beguiling shadows on her face, deepening the clear wells of her eyes, gleaming on the moisture that appeared on her lips when her tongue darted out to wet them. Feeling his control begin to slip, Rogan forced himself to look around the familiar room. Not even to himself would he admit what he was searching for. Hoping against all that was holy he wouldn't find.

Under the sloping eaves, his bed looked broad, high and inviting. There was a small glass of Joe Bell flowers on the bedside table, and it affected him strangely.

He looked from the flowers to his wife, who seemed frozen in place. "Pretty," he growled, meaning the flowers. Meaning both. Meaning he was so damned confused he didn't know what he meant!

As if freed by the sound of his voice, Kathleen began to gather up her belongings, her comb and brush, a pair of tan kidskin boots that were worn nearly through at the toe. She reached for the white muslin night rail that had been spread across his pillow, only to have Rogan sweep it out of her reach.

"Give me that! I told you if you'd just wait a minute, I'd clear out my things!"

"You won't be needing this."

"Rogan, it's late and I'm in no mood to play childish games."

Shifting his position so that he was between her and freedom, he continued. "But then, the games I have in mind aren't the least bit childish, darling. I think you know that."

Her braid had come loose halfway up, and he reached behind her and quickly unplaited the rest of it, allowing her hair to play over his fingers. She protested, but he only smiled. Forking his fingers through her hair, he held her head and leaned closer, so close he could feel her erratic breath warming his face. "The day you can tame all this wild silk," he whispered, "will be the day the rivers run uphill, little Primrose."

She tried to jerk her head away, but he held on to her hair. Even her defiance aroused him, and God knows he'd been aroused enough just thinking about what he was going to do to her. Whatever she was, whatever she'd been in the past, he told himself, she was his now. And he was damned well going to make sure she knew it! After this night's work, she wouldn't be feeling quite so fancy-free.

"Quit trying to run away from me, Kathleen."

Even in the dim light of the single lamp, gray eyes blazed into black. "I beg your—"

"Don't," he warned softly. "Beg my pardon one more time, and I'm apt to turn you over my knee and give you a lesson in manners the way I learned them."

"I think you've quite lost your mind."

He shook his head, teeth gleaming whitely in the dark shadows of his face. "No, ma'am, I've only just found it. This is something I should've done much sooner, but instead, I listened to Josiah. He said you needed time." He'd said a lot of other things, too, but Rogan was no longer certain the old man knew what he was talking about. "Well, I'm done listening. We're wed now, woman, and there's no undoing that. I've waited long enough to claim what's rightfully mine."

We're wed...rightfully mine... The words echoed in Kathleen's head as if they'd been hollered into an empty cistern. Once when she'd been about ten there had been a long, dry spell. All the cisterns around Pelletier's Mills had run dry. She had lifted the wooden lid and leaned down into the dank cavern and shouted, "I am too, pretty!" A chorus of *too pretty, too pretty, too pretty* had reverberated for long moments afterward. For nearly half a day she'd believed it, until she had made the mistake of boasting to her grandmother.

Now, standing rigidly before her husband in the chilly sleeping loft, surrounded by the scent of raw wood paneling, lamp oil and something far more subtle, something infinitely exciting, Kathleen shook her head. She knew better than most that dreams were only for dreaming, never for believing in. "Rogan," she whispered, "I don't think you really want to do this."

"Don't I?"

It never occurred to her to pretend she didn't know what he had in mind. She'd seen that same gleam in Morton's eyes more times than she could count. The difference was that with Morton, even though he had never managed to carry out his implied threats, she had felt soiled. Soiled and frightened, and slightly nauseated.

With Rogan she felt…something altogether different.

"Don't I, Primrose?" he repeated. Then, with all the gentleness in the world, he reached out and removed the comb and brush from her cold fingers. He lifted her shoes from the other hand and set them on the floor beside the bed.

Her eyes were enormous, and in spite of himself, Rogan felt a reluctant tenderness well up inside him. It was quickly overtaken by another, more powerful feeling. Without another word he lifted his hands to her face, shaping it between his two palms, touching the fluttering pulse at her temples, her high, rounded cheekbones, the hollows beneath them. His thumbs playing along the delicate ridge of her jaw, he murmured, "Don't I, love? I'm just now beginning to realize how much I do want it."

The sound of her breathing was loud in the silence—or was it Rogan's? Knowing that if he once made love to her the way she'd dreamed of his doing, she would be lost forever, Kathleen tried to hold back, but it was no use. He was stronger physically. His will was stronger. And how could she fight against something she wanted so desperately?

"Come here, Primrose," Rogan commanded softly.

Wasn't she already as close as she could possible be? Her toes were caught between his two booted feet, her face held in his hot, hard hands, everything in between in astonishingly close alignment.

Love me. Only love me, Rogan, for that's all in the world I'll ever want. "Rogan," she managed to gasp, when his hands moved from her face to her shoulders. One slid over her back and down to her waist, pressing her so tightly against his hard chest that she could feel her breasts swelling in response.

The other hand moved up the side of her throat, over the high buckram-lined collar of her gown, until his fingers spread around her jaw, tipping her face to meet his.

The moment before his mouth closed over hers she heard hundreds of soft, sweet explosions, like flurries of soap bubbles going off in her head. How strange... She could even feel them, and they were not in her head at all, but in the most intimate parts of her body!

His lips caressed, lifting, brushing, dragging gently against the moisture of her own so that she found it impossible to keep them properly closed. She tried, though. Desperately, she clamped her lips together, frightened by the reckless urge she felt to open her mouth and discover the taste of him—of his skin, of his lips, of his tongue...

"Open for me, Primrose," Rogan whispered against her mouth, causing the most delicious sensations to race down her spine. He lifted his head and stared down at her, his narrowed eyes glowing in the flickering lamplight. Then slowly, deliberately, he lowered his head again. Her eyelids fluttered. Her mouth softened, ready, willing—nay, *eager* for his kiss.

Only he didn't kiss her. Instead, with just the tip of his tongue, he traced the line between her lips, then stepped back.

She would have fallen had she not clutched the bedstead. If she'd dared to hope her limbs would support her, she might have fled, she told herself, knowing the lie for what it was. Whatever came next, tonight or a hundred years from now, she could no more run away from this man than she could leap the ocean.

"Wh-why did you do that?" she asked finally, when it seemed as if he would go on staring at her forever.

"Do what?"

"You know. That. Lick me." She wanted to look away from him, but her eyes, no more than any other part of her body, seemed inclined to do her bidding.

"Maybe I wondered if you tasted of vinegar or sugar." He seemed strangely watchful. Did he suspect her secret? "Or maybe I was just serving you fair warning."

"W-warning?" She clutched the tall walnut headboard until her fingers threatened to cramp. Releasing it suddenly, she clasped her hands, found them to be damp and unconsciously wiped them down her skirt.

Rogan's gaze followed the movement of her hands as they smoothed the soft faded material over her slender hips. She had left her apron in the kitchen, he noticed, but she was still wrapped in too many layers. Her gown covered her from her chin to the tops of her shoes, and all the way down to her wrists. God knows what she had on underneath all that. He intended to find out, though. Starting now.

"Take off your clothes, Kathleen." Her mouth fell open, and he fought against the temptation to take advantage of it.

"My—take off my—Rogan, *what* warning? I demand to know what your intentions are!"

Eyebrows dark as a crow's wings lifted quizzically. "You demand? Woman, this may come as a surprise to you, but you're in no position to be demanding anything. Now take off your gown, or I'll do it for you, and I warn you, there's a limit to my patience."

Her eyes never leaving his, Kathleen lifted a hand and felt for the covered buttons at the back of her neck. "Patience!'' she muttered, ''I've yet to see a sign that you even know the meaning of the word.'' Oh, why did he have to go and spoil it? For just a moment, she'd almost dared to dream!

''Stop nattering and get on with it.'' He had begun to unbutton his shirt, and Kathleen found her hands were trembling almost too much to find the buttons, much less to twist the pesky little things through their respective loops. Just as Rogan finished tugging his shirt free of his trousers, she gave a cry of frustration, spun around and headed for the stairs.

He caught her before she'd gone more than three steps. ''Oh, no, you don't, woman. I came home to bed my wife, and bed her I will!''

She refused to turn and face him. ''Why?'' came the muffled plea.

Tell me you love me. Tell me, damn your eyes, tell me!

Not even to himself did Rogan want to admit that she sounded tired and baffled and trapped and truly mystified. He found, somewhat to his dismay, that he hadn't the heart to tell her the real reason it suddenly seemed so important to stake his claim to what was legally his property.

''Why? Why do you suppose, Primrose? Maybe it's because I've spent too much time wondering what your hair would look like unbound, what it would feel like sweeping across my naked body.'' He thought he heard her gasp, but she still refused to face him. ''Or maybe it was because once I had a taste of your lips, I found I was hungry for more. Maybe because I knew even that wouldn't be enough. I want to know what you look like when your eyes are dark with passion, when your cheeks are flushed with it. I want to know what it feels like to have your long legs wrapped around my—''

''Rogan!''

''Naked body.''

"You mustn't talk that way! It's not—it isn't seemly."

"You're my wife," he reminded her, drawing her imperceptibly closer. "I'm your husband. It's seemly. It's what marriage is created for."

"But not ours!"

"Yes, ours, my little prickly pear," he whispered against her neck, and he swung her into his arms and turned toward the bed. "A man might tell himself he's marrying because he needs a housekeeper, or a mother for his motherless children, or a nurse for an aging relative, but deep inside, he knows what he's doing. He knows all along."

Which was about as fancy a way of saying absolutely nothing as ever a man had invented, Rogan congratulated himself. Have her he would, but be damned if he was going to put himself in the position of being owned, by her or any other woman. A man would have to be crazy to let himself get caught in that kind of trap.

Unwilling to open her eyes, Kathleen felt herself lowered onto the bed. Her mind was in a whirl, her body quivering from the feel of his powerful arms around her. The clean, masculine scent of his body owed everything to who and what he was, and nothing at all to artifice, and she found it incredibly intoxicating.

"Now finish taking off your gown, sweetheart."

"My—I forgot to bring my buttonhook upstairs."

In the process of tugging off his boots, Rogan turned to smile at her. "All right, turn around. I don't mind playing lady's maid, not when there's such a sweet reward in store for me."

The thought of how many times in the past he must have done just that was surprisingly painful. For all she knew, he might have said those very words to a hundred other women. Beautiful women. Women who knew exactly how to please a man so that he would come back again and again.

Turning her away from him, Rogan made short work of the row of small buttons down her back, his deftness only increasing her suspicions. As for the suspicions themselves, they made her sad rather than angry. She would have given anything she possessed at that moment to be so lovely, so skilled, that he would never again look at another woman. If only she'd listened when Alice and her friends had whispered and giggled over those wicked books Patrice had lent them. If only she'd bothered to read a few...

If only she were beautiful.

"Rogan, I'm afraid I'm not—"

"Shh." He placed a finger over her lips. Drawing her gown and the straps of her chemise over her shoulders, he placed a kiss on the soft swell of her breasts. His lips still pressed to her skin, he murmured, "Tonight is all that matters, and that belongs to me."

She'd wanted this, she reminded herself. She'd dreamed for ages that someday he would come to love her, only now that he had, now that it was going to happen, she wasn't too sure she was ready. Was it possible to want something so desperately and be afraid of it at the same time?

"Ah, God, you're so—" Rogan began, then broke off to remove her stockings, rolling them slowly down her calf with the palm of his hands and then circling her ankle with his thumb and forefinger. "I never imagined..."

You never imagined what? Kathleen wanted more than anything to know, but was afraid to ask.

Hurriedly pulling the quilt over her breasts, she begged him to blow out the lamp, but he refused. "Let me look. You'll never know how many times I've pictured you this way, my little rose."

She had pictured him, too, only she would have died rather than admit it. All the same, there was no way on earth she could have prevented herself from watching as he

removed all his clothing. First the shirt, then the belt and
boots, then the trousers. Finally he stood before her in a
suit of underwear that did little to disguise the startling
differences between their bodies. And then that, too, was
disposed of, and before she could gather her wits enough
to look away, he was standing there naked, just as bold as
you please.

Dear heavens, the man was—

Were *all* men made that way? How on earth did they
ever get their trousers on?

"Oh, my mercy," she whispered, burying her face in the
bolster.

A moment later she heard him laugh softly, but even in
her state of shock it seemed that he'd sounded a bit per-
plexed. Almost as if he'd been surprised that *she* was surprised.

Determined not to let him know how fearful she was,
Kathleen forced herself not to jump out of bed and flee
when he lifted the quilt and climbed in beside her. More
than once she'd heard her grandmother say that little Kathleen might be plain, but she had the Stevens backbone, and
when it came to enduring a woman's lot in life, a backbone
was better than a dozen pretty faces.

Rogan spoke her name, and the Stevens backbone stiffened even more. He came up on his forearms and leaned
over her, and she squinched her eyes up tight, hoping he
might think she was asleep.

"Rogan, I've changed my mind. I believe I'd rather sleep
downstairs on the sofa, if it's all the same to you." Her
voice sounded as thin as penny-a-yard muslin.

But then, just as if she'd never spoken, he began to kiss
her. He placed burning, moist little kisses on her lips, her
eyes, the sensitive place under her jaw, then her lips again.
"Oh, my," she whimpered helplessly.

He lifted his head, angled it another way, and said, "Now open your mouth for me, darling."

And she did. In the softness of the big old sleigh bed under the sloping eaves, they spoke little more. No words were needed by the time Rogan began to remove the last of her clothes. As he untied her petticoat and eased it off, then unbuttoned the waist of her white muslin drawers and drew them over her hips, she began to tremble. Then he leaned over and buried his face in her belly, and she thought she was going to burst into flames.

Frantic with the most urgent need, she followed him willingly as he led her down pathways she had never dreamed of, taught her things about her own body she'd never learned in all her eighteen years.

And things about his that made her feel wicked and wanton and wonderfully desirable.

"Rogan, what are you..."

"Shh, be patient, darling. I know, I know, I've waited long enough, but half the pleasure's in the waiting." He stroked her breasts, suckled them until she was thrashing wildly, then paid equal homage to every inch of her throbbing body.

She pleaded with him to make it stop, make it go away, to end this awful hunger that was driving her frantic, but he only smiled, his face strangely alien in the half light, all sharp angles and high color and glittering, feverish eyes.

Finally, when she was on the verge of unconsciousness, he spread her thighs and knelt between them. When she tried to speak, tried to tell him how she felt, the words got all twisted up, and she could only sob, "Please—please."

He kissed her then, a fierce kind of kiss that only added fuel to the flames that were consuming her. "Never forget that you belong to me," he whispered harshly as he lowered his body onto hers.

She grasped his shoulders, wanting to urge him on, wanting to assuage this awful, aching hunger inside her, but he was sweating, and her hands slipped off his shoulders. She felt something hard begin to probe her most private place. Instinctively, she tried to buck him off, suddenly terrified of what was happening to her.

With a rough oath, Rogan slid his hands beneath her hips, holding her in place, and drove himself inside her. She heard him groan softly, swear, then he lowered his head to her shoulders.

Kathleen was beyond seeing, beyond even wondering why he should have done this awful thing to her. He had hurt her! In the most intimate place possible, in the most intimate way imaginable, he had hurt her badly.

"Oh, no—God, I *knew*," he whispered roughly. He was lying atop her, the full weight of his body pressing her down. Sobbing, she shoved at him with both hands, but he was slippery and her hands slid off. She cursed, bewildered, hurt and frightened, and he eased his weight onto his arms so that she could at least breathe.

But she couldn't escape. She was still impaled on that— that *thing!* It had been the thing that had hurt her.

Perhaps he'd broken it. She hoped he had! It would serve him right!

"Love, I...can't...stop," he groaned, and before she could free herself, he began to move inside her. Horrified, she waited for the pain to come again...but it didn't. Discomfort, but no real pain. What was she supposed to do now? How long was this business supposed to last? Until he grew tired?

Eyes shut, his face the mask of a stranger, Rogan moved over her, driving into her harder, deeper, faster, until something warm and wild began to uncoil in the pit of her belly.

"Please, Rogan—stop!" she sobbed. "I don't want to do this any more!"

But he pounded on, then suddenly he shuddered and

gasped, collapsing on top of her for a second time. For a single moment he lay there, his skin burning hers, then he reared up and stared down at her, a grimace of something akin to pain on his face.

She thought he muttered an apology, but before she could sort out the words, he had rolled over onto his side, taking her with him. Naked, trembling from a mixture of shock and fear, she allowed him to hold her because she honestly didn't know what else to do. Was this it, then? Was this to be her duty? A wife's role in her husband's life?

"Kathleen? Are you asleep?"

She shook her head, unable to speak. His hand was stroking her back, his fingers tangling in her hair.

"I can't tell you how sorry I am. I shouldn't have hurt you—I knew better, but—" And then, breaking off, he swore again.

She ached in ways that she had never ached before, but finally she slept, unaware that he lay until the hour before dawn, staring into the darkness, calling himself every kind of a name for having ever doubted her. For having hurt her. For being a stupid, inarticulate, blundering fool!

He would start all over again, win her trust, and in time, perhaps she could forgive him for ever doubting her. God knows, he would never be able to forgive himself.

When Kathleen opened her eyes the next morning, Rogan was standing over her. Dressed in his usual black trousers and jersey, he might have been a stranger for all the warmth that showed in his face.

She eyed him warily, clutching the covers under her chin. He was wearing his cap, which must mean he was leaving her again. Was this to be her fate, then? From time to time he would come home and...do that thing to her, then go off and leave her here alone? For a little while before she'd fallen asleep, she'd dared to hope that maybe he was coming to love her. Surely he must like her a little bit, at least. That was a beginning. In time, perhaps...

Seeing her there, Rogan would have given all he possessed to go back to yesterday and wipe out what had happened. But he couldn't. There was no way to turn back the clock, to undo what he had done. All he could hope to do was to make it up to her.

He had woken in the middle of the night and stared at the ceiling, wondering how he could have been such a fool. How could he have ignored the words of a man he had known and trusted all his life? How could he have allowed a woman of questionable integrity and even more questionable morals to poison his mind against his own wife?

Looking now at those clear gray eyes, he felt like the lowest form of life. Because he *had* known. Deep down, he had known all along that she was good, that she was innocent, that she was none of the things Patrice implied, but in his rutting arrogance he'd destroyed all that. He'd listened to others when he should have listened only to his own heart, and now it was too late to undo what he had done.

And God help him, he knew that in one way he didn't want to undo it. It had been an experience unlike anything he had ever known before. Deeper, richer, more profound than a mere mating of two bodies. How could he make her understand that, when he didn't understand it himself?

He didn't know how to begin. He only knew that if it took the rest of his life, he would make it up to her. Now, seeing the fear in her eyes, he warned himself to go slowly. The first step was to win her trust. If that took a lifetime, so be it. It was the only way he knew to begin.

Clutching the brim of his hat in his sweating hand, he said sternly, "Kathleen, I'd like you to know that you have my respect." Oh, hell, that had sounded cold, uncaring, and that was the last thing he felt! But he could hardly blurt out his true feelings, not without frightening her even more. He cleared his throat. "I—uh, I give you my word that you have nothing to fear from me, ever again." And when no response was forthcoming, he panicked. "Dammit, you're my wife! I wasn't sure—that is to say, I know you were surprised. Uh…hurt, that is. Oh, the devil! Leastways, you know your proper place now," he said grimly, and turned away.

Beyond words, Kathleen continued to stare at him. Not until he'd let himself quietly out the front door did she remember the shirt she had spent so many hours carefully stitching for him. Not that if mattered now. Not that anything could ever matter now.

Chapter Fifteen

Kathleen *knew* her proper place. If she'd begun to hope that that place might turn into something considerably more rewarding than she'd expected, she'd had her hopes shattered beyond all redemption. Rogan had married her so she would look after Hetty. Evidently, somewhere along the way he'd remembered that wives had other duties, and sought to remind her of hers.

Well, she'd been reminded. Regardless of what he'd promised her in the beginning, regardless of how Josiah had told her it would be, she had been foolish enough to dream. And in dreaming, she'd let herself fall victim to the world's oldest trap.

Oh, she was in love, all right, there was no denying that. But she wasn't in *like*. Truly, she detested the man! What's more, if she kept on reminding herself how much she detested him, sooner or later she would come to believe it.

Although to be quite fair, aside from all that business about honoring and cleaving, which had meant nothing to either of them, she'd have to admit that Rogan had kept his bargain to the letter. She had a home, and a fine one, at that. She had someone who needed her, who depended on her, and that was important. So unless he changed his mind and asked her to leave, she had the security every woman needed in this world, as well as the assurance that he would never bother her again.

Standing at the back door, she scraped the leftover eggs into Rags's bowl and lingered to stare blindly out at the rain. She had everything a woman could ask for, didn't she? She told herself it was enough, but in spite of everything that had happened, in spite of the way he'd led her on and then hurt her, later tossing her the cold coin of his "respect" as if in payment, she was shamed to admit that she still wanted more.

Well, she thought, closing the door against the bleak winter day, she'd get over it. One did, no matter how many times it seemed the world had fallen apart. She was a sensible woman, not some silly child. The Stevens backbone had withstood worse than this and never let her down.

As if sensing Kathleen's distraction, Hetty began to act up, demanding constant attention. It was a blessing in a way, for at least it took Kathleen's mind off her own troubles.

The first episode could have been an accident. Anyone could drop a basket of eggs on the floor, then spill coffee on top of the mess. Hetty's poor knotted fingers weren't as agile as they could have been, after all.

But as time passed and certain things disappeared and still others were broken, Kathleen began to wonder. Matters came to a head late one afternoon when she noticed that one of Hetty's favorite hens seemed to be afflicted with mites. Closer examination sent her hurrying to the shed to fetch a tin of coal oil and an old discarded dish towel, which she tore into strips just outside the henhouse door.

Selecting a long strip with which to bind the poor creature's swollen leg, she saturated it with oil. Then, leaving the tin and the rest of the rags outside, she ducked inside the henhouse, wishing she'd noticed it earlier in the day. It got dark so early this time of year, there was scarce time enough to do all that needed doing.

Taking only a moment for her eyes to adjust, she picked her way to the far corner, wishing she'd thought to bring a lantern, although oily rags and lighted lanterns were not the wisest combination. She'd just have to hurry, that was all.

The roost was at the far end from the door, and Kathleen didn't relish dealing with the ill-tempered dominique. Carefully, she picked her way over the rough plank floor, wrinkling her nose at the rank odor. She made a mental note to add raking out the henhouse to her long list of chores. Lately, Hetty seemed to forget more often than she remembered.

By the time she'd captured the poor creature and poulticed her affliction, both Kathleen and the hen were thoroughly out of sorts. Kathleen was also filthy and bleeding where the stupid old bird had fought her.

Then, in the midst of the ruckus, with feathers flying and chickens squawking and flopping about on the roost, what little light that came through the door was suddenly shut off.

"Oh, drat! Of all times for the door to blow shut. Hush up, you silly birds, or I'm going to wring every neck in the henhouse!" Carefully holding her skirts up with one hand, she felt her way past the nest boxes, praying her feet wouldn't slip out from under her. "Smelly, brainless, silly—ouch!"

Now she'd caught a splinter! Beginning to feel extremely martyred, she paused to get her bearings, and it was then that she smelled the smoke.

Smoke? She sniffed again to be sure, but even in the fetid atmosphere of the henhouse, there was no mistaking that odor. Oh, my mercy, hadn't she warned Hetty not to add any wood to the fire? The poor old thing seemed to think biscuits wouldn't brown unless the whole stove was cherry red. It was a wonder she hadn't long since melted the stovepipe!

Cautiously, Kathleen hurried as fast as she dared toward the door, her nose twitching at the acrid mixture of chicken offal and smoke. It smelled almost like...

Burning rags? Coal oil?

Dear Lord, it was! And what's more, it seemed to be seeping up through the floor, which was a good five feet off the ground to keep from being flooded every time the tide came up in the Green Pond.

But surely there was nothing under there to burn. The chickens had long since scratched up the last stalk of dried grass. And even if a spark from the chimney happened to blow all the way from the house and catch fire, it would smell of feathers and manure, not old rags and coal oil.

Relief poured over her as she reached the door, its shape illuminated by a rim of light from the late afternoon sky. Coughing and trying not to breathe, she pushed.

And pushed again. "Drat! *Dammit!*" The thing was stuck! The bar must have tumbled into the slot when it had blown shut.

While the smell of smoke grew stronger until her eyes were burning and her throat was raw from coughing, Kathleen alternately rattled and pounded on the door, calling out for Hetty—for Amos—for anyone to let her out.

It was Marthenia Willis's old yellow dog she had to thank for her release in the end. The hound set to barking until Amos heard her all the way over at his house, and came to investigate.

"Lord love ye, young'un, how'd ye come to be in such a fix?"

It was several minutes before she could answer him. Busy filling her lungs with good air and scraping off her shoes as best she could with a stick, she merely shook her head. "I haven't the least idea," she said finally. By the time Hetty had come to join them, Amos had gone under the henhouse, where a few rags and twigs still smoldered, and dumped a pail of sand over the coals.

He grunted as he rejoined the two women. Hetty stood by silently, looking from one to the other. "Downright peculiar, if ye ask me," he grumbled, dusting off his hands.

"I left a tin of oil and some rags outside while I went in to poultice one of the hens. I reckon the wind that blew the door shut blew the rags under the henhouse, and they just sort of—" she shrugged, looking from Hetty to Amos "—caught up," she finished, when no help was forthcoming from either quarter. "I probably leaked some oil on them, I don't remember. I've heard of oily rags just bursting into flames like that, haven't you?"

"Not out in the open, I've not," said Amos.

Hetty spoke up then. "Smoke'll get rid of mites quicker'n anything. I'da told you if you'd asked me. Some folks don't ask a body nothing, they just move in and take over and next thing you know, the old folks is out in the cold."

At that blunt pronouncement, both Amos and Kathleen turned to stare. It was nearly dark, for it was early December, and quite cold, even with the wind out of the southeast. "Old woman, you got a short memory and a wicked tongue," Amos declared.

Hetty cackled, and the sound brought chill bumps to Kathleen's already chilled body. "Just you wait, Amos McNair, just you wait! One o' these days that boy o' yourn'll bring home one o' his fancy pieces, and then we'll see who's got a wicked tongue!"

Over the next few days, Kathleen and Hetty sidled around one another like two strange dogs fenced into the same yard. Gone was the comfortable rapport that had sprung up between them. More than once Kathleen heard the old woman muttering something about "fancy pieces," and she finally concluded that Hetty must have found out what happened that last time Rogan had come home. Although how that could be, she didn't know, for he'd come home after Hetty had gone to bed and left again before she'd got up.

Kathleen didn't know whether to be amused or irritated. Did a wife qualify as a fancy piece if she made love with her husband?

Not that love had been involved. Leastwise, not on Rogan's part. She'd been around that rutting old rooster of Hetty's long enough to know the difference between lust and love. He mounted his hens every chance he got. In between times, he chased them away from the trough and attacked them if they dared utter a squawk of complaint.

As December waxed, the tension between the two women seemed to fade, until Kathleen wondered if perhaps she'd imagined it. Other than taking great care not to step on Hetty's toes again, she sensibly decided to forget the whole thing. Having to tiptoe constantly around the old woman's pride took time, often stretching Kathleen's patience to the limits, but for the sake of peace, it was worth it.

Then, suddenly, Christmas was only two weeks off. Just as Kathleen had been beginning to get over missing the children so much it hurt, the Styron children from across the road came gathering red-berried yaupon for decorations, their laughing, teasing voices ringing out clearly in the cold air, and she was reminded all over again of what an empty holiday this would be, with no one of her own.

Oh, she'd made new friends, of course. And she had Hetty, who, although she was hardly a child, was remarkably childlike in some ways. In spite of everything, Kathleen had grown exceedingly fond of the old woman.

She thought about Rogan whenever she was too tired to keep up her guard. It was pointless, and she despised herself for being so weak, but she couldn't help but wonder where he was, and if he ever thought about her.

"He's probably all the way up in Baltimore," she muttered sharply as she chopped dried apples for cake. "Probably celebrating the season with a different pretty woman every night!"

Or, even worse, the same one.

Well, let him celebrate. Selfish or not, Kathleen was glad he wasn't likely to come barging in and spoil her holiday. She'd planned a nice roasted goose for Hetty and Amos and herself, with rutabagas and onions smothered in gravy. She'd made a fig pudding with nuts and currants, and every day she drizzled rum over it and wrapped it back in its muslin sack.

Let him celebrate in some big fancy city with a dozen fancy women, what did she care? He'd probably give them all a yellow bonnet, too. No doubt he bought the things from a jobber for all his fancy women friends!

She'd tried on her own bonnet at least a hundred times since he'd brought it to her, but never where anyone could see her. Sometimes she would stand for ages in front of the small mirror in her bedchamber, tilting her head this way and that and trying to see some sign that clothes made the man. Or in this case, hats made the woman.

It was no good. The same old face stared back at her, and no amount of silk flowers could ever turn it into the kind of face that Rogan could love.

One evening some five days before Christmas, Hetty came to the supper table all gussied up in her new yellow silk gown. It was the first time she'd put it on since Kathleen had fitted it on her.

Oddly touched, Kathleen felt tears threaten and forced

them back. "You look lovely, Hetty. I wish Rogan could see how fine you look."

Hetty gave her a sly look that defied interpretation. But then, Kathleen had long since given up trying to understand the old woman's moods. "Reckon this is one frock that won't get sewed under covers."

Kathleen didn't even attempt to figure that one out. "Your hair looks so pretty. I'd give anything if mine would curl that way." Hetty's hair had grown out to a respectable two inches by now, and curled around her wrinkled old face like a soft white halo.

"Shave it off. Might come back like mine did. Mine weren't always like this, y'know. Used to be brown."

Hiding her smile, Kathleen filled two plates and set them on the table. She poured coffee in two blue willowware cups and added sugar to one and the thin milk produced by George Styron's cow. Taking her seat, she bowed her head and murmured a word of thanks.

Hetty added her amen. "You bake me a cake today, girl?"

"Did I? Why, no. We still have some of that persimmon pudding left, remember? I'm planning on baking an apple cake, and there'll be fig pudding for Christmas."

"Pshaw! I told you I wanted a Lady Baltimore cake for my birthday. I always have a Lady Baltimore cake, you know that."

Kathleen felt as if she'd stepped off a fast train without waiting for it to slow down. "This is your *birthday?* Hetty, why didn't you tell me?" Oh, my mercy, she had really cooked her goose this time! Just when she thought she might have redeemed herself for being her husband's "fancy piece," she'd gone and blundered again! And this time, it was no small blunder. "Hetty, I thought your birthday was next week."

The truth was, she hadn't thought about birthdays at all,

her own having passed unheralded more than three months before. *Forgive me for lying, Lord, I'll make it up to you, but don't let her think I clean forgot. She'll be so hurt!*

Her lapse evidently tolerated, if not entirely forgiven, Kathleen set about planning a hasty birthday party, inviting Amos and all the neighbors as far north as the church. A few looked at her as if they thought she was daft, and a few outright refused. She didn't need Amos to explain that Hetty had alienated them all at one time or another. She was fast coming to realize that in accepting Rogan's bargain, she'd been handed a devilish hard task.

"All right, so that's Ed and Janie Burrus, Marthenia, Mary and Caleb Stowe, Chrissy Jane and Bunyan, and the Ballance girls from down the road, and what about the Austins, up by the church?"

"I'll stop by on my way up the road. You need anything from the store?" Amos asked.

"Mr. A.J. had everything I needed for Hetty's cake. I just wish she'd asked for an apple cake instead of a Lady Baltimore."

"Last time it was a coconut cake. She sprung it on Marthenia on Ash Wednesday, and it a-blowing up a gale. Had 'er a birthday party, though. Hetty's right partial to birthday parties. Some years, she has two or three. Some years, she clean forgets."

"But isn't this her birthday? I thought…she said—"

"Doubt if she even remembers any more. A body don't need a party to know the years is piling up. Hetty, she just has herself a birthday whenever the spell comes on her."

So Kathleen had sent invitations by word of mouth and polished up the house, which was already decorated with cedar and yaupon for Christmas. Hetty had her birthday party, and wore her yellow gown. As delighted as a child, she pounced on her gifts, several of which Kathleen recognized as having come from Rogan's house in the first place. A silver spoon that matched the rest of his mother's silver and a footed green sugar bowl she could have sworn she remembered seeing the first week she'd come to live there.

All pronounced the birthday cake a huge success, which helped make up for the fact that Kathleen had spent the entire day working on it. She'd spent the last of Rogan's money on three yards of bright red calico, after visiting all three stores. But it was Amos who brought the best surprise of all to the party. Callum had come home for the holidays, arriving on the packet only hours before.

The two McNairs lingered after the other guests had gone home, and while Kathleen washed the dishes and Hetty dozed in her chair, all her gifts piled in her lap, Callum told Kathleen and his father where he'd been and what he'd been doing since last he'd seen them.

A highly expurgated version, Kathleen suspected. What an endearing scamp he was! And how strange that she, who had never before had a single beau, should end up with the two handsomest men in creation, one for a husband and one for a best friend.

"Callum, that's got to be illegal," she exclaimed in response to a tale involving a Georgia gold mine, a Louisiana senator and a floating bawdy house.

"Why, no, dear heart—leastwise, not every single count in every state in the Union, which is one of the great advantages of owning one's own ship, even if she is only a stern-wheeler plowing up the mud in the Mississippi River. We can't all be blue-water captains like your worthy husband. Which reminds me, love, when's he due in?"

Kathleen rinsed the last teacup and reached for the drying towel. It would never have occurred to her to ask a man's help, any more than it would have occurred to one of them to offer. "He's not," she said flatly as she commenced to dry the mountainous heap of clean dishes.

"Oh, he'll be here. The Rogue never misses a Christmas home, not since his pa died."

In other words he wouldn't dream of leaving Hetty here alone over the holidays, Kathleen thought as she dried and stacked, dried and stacked. But then, Hetty was no longer alone. Wasn't that why he'd taken himself a wife?

"Kathy?" Callum spoke softly, as both elders were dozing in their chairs. "Cat got your tongue?"

"Did you ask me a question?"

"I asked when you were expecting Rogan in."

"And I said I'm not. Do you want more coffee?"

"No, I don't want more coffee. What's the matter, love, does your belly hurt? Are you having your monthlies?"

She gawked at him, horrified. "Callum! How dare you!"

He chuckled. "I heard you were prissy. I didn't believe it. First time I saw you, you had your skirts up around your knees, and I said to myself, any woman with legs like that has got to be wild and beautiful. Turned out I was right."

Kathleen was beyond blushing. She'd quickly learned that with Callum, neither anger nor indignation made a dent. He was simply one of those charming rascals who said precisely what he felt like saying, and the devil take the ashes. More often than not, he got away with it.

The last time he'd been there, she'd found herself telling him things she'd never told another living soul, things she'd never even told her own sister.

But then, Callum was a better listener than Alice had ever been.

"You're not worried about him, are you? If he'd run into trouble, you'd have heard. There's ships passing here every day, and not a one of 'em but what wouldn't get word to a man's family in case of trouble."

"I'm not worried," she said, her jaw clenched as she scrubbed at the pattern in the bottom of a teacup with the towel. "If you want to know the truth, I haven't given the man a thought since the last time I laid eyes on him."

Leaning back in his chair, Callum grinned lazily. "Yes'm."

"You don't believe me?"

Thumbs hooked in the armholes of his satin brocade vest, Callum chuckled outright. "Yes'm, I guess you're right. I don't believe you."

Kathleen sputtered and broke into laughter. "All right, so I might've thought about him once or twice. After all, I'm living under his roof, beholden to him for everything I own."

"Everything but your pride," Callum said softly, causing the smile on Kathleen's face to evaporate.

Eyes wide and hauntingly sad, she stared at him. "Can you see right into a body's head? I keep telling myself that I still have my pride, but I don't know. Lately, I'm not even sure I can count on that any more."

"Does he know how you feel?"

Looking away, Kathleen hunched her shoulders. "Mercy, I hope not!"

"That's pride talking. Try honesty, you'll get quicker results."

"All right, I love him. There. I've said it. Now do I get to live happily ever after?"

"Say it to him, not to me, love."

Kathleen sighed. Funny how little an endearment from Callum meant to her, and how much one meant coming from Rogan.

From the chair closest to the stove came a long, broken snore. Amos had had a tot more than his share of rum tonight, but he'd seemed to enjoy it. Hetty shifted in her chair, mumbling something in her sleep, and Callum moved quickly in time to rescue the pile of treasures before it slid off her lap.

"We'd better get these two to bed. Want me to help you with the birthday girl?"

Kathleen bent over and kissed the halo of white curls. "No, I can manage. Settle Amos on the sofa with a quilt and a pillow, if you'd like."

"Thanks, but he'll be better off in his own bed. I can sleepwalk him home. Won't be the first time I've done it for him, nor him for me." He looked as if he wanted to say more, but all he said was, "I'll see you tomorrow."

As Christmas day drew near, Kathleen tried not to let herself hope, but she couldn't help glancing out the window a dozen times a day, or standing on the front porch, wrapped in the black woolen shawl Rogan had given her and looking down along the winding road that led to the wharves. If he came, it would be along that road. From the fork up by Homer Styron's, along the shoreside to the turn-off, past Mr. A.J.'s store, past Smith's house, past George Styron's...

Of course, he wouldn't come. She knew that.

And even if he did, it would be only for Hetty's sake. He wouldn't want to disappoint Hetty. But of course, he wouldn't come.

Callum took upon himself the task of cheering her up, although Kathleen could have sworn she'd managed to hide her despondency. It wasn't just a matter of missing Beaufort, missing Alice and the twins and Caleb and baby Margaret. Her parents had died three weeks before Christmas. Her grandmother had died two days after. December held sad memories for her. Rogan had nothing to do with her dragging spirits.

She played poker, practiced her cheating and still lost. She laughed, but the shadows still lingered in her eyes. It took Amos's wretched fiddling and Callum's attempts to teach her to waltz to make her laugh until the tears ran down her cheeks.

Earlier, they had dined on boiled drumfish with potatoes and cracklings and onions, which all pronounced the best they'd ever tasted. Leaving the dishes on the table, Callum had lured them into the sitting room and rolled up the rugs.

"Tune up first, Paw." And then in an undertone to Kathleen, "Not that you can tell much difference."

They waited until Amos got warmed up, and while Hetty sat in her rocker, clapping her hands and tapping her feet, Callum led Kathleen into a courtly waltz to the unlikely strains of "Turkey in the Straw." Before they'd circled the room the second time, she was laughing helplessly, completely oblivious to the longing in Callum's eyes as they moved over her flushed face.

"I warned you," she gasped, leaning her head against his chest so that she could watch her feet. "The only dancing I've ever done is walking the floor and jiggling Alice's babies when they had the colic."

"I hope you appreciate the difference," Callum said with a wicked grin, no hint of anything other than amusement on his handsome face.

"You don't see a napkin tossed over my shoulder, do you?"

He looked properly horrified, and then, laughing, caught her to him and spun her around until her feet left the floor. Which was just as well, as they were hopelessly tangled by that time.

As Amos sawed relentlessly on the ancient fiddle, Kathleen and Callum danced and laughed, while Hetty clapped, tapped and sipped her rum toddy. *Why can't I love him? He's all the things any woman with a grain of sense would want in a man.*

But he wasn't Rogan.

Hetty's moss rose dishes were rattling in the old pine

china cabinet, and Kathleen was ready to plead for mercy when she happened to glance across the room. Afterward she knew she must have sensed something wrong. "I do believe she's fallen asleep," she whispered, slipping out of Callum's arms to go to Hetty.

Amos lowered his bow. She thought he might have said something but by then she was truly alarmed.

"Hetty? Hetty, wake up. Callum, do something! She's not—she doesn't seem to be breathing right."

Callum knelt beside the rocking chair and removed Kathleen's hands from the old woman's shoulders. He placed two fingers on her wrist, and then at the side of her throat. Finally he lifted one of her wrinkled old eyelids. "She's not breathing at all. I'm afraid Hetty slipped away while we were dancing, Kathy. She won't be back."

Chapter Sixteen

Christmas was a day of mourning. On the following day, it took more than an hour for the church bell to toll out Hetty's due, one peal for each year of her life, or as nearly as anyone could guess. The church was more than a mile to the northeast, and what wind there was blew out of the west, yet the sound carried clearly, each lingering note a reminder.

Henrietta Beshears Rawson was laid to rest in her yellow silk gown and a rusty black lace shawl and thin gold bangle Kathleen had found among her things when she'd gone looking for an unmended pair of stockings. Kneeling beside the old pine chest in the cluttered back chamber, Kathleen had ached for the young woman Hetty once must have been, a woman who had married a mariner and come to this bleak, barren island with a black lace shawl, a gold trinket and a heart full of hope.

Or was the ache in her heart for another mariner's bride?

The women of the neighborhood had come to help with the laying out, bringing food to the house of mourning. Kathleen, dressed in her best black taffeta and the bonnet Rogan hated so much, watched as six men, all of whom she knew, if only by name, walked beside the cart that carried the plain cypress box to a nearby knoll overlooking another of the countless ponds that dotted the marsh. For the hundredth time she wondered how she could have allowed it to happen. Or how she might have prevented it.

"My, she did look fine, didn't she?" murmured Chrissy Jane Stowe. "All dressed up in that yellow silk frock like she was going to a play party."

Kathleen thought of the beautiful yellow hat Rogan had given her. She wished she'd had the nerve to wear it. She had a feeling Hetty would have appreciated it. "I still can't believe it. She's never been sick a day since I've been here."

They trudged along the rotted road, high-button shoes and flat-heeled boots alike digging into the sand as they followed the small congregation to the burial site. A bald eagle that had been hunting along the shoreside glided silently overhead, casting a fast-moving shadow over marsh and funeral party alike.

"I reckon Rogan, he'll be some broke up," said 'Lizer Styron. She'd brought over a boiled ham and taken the bed linens home with her to wash. "Have you sent for him yet?"

Her sister-in-law, Achsah, who lived across the creek, said, "Dosher set out directly the word come yesterday. Said he hears tell the *Witch* was headed down from Norfolks. If she come through the big ditch, he'll likely catch up to 'er in Elizabeth City."

Kathleen knew that the big ditch referred to the Dismal Swamp Canal, which meant he wasn't so very far away, after all.

"If the wind holds fair, they could be here by morning."

"I'd sooner wait than sail that sound after dark. Them shoals can make up in a minute, and before you know it, you're hard aground where yesterday there weren't nothing but channel."

"I declare that yellow silk looked some pretty against that green and brown quilt we lined her coffin with. Minded me of a ditch bank full o' daisies."

The soft murmur of the women's words became a background to Kathleen's thoughts as she stood silently beside the grave the men had dug late on Christmas day. This morning, water had stood some two feet deep in it, and Callum had shoveled some of the sand back in. The water would rise again. No one pretended it wouldn't, but Kathleen couldn't have stood to lay Hetty to rest in a wet grave.

Rogan, I'm so sorry. I should never have let myself get carried away, but Amos was fiddling so hard, and Hetty was laughing and clapping, too. And then I looked around, and it was too late.

A deep bass voice rumbled in the cold, clear late afternoon. There was an occasional muttered amen, and she could hear several of the women sobbing quietly beside her. As the sounds ran together in her mind, Kathleen wondered how she could ever face Rogan again. If only she'd been watching instead of frolicking around with Callum, she might have prevented it.

It wasn't as if Rogan had asked so awfully much of her. He had never demanded that she be a perfect housekeeper, although she did try. He had never once suggested that she might give him a son to inherit his ships...although God knows, she would have given him a baker's dozen if only he'd wanted her to!

Certainly he had never asked her to love him. That had been her own idea, and now that she'd started, she couldn't seem to stop. He'd asked only the one thing of her, and she'd let him down. While she'd been prancing around without a care in the world, his beloved Hetty had up and died.

Suddenly, Kathleen came to her senses and realized that everyone was looking a her. "Earth to earth, child," Amos instructed softly, and having been through the ritual more times than she cared to recall, she bent and picked up a handful of damp sand and scattered it over the cypress box.

Chrissy Jane began to wail. Achsah said, "Oh, Lordy, Lordy, she was a trial, but I'll sorely miss her," and she sobbed, too.

Numbly, Kathleen allowed her arm to be taken by Amos. Her eyes were dry. She was utterly heartless. No wonder Rogan couldn't love her. She didn't deserve to be loved. Here Hetty had been laid to her final rest, and to her everlasting shame, all she could think of was how it would affect her own life. What to do first, pray for Rogan's forgiveness? Or drag out her trunk and start packing?

Five days later, there'd been no word from Rogan. Dosher had returned the day after the burial with the news that the *Arduous* had limped into Newport News after losing a deck cargo and part of a mast in a storm at sea, and Rogan had turned back to meet her. "I sent word by Tom Scarborough, aboard the *Relentless*," Dosher told her. "She's running regular up through the ditch hauling for Moses Patterson, and Tom said he'd pass the message when he come abreast the *Witch*, so I reckon Rogan's heard by now."

Kathleen had all but forgotten that aside from the *White Witch*, Rogan also owned the small steam packet, *Relentless*, and a part interest in the four-masted schooner *Arduous*. Which meant that aside from being a strikingly handsome man who, from all reports, had always had a great following among the ladies, he was also a successful and probably even a wealthy businessman.

If she'd been depressed before, she was cast into the very depths at that thought. Why couldn't he have been an ordinary man? Then she might have stood a chance. Not that she would have expected him to love her. There was nothing particularly lovable about her. Nothing at all special. Certainly nothing that would compete with all the beautiful women he was bound to know in every port between Beaufort and Baltimore. No wonder they all wanted him. Who wouldn't?

If Kathleen longed for his coming, she dreaded it even more. Considering the way they'd parted, it would have been hard enough to face him again without this. It was beginning to look as if he didn't plan to come home at all, but she knew that sooner or later he would have to.

Wandering into her room, she took down her hatbox and lifted her precious yellow silk bonnet from the tissue. Settling it on her head, she stared at herself in the mirror. "Curse the wretched man," she muttered, wishing she could bring herself to forget him.

The tip of her nose turned red. Her chin wobbled. "Oh, my mercy, if you're not the sorriest spectacle I ever saw," she muttered, dragging her sleeve ruthlessly across her wet cheeks. Not that she was crying. She *never* cried. It was totally impractical.

Calling on the determination that had got her through the ordeal of losing both her parents, being torn apart from her sister and taken to live with a grandmother who didn't want her and all that had followed her grandmother's lingering illness and death, Kathleen made up her mind to get on with her life.

The very next morning she set about returning dishes to all the neighbors who had brought food, a task that took almost an entire day by the time she'd walked all the way up the road past Homer and 'Lizer's house near Windmill Point, to the Austins', way up past the Sand Hills, then back along the shoreside. She thanked them all kindly, refused invitations to come set a spell, to stay for supper, to come sleep in the trundle if the thought of staying in an empty house bothered her.

There were invitations from people she'd barely swapped a dozen words with before Hetty's death, but Kathleen had lived among these quiet, self-sufficient bankers long enough to know that she would never be left in need. There would be fish and wildfowl hanging outside her kitchen door once or twice a week. Wood would miraculously chop itself and lie down in neat order out by the shed after a hard cold spell. Amos would keep an eye on her, and what he couldn't do personally, he'd see that someone else did. The bankers were used to women being left alone. It was a way of life among mariners' wives.

They all asked about Rogan, and Kathleen, her smile frozen in place, replied that he would probably be coming home to pay his last respects once he settled the business with the *Arduous*. It was better than telling them that with Hetty dead and buried, he had no reason to come home at all.

"Lawsy, I know how that goes," declared one woman, standing on her front porch with her apron extended to cover her swollen belly. "Four cent out of ever' nickel Robert makes goes into that blessed boat of his. He comes home just long enough to eat and to—" To Kathleen's amazement, her weathered face flushed. "Long enough to eat, and that's all. I swear, if that boat o' his could cook, he'd ha' married her!"

Laughing for the first time in a week, Kathleen turned toward home. She had learned from talking to another woman who was in the family way, and whose husband sailed on the *White Witch*, that Rogan paid out an extra share whenever one of his crew had a baby.

"Otis 'n' me, we got five, not countin' the one on the way. If Cap'n Rogan weren't so good to us, Otis could probably buy into a boat of his own with what he's given us above Otis's pay."

Rogan. Wherever she went, she heard his praises sung.

He was a credit to his raising. He was generous to a fault. It was a hard life for any man, but those that didn't break were the better for it.

When so much time had passed with still no word, Callum had set out across the sound to track him down. In a way, Kathleen missed him almost as much as she did Rogan. In another way, it was a relief to have him gone. He and Amos had practically adopted her, dropping in at all hours of the day on the flimsiest of excuses to be sure she wasn't moping.

Kathleen had scoffed at the idea. She might be stricken with guilt now and then, particularly when Callum provoked a smile against her will, but she was far too practical to mope. To prove it, she tackled the stacks of boxes and bundles in Hetty's room that the poor old dear had never allowed her even to dust.

The rooming house was far from luxurious, but it was one of the cleaner establishments on the waterfront. Besides, it was convenient. Sending Dick to finish the run in the *White Witch,* Rogan had taken a room there when it had become apparent that he would have to meet with various claims adjusters and brokers, since the other owners of the *Arduous* were in Seattle discussing a deal with a logging outfit.

It was there that Callum finally tracked him down. "I'm sorry as hell to have to bring you the news, Rogue. We sent word right off, but we had no way of knowing you'd sent Dick on with the *Witch* and stopped off here."

If Rogan had suffered a blow, he'd covered it well. But then, thought Callum, he'd always been one to play his cards close to his vest, even when he was among friends. "I reckon you'll be wanting to get on home to your wife?" He waited for a reaction, and when none was forthcoming, he continued. "We can probably connect with the mail boat if we hurry."

"I'm meeting with a man from Lloyd's at four this afternoon. I still have to make arrangements for the crew, or we'll not have a hand left by the time we get ready to sail again." Rogan ceased his pacing and stood at the window overlooking the harbor. He'd been shocked, yet not surprised. Saddened, yet already he was beginning to accept the loss. Hetty, bless her, had changed so over the past few years that she bore little resemblance to the woman who had dragged him up by the scruff of the neck and managed to turn a wild young hellion into a fairly respectable citizen. It hurt like hell to lose her. But then, he'd been losing her for years. It might have hurt even more to watch her change beyond all recognition. Soon she would have been unable to take care of her personal needs, beholden to strangers...

No, not to strangers. To Kathleen.

"How's my wife bearing up?"

"Uh, that's something I've been wanting to speak to you about. Now I don't want you to take this the wrong way, Rogue." Callum smoothed a hand down the revers of his pearl-gray worsted coat. He was tempted to back out, but dammit, she was hurting! And if he couldn't have her for himself, at least he could do this much for her. Clearing his throat, he said, "The thing is, Rogan, I thought maybe now that—ah, that is, now that you and Kathy—"

With a sudden release of pent-up energy, Rogan spun around and glared at his friend. "Now that Kathy and I *what*? Exactly what the devil are you driving at, Cal?"

Here we go, ladies and gentlemen, place your bets!
"Look, you know how it's always been with us, Rogue. In the past, that is. I mean, not with Kathy—that's different." He ran a finger along the stiff edge of his collar, wondering why the hell he hadn't just written a letter telling Rogan that his stepmother had passed away, and that, by the way,

if he didn't need his wife any longer, could Callum have her? It would have served the same purpose, and he could have remained safely out of the direct line of fire.

Sensing an ominous quietness in the room, he sorted through his options and said cautiously, "Well, the thing is, Kathy's all alone now."

"So?"

"So... Well, a woman don't need to be alone, Rogue. Not a woman like—"

"Women have always been alone. Why should my woman be any different?"

"Because, dammit, she is! She just *is,* that's all!" There was a ring of truth in the statement that startled Callum perhaps even more than Rogan.

"If a woman can't get along without having a man living in her apron pocket, then she damned well ought to marry a farmer or a storekeeper!"

"Still, Kathy—"

"Her name is Kathleen. Kathleen Rawson. She married me knowing damned well what I was!" Rogan's eyes had narrowed to glittering slits. His face, perennially bronzed from a life at sea, had turned an unnatural shade of gray. If Callum had happened to look just then, he might have seen the muscle clenching beside that angular jaw and begun considering ways to defuse the situation.

But he didn't. Instead, he forged on with the plan he'd devised, the plan that would bring Kathy and Rogan together and keep himself from doing something dangerously foolish. Like falling in love with his best friend's wife.

"Look, it's always been a game with us before, Rogue. But this time I'm not playing. I want her. I wanted her the first time I laid eyes on her, and I mean to have her. Naturally, I don't intend to marry her, so whether or not you want to apply for a divorce is up to you. It won't make a speck of difference to Kathy and me. Look at it from her standpoint, Rogue," he urged. "She's buried alive there on the island with no man, not even a baby to fill her time. At least I can take her places, show her a life she's never even dreamed of. I can dress her the way she deserves to be dressed, and give her jewelry and a maid to help her with her hair and her clothes...when I'm not there to help her, that is." He grinned, calculating the effect of his argument. Should he turn up the heat another notch?

Sure, why not? In for a penny, in for a pound. "You see, I know she already likes me. Once you're out of the picture, it'll be a cinch to make her forget any girlish fantasies she might've harbored. Oh, she might think she's in love with you now, but that's just because—well, hell, how would I know? You're not my idea of a hero." He assayed a laugh that didn't quite come off.

Damn, he was sweating! He *never* sweated! "Poor little fool, she probably thinks you're romantic. You know—tall, dark and absent? The stuff a maiden's dreams are made of? But Kathy needs more than dreams, Rogue. She deserves more, and I intend to see that she—"

Rogan's fist shot out with no notice. One minute Callum was standing on his well-shod feet; the next, he was lying flat on his fashionably clad backside.

"Aw, hell! Why'd you have to go and do that?" Callum rubbed his jaw and examined his hand for blood. No slouch when it came to fisticuffs, he was well able to defend himself against the average man. But Rogan was no average man. He had the strength of an ox, a tricky fuse and a right cross that exploded like a bolt out of the blue when a man least expected it.

Nor did that cast-iron face of his betray the slightest trace of remorse as he glared down at his fallen opponent. "Stay away from my wife," Rogan warned, each word sizzling like hot lead dropped into a pail of cold water.

"Well, now, that might not be so easy. Y'see, I told Paw I'd be back in a week's time. That was last Thursday."

"Amos knows better than to hold his breath waiting for you to keep your word. I'll be heading south in—" he hesitated, doing some rapid calculations in his mind "—in two days' time. Give me your word you'll stay here until after I've gone, or I'll damned well strip you down to your longhandles and press you aboard the first ship bound for China!"

Propped up on one elbow, Callum grinned unrepentantly. "Sounds to me like you're running scared, friend. What's the matter, can't you take a little competition?"

Rogan gave him a look that came close to severing the bonds of a lifelong friendship. "Maybe I'm just afraid I'll wind up getting my neck stretched for ridding the world of one more home-wrecking, wife-stealing son of a bitch."

Nearly two weeks had gone by. Rogan wasn't coming. Surely he'd had the word by now. Two men had gone after him. A man who owned three ships and kept a more or less regular schedule couldn't be all that hard to track down.

He didn't want to come home, Kathleen told herself, the meager hope she'd harbored against all reason finally snuffed out. He knew she was here all alone. He knew she must be wondering about her future now that the reason for their marriage no longer existed. If he'd had the least bit of feeling for her, he wouldn't let her dangle here this way.

She had given him every opportunity, made excuses for him when she'd long since run out of hope. Now, sitting amidst the stacks of clothing she'd found sandwiched between the covers of Hetty's quilts, she told herself that if she had a grain of pride left, she would refuse to wait for him to come and send her packing.

He'd likely offer her money. Maybe he would even divorce her! It was going to be hard enough to find a place to stay and a job that would support her without that particular stigma to overcome.

Of course, if she just up and left on the mail boat before he showed up, he wouldn't be able to divorce her. Could a man divorce a wife he couldn't find? She frowned, wondering how she could find the answer without giving rise to suspicion. No one she knew had ever been divorced.

On the other hand, what difference did it make? If she could get far enough away, she could simply change her name and pretend to be a widow. Goodness knows, since the war, there were enough of those around so that one more wouldn't arouse any suspicions.

Morosely, she plucked away one more of the loose, colorful threads that still blemished a perfectly good man's black wool coat. It was obviously Rogan's and practically new. She'd found it when she'd been trying to pack away all Hetty's quilts and discovered that some of them were so stiff they couldn't be folded.

She had felt the lumps, grown suspicious and gone after her scissors, and the result was a heap of clothing of all sizes and conditions spread over the bed. Entire garments had been laid one overlapping the other, tacked in place, then sewn between patchwork tops and calico bottoms to make up more than a dozen different quilts. No wonder the blessed things were so heavy! No wonder Rogan had seemed puzzled by the way Hetty had dressed. That plum-colored merino was new and expensive and just her size.

And the poor neighbors; no wonder they'd always hurried out to their clotheslines when they'd seen Hetty and Kathleen coming and begun gathering in their wash. She'd thought nothing of it at the time.

Poor Hetty. Kathleen had only known her for a few months, but she missed her more than she would have thought possible. The house seemed so empty without her.

Bully didn't crow much anymore. The hens had stopped laying. Of course, this time of year, they usually did, but even Rags had deserted her to take up over at Amos's.

Kathleen got to her feet, brushed the loose threads off her apron and wandered out to the sitting room. Since the weather had turned so cold, she'd taken to living in two rooms and cooking on the hob rather than waste precious firewood keeping the big stove in the kitchen going.

If she was lonely, that was only reasonable. If she was restless, that, too, was understandable. Everywhere she turned there were reminders of Rogan. He'd stood in that particular doorway, filling it with his broad shoulders, making her ache to walk into his arms. He'd sat in that particular chair, with the lamplight casting sharp shadows on his angular face, sprawled across the feather tick in the loft, his body glistening with sweat and his head beside hers on the pillow after they had made love.

Most of all she remembered him that way. A familiar stranger, dearly beloved, yet still as distant as the moon.

She'd begun to read his books. Achsah Burrus had returned seven leather-bound volumes of essays and a scientific treatise, saying that Hetty had given them to her two years before when she and Dosher had lost their first baby. "Poor Hetty, she was some bad about that. Reckon she'd have give away everything in the house if she'd lived long enough. Didn't do no good to take it back, because she'd just give it away again. She got mad at Edmund one day and threw his pipe and his crutch in the Green Pond. Dosher had to fish 'em out again with a clam rake. Poor Edmund claimed his pipe never did draw worth shoot after that."

Oh, yes, now she could smile about all poor Hetty's foibles, but being locked in the henhouse and having a fire set underneath it hadn't been all that funny at the time. Or having to convince the poor old dear that they didn't really need six boxes of brace buttons, and then convince Mr. A.J. to take them back and credit their account at the store. Or having to go around to the neighbors and ask them to come and identify any clothing of theirs that Hetty might have sewed inside one of her infamous quilts.

The feeling of rootlessness that had been growing in her ever since she'd known she would have to leave returned with a vengeance. Packing. She really should get down to it now that Hetty's things were in order and the house was shining like a new penny. She'd gone over every piece of furniture, including those that had been returned, with oil polish until they gleamed like satin. There'd been a perfectly good Nottingham lace tablecloth and a framed picture of moonlight on the ocean with a silhouette of a ship among the boxes she'd found in Hetty's bedchamber. She'd hung the picture and spread the cloth over the gate-legged table, and now she wandered around, lacking anything better to do, until she'd chewed her fingernails right down to the tender.

Sighing, she crossed to the shelf above the row of pegs on her bedchamber wall. She took down the hatbox, lifted out her precious yellow bonnet with its fragile burden of silk flowers and set it carefully on her head.

"She wears her clothes as if they were thrown on her with a pitchfork," she murmured to the image in the speckled mirror. She'd read those lines just yesterday in one of Rogan's books. Jonathan Swift, if she remembered right. He might have been speaking of her.

Still, the hat was beautiful, as long as she ignored all the rest—the drab hair, the freckles, the colorless eyes and the mouth her mother used to tell her she'd grow up to one day. She never had. If Rogan had given her the yellow silk gown, and she'd put it on for him, he'd probably have popped a gusset laughing.

She was still muttering about silk purses and sow's ears when someone rapped sharply on her front door.

Amos? He never stood on formality, and the women usually cracked the door open and called out.

Rogan! The yellow hat forgotten, she opened the door and stepped back, one hand flying up to cover her heart. "Oh, my mercy," she whispered.

"Kathleen? Were you going out?" He eyed the unseasonable bonnet, and she snatched it off her head.

"Whether I am or not is none of your concern, Morton. What are you doing here?"

He made as if to step past her, but she barred the way. Wrinkling her nose at the bay rum and bourbon smell that always used to make her cringe, she demanded once more to know what he wanted. Once, a long time ago, when she had first gone to live with Morton and Alice, she had thought him handsome, being too young to see the weak chin and the way he had of constantly shifting his eyes whenever he talked to someone.

"Considering the season and all—"

"What season? Christmas was weeks ago. I sent the children cards. Did they get them, or did you throw them away?" She had spent hours poring over the meager selection at the local stores, choosing just the right card for each child.

"How can you think I'd do something so coldhearted?"

She continued to watch him, her level gaze unwavering, until he cleared his throat and turned to stare into the distance. "If you don't believe me, then maybe you'll believe Alice."

"I haven't heard a word from Alice since she—since that day. I left a letter, so it's not as if she didn't know where to find me." She lifted her chin, unafraid to show her loathing. This was her house. He had no power over her here.

"Yes, well, as to that, I explained—"

"Horse biscuits! You know as well as I do there was nothing to explain! Nothing except the way you'd been touching me, and sneaking around looking at me, and—and trying to kiss me until I was scared to be alone in the house with you! Is that what you explained to Alice? Is that why she sent me away?"

Arms crossed over her chest, Kathleen continued to bar the door, oblivious to the cold wind that blew in from the northeast. From the smell of his breath, Morton was in no danger of freezing, even without his elegant tan topcoat and beaver hat. "Well?" she prompted.

"Just ask her. All you have to do is ask her."

"Oh, and just how do I do that? I haven't noticed any telegraph wires between here and Beaufort, have you?"

"I brought her to you."

"You *what?*" Narrowing her eyes, Kathleen glanced past him, then back again. She didn't trust him any more than she ever had, but then, why would he lie about something that could be so easily disproved? "Where is she?"

"She stayed aboard the boat. You know she's in the family way again, but things aren't going too well, so—"

"What do you mean, not going well?" Heedless of her own feelings, she grabbed his arm and pulled him into the house, slamming the door behind him. Spinning around, she demanded, "What do you mean, Alice is not doing well, Morton? Has she lost the baby? Is she still having trouble keeping anything down? Is she—"

"No, no, now you mustn't worry so, little sister, it's not all that bad. It's just that it's twins again, and there was this doctor up in Virginia—"

"You took her to Virginia? This late in her time? Morton, you're a fool! What did he say? Is she going to be all right? Who's looking after the children?"

The smell of alcohol was even more potent inside the house, but Kathleen ignored it. Morton had always enjoyed a drink after his supper. Several, in fact, and sometimes he didn't wait until the evening meal.

"Happens we have a jewel of a woman, a widow from Harker's Island, but why not let Alice tell you all about it? I promised her I'd bring you right back."

She didn't have to think twice. Throwing on her coat, she banked the fire and adjusted the damper. Leaving a single lamp lit, she followed him outside.

Morton made an effort to draw her out, but Kathleen refused to be drawn as they walked the parallel ruts that led to the docks. "I rowed myself ashore," he said as they passed the store. "Don't mind telling you, I haven't done that kind of work in many a day."

If that small confession had been calculated to disarm her, it fell far short of the mark. All she could think of was seeing Alice again and hearing about the children.

Morton hurried to keep up with her, hating the feel of deep sand underfoot. God, what an uncivilized place! Approaching the wharf, he ignored the two fishermen who'd grudgingly given him directions to the Rawson place. He'd had the devil's own time convincing them that he was Kathleen's brother. Damned narrow-minded heathens! Finally, one of the ignorant clods had told him how to find her, but only after he'd spun them a tale about meeting her new family.

"No family left. Old woman died. Her man's not come home yet."

He'd barely been able to understand the barbarian, so thick was his brogue, but he'd made out enough. Kathleen was alone. He wouldn't have to invent some excuse to get her away from that great hulking bruiser she'd married. Patrice had said he'd probably be gone.

He'd even considered barring the door and taking her right in her own bed, until he remembered what a scrapper she was. If she started screaming, the place would be overrun with these damned savages before he could even get her drawers down! He hadn't cared at all for the way they'd stared after him when he'd set off down the road.

Easing himself carefully into the small open boat, Morton reached up to assist Kathleen, but she evaded his hands and leapt down herself. "Where is this boat of yours? Why didn't one of the crew row you ashore?"

Morton wrestled clumsily with the oars then shoved them away from the dock. His stroke was uneven, as if he were afraid of splashing his fine worsted coat and those dun-colored trousers of his.

He didn't bother to reply, and Kathleen stared back at the rapidly diminishing shoreline. Had she completely lost her wits? What was she doing out here in the middle of the Pamlico Sound with a man she trusted just about as far as she could throw him? It was practically dark, and for all she knew, Morton could be lying through his teeth.

Maybe there was no housekeeper. They'd never been able to keep one before. Maybe they needed her, and he meant to take her back to Beaufort with him!

Chapter Seventeen

Twice before they reached their destination, Morton tippled from a silver flask he carried in his coat pocket. The first time he took a quick nip, thinking she wasn't watching. Kathleen's lips tightened, and she made up her mind to insist that one of the crew members row her ashore once she'd seen her sister.

The second time he fumbled with the cap on the flask, they were nearly at the yacht, an elegant little sloop with fancy scrollwork and a furled rig. Morton leaned forward and offered her a drink. "Come on, little Kathleen, be a good sport. This'll thaw you out."

"I don't need thawing, thank you. Morton, whose yacht is this?" Morton was comfortably fixed, but surely he wasn't able to afford a yacht and crew.

"B'longs to a friend. Hardware supplier, y'know? Had business in Virginia, invited me along."

"I thought you were taking Alice to see a doctor." Her eyes narrowed as Morton began to swear under his breath.

"Alice is not aboard at all, is she? You lied to me! Turn this thing around, Morton. If you don't, I will."

"Now, don't be like that, Katie dear. Don't you want to see your sister?"

"If she's actually with you, I'll see her tomorrow. Some-one from the village can row me out at first light."

Morton took time for another pull at his flask, wiped his lips on the back of his hand, nearly dropping an oar in the process, and shook his head. "You don't b'lieve me, do you? After I took you in and treated you like you was my own fam'ly."

"Huh!"

"Besides, we'll be headed home first thing. Had trouble enough making 'em lay over, as it was."

He was lying. She knew good and well he was lying! How could she have been so stupid as to have put herself in this precarious position? Where was her common sense? She should have known it was completely out of character for Morton to exert himself on behalf of anyone. Even if he did, he'd never have risked ruining an expensive suit unless he hoped to gain far more than he lost.

"We're a'most there now, so why don't you sit back down and stop rocking the boat, hmm?"

"You're inebriated!"

"You're in*nee*briated," he mocked, nearly losing an-other oar as he shifted to tuck away the flask.

One deep sweep sent them bumping against the gleaming hull of the little sloop, nearly tumbling Kathleen overboard. While Morton attempted to bring the small boat alongside, Kathleen lurched toward the bow and grasped hold of the yacht's low railing. Propelled more by anger than fear, she flung herself aboard and was screaming for help before she had regained her balance.

"Help! Please, someone!" she cried, running forward to peer into a dark companionway. Hearing her brother-in-law fumbling in the launch, she wheeled around. "Morton, you set one foot on board this thing, and I'll crown you over the head with—" Frantically, she glanced around, finding no handy weapon in the fast fading light. The deck was tidy to a fault. "With my boot heel!"

"You self-righteous prig, it'd serve you right if I—ow, dammit, why'd you go'n do that?" he wailed plaintively as he nursed the fingers she had stomped.

"Stay away from me," she warned, then, peering through the gloom, she called out again for help. For someone. For anyone who could hear her.

They were alone. She knew it even before she saw the evil smile on Morton's sweating face as he struggled to climb aboard the sloop. "Stay away from me," she warned again. "Look, let me go and I'll never tell a soul that you tried to kidnap me. I promise you I won't."

"Like you didn't tell that santimoni—that sanctimonious bastard, Dunwoody? Like you didn't tell that whinin' Rhodes bitch?" He made another attempt to fling himself over the rail and swore when he fell back. She wasn't about to direct him to the place a few feet forward that was designed to accommodate boarding.

God, what a fool she'd been! Edging away from him, she wondered if she could wait until he set foot on board and then rush forward and fling herself into the launch. "Morton, don't you dare—!"

"You tol' Trice, an' she tol' th' whole damn town! Went an' blabbed her fool head off, an' now Allie's mad at me, an'—"

"I didn't tell Patrice anything, she saw for herself! So did Alice! I'm warning you, Morton—" She broke off, furious at being put on the defensive. "Why am I doing this? I don't owe you any explanations!"

Gauging her chances, she waited until Morton managed to pull himself on board, then she made a desperate lunge. With amazing agility, he leapt after her and managed to grab the tail of her coat. Without pausing to think, she freed her arms. Off balance, he staggered back, taking the coat with him. While he was trying to regain his feet, Kathleen flung herself over the rail, praying belatedly that the launch was still alongside.

It was. Or near enough. Her foot struck the near gun'ale and slipped, and she fell across the center thwart, but she was on her knees in an instant. It took but a moment to untie the leader, but that was nearly a moment too long. Before she could push off from the sloop, Morton was clambering over the railing, mouthing obscenities and threatening to teach her the lesson she'd been asking for all these years.

"Temptin' me, always temptin' me, laughin' behin' my back! I know your game, girl," he raved. "Wi' that old bitch next door trollin' her bait in front of me ever' time I set foot out th' door, and you, twitchin' your fancy li'l behind in my—in my face, 's no wonder I can't sleep! Allie, snorin' like a farrowin' sow…damn' Trice tryin' t' lure me back in 'er bed, an' you—"

"Leave me out of it!" With one might effort, Kathleen pushed the launch away from the hull, and it drifted out on the black water, catching the current. "Morton, I'm warning you, if you do anything to hurt my sister, I'll—" Panting, she waited to catch her breath, trying to think of some effective and believable threat.

There wasn't a single light except for the anchor lights showing anywhere on the sloop. How could she have *believed* him! How could she have been so *stupid!*

"Come back an' lemme take you home, Katie. It's dark. No time f' li'l gals t' be wannerin' around alone. Katie? Can y'hear me?"

She could hear him, all right. She could barely see him, reeling around on deck like a scarecrow in a high wind, but she could sure enough hear the lecherous sot! For a moment, she hesitated, lifting both dripping oars from the water. If he fell overboard, fully clothed and inebriated, he would surely drown. And while Alice and the children might be better off without him, for the Chadwicks would see that they were well taken care of, it would be just one more burden for Kathleen's already overburdened conscience.

The night was cold and perfectly still, not a ripple showing on the water. Lights from several ships anchored in deeper water gleamed across the surface like long yellow worms, and she could just make out the lanterns that marked the entrance to the harbor.

She was still undecided when she heard a filthy profanity, followed by the slamming of a door. He might break his neck tumbling down a companionway, but at least he wouldn't drown.

Turning the boat, she began to pull toward shore. Belatedly, the thought of her narrow escape overcame her, and she began to tremble, but soon even fear was forgotten as the cold bit into her bones.

She'd left her coat on board. "Good riddance," she muttered, and pulled harder, ignoring the assortment of bruises and abrasions she'd received when she'd tumbled into the launch.

She'd been rowing for what seemed hours, but could have been no more than ten minutes, when she heard a sound that caused her to lift both blades and hold them dripping above the surface. It was pitch-dark. There was no moon showing, only a few million stars that were too cold and distant to offer much in the way of comfort.

Had she actually heard something, or had she only imagined it?

Before she could make up her mind, she heard it again. A distinct thump, splash.

Morton? Could he have followed her? She opened her mouth to call out, then shut it again. It could be the crew of the sloop returning. Morton had probably sent them away on some fool's errand so as to get her aboard without being detected. The less anyone knew of this night's deeds, the better off she'd be. Heaven help her if the threat of scandal ran her away from a second town!

Silence. Perhaps she'd only imagined it. It might even have come from shore…one of the men doing something aboard his boat, probably. She had made up her mind to slip ashore and hurry away before anyone could see her when she sneezed. And then sneezed again.

"Kathleen?"

She froze. That had sounded almost like…

No, that was crazy. Rogan was hundreds of miles away. Even if the *Witch* had finally come home and he was on his way ashore, he certainly wouldn't be expecting to find her out here in the channel after dark.

"Kathleen, is that you? Dammit, answer me!"

"R-Rogan?"

And then somehow, their two boats were bumping sides, and he was swearing at the lack of light and at his bruised fingers, pinched between the two gunwales, and at her for being fool enough to go with that bastard, Kingsley.

"How did you know?" she asked when he had lifted her bodily into his boat, plopped her on the aft thwart and taken up the oars again, leaving Morton's launch adrift.

"How the hell do you think I knew? Homer and Dosher were wearing ruts in the dock when I got in, worrying about you. Dosher was all set to go after you himself when I got there."

"B-but—but how did you know where— And where's the *White Witch?* When d-did you get in?"

Rogan was sweeping them shoreward with deep, silent strokes. Kathleen clutched the gunwales and tried to control her shivering. She was so rigid by now that if she had tried to move, she probably would have shattered.

"You're cold." With that flat observation, he drew both

oars across his lap, peeled off his warm melton coat and slung it around her, nearly capsizing her in the process.

Too grateful to protest, Kathleen huddled in the welcome warmth, drawing comfort and security from the lingering scent of his body. "You d-didn't answer my questions." Even though she was no longer quite so cold, her voice was still frozen.

"The *Witch* is lying off Windmill Point. We dropped anchor less than an hour ago. Is that what you want to know?"

It wasn't. At least, it wasn't all she wanted to know, but the rest would have to wait. Having already resumed his distance-devouring stroke, Rogan ignored her, and Kathleen had to content herself with being able to watch the shadowy form against the night sky. He had come back. That was all that mattered. Smiling, she buried her head in the deep collar and inhaled the intoxicating essence of wool, soap, tobacco and Rogan.

Not until they were at the house, fires roaring in both the range and the sitting room hearth, with two kettles and several pots of water set to heat, did Kathleen begin to worry. She'd been so relieved to have escaped, so unbelievably glad to see Rogan again, that she'd shut her mind to anything beyond that.

There'd been a horse—Dosher's, she thought—waiting at the dock. Rogan had hoisted her atop the creature, then leapt up behind her, all without benefit of anything faintly resembling a saddle, and they'd made short work of the trek home. Neither of them had spoken a word.

Now he towered over her, looking unnaturally pale and too grim for comfort. She eyed him warily and tried to think how to begin.

"Why, Kathleen? Just tell me that much, why'd you go with him? It was Kingsley, wasn't it?"

Having finally thawed out, she was suddenly too tired to

pick her words carefully. "Morton," she said, and she yawned. "It was Morton."

"Wake up, dammit! You're not going to sleep before you've told me what you were doing out there with that—"

"I was going to see Alice. My sister Alice. Only—" She yawned again. "Only she wasn't there."

"Would you care to explain that?" He was scowling at her, and tired or not, that put her back up. She'd done nothing to deserve his anger.

Well, there was Hetty, of course, but she rather thought this was about something else. "Not really," she said tiredly, then scuttled back against the cushions as he moved in so close his boots bumped against her shoes. "I'd just as soon wait until tomorrow."

"And I'd just as soon get the talking over and done with."

Over and done with. That didn't sound too promising. Swallowing hard, Kathleen sat up straight, focusing her gaze on the part of him that happened to be in her direct line of vision, which was his crotch. Closing her eyes quickly, she groaned and said, "Oh, all right, if you must know, I'd been wondering about the children, how they were and all, and whether Alice had had her baby, and— Look, would you move back? You—you're blocking the heat from the fireplace."

He took one step back, crossed his arms over his chest and continued to glare down at her. It was better, but just barely.

"I'm waiting, Kathleen."

She licked her lips. "Where was I?"

"You were missing your family," he prompted, his voice deadly calm.

"All right, I admit I was foolish to believe him, but you see, I'd been here alone for so long, and I wondered—that is, I didn't know if you were—" Frantically, she sought a way to explain how she'd felt, not knowing what the future held or if she even had a future. With him, that was. And a future without him was no future at all, but she could hardly tell him that.

"Go on. You were wondering what?" Rogan had been so terrified when he thought he'd lost her that he hadn't yet recovered.

"I was wondering...well, with Hetty gone and all, I didn't know what I was supposed to do." Lifting her face, she met his eyes squarely. There, she'd said it. If he wanted to put her on the next packet out, she could hardly blame him.

She waited for him to pronounce her sentence. Some of the harshness seemed to go out of his face, but he remained silent. She began to fidget. Then before she could help it, the words were spilling out of her like dried beans out of a split sack, and she was telling him how it had been—Amos's fiddling, Callum's trying to teach her to dance and Hetty, laughing and clapping one minute and gone the next. She tried to tell him how heartsore she'd been, knowing how Rogan had loved her. She told him about the neighbors' coming to her aid, and how nice Hetty had looked in her yellow gown, and about the quilts and the books and the furniture.

Halfway through the telling, Rogan lowered himself onto the cushion beside her, extending his long legs across the rug and an arm along the back of the sofa.

She leaned forward, afraid to touch him. Sitting stiffly upright, she hurried through the last of the telling. "She didn't suffer any, Rogan. She was laughing right up to the last. Believe me, it's a far better way to go than having to suffer for years until you're so mean and bitter that no one wants to come near you."

"Your grandmother?" he asked, his deep voice edged with a soft roughness.

She nodded. "How did you know?"

"Dunwoody."

"Did Patrice—that is, when you left here that time after the storm, did she tell you...anything?"

Rogan considered telling her the truth and decided against it. There'd been no truth to the woman's wicked tale. He'd known that in his heart, even though he'd let himself be tainted by her malice. "Nothing important," he said. "Kathleen, I owe you an apology. What I did—well, there's no way I can undo it, but I want you to know I'll never lay a hand on you again." He hesitated, almost as if waiting for her to speak. She made the mistake of meeting his eyes, and she was lost.

"Kathy? You can have it any way you want to. I won't pretend it'll be easy, but I give you my word, I'll take good care of you for as long as I'm able. If anything happens—if my ship goes down, I'll arrange things so that you'll never know need, I promise you that."

"I'm your responsibility, you mean. Like a—a duty."

After only the briefest hesitation, he nodded. "If that's what you want."

Duty. What a lukewarm offering. But was that truly all he was offering? He'd promised to go on with their marriage, even though it wouldn't be easy. On the other hand, his eyes were promising...

No. She couldn't afford to believe what she saw there. It wouldn't be the first time she'd let herself believe something only because she wanted so desperately to believe it.

"Rogan, how did you know where I was?"

He shrugged, and his arm shifted so that it was resting lightly over her shoulder. "It was the first thing I heard when I came ashore. Didn't I tell you how Homer and Dosher were so worried about this smooth-talking sharpster who'd come nosing around, claiming to be your brother? They took him at his word and gave him your direction, but when you went off with him that way, they began to have doubts. They were just thinking about going out after you when we got in. From the way they described him, I guessed who it was and sent my crew on home. Dosher insisted on leaving his horse at the dock in case I needed help in a hurry, and you know the rest.''

And she knew the rest. That is, she knew everything except the most important thing of all. ''He lied to me, you know. He claimed Alice was on board the sloop, but she wasn't. When we got there, I discovered he'd sent the crew ashore, and then I knew it was all a trick, and so I left him there and came back.'' She shuddered.

''It's over now. You're home.'' His arm eased around her shoulder, and he drew her closer.

Kathleen allowed herself to be held. Home. If only she could believe it. ''Rogan, what you said before? About taking care of me? About it's not being easy, but—''

''I think maybe that didn't come out quite the way I'd intended. What I meant to say was that it wouldn't be easy to—that is, not to—'' Breaking off, he leaned back, one hand forking impatiently through his dark hair, the other stroking her arm, which was now quite warm, thanks only in part to the leaping fire.

Some intensely male element in his makeup had always drawn him to the sea. The same male element kept drawing him back again and again to this one woman. Just when he'd thought his life was set on its proper course...

Hope began to flicker in Kathleen's heart, and she tried to snuff it out. This was no time to let herself get caught up in a fairy tale. ''Rogan,'' she began, but before she could put her doubts into words, he stunned her by asking pointblank if she was in love with Callum McNair.

''Am I—with *Callum?*''

His arm tightened until his fingers were biting into her flesh. ''I damned well wasn't talking about Amos. Well?

Are you? Because if you are, then I'd better warn you, he don't mean to marry you, and even if he did, I wouldn't let you go.''

"I—you wouldn't?" Bemused, she blinked at him, afraid to let herself hope, unable to prevent it.

"We made a bargain. I've held to my part."

"Oh." Then it wasn't that he was jealous, it was Hetty. "Rogan, I'm truly sorry. I wouldn't have had this happen for the world." Sighing, she tried to ease herself away from his arm, but it was difficult when all in the world she wanted to do was lose herself in his warm embrace and beg him to try hard to love her. Instead, she collected herself enough to tell him how deeply she regretted having let him down. "I can't say how truly sorry I am. Cal and I were dancing and laughing, and—well, it just happened before we knew it, and there was nothing we could do."

So she did love the smooth bastard! Rogan didn't want to hear this, not now. Not ever! He shut his eyes against a sudden burning. Damned fireplace was smoking! He'd been meaning to clean out the chimney. "It's all right, love, I understand," he lied. Drawing in a deep breath, he smelled only furniture polish and the faint odor of roses that had haunted his dreams for too long. All right, so it wasn't a smoking fireplace.

"You don't have to explain," he said gruffly.

"I only wanted you to know how much I cared—I mean, it's not as though we were strangers. We lived together, after all." He winced at the sudden pain of that revelation. So it had gone that far. "Living under the same roof, a body can come to love someone, no matter what their faults. And I did. And I'm sorry, truly sorry."

Head bowed, he held her against him, unable to let her go even on learning by her own admission that he'd lost her just when he'd come to love her.

No, that wasn't true. His feelings had been growing all

along. Recalling the brave set of her chin as she'd set sail
with a stranger, leaving behind everything dear and familiar—remembering the way she'd been with Hetty, the kindness, the generosity, the care—watching her somber gray
eyes light up like sunshine breaking through the clouds,
hearing the sound of her laughter, was it any wonder he'd
come to love her?

No, it hadn't been sudden. It had been there all along,
like a seed planted in the darkness, just waiting for warmth
and light to germinate and flourish.

"I understand," he repeated, wondering how a man
could live to be nearly thirty years old, could know as many
women as he had and still make as many mistakes as he
had made with the only woman who had ever mattered. It
defied reason.

Releasing her and moving away was perhaps the hardest
thing he'd ever done in his life, but he was afraid that if
he didn't do it now, he wouldn't be able to. "Reckon the
water's hot by now. I'll tote it into the bathing room for
you, and while you soak out the chill, I'll make coffee. Are
you hungry?"

Kathleen felt the tip of her nose prickle. She lifted her
chin and willed herself not to weep. Hungry? Oh, yes, she
was starving, but not for what he was offering. With a
dignity that came harder than anything she'd ever attempted, she offered him her most gracious smile. "No,
but a warm bath would be lovely, Rogan. Thank you."

She waited until he poured two pots full of scalding water into the porcelain tub, added a few drops of attar of
roses then twisted the single faucet and set cold water gush-
ing in to dilute it while she undressed. By the time she'd
removed the last of her clothing, the temperature was just
right. Moving woodenly, she reached for her jar of Rosa-
mund's Cold Cream and General Beautifier and spread a
thin layer over her face. She'd been using it for more than

a year to no avail, but hope and old habits died equally hard.

With her braid pinned on top of her head and her fringe held back by a ribbon to keep it out of the cold cream, she settled into the fragrant warmth with a sigh that held more regret than relief.

A few feet away, Rogan paced. He lighted a cigar, then tossed it into the fire. It occurred to him that the room looked different from the last time he'd seen it, but it took him a moment to figure out why. This was the way it used to look, a long time ago. Furniture gleaming with care, sparkling glass in the windows. That old lithograph of Hetty's...and his books! So she'd finally found the things!

As quickly as it had arisen, his interest waned and he stared at the bathing room door. Damn that maddening female! She had married him for better or worse less than six months ago. Now, just because she'd had her head turned by a handsome face and a bit of fancy tailoring, she thought she could waltz off and forget all about their bargain.

Well, we'd just see about that.

Burdened with more emotions than he could readily sort out, Rogan gave in to the easiest, which was anger. Without further thought, he flung open the door to the bathing room, prepared to do battle for what was rightfully his. "Dammit, Kathleen, I—" As quickly as it had arisen, his anger seeped out and he stood there beside a heap of crumpled clothing and stared.

The water held a greenish cast, distorting her lower body. But there was no disguising the part of her that rose above the steamy, fragrant cloud. Underneath a pink ribbon that wound through her dark hair, Kathleen's face gleamed like polished ivory. Her eyes were enormous. Without her usual high collar, her neck looked almost too delicate to hold the weight of her head, much less the tumbled mass of her hair.

Quickly, she crossed her arms in a familiar protective gesture, but the image of those small, perfect breasts, their tips glistening like freshly washed berries, was indelibly etched on his mind. And then his gaze wandered lower.

"Rogan, you have no right to—"

"What happened? You've burned yourself again. God, darling, how'd you ever manage to burn yourself *there?*"

Kathleen blinked, feeling her cold-creamed lashes stick together. "Burned myself? Rogan, are you feeling all right?"

Without bothering to answer, he went down on his knees beside the tub, leaning over to peer at the part of her that was covered by the bathwater.

Kathleen drew up her knees and scowled at him. "Would you please allow me my privacy?"

Completely disregarding the sleeve of his woolen jersey, he reached under the water and pressed her knees down. She fought back. "Rogan! Stop that! You have no right—"

"Does it hurt bad?" Gently, he pried her arms loose and held them aside, staring at a reddened place just below her right breast.

Ducking her head, Kathleen followed his gaze and gasped.

A short while later, having wiped her face clean of the beautifying cream and dried off her body over her rather halfhearted protests, Rogan carried his wife, wrapped only in a blanket, up the stairs. Each time she tried to tell him that her own bed would do well enough, and that she really needed her night rail if she weren't to freeze to death, he ignored her. She might as well not have spoken.

The loft was cold, for the heat from the fire had not had time to climb the stairwell. With one arm he folded back the quilt. One of Hetty's oldest, it was neither too lumpy, nor too heavy. He laid her on the bed, blanket and all, a look of concern on his face.

"Does it hurt?"

"Does what hurt?"

"Your...burn?" He hovered over her until she was sorely tempted to tell him that what hurt the most was not where she'd cracked her ribs when she'd tumbled into the launch. What really hurt was that he was so blind to her real needs and wants.

"It's not a burn, it's a bruise. I'll probably be all colors come morning, but it doesn't hurt all that much." *I need you to want me, you great dim-witted ox! I want you to need me!*

"How?"

"What does it matter?" she cried impatiently, trying to battle herself free of the blanket. He had taken command so swiftly after lifting her from the tub that she hadn't been able to think, much less argue. He had stood her on her discarded garments, which were now all wet, and tenderly blotted her all over with a towel. And like a fool, she'd stood there and let him do it. By the time she'd recovered her wits enough to protest, he was winding her up in a blanket, and when she'd tried to make him listen to her, he'd shushed her as if she were a witless child.

Drat! Was the man bound and determined to have someone weaker around so that he could take command of his home the way he did his ship? "Rogan, listen to me, I don't need someone to tell me how to go on, and I certainly don't need looking after. I've been taking care of myself for a good many years now, and while I'm sure you mean well—"

"Mean well! God, was ever a man so damned by faint praise."

"Well, I never meant to hurt your feelings, I only meant—"

"It's not my feelings that's hurting, you know." His smile was wintry, a mere twist of his lips, but she found herself as caught up as ever in whatever it was that made this one man in all the world so dear to her. "You want me to fetch the turpentine?"

"Turpentine?" She was bound up like a mummy. He had shifted her so he could sit beside her, his thigh pressing against her side.

"For your bruise," he explained.

"Oh." With every cell in her body clamoring its answer, she made the mistake of meeting his eyes, and now she was trapped. "No, I don't think it needs anything. Maybe tomorrow…"

"Good." It was more a sigh than anything else. "I've never made love to a woman who reeked of turpentine, but if you'd needed it, I'd be willing to do it."

"Willing to make love to me?" Eyes still clinging, they were speaking softly, with no particular emphasis, as if the words spoken were secondary to the words unspoken.

"Willing to rub your bruise with turpentine." And then he began to unwrap her, as if she were a priceless gift, and because she was helpless to do anything else, Kathleen let him. How could she fight the both of them? In spite of what had happened the last time he had made love to her, she felt herself drawn closer and closer to the fire that was in him, loving the way he could make her feel with his looks, his soft words, his touches…

As for what came next, it only hurt for a little while. It was a small price to pay for all the wonderful feelings he aroused in her before he did that other thing.

"Kathleen," he whispered. "I have to kiss you."

"That would be…nice." He had partially uncovered her by then, so that her arms were free. Should she place them around his neck? She didn't want to seem too forward, but the feelings that were racing through were so unsettling. She couldn't even breathe properly, much less think.

But then his lips were on hers, and breathing no longer

seemed so important. Every shred of her being was caught up in the wild wonder of Rogan's arms around her, his mouth on hers, his warmth and weight bearing her down into the deep softness of the feather bed.

"It'll be good this time, love, I promise," he whispered a long time later, his face buried in her throat.

"I don't mind the hurt, Rogan, I only want to please you." Somehow, he had removed his jersey and folded back enough of the blanket so that his chest was pressed against her breasts. She could feel herself swelling with pleasure, feel the same strange sensation coiling inside her that she'd experienced the last time.

His eyes black as burnt pitch, he stared at her for what seemed an eternity. Then he stood and quickly removed the rest of his clothing. Kathleen told herself not to look, but she couldn't help it. He was so beautiful. Even that part of him that would soon cause her pain. So bold, so proud, so...everything a man should be.

"I promised myself I wouldn't do this," he said as he came down beside her. His voice grated as if he were hurting. Instinctively, she drew him to her, wanting to give comfort, to give pleasure, to give all that was in her power to give.

"Kathleen. Primrose. Listen to me, love. If you'll stay with me, I vow to spend the rest of my life making you forget him. He's not good enough for you." He shook his head, a wry smile flickering briefly. "Oh, hell, I'm not good enough, either, but I found you first, and I can't let you go."

"Rogan?"

"We'll work something out, I promise you. If you want to live somewhere else, I'll build you a home anywhere you say. And clothes—"

"Rogan?"

"You'll have the finest clothes money can buy, as many

as you want, in all colors. Anything but black, that is, but if you truly want black, then I'll not—"

"Rogan!"

Startled, he propped himself on one elbow to stare down at her. Her face, softened by the scented cream and the bath, was flushed, and her eyes glittered like raindrops.

Oh, Lord, she was mad as hell, and it was all his fault. The first time in his life it really mattered, and he couldn't even command his own tongue! All he'd wanted was to soothe her into giving him time. Given enough time, he knew he could make her forget McNair, only as usual, he was making a royal botch of it.

"Yes, ma'am. Did you have something you wanted to say?" he asked meekly.

"I love you."

"Kathleen, I'm sorry, and I promise… You *what?*"

"I thought you'd better know before you made me too many promises. I should think a man could land himself in all kinds of trouble that way."

Stunned, he continued to stare at her. Her eyes were glittering, her lashes sparkling with tears. Groaning, he began to kiss them away. "Are you saying that because you know it's what I want most in the world to hear?" he asked between tiny searing kisses.

"No," she whispered helplessly. "I said it because I couldn't hold back any longer. Did you? I mean, do you? Want to hear it, that is?"

Rogan began to laugh. Suddenly, he was lying on his back and she was on top of him, and he was laughing so that she was forced to wrap her arms around his middle to keep from being rocked off.

"Oh, darling, my little love, have I really managed to weather the storm and reach safe harbor? God, you don't know how many times I thought I'd foundered!"

Sensing the truth in her heart, she still needed the words.

Calling her his love and his little darling and his Primrose—those were all very well, but men did that sort of thing, and it didn't necessarily mean anything. Callum called her love and dear heart more often than not, and he certainly wasn't harboring any tender feelings for her.

"Isn't there anything else you want to tell me?" she ventured, more than a little shocked at her newfound boldness. He felt solid and warm and wonderful against her body, and she was having increasing trouble keeping her mind on what was being said instead of what was being done.

"Oh, my, yes," he murmured into her hair. Deftly, he removed the pins and worked free the braid, then he spread her hair over them both, stroking it slowly from the top of her head, down her back...and beyond. "Did you know I was real partial to dark brown hair?"

She shook her head, and as if to prove his words, he traced a length of her hair over her shoulder, past her arm, to where it was caught under her breast. "And did you know I've always had a powerful weakness for gray-eyed women?"

By this time his hand had moved between their two bodies, causing her to draw in her breath in shuddery little gasps. When it began to slip down toward *that* part of her body, she couldn't have spoken if her life had depended on it.

Gently, he turned her onto her back, then he was lying half on top of her, half beside her. Staring up at him, Kathleen could feel him moving against her belly, hard, hot and demanding. Instinctively, her hips began to move. She was afire with a wild hunger that swiftly overcame all else. Hearing a small whimpering sound, she realized that it was her own voice.

"Hush, love, let me pleasure you," Rogan whispered,

and his hand moved over her belly, burrowing between her tightly pressed thighs.

"Please, please," she cried, without the least notion of what she was pleading for. It was happening all over again—the rainbows, the soft wild explosions inside her, the glowing, growing, expanding feeling of— "Rogan!"

"I'm here, darling, I'm right here." And he was. His hand moved again, then he lifted himself over her, and while she was still dazed by a pleasure more intense than anything she'd ever experienced, he came inside her.

She gasped, feeling an exquisite pressure that was part pain, part pleasure. Before she could accustom herself to that, he began moving.

"Relax, my own love, it's all right," he murmured, and she clutched his shoulders, staring wide-eyed up into his face.

He kissed her then, and against her lips he encouraged her to let go, to let it happen. And trusting him, she did. A moment before he stiffened and cried out, she felt herself begin to leave her own body.

A long while later, they lay together, her head on his shoulder, his arm holding her to him, her leg caught between his thighs. "Did I hurt you, precious?"

Almost too drowsy to speak, she murmured, "If you did, I never noticed it. That was…"

"Wonderful?" he prompted with a whimsical smile. Reaching down, he drew Hetty's quilt over them both.

"That, too. It was…"

"Painful?"

"Oh, no!" She sounded shocked. "It was—"

"Worth repeating?"

She smiled, her lips moving against his salty, damp chest. "Well, I've never cared to be thought greedy, but…"

Rogan chuckled. Greedy was the last word in the world

to describe this wondrous creature he had married. It would take a lifetime to tell her all the ways in which she was infinitely more precious to him than anything else in this world or the next, but then, they had a lifetime.

"Unfortunately for you, you married a greedy man. I reckon we're just going to have to work things out between us so that I don't have to do without you for more than a few hours a day."

Kathleen lifted her head to get a better look at his eyes. "We are? Rogan, I don't see how that's possible, even if we wanted it." So far, she had no real assurance that they both did want it, although every instinct she possessed told her she was finally home in the truest sense of the word. "I've always heard it said that mariners' wives spent most of their days alone."

Cupping her face in his hands, Rogan smiled at her, his eyes already gleaming once more with passion. "If you'd hoped to have an easy time of it, lolling about, gossiping away your days with the other women, you're in for a disappointment, Primrose. Seems this mariner has developed a powerful hunger to have his woman by his side. What would you say to sailing with me now and again?"

"What about the chickens?"

"Give 'em to Amos."

"And the cat?"

"Drown the beggar!"

She grinned. "Then I reckon I don't have any real objection, if you're sure you want me."

Rogan leaned over, blew out the lamp and reached for her again. "Let me just set your mind at ease on that point, love."

And he did.

* * * * *

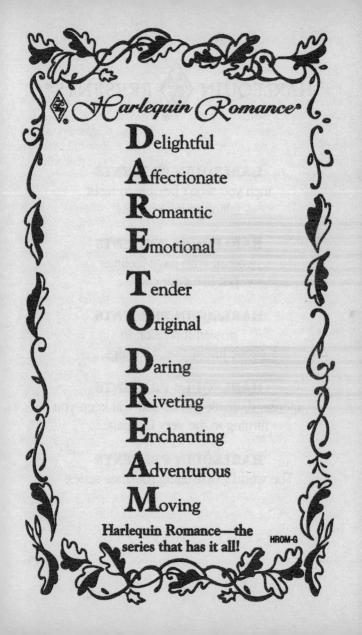

Harlequin Romance®

Delightful

Affectionate

Romantic

Emotional

Tender

Original

Daring

Riveting

Enchanting

Adventurous

Moving

Harlequin Romance—the
series that has it all!

HROM-G

HARLEQUIN ◆ PRESENTS®

HARLEQUIN PRESENTS
men you won't be able to resist
falling in love with...

HARLEQUIN PRESENTS
women who have feelings
just like your own...

HARLEQUIN PRESENTS
powerful passion in
exotic international settings...

HARLEQUIN PRESENTS
intense, dramatic stories that will keep you
turning to the very last page...

HARLEQUIN PRESENTS
The world's bestselling romance series!

Harlequin® Historical

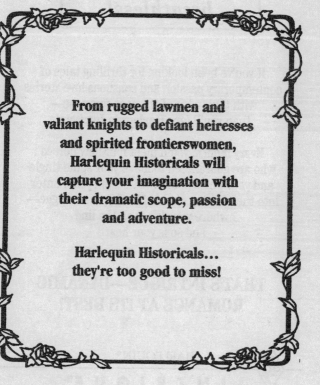

From rugged lawmen and
valiant knights to defiant heiresses
and spirited frontierswomen,
Harlequin Historicals will
capture your imagination with
their dramatic scope, passion
and adventure.

Harlequin Historicals...
they're too good to miss!

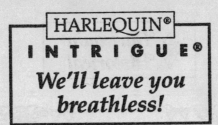

LOOK FOR OUR FOUR FABULOUS MEN!

Each month some of today's bestselling authors bring four new fabulous men to Harlequin American Romance. Whether they're rebel ranchers, millionaire power brokers or sexy single dads, they're all gallant princes—and they're all ready to sweep you into lighthearted fantasies and contemporary fairy tales where anything is possible and where all your dreams come true!

You don't even have to make a wish...
Harlequin American Romance will grant your every desire!

Look for Harlequin American Romance
wherever Harlequin books are sold!

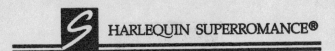